Mrs. Lieutenant

A SHARON GOLD NOVEL

Phyllis Zimbler Miller

*They had their
whole lives to look
forward to – if only
their husbands could
survive Vietnam.*

Chapter opening quotes from Mary Preston Gross' Mrs. Lieutenant (Third Edition).

ISBN: 1-4196-8629-1
ISBN-13: 9781419686290
Library of Congress Control Number: 2007910208

Visit www.booksurge.com to order additional copies.

To the memory of
Elaine Siegel Masser
AEPhi sorority sister, college roommate, friend

With affection for
the wives of AOB 21
13 May 70 – 16 Jul 70

Phyllis Zimbler and Mitchell Miller at the Coronation Ball at Michigan State University on Saturday, November 18, 1967, sponsored by the Cadet Officers Club and the Arnold Air Society.

Phyllis Zimbler Miller is a former Mrs. Lieutenant and lives with her husband in Los Angeles. The co-author of the Jewish holiday book "Seasons for Celebration," she has written a success guide for teens (www. flippingburgersandbeyond.com). She welcomes messages and visitors at www.mrslieutenant.com.

Acknowledgments

With gratitude to the four women who have been the strongest supporters of this book: Loretta Savery, who for many long years has cheered on this book; Susan Chodakiewitz, who is my exercise partner, business partner, and confidante; and my two daughters – Rachel and Yael – for whom I've written this story.

And thanks to my husband Mitch, who made me an officer's wife.

My sources for putting this story in historical context are "Day by Day: The Seventies," Volume 1, 1970–1975, by Thomas Leonard, Cynthia Crippen and Marc Aronson, and "The Vietnam War: An Almanac," general editor John S. Bowman with introduction by Fox Butterfield.

And, of course, in the spring of 1970, Mary Preston Gross' Mrs. Lieutenant (Third Edition) taught me how to be a proper officer's wife.

PART I – ACTIVE DUTY

SHARON – I – May 4, 1970

"It has been said that when a man acquires a commission, the government has gained not one, but two – the officer and his wife."

They drive around the western edge of Lake Michigan, past the industrial suburbs of Chicago, down into the flat farmland of Indiana, their tiny convertible a bright yellow bug boring through the cornfields.

Sharon Gold moves her cramped right foot, and the Farberware coffeepot bangs against her shin. Then the brown paper grocery bag with its open boxes of cereal and crackers shifts across her seatbelted lap. For the 10th time in the last two hours she glances around the densely packed interior of the Fiat Spider, a car that seemed truly wonderful when Robert bought it last summer, before they had to rely on it as a moving van.

It certainly can't be said that they have all their earthly possessions with them. When you have a car as small as a Fiat, you take only the barest necessities: Suitcases with summer clothes and bedding tied atop the luggage rack. A few pots and pans and shoes in the minuscule trunk. In the well behind the two seats are stashed a tiny black and white television, already several years old when her parents passed it on to them, and the Singer sewing machine presented in the hope that she might someday learn domestic skills. Their wedding gifts, their books and her stereo and albums, and the rest of their clothes remain at her parents' home, moved there from Robert's one-room apartment on Sheridan Drive they shared after their wedding.

The branch transfer to military intelligence from infantry has come through! Robert's orders are to report to Ft. Knox, Kentucky, for nine weeks of Armor Officers Basic to fulfill the requirement of a combat arms course before military intelligence training. "Why combat arms training?" she asked him when he received his new orders. "Surely you'll have a desk job. That's the whole point of getting the branch transfer." Robert didn't answer.

Her purse holds the official army reporting packet sent to Robert. The orders for Ft. Knox say nothing about his wife. Robert reminded her of the old army joke: "If the army had wanted him to have a wife, they would have issued him one."

Her purse also contains the journal she bought yesterday. She's a firm believer in the expression that, when you are handed lemons, make lemonade. Since she wants to be a writer, she's going to record her experiences in the army. Maybe she can write articles or short stories about this alien environment and sell them to a newspaper or magazine.

"You think your parents are still upset?" Robert asks.

Sharon glances at him, acutely aware of his altered looks. His long sideburns shaved off; the rest of his dark hair trimmed by the barber so close to his scalp that the waves usually framing his broad face have disappeared.

Is he asking about her insistence on coming with him to Ft. Knox? Or about something more basic – Sharon marrying him right before the start of his two-year active duty commitment?

At last night's dinner Sharon's mother passed the platter of roast beef for the second time. "Wouldn't it be a better idea for you to wait until Robert has gone down to Kentucky? Checked on the housing situation? Then you could fly down to join him when he's found a place for you to live."

This plan has been proposed before. Sharon's mother first put it forward when she and Sharon lunched at Marshall Field's after a morning of shopping in the mammoth State Street department store. Her mother had actually been somewhat tactful, pointing out how much difficulty Sharon might have relating to the people she would meet at Ft. Knox. "Remember when you decided where to go to college?" she said. "You didn't listen to us then about going to the University of Illinois – you insisted on going to Michigan State – and look what happened!"

All around the department store dining room the lunch crowd enjoyed the food. Sharon grasped her water glass. Presumably her mother meant the two roommates at MSU that Sharon had been assigned her first term – the WASP from the upper-class Detroit suburb of Grosse Pointe and the Catholic from the Hamtramck working-class section of Detroit, both prejudiced against Jews – and then, second term, the hostile roommate off a farm in central Michigan who had never met a Jew before. Or perhaps her mother meant meeting Robert. Sharon didn't ask for clarification.

At the dinner table last night her father studied his refilled plate while her mother repeated her position. As a successful real estate attorney, he identified those occasions in which keeping quiet could enhance a negotiation.

Sharon took the platter out of her mother's hands and passed it on to her brother Howard without taking seconds. "Relax, Mom. I keep telling you, I can always stay with Grandma and Grandpa in Louisville. At least then I'll only be an hour away from Robert."

Her mother had the last word: "Two days with your grandparents will be too much."

She looks at Robert now, his eyes on the road ahead. "I think they accept my coming with you."

"If they do, why did they get your brother to show up and try to talk you out of going?"

Sharon studies her husband's face. His tone isn't belligerent, but she can't read his expression.

In fact she suspects Howard did receive an official summons from his studies at the University of Illinois to say good-bye to his only sibling. His assigned mission probably included trying to dissuade her from her "ridiculous" plan to go with her husband. If so, her parents wasted their train money and Howard's time.

Howard, her younger brother by two years and several inches taller than her 5'5" height. There is a clear family resemblance with their light brown hair, narrow faces with strong noses, and dark eyes, not to mention their good complexions thanks to a rigorous dermatologist who burned off their blemished skin with dry ice treatments. And their opposition to the Vietnam War is equally strong.

Finally she says, "It was nice to have a chance to say good-bye. I don't know when we'll see him again."

Robert snorts, flipping one hand momentarily off the wheel. "It would have been better if he had left his 'make love not war' paraphernalia at school. He overdid it."

Sharon leans toward Robert, about to say something. Instead she stares straight ahead.

Robert glances over at her, then returns his eyes to the road. "How will you feel if he's drafted and goes to Canada? You may not be able to see him for years."

Not see Howard for years? Robert insists that Howard has the luxury to be anti-war due to his college deferment along with his high lottery draft number based on his birth date – 239 – drawn five months ago in the December 1st draft lottery. Robert's lottery number was 16, making his college commitment to ROTC – Reserve Officers Training Corps – appear to be a prescient choice. Even an anti-war protestor like herself realizes it's better to be entering the army as an officer rather than at the lowest enlisted rank.

"Do you really think Howard would go to Canada?" she says.

"You'll have to ask him yourself."

Sharon can't predict what her younger brother would do. Even if Howard says he'll never flee to Canada, he still might.

Robert hums along with the song on the radio – Kenny Rogers singing "Ruby, Don't Take Your Love to Town." Sharon wants to ask Robert to switch the channel, not to listen to the song of a paralyzed

Vietnam vet whose woman has to go "to town" to get physical love. War is wrong, so wrong! Robert can get killed!

She wills the tears not to start and studies the farmland all around them. The top of the convertible is up to prevent their possessions from flying out, and the open windows let in the pungent odors of grass and cattle. She shrugs the smells away. She does not like the country. Too few people around and too few things to do.

Her hair blows around her head. The microscopic hairs on Robert's head don't move a fraction. Her mother whispered to her last night, "Why is his hair so short?" Obviously her mother doesn't know anything about the army. And the nightly television news shots of men fighting in Vietnam are too blurry to see the men's hair length.

Sharon yanks her mind away from the thought of men fighting. To calm herself she silently recites the opening lines of the Prologue to Chaucer's "Canterbury Tales," a relic from her English literature classes in college: *Whan that April with his shoures soote/The droghte of March hath perced to the roote* ...

In the midst of these Middle English words the last line of a Milton sonnet pops into her head: "*They also serve who only stand and wait.*"

Sharon fingers the bag on her lap. Is this also heroism? And will she be prepared if a sacrifice is required?

The radio signal from Chicago suddenly dies out. They must be approaching Louisville. She fiddles with the knobs to find a local channel.

She knows she's found a Louisville station when she hears: "Pete, what did you think of Dust Commander's winning time of 2 minutes and 3 2/5 seconds?"

"Chuck, I think Mike Manganello was a hell of a jockey."

"I agree with you, Pete.

"And for you listening out there today who may have been in outer space this past Saturday and not near a radio or television, we're discussing this year's Kentucky Derby, a 1 1/4 mile race for three-year-old horses run at Churchill Downs race track here in Louisville.

"So, Pete, let's talk about some of the other horses who gave Dust Commander a run for the money."

Sharon pictures spectators leaning over the railing along the race track. Their lips move but she hears nothing. Instead of horses thundering down on top of each other, their jockeys bunched close over them, Sharon sees her own life ahead on the racecourse, the obstacles past the turns still unknown. How will she ever fit into a military environment?

"This just in," a different voice erupts on the radio. "The National Guard has fired on Kent State University students protesting the Vietnam War and Nixon's incursion into Cambodia. Some shootings have been reported. We'll have more as soon as it's available."

"The National Guard fired on students!" Perspiration dots her palms. Howard could have been there; she could have been there.

"Find another station," Robert says. "See if there's any more news."

The police siren comes out of nowhere as she jerks the knobs along a static-filled band.

"We've got company," Robert says.

Sharon flicks the radio off and peers behind them. A police car right on their tail signals them to pull over. "Were you speeding?" she asks.

Robert brings the car to a stop on the shoulder and looks at her. He turns back to the driver's side window.

A tall police officer in his early 30s comes alongside Robert. His hat, low over his forehead, covers his eyes. "May I see your license?"

Robert pulls his wallet out of his back pocket and hands over his driver's license.

"From Chicago," the officer reads.

Can he tell they are Jewish? Will he throw the book at them because he hates Jews? They are in the South now, and everyone knows about prejudiced Southerners.

The officer leans closer, cigarette smoke pulsating off his uniform. "Now why were you doing 60 in a 40-mile-per-hour zone?"

Robert squirms. "I didn't realize the speed limit had dropped, sir."

"Yep, you're right outside Louisville" – he pronounces it Loullville like her grandmother – "and this here is a speed trap." He grins, stretching his suntanned face.

"Then you caught us," Robert says.

The officer peers into the car, stuffed with all their things. "Where you folks going?"

"To Ft. Knox, sir."

The officer smiles again. "The Golds going to the gold."

What does he mean? Oh, yes, the gold at Ft. Knox.

"Reporting for active duty – Armor Officers Basic," Robert says.

"An officer, huh?"

"Yes, sir."

The police officer straightens up and gestures down the road to Louisville.

"If you promise to follow the posted signs from now on," he says, "I'll let you off this time. Have to support our boys in uniform."

President Nixon calls
student protestors "bums"
and those fighting in
Vietnam the "greatest"...
May 1, 1970

KIM – I – May 4

"If the wife is well informed as to what is expected of her, the
probability is greater that the officer will have an easier and
more successful career."

Kim Benton places her pet white rat Squeaky in his metal cage under the sagging bed and out of Jim's sight. It is a small motel room, and it smells of hair spray and shaving cream and liquor and sex. Tomorrow if they are lucky they'll find an apartment.

When they crossed the state line today into Virginia, Jim leaned over and kissed her. "Welcome to being out of North Carolina for the first time," he said.

She hadn't felt any excitement, just anxiety. And the anxiety had less to do with the new state, she knows, than with the reason for the move.

She glances into the bathroom, where Jim stands shaving, his serious, good-looking face reflected in the mirror. She refused his parents' offer to stay with them while Jim drove up here to Ft. Knox and found housing. His parents have the same fear of Northerners that she does. They thought it would be better if Jim made all the arrangements before subjecting Kim to such changes. It took a lot for her to say no to their offer, especially with Jim encouraging her to accept.

She waited once before, a long time ago, for the most important people in her life to return from a short trip. They hadn't. And now she can't bear to be separated from her husband, even for a few days. For a moment her mind darts to the terrifying thought of a year's separation if he is sent to Vietnam. Just as quickly she thinks of something else, anything else, to prevent the pounding headache that always accompanies her deepest fears.

"Honey, I'm ready," Jim says as he comes out of the bathroom.

He must have seen the expression on her face, because he puts his arms around her. "Everything's going to be fine."

She smiles up at him. "You're bleeding. Did you nick yourself shaving?"

She raises her hand to wipe away the blood. But before she can, he says, "Let's just go."

The blood droplet hits the floor as she follows him. No need to stop and wipe it up; it doesn't even show among all the other stains.

PHYLLIS ZIMBLER MILLER

In the car Kim reaches for the map as Jim starts the engine. "I know where to go, honey," he says. He backs the car out of the motel lot and turns towards Ft. Knox.

The air still drips the heat of the day. Kim brushes perspiration off her forehead and searches the sky for signs of rain.

"It was sure nice of our preacher to arrange this introduction," Jim says. He hums a tune, something familiar, perhaps a church hymn, she can't quite recognize it.

Actually, this meeting worries Kim. The preacher of their Southern Baptist church contacted a captain and his wife from their hometown stationed at Ft. Knox. The couple wrote Kim and Jim inviting them for dinner this first night. Bill and Susanna Norris are a few years older than she and Jim, so she and Jim don't know them. Will Kim embarrass herself with her ignorance?

"They live in post housing for officers – but it's not really on the post," Jim explains as he turns away from the sign pointing to the entrance to Ft. Knox. "We won't be seeing the actual Ft. Knox tonight."

Kim isn't disappointed. She is in no rush to see an army post.

It's not yet dark, and she can clearly see the houses they drive past. The ranch-style semi-detached red-brick buildings look nice, with kids' bikes in the driveway and an occasional small camper parked in

15

front. Trees and some scraggly flowers break up the monotony of identical lawns.

Jim stops in front of one of the buildings. When they reach the front door, a sign announces "Captain William Norris."

A little girl of about three with two brown braids and a pink gingham dress stands in the open door. Right behind her comes a woman with shoulder-length blond hair and a cotton patterned dress covering a plump body. "Welcome to Ft. Knox," she says. "I'm Susanna Norris. Bill will be right here. He's just chasin' Billy Jr. 'round the yard out back. And this is Patty."

"Hello," Kim says.

Patty says nothing.

"Patty, mind your manners! Say hello to Mrs. Benton," her mother says.

Patty still says nothing as they all walk into the living room. She's shy Kim thinks.

"Patty! Pay attention to me!" Susanna's voice increases in volume. She grabs Patty by the arm. "Say hello."

"'ello," Patty says, then sits down next to her mother on the couch.

Susanna smiles at Jim and Kim. "We expect our children to have good manners. I was raised without parents but I know how important manners are."

"Sure are," Jim says.

Relief edges up Kim's chest. Thank heavens Jim doesn't say anything more.

Susanna nods in appreciation of Jim seconding her opinion. "My daddy died when I was just Patty's age and my brother was as little as Billy Jr.," Susanna says. "My mama had what my granny called a drinkin' condition."

Susanna twists around to Patty. "Stop that wigglin'," she says, slapping Patty on the arm. "Now sit still."

Kim's stomach wobbles. Patty hasn't been doing anything wrong. How quiet can a little girl sit?

Susanna turns back to them. "One day my mama just didn't come on home. My granny raised us as best she could, but she wasn't one for talkin' to kids or showin' any love."

Has slapping her own daughter shown love?

"Hello, everyone, I'm Bill Norris," says a tall thin man coming into the room with a baby boy in his arms. The roly-poly child is as blond as his father and mother. Where does Patty get her brown hair?

Jim immediately stands. "Good evening, Captain Norris."

The man waves Jim back to his seat. "Just call me Bill. We're informal here at home."

Kim smiles her hello.

"Can I get you anything to drink?"

"No, sir, we're fine," Jim answers for both of them.

Susanna turns to Bill. "The chicken and dumplin's will be ready in a few minutes. We're just gettin' to know each other."

"It was very nice of you to have us for dinner," Jim says.

"Our pleasure," Bill says.

Jim glances at Kim, his eyebrows raised. He wants her to say something.

"How did you two meet?" she asks.

Susanna beams, taking Billy Jr. from her husband's arms and bouncing him on her knees.

"We met in senior year of high school. His folks had just moved to town. It was love at first sight..." – she glances at her husband – "... and a way to escape my granny's house."

"I was just as poor and ignorant as she was, but I was enlisting in the army right after high school graduation. I had a future." Bill grins.

"We got married on a two-day leave from basic training," Susanna says as Billy Jr. gurgles his appreciation of the horsey ride. "I got pregnant on our weddin' night. Neither one of us knew a darn thing about sex or birth control."

Again that flush of relief. Kim could have been as ignorant as Susanna on her own wedding night.

"What did you do?" Kim asks.

"Bought a washin' machine and dryer. Bill got to go to OCS – Officers Candidate School. I took in wash from the other men and it helped support me and the baby."

Jim turns to Bill. "Weren't you worried about your wife talking to all those single men? You never know what single men might be after."

A stab of pain above her left eye. Please may he not start.

Bill leans forward as if he can see through Jim, then he says, "I'm talking about my buddies. In OCS – OCS is hell on wheels, 120 days of pure hell – you can't survive if you can't trust your buddies and they can't trust you. There's a motto – 'Cooperate and graduate.' You'd do well to remember that." He leans back.

"And once I finished OCS it was better. We had more money on a second lieutenant's salary and we were entitled to housing. Susanna could stop doing laundry for the men."

Mercifully Susanna turns to her husband before Jim can say anything more. "Then you went to Vietnam and I was left alone with a baby who cried all the time."

Bill stands up and grins. "That's what army wives put up with. Now let's eat before we scare these newcomers. Jim won't have to think about a Vietnam tour for a while."

He turns to the two of them. "You can both enjoy your time at Ft. Knox."

At Kent State University
R.O.T.C. building attacked
and burned to the ground ...
May 2, 1970

DONNA – I – May 4

"Your knowledge and practice of Army customs will enable
you to eliminate and avoid many misunderstandings
and uncertain moments that are apt to arise when you
unintentionally disregard a practice or custom because of
lack of knowledge or uncertainty."

The reflection of the oval-shaped face with its slightly brownish skin tone in the bathroom mirror is certainly her own Donna Lautenberg thinks. Yet her face doesn't give away any hints as to how she feels, standing here like this, anticipating her husband's first day of active duty. It isn't that she's having deja vu. It's just that she feels ... different, a shiver of apprehension running up her back.

Will she fit in? Can she play by a whole new set of rules? After all those years of being an "army brat" of an enlisted man will she finally be accepted now that she is married to an Anglo and an officer, or will she still be a Puerto Rican outsider?

She continues to study her face, the face that reminds her of the other important people in her life, the face that reminds her of where she's come from. She'll write her brother tomorrow. She won't tell him about her fears of fitting in. He has enough to worry about.

"This apartment's not bad," Jerry says, coming into the bathroom behind her and putting his arms around her. He presses his muscular body up against hers and she feels his "excitement." He leans over and kisses her right ear, then looks at her face.

"Maybe you shouldn't have come with," he says. "It's only for a few weeks and I know how hard this must be for you."

She hugs him back, then pulls away and goes into the bedroom. There, lying on the bed, are six tiny yellow roses, still in their green tissue paper.

Jerry follows her out of the bathroom. She swings around and kisses him. "When did you get those? How did you know? You're so wonderful!"

He grins. "When I went out to get the milk. They're perfect for our first night in our new apartment."

She kisses him again.

"Come on, let's test the bed," he says. "That's the only thing that matters."

✲ ✲ ✲

The shots scatter the students. They run, their breath jammed in their throats, anticipating the thud that can bring them crashing to the ground. A National Guardsman aims his rifle at Donna.

The blast wakes her.

She shakes her head in the early morning light. She knows the nightmare is of Kent State, a place she never heard of until the news yesterday.

In her mind she now sees the student protest against ROTC at Jerry's college as he once described it to her: Right after winter break, in January of 1968, when the students returned to campus, their bellies stuffed with home cooking and their pockets jangling with Christmas cash.

On the first day of classes the protesting students converged upon Jerry and the other marching ROTC students with banners displaying peace symbols and chanting, "Hey, hey, LBJ, how many kids did you kill today?" The ROTC cadets tussled with the protesters. By the time the campus police arrived, Jerry had a broken arm – and later a reprimand from his ROTC instructor for "engaging with the enemy without orders to do so."

Two months after that protest President Johnson surprised everyone by announcing he would not run for reelection and ordering a reduction in the bombing of North Vietnam. And another two months later peace talks started in Paris. Not that those talks have accomplished anything in two whole years. American military personnel are still dying daily halfway across the world – and now

American students are being shot to death on college campuses.

Donna looks at Jerry still asleep, then eyes the six yellow roses spotting the floor, knocked there by last night's "testing."

She climbs out of bed and steps over the flowers on her way to the bathroom. The diaphragm has been in long enough.

She ties on a robe as she thinks about Jerry. He's the best thing that ever happened to her, something so unexpected and sweet that it still makes her feel giddy when she pictures their first meeting. Even now.

She isn't superstitious, really she isn't, she just doesn't want to tempt fate by dwelling on her good fortune.

This morning she has to unpack before she writes her brother. After she and Jerry moved their suitcases and boxes into this furnished apartment yesterday evening, she'd been too tired to do anything else. "Let's leave everything for tomorrow and take it easy our first night at Ft. Knox," she had said.

The doorbell rings. Did the apartment manager forget to tell them something yesterday? Donna hopes the bell doesn't wake Jerry.

Outside the front door stands a short man wearing a Western Union uniform that pulls across a beer barrel chest. A yellow envelope dangles from his hand.

The next thing she knows Jerry has his arms around her and they are sitting together on the floor of the living room. "What happened?" she asks.

"You fainted."

Donna struggles out of his arms and stands up. Jerry, in a bathrobe that hangs open in front, stands too. "Why would I do that?"

"There was a man – it was a mistake – looking for someone named Holden to deliver a telegram to. You took one look at him and fainted."

This is bad, very bad. She'll never make it as an officer's wife if she overreacts to everything.

She takes a deep breath and kisses Jerry. "Maybe I'm hungry," she says.

He kisses her back. "Let's have breakfast."

She walks into the kitchen. The familiarity of a sink, refrigerator and stove calms her.

As she takes a skillet from the packing box perched on the tiny counter, she makes a resolution: For now she'll only think of the present.

She'll banish the past and future from her mind.

Ohio National Guardsmen kill
4 and wound 11 at Kent State
University ...
May 4, 1970

WENDY – I – May 5

"... it is true that a wife has no rank, but she does have position created by her husband's rank, which is respected and accepted by Army custom."

"Mama, it's me," Wendy Johnson shouts into the telephone mouthpiece. "Nelson and I are at a gas station outside Ft. Knox. We're just filling up and then we're going to go see about finding a place to stay."

She listens to her mother's words of advice – "remember you're in the white world now," listens as she has always listened, then promises to call tomorrow and hangs up. She comes out of the phone booth and slides into the passenger side of the Mustang.

"What'd your mama say?" Nelson asks.

"The same as always. And we're to call as often as we can."

"She sure is a broken record, your mama."

"She usually has good advice, advice we can't afford to ignore."

Nelson lifts one hand off the steering wheel and pats Wendy's left arm. "Sweetie, it's going to be fine. Heck, I'm an officer of the United States Army. I will be treated with respect and saluted and looked up to by the enlisted men and the rest of society."

Wendy turns away from her husband for a moment so he can't see her eyes. It isn't his fault she's from such a protected environment that she hasn't been subjected to much racial prejudice. Now for the first time she might have to face what being a black in America really means. The thought terrifies her.

The night before they left South Carolina her papa called her into his study, the room that has always been the most comforting for Wendy, surrounded by his medical texts and medical school degrees and certificates. He sat behind his oversize mahogany desk in his red leather chair and she sat in a matching armchair facing him.

"Honey," he said, "your mama and I have always tried to do the best for you. We've done some things right and I'm sure a whole lot of things wrong. And maybe some of those things we thought we did right were really wrong."

What was he leading up to? She rubs her hands along the red leather armrests.

"We wanted you to be proud, proud of yourself and your race. And to do that we chose to protect you as much as we could from the real world as you were growing up."

He fiddled with papers on his desk, creating several small piles from a single large one as if laying bricks end to end, then returned his attention to her.

"Your mama and I kept as much as we could from you of the truth about the treatment of black people in America. We didn't want you to know how bad it can be."

He paused again and Wendy thought about her rudimentary school learning of the slaves in the South, the aftermath of Reconstruction, and the civil rights movement. It had all been pretty much book learning, because in her own black community – and then later at an all-black college in Texas – she led a rather sheltered life, not exposed to the rest of the world. This move to Ft. Knox would be her first time truly in the white world.

"When I was in the army in World War II," her papa was saying, "it was strictly segregated units. It wasn't until the Korean War – and that's only 20 years ago – that there were integrated units. And I'm afraid," he said, his speech slowing, "that the army may not have changed as much as we would like it to have."

"Do you think Nelson will have problems?" Wendy asked, holding her breath to see how much her papa would say now that he had started down this "truthful" path.

"It will depend on a lot of factors," he said, "including how you both handle yourselves. You and Nelson will have to wait and see."

Her father then stood and came around his desk to hug her. "Your mama and I wish you and Nelson all the best," he said.

That night when she and Nelson got ready for bed, Nelson asked, "What did your papa want with you in private?"

Wendy stood with her nightgown still in her hands, her nude body outlined by the glow of the lamp behind her. She opened her mouth to tell her husband, then changed her mind. Nelson always chided her for her naiveté. And she was naive – why shouldn't she be? As her mama once said, "Why hear bad news? It only makes you feel bad and you usually can't do anything about it."

In the same way Wendy hadn't really thought about blacks in America, she had refused to think about Nelson's army commitment. Why think of it ahead of time when she couldn't do anything about it? And even if her father's words had worried her, she wasn't about to admit this to Nelson. He'd just say something like "You're finally catching on."

Instead she smiled and said, "He wanted to say good-bye and wish us luck." Then she got into bed.

She knew the moment Nelson slid in beside her he'd forget the conversation, instantly immersed in his nightly exploration of the mysteries of her body. They had only been married four months.

Now here they are outside Ft. Knox, Kentucky, about to look for an apartment for themselves for the first time. They lived with her parents after their December graduation and wedding. Nelson worked in her papa's office and she practiced cooking and keeping house with her mama while waiting for Nelson to go on active duty.

The minimal active duty information they received from the army lists a housing office. Nelson stops the car at the entrance to Ft. Knox – they are here! – and asks the soldier there for directions to the office.

"That's an MP – a military policeman," he explains to her as they drive onto the post.

Wendy nods, then watches out the window. Wooden buildings perch haphazardly on green lawns, trees shading the buildings. The overall effect reminds Wendy of her college campus, and she resists the impulse to twist her head around, searching for the campanile at the center of the college quadrangle.

They follow the signs to the post housing office, where Nelson introduces himself to the clerk: "I'm Lieutenant Johnson. I understand you have a list of available units."

The clerk hands Nelson a manila envelope. "The list is inside. The ones with vacancies as of yesterday afternoon are marked," she says. "The one over in Muldraugh north of the post – Hansen's Apartments – is a good one. You should try there first."

Back in the car, they study the list and the accompanying map. Then they drive to Muldraugh and pull into Hansen's – a paved central parking lot surrounded on three sides by two-storey motel-like units. Sprinkled across the lot are a handful of cars, but no people.

The sun has already begun to fry the air, the moisture oozing onto their skin. Overgrown wild grass, edging the buildings, stands motionless. Food odors transmit signals from the closest units.

A hand-lettered OFFICE sign points to their right. Wendy fans herself with the housing list as they enter the office, where a man in a dirty t-shirt sits at a desk holding a bottle of beer.

"Hello," Nelson says, not offering his hand. "I'm Lieutenant Johnson. This is my wife. We've come about the unit to rent."

The man doesn't stand. He just stares at them, then grins. Watching him, Wendy's neck hairs itch.

"Sorry to say, that's been rented. I was just about to call the housing office and tell 'em."

Nelson says nothing. Wendy says "Thank you" as she follows Nelson out of the office.

"Damn!" Nelson says as they drive out of the parking lot.

"What's the matter?"

"I'm sure that unit's not rented yet; he just wouldn't rent to us."

"Why not? He knows you're an officer."

Nelson turns his eyes on her, then swings his eyes back to the road. "An officer yes, but still a black man," he says. "Hell, I don't know if it's going to be any different here than elsewhere. We're still going to be treated like shit."

Wendy stares out her side window while she wipes away the tears trapped in her eyes. "Can we go back to the housing office and complain?" she asks. "Maybe they can convince that man to let us rent from him."

"I don't think so. We should just try the trailer park on the list and not waste our time with the others."

Wendy gasps. "Live in a trailer?" White trash does that back home. She isn't going to live like they do.

And how can she tell her mama what kind of place she and Nelson rented? If her mama finds out, she and her papa might arrive on the trailer's doorstep and demand Wendy pack up and return home with them.

"It's our best bet. People will be more willing to rent to us if we're not living right next to some white folk, sharing a common wall and everything. I'm not up to taking a lot of this shit. It's only for a few weeks."

A few weeks! A few weeks of living in a tiny, dirty trailer with a little patch of gravel in front of a rickety metal doorstep? A few weeks of being totally isolated there, all alone, except when her husband comes home in the evenings! How will she ever survive?

As Wendy tries to decide what to say to Nelson, that little familiar flutter ripples through her. It's been there since the first time she laid eyes on Nelson.

She smiles to herself. She'll put up with whatever it takes to stay with her husband – she isn't going home.

"Where's the trailer park?" she asks.

Anti-war leaders call for
national university strike
to protest the war ...
May 4, 1970

SHARON – II – May 5

"... be proud of the fact that you are making an effort to contribute to the esprit de corps that is developed when we serve with the United States Army as part of a happy, congenial and proud family."

Sharon and Robert leave her grandparents' apartment and take the road south of Louisville, wandering past fast food places and used car lots. Although early in the day, the humidity fills the Fiat, now lightened considerably by the stashing of their belongings with her grandparents.

Her grandmother is really her step-grandmother, a Jewish woman who grew up poor in the cotton fields of Mississippi, where, she claims, she often played with the "colored" children. This morning Sharon had been tempted to ask if blacks still rode in the backs of buses in Louisville. Instead she and Robert graciously accepted the offered breakfast of hot – in this heat? – oatmeal and then hit the road.

She flicks the radio on and twiddles the knobs. They watched the news last night at her grandparents' apartment. Rows and rows of helmeted armed National Guardsmen rushing unarmed student protesters. The sounds of the shots buried in the chanting and screaming. The slumped bodies lying on the ground unmistakable. Four students. Add them to the total of war dead.

"...256 *Vietcong captured*," the cast of the Broadway musical "Hair" sang when Sharon and Robert had seen the production in New York the night after their Chicago wedding. Yet the musical's "Age of Aquarius" with its promise of "harmony and understanding" doesn't seem likely to materialize any time soon. *Then peace will guide the planet/And love will steer the stars.*

Sharon twiddles the knobs harder and still finds only commercials on the radio. She swats the knob into the "off" position, then brushes at the clammy film of moisture shimmering across her face and sliding down her neck.

The face she sees is always indistinguishable:

The perspiration drips down his face, oozing into his eyes and sliding over his mouth. He swipes at the beads dripping from his nose with the arm of his filthy fatigue shirt. "This heat is unbearable," the armor officer says to the 19-year-old enlisted man quivering beside him inside the tank. "How do the Vietnamese survive?"

The officer pops the hatch, standing upright in the commander's seat to check the terrain. The enemy hides somewhere nearby.

The explosion lifts his body up into the air, twisting it around before dumping it on top of the tank, his sweat-stained face turned downward as if searching for the softest place to land.

The 19-year-old screams.

Robert doesn't notice her panic – he's busy pointing at a sign on the highway indicating the approach of Ft. Knox.

"You better start learning to recognize officer rank insignia. It's important for you to know," he says.

Is this really happening? The National Guard kills four students protesting a war that the U.S. has no hopes of winning and she's about to become an officer's wife?

She must concentrate on the present. She takes a deep breath and considers what she knows about officer ranks: 1) Robert as a second lieutenant is the lowest level of officer; 2) Within the two years he will be serving he can expect to automatically become a first lieutenant. "What's after first lieutenant?"

"Captain, then major, then lieutenant colonel, full colonel, and several ranks of generals. The generals you won't have to worry about – you won't see a lot of those. For the others, you should know who's who."

Sharon peers towards the Ft. Knox entrance as Robert moves over into the highway's left turn lane. Suddenly a huge semi-trailer hauls towards them – in their lane!

"Shit!" Robert jerks the wheel and they spin out of the semi's path.

The five-ton truck couldn't stop. Something wrong with the brakes. The family in the Rambler station wagon didn't have a chance. Just facts on the evening news. To Sharon, hiding in her dark closet, it is the end of her life too.

Sharon releases her clenched hands. She says nothing.

At the entrance to Ft. Knox a uniformed soldier waves them to a stop. He wears an armband with the letters MP. Robert displays his orders.

"Welcome to Ft. Knox, sir."

Following the MP's directions, they drive onto the post and head towards the housing office. Wooden frame buildings and trees dot grass lawns, almost like the Jewish camp she attended two summers in Wisconsin, where the counselors lorded it over the campers in probably the same way the officers lord it over the enlisted personnel. She hates that claustrophobic feeling of someone else being in control of one's life, Big Brother watching every move. And now THE ARMY controls her life.

Before leaving Chicago Sharon read the brief entry for "Fort Knox" in her childhood "World Book Encyclopedia." The post – named for Major General

Henry Knox, the first secretary of war – covers 110,000 acres 35 miles south of Louisville. Ft. Knox houses the United States Army Armor Center as well as the depository since 1936 of billions of dollars worth of gold.

"Where's the building with the gold?" she asks Robert.

"We'll find it later."

Sharon inhales. "What else should I know?"

"Officers wear their rank on their shoulders – or on their collars when they're wearing fatigues."

Fatigues. The olive green shirt and pants worn in combat. Every night on the news all of America can see men in fatigues, often soaked in blood. The bloodstains don't show up clearly on black-and-white television.

Robert swats a fly away from his face. "Second lieutenants have one gold bar. First lieutenants one silver bar. Captains two silver bars. Majors one gold maple leaf. Lieutenant colonels one silver maple leaf. Full colonels one silver eagle. Generals gold stars, one for each rank – one-star general, two star, etc."

How confusing, and this is only the officers' ranks. "What about enlisted men?"

"Enlisted men always wear their rank on their sleeves. You won't have to learn their ranks. Officers aren't supposed to fraternize with the enlisted men."

Just lead them into battle, often to their deaths Sharon thinks.

The sign indicates the housing office straight ahead. Inside, a woman in a polyester pantsuit glances up from her desk behind the counter.

"May I help you, Lieutenant?" Robert has worn his Class A uniform from ROTC to look more official. Obviously this woman can read rank insignia.

"I'm Lieutenant Gold and I'm reporting for Armor Officers Basic. You have listings for available housing off base."

The woman stands up and walks towards the counter. "If you were here alone, we'd quarter you in Bachelor Officers Quarters. As you have your wife with you, we can give you some leads on housing in the surrounding areas. I caution you, the places may not be what you're used to." She hands Robert a manila envelope. "Here's your information packet. Welcome to Ft. Knox."

"What does she think we're used to?" Sharon asks as she and Robert return to the Fiat. "She certainly couldn't tell from what I'm wearing – a simple summer dress. And the uniform is the same for everyone."

Robert grunts. "Maybe they've had complaints from new lieutenants before." Then he grins. "Or maybe because I didn't say 'you all.'"

They drive back out of the post and, starting with the first place on the list, turn onto the highway that leads south towards Elizabethtown. Inside the town limits small and medium-size houses line the roads. Bright flowers decorate many of the front lawns, the air as hot as everywhere else.

They follow the map provided by the housing office and stop in front of a brick ranch-style house. Robert rings the doorbell. After a few seconds a thin man in his early 50s dressed in casual clothes answers the door.

"Hello," Robert says. "We're interested in the apartment listed with the housing office."

The man looks Robert up and down. He doesn't even glance at Sharon.

"You wouldn't be happy here, Lieutenant."

"I'm sure the apartment is fine," Robert says.

"I'm sorry, sir, but I really can't rent you the apartment." The man closes the door in their faces.

"We didn't even see the apartment," Sharon says. "How does he know we wouldn't like it?"

Robert walks back down the sidewalk without saying a word. Sharon follows and gets into the car. Robert starts the engine, then speaks as he pulls away from the curb.

"He's obviously a former enlisted man."

"How could you tell that?"

"From the way he called me 'sir.' He doesn't want to rent to an officer. Makes him uncomfortable."

"Uncomfortable! We wouldn't be living with him. Just renting his apartment. How dare he be so rude to us!"

Robert flicks his eyes towards Sharon. "We have a lot to learn."

Hours later they drive back to the housing office. They have seen trailers not fit to live in, apartments so small they couldn't have turned around without bumping into each other, and plain dumps. For this she insisted on coming with Robert?

"Maybe there'll be some new listings now," Robert says.

"Since this morning?"

The clerk greets them like long-lost friends. "One of the best apartment complexes in the area – Hansen's Apartments – has an opening. I didn't tell you this morning because I thought someone else was taking it. But it's still available. Hurry over to Muldraugh and see about this one."

They look at each other. What does this clerk consider a good apartment?

Muldraugh lies north of the post. They easily locate the place. The town isn't big enough to get lost. The complex looks just like a motel, with three buildings surrounding a parking lot.

A man in his late 40s with arm muscles bulging under his dirty t-shirt meets them in the office. "Lieutenant, I have just the apartment for ya."

The man comes out from behind his desk. In his right hand he holds a shotgun. Sharon recoils against Robert.

The man looks at her, then grins. "I was just goin' out to hunt stray dogs."

Stay calm she tells herself.

They follow him up an outside staircase to a furnished second-floor apartment with a minuscule living room, dining area and kitchenette. An equally small bedroom and bathroom complete the unit.

It's clean and neat. Sharon nods.

"Can I speak to you for a moment – in private?" Robert asks her.

The man throws them a look and goes out onto the balcony, his shotgun still slung down his side.

"There's no shower, only a bath," Robert says. "I can't stand not having a shower."

"You'll just have to. I'm not about to give up this decent apartment. Who knows what else we'll find?"

Robert goes out onto the balcony and Sharon watches him shake the man's hand – the one not holding the shotgun. "We'll move in tomorrow," Robert says.

"I figure ya all'll get together with ya neighbors," the man says, jerking a thumb towards the apartment next door.

Sharon wonders what he means as she watches Robert follow him down the stairs. When the men get to the bottom of the stairs, she leans over the railing, studying the other two buildings, one on each side of her.

She is actually here and going to stay. She takes a deep breath and steadies herself against the railing.

✯ ✯ ✯

The next afternoon a knock on the apartment door interrupts Sharon as she is unpacking their few kitchen utensils, brought from her grandparents' apartment in Louisville this morning. Robert stays in the bathroom putting away their toiletries. She goes to the door and opens it to a tall woman with dark hair and a wide smile.

"Yes?" Sharon says.

"I'm Anne Grossman and I live next door. I've come to say hi and invite you over."

Grossman can be a Jewish name, but Sharon doesn't expect to find many Jews down here. Is Anne Grossman Jewish? And is that what the apartment owner meant about them getting together with these neighbors?

"I'm Sharon Gold."

The woman smiles even wider. "My husband Michael will be home soon. Why don't you and your husband come over around 8? We can watch tv together."

Watch tv together? Is this army code for some other activity or does this woman really mean it? In either case Sharon wants to meet people.

"We'll do that. My husband's name is Robert," Sharon adds.

"We'll see you and Robert at 8 then."

As Sharon closes the door behind Anne, Robert comes out of the bathroom. "Did I hear voices?"

"We've just been invited over at 8 this evening by our next-door neighbors. They might be Jewish."

Robert smiles. "Don't bet on it. Anyway, come on, let's go to the post. We just have time to get your dependent's ID card before the office closes for the day."

She is about to officially become an officer's wife.

They make tuna sandwiches for their first dinner in their new apartment, having stopped by a grocery store on Dixie Highway on the way back from the post. The army dependent ID she got today can't be used at the army commissary until Robert officially goes on active duty May 8th.

After dinner Robert says, "And just don't blabber away. You have to be careful what you say, particularly about Vietnam."

"What do you think I'm going to say? That I'm against the war? That I don't want you to go there?"

He kisses her. "Just remember we're playing by a different set of rules now. And since we're the new kids on the block, we'd better keep our mouths shut."

She straightens her short skirt and checks her blouse in the mirror. She has on a skirt because perhaps it is incorrect to wear pants when making a social call. She hasn't put on nylons with her sandals. Too hot.

A second after Sharon and Robert knock, Michael Grossman opens the door and invites them in. Sharon suspects that, even with the television blaring, these neighbors can hear well enough through the thin walls to know when she and Robert left their apartment. Now neither Anne nor Michael turns the television off or the volume down.

Of medium height with dark hair and dark eyes, Michael looks as if he could be Jewish. He gestures to the television encased in its own mahogany cabinet.

"Isn't it a beauty?" Michael says. "Everyone in the complex loves it."

The television flaunts a big screen – probably the biggest she's ever seen.

"Did you bring it from home?" Robert asks.

"Absolutely!" Anne says. "We told the army it had to be shipped down here. We didn't care what else they shipped. The television had to come."

Sharon stares at the television. She hates watching the news from Vietnam roll across the screen: The helmeted soldiers in their splotched fatigues carrying their dead and dying comrades in litters, running for helicopters that just as likely won't make it to a field hospital in time. The images followed by the usual announcements: How many have died today in Vietnam. What new battle has brought the death toll of Americans even higher.

How can these people want to see the battle scenes on such a large screen, making the figures even more lifelike? Are they really that removed from reality?

She glances at Robert and remembers his warning. She says, "We didn't ship anything. We didn't know the army would ship anything for us."

Anne and Michael stare at them as if they are children. "Of course they have to ship some things. Didn't you find out what you were entitled to?"

Sharon and Robert look at each other, then back at their hosts. They say no in unison. Their hosts' facial expressions clearly say what they think of such imbecilic behavior.

"You're Jewish, aren't you?" Anne says. When they don't answer immediately, she goes on, "Michael is Jewish, I'm Catholic."

What can possibly be a courteous response to this admission? Sharon doesn't approve of "mixed marriages." Her parents always told her and Howard that they had to socialize with and marry Jews. What shall she say now to Anne? Michael saves her from replying.

He turns to Robert and says, "I'm working on a medical discharge. I have some pulled tendons in my right knee – I figure if I play this right, I can get out of the army now."

Not have to go to Vietnam is what he means, Sharon knows. She watches Robert's face. His expression doesn't change and he says nothing.

Michael now turns to Sharon, "What's your favorite at this time of night?"

It takes a moment to realize he means television program.

Two hours later Sharon and Robert lay naked under the sheets, having survived watching Anne and Michael's favorite television programs.

"Robert, shhh. They can probably hear every sound through the wall."

The bed creaks, and the headboard pushes up against the wall – only thin plasterboard separates them from the headboard of Anne and Michael's mirror-image bed next door.

"One more state we've done it in," Robert says.

His hands tiptoe across her breasts. She forgets about the neighbors – and their giant television.

*Governor Reagan closes
down entire California
university and college
system in effort to cool
student tempers ...*
May 6, 1970

KIM – II – May 6

"Play the game according to the rules and do not try to change them."

Kim unpacks the black-and-white photo in its battered metal frame, placing it on the small table next to the bed in the furnished apartment. The uneven table legs cause the picture to slant to one side, making the man standing against the wooden frame house seem shorter than the woman next to him, her hand resting on his arm.

The first time Jim saw the picture he offered to buy her a new frame. Kim refused, saying she liked the old frame. She lied. She hated the poor frame, hated the thought that this was all that she had. Yet she can't give up any part of the only thing she'd ever been given as a young child just for herself.

Jim comes into the room with a carrying case. He takes the gun from the case and places it in the nightstand drawer. "We're all set now," he says.

Kim slides Squeaky in his cage into the closet, leaving the door open a crack for air. Best to keep Squeaky out of Jim's sight. He sometimes accuses her of paying more attention to the pet rat than to him.

Then she avoids Jim's eyes and instead speaks to the photo. "Why can't we get a phone?"

Jim sits down on the bed and pulls her to him. "Honey, we've been through this already. It's only for a few weeks and we can save the money. Who are we going to call except my parents and your sister? And we can call them from a pay phone every Sunday."

She says nothing. They were lucky to get this apartment – nicer than the student housing apartment they had. This is the first one they saw up here, and they took it immediately.

"Can I take the car to the store? I need some more things."

"Just come right back."

Kim takes her purse off the bed and leaves the apartment. She wasn't sure Jim would let her go by herself. He might have thought she didn't yet know her way around. When they had first married and lived in student housing, he worried she'd get lost on campus. He drove her almost everywhere she wanted to go rather than let her walk or take the bus.

Now she noses the Ford into a place alongside an old Chevy in front of the little store up the road from the apartment. She'll get some ingredients to make sugar cookies. This should please Jim.

Two clerks stand behind a counter covered with items for sale. A man in olive green fatigues and combat boots faces the two clerks.

"Where can I find the baking items?" she asks the older of the two clerks. He points to the far corner along the street side of the store.

The soldier turns toward her. "Honey, I could sure help you find the sugar."

Kim ignores him as she walks toward the baking goods shelf with the soldier trailing behind her.

"Hey, honey," he says, "I'm talking to you."

She takes a small bag of flour and a box of sugar off the shelf along with a can of baking powder. She has salt, vanilla and butter at the apartment.

Although he has said nothing more, Kim can hear the man's footsteps behind her as she returns to the counter.

The older clerk is no longer there. She hands her packages to the younger man. He smiles at her. There is something not quite right about his eyes and the way he moves sort of slow. When he asks her if this is all, his voice sounds slurred.

The soldier bumps against her. "Excuse me, mam," he says. "I'm just trying to be friendly." His breath smells of beer.

She doesn't answer. The clerk says, "She don't want to be bothered. Go away." He makes shooing motions with his hands.

"No one tells me to go away!"

"Go away. Go away," the clerk says.

Kim stuffs her hand into her purse to find some money and leave. But the soldier runs out the front door. She now counts out the exact amount, smiles at the clerk, and says "thank you." At that moment something explodes behind her!

She jumps, then swivels towards the bang. The soldier stands in the doorway, a rifle in his hands. He whirls and runs out. Kim turns back toward the counter as the clerk moans and slumps over. A circle of red slowly balloons across the counter, mixing with the candy and gum lined up in neat rows.

She screams and screams! From somewhere the older clerk appears. He looks at her, then at the other clerk. Then he screams too. "Jesus Christ! He killed Marvin!"

Kim sinks down onto the floor and rocks back and forth on her knees. The older clerk explains, "Marvin was harmless – just a bit touched in the head. He didn't mean nothing." She keeps rocking.

The clerk says, "I have to call the MPs. It won't be that hard to find the guy. His name was on his fatigues. You'll just have to wait to give a statement, then you can go home."

"No, no!" She jumps up and runs out the door, clutching the grocery bag to her chest. She drives off as the balloon of blood spreads itself farther and farther in front of her eyes.

She can't believe what has happened. It is like a movie, or maybe the news on television. What will she tell Jim? He'll be able to tell she's upset, that something has happened. He'll think the worst if she says nothing.

She'll tell him ... the truth, someone shot the clerk. She won't tell him why, won't say the soldier had been pestering her, the clerk had tried to protect her, that she's responsible for his death.

She parks the car in front of their apartment and bends her head over the steering wheel.

The first stabs of a migraine jab above her eyes.

She must go in. She has sat here too long. Jim could come out of the apartment any minute looking for her.

She opens the apartment door and puts the grocery bag down on the table. "What took so long?" Jim says.

Then he must notice her tear-streaked face because he flings himself off the couch. "Did

someone mess with you? Who did it? I'll kill him."
He turns towards the bedroom where the gun is as
she screams, "No, no! Sit down and I'll tell you!"

She clasps her hands together. "The clerk at the
store was killed by a soldier. The soldier just shot the
clerk."

"While you were there?"

She nods, staring at her hands.

"Oh, honey, it must have been terrible for
you," he says. He jumps up and hugs her. "Some
of these guys, they get crazy, all that killing they
see in Vietnam, makes them do crazy things. " He
nods his head as if agreeing with himself that this
happens.

"Besides, even down home people do go crazy
with their guns," he says. "Happens all the time.
Just sorry you had to be there." He asks no other
questions.

During the next few days she stays in the
apartment, afraid to go out except when she has to
go with Jim to the post to get her ID. While there
Jim insists she call Susanna Norris to thank her
for the dinner and tell her where they found an
apartment.

Now, on the first day of Jim's AOB class, Kim
sits in the living room, hot even with the room air

conditioner running, and crochets little squares of green yarn and yellow yarn that will become an afghan for her sister Diane's Christmas present.

And over and over again Kim wishes for a phone. She wants to call her sister, be reassured that things are fine at home. Without a phone here she would have to go out to make the call, the closest phone at the little store. And she sure isn't going there – not ever again.

Kim squeezes her eyes shut to block the mental picture of the ballooning blood just as the doorbell rings.

"Hi," Susanna says, ushering her children through the door. "Thought you might like a little company."

Kim doesn't tell Susanna what happened. Instead she sits listening to Susanna chatter about life as an army wife. "And it was so much fun meetin' Bill in Hawaii. You know, for R & R after six months in Vietnam. Patty and I loved the beaches. And at night Bill and I really pumped those bed springs."

Kim has never met anybody who talks so much, who tells all the details of her life without hardly even knowing the person she's telling.

Susanna fans her face and pops a bottle in Billy Jr.'s mouth. "Just wait till you're invited to your first official function. It'll be so much fun to meet everybody."

Kim's thinking how much agony it could be, worrying about saying the wrong thing or doing the wrong thing, when Patty slips off the couch and walks to the kitchenette. "ooies!" she says.

"That's how she says cookies," Susanna says to Kim. Then Susanna says, "Patty, come back over here. It's not polite to ask for food."

Patty stays where she is, repeating "ooies" over and over. Kim doesn't know what to do. Should she offer cookies to the child or would that be interfering with the mother's authority? As a child she learned all too well the consequences of interfering with an adult's authority.

And then Susanna gets up, switching Billy Jr. from one hip to the other, and walks over to Patty. Susanna bends down and slaps Patty. "No cookies. Now come back and sit down quietly." Patty follows her mother back to the couch.

Kim's chest lurches. She stands up. "I have some cookies I'd be glad to give her."

"No," Susanna says. "She didn't come over here when I told her to so she can't have any cookies."

The tears in the child's eyes shine up at Kim. She feels as if she herself has been the one slapped. She herself ... Kim switches her mind back to Patty. The child looks so miserable that Kim asks, "Can I show my pet rat to the children?"

"Rat!" Susanna says. "Absolutely not."

She stands up and says, "It's time to go. Billy Jr. needs a nap."

Kim waves good-bye to them from the door. "Thanks for stopping by," she remembers to say, glad they are leaving. She doesn't want to have to talk to anyone or to feel badly about anyone else. She just wants to feel safe.

Now Kim hears the Ford outside. She opens the door before Jim can insert his key.

"How was it?" she asks.

"Nothing much happened in class," he says.

He closes the door. "A guy from my class – Robert Gold – invited us over tonight. He's from the North, but he seems like a nice guy. He lives right near here and he says you and his wife might like to meet."

"He invited us over without knowing us?"

Jim nods his head. "Guess they do that, so I said yes."

A warning jab above her left eye. She doesn't want to go out and she certainly isn't prepared to meet any new people yet, especially ones from the North!

She wants to scream at Jim that he shouldn't have said yes without asking her first – especially when she is still upset – but she doesn't want to start a fight. She'll take some aspirin and get through it.

At least no one will be shot and killed in front of her eyes.

House rejects proposal
for July 1 cutoff date
for funds to support
U.S. troops in Cambodia ...
May 7, 1970

SHARON – III – May 13

"It will certainly be more advantageous to both of you if his record reflects a man and wife who were sincere in their efforts, could meet and enjoy new people, able to adapt to different and new circumstances, and who displayed an attitude of cooperation and respect."

At dinner time Sharon leans over the balcony railing to watch for the yellow blur announcing the Fiat's arrival. The sizzling sun fries the few cars mired in the asphalt parking lot.

In her mind it is morning again, the alarm clock's shrill ring waking her. For a moment she doesn't recognize where she is. Then she remembers and also what today is – the day Robert reports for the Armor Officer Basic training course. She rolls over to reach for him – he isn't there! A wild fear sweeps over her that the army has already swallowed him.

"Robert!" she calls. The apartment so small he can surely hear her wherever he is.

"I'm in the bathroom," he says.

He comes and sits down on the bed. "What is it?"

He seems so calm, so self-assured, that she doesn't want to mention her fears. "I just wanted a good-morning kiss."

"I'll give you more than that," he says, reaching under the sheets for her nude body. "Then we have to get going."

A few minutes later she slips out of bed and, shrugging on her robe, goes into the tiny kitchen to get coffee started and the cereal set out. Robert joins her at the table, a rosy flush on his chest visible between the edges of his robe. They eat in silence except for "Please pass the milk" and "May I have more coffee?"

"I'll be right back," Robert says, heading for the bedroom.

He'll be putting on his uniform, checking one last time, she knows, that his boots are shined, his insignia pinned on correctly.

She'll write in her journal today, she tells herself. She hasn't written anything – the pages all virgin white. Yet today she'll record her feelings of watching her husband leave to become part of the war machinery.

Robert reemerges from the bedroom in his uniform, carrying his uniform hat, and stands in front of her for inspection. She wants to say "good luck." The words stick in her throat – don't these words imply the opposite is feared? She says: "You look terrific."

And he does look terrific if you like men in uniforms.

He kisses her good-bye at the front door. She stands on the balcony and watches him down the stairs to the car. He waves and mouths "I love you." Then he's gone.

She is without wheels and all alone.

She picks up the journal. There's a knock on the door.

Anne announces: "I want you to meet Elizabeth, one of our other neighbors."

Humidity droplets slide down Sharon's bare arms and legs in the few short steps to a downstairs apartment in the building on the right. The landlord waves as Anne knocks on Elizabeth's door.

Elizabeth is a small woman with blond hair pulled into a tight French twist and expertly applied makeup. She wears a flower-print dress, nylons, and heels, not the shorts, top, and sandals both Sharon and Anne have on.

A large wall-hung wedding portrait in a gilt frame overpowers the small living room. Elizabeth in a Scarlett O'Hara gown and her husband in his army uniform stand together under crossed swords.

Elizabeth follows Sharon's eyes. "Mama said I had to bring it. Wouldn't be a proper home without it. I also brought my silver. An officer's lady has to be ready to assume her duties."

Anne laughs. "Can you tell she's a Southerner? Even if she didn't have an accent. These Southerners are in love with the 'noble duty' of the army – that's why so many officers are Southern – even if it means going to Vietnam."

There, someone has said the word – Vietnam.

Elizabeth smiles. "How can a man get ahead in the army if he hasn't had at least one combat command? If my husband decides to go Regular Army – make the army a career, he has to get ahead."

Sharon mentally runs through any number of responses to this statement. No words leave her mouth. She has promised Robert.

Now, as she waits for Robert to return home, Sharon again thinks how Southerners are truly crazy. Robert told her Southerners make up a disproportionately large percentage of the army officer corps. This love of the military, can it really come from losing the Civil War and thus wanting to prove their manhood?

Below her a young woman dusts off a huge Chrysler. "Why are you dusting the car?" Sharon calls down to her.

"My husband just washed it yesterday," the woman says, "and I promised to dust it off if I drove it anywhere."

Unbelievable! Along with the soap operas that Anne and Elizabeth watch faithfully each day – "Whose program is it now?" they had said to an amazed Sharon – this seems to be the main activity for army wives: waiting for their husbands to come home and keeping their apartments, clothes and cars "spit-shined."

The Fiat appears in the open area between the three buildings. Sharon races down the stairs. Robert gets out, looks around as if checking who else has arrived home, and locks the car door. He kisses her hello.

"How was it? What did you do?"

"Cool it," he says out of the side of his mouth. "Wait until we get upstairs."

They walk up the outside stairs of the building, then down the outer balcony to their apartment door. Sharon unlocks the door and lets Robert enter first, then she follows him back to the bedroom, where he immediately sheds his uniform.

"It went okay. There's about 30 of us in the class. We filled out forms and listened to lectures. Not much action yet."

She doesn't want Robert to see any "action." She wants him to spend a quiet two years in the army behind a desk somewhere – if possible in Washington or some other big city – where she can pretend to herself he's not part of the war machine.

"What were the lectures about?"

"Mostly administrative details, TDY pay, uniform allotment."

"What's TDY?"

"Temporary duty. That's what this assignment is for me. Same as going to Ft. Holabird for MI – military intelligence – training will be temporary. The assignment after that will be a permanent one."

"And we'll get housing provided then, right?"

He turns away from her, places his insignia on the dresser. "If it's an accompanied tour."

"What's that mean?"

His back is still towards her. "Unaccompanied tours are to combat areas – Vietnam."

Sharon sits down on the edge of the bed. "Did they say anything about the chances of your going to Vietnam?"

Robert shakes his head.

She leaves the bedroom to serve dinner and Robert follows her, turning on the television in the living room. "Please don't watch the news," she says.

"I just want to see what's happening in Israel. I'll turn it off right after that."

Sharon walks back into the bedroom. She turns on the radio to listen to music and drown out the television. She doesn't want to risk seeing or hearing the news of Vietnam come on before the news of Israel.

At least the War of Attrition in Israel is one war of which Sharon can approve. It's a fight for survival waged by the country's own inhabitants. And no American troops have been sent there to fight.

A few minutes later Robert comes back to the bedroom. "I'm done watching the news now. And, listen, I invited a guy and his wife over tonight – Jim and Kim Benton. They live in the next complex."

Sharon stands up. "That's great. I want to meet some people. What time are they coming?"

"About 7:30. I said it would be nothing fancy, just coffee, or I'm not sure he would have agreed to come. Jim seemed surprised we would invite strangers over."

"Where do they come from?"

"Somewhere in the South."

Sharon has prepared for the Bentons' upcoming visit, straightening the sofa cushions and checking on the supply of cold pop. Still the knock on the door startles her. She hasn't realized she is so nervous about this visit – what will they think of her and Robert? Do they dislike Jews?

Robert answers the knock as Sharon stands behind him. Both Kim and Jim are tall, slender blonds with light eyes. They look almost like brother and sister.

"Come on in," Robert says, motioning them to sit down.

"Would you like some coffee?" Sharon says.

"Not right now," Jim says as he and Kim sit down on the sofa. "It's a little too hot."

"How about some pop? I've got some Dr. Pepper and some Coke."

"Thanks, that'll be really great," Jim says. "We'll both take a Coke."

"I'll have one too," Robert says, jumping up to help her.

"Where do you come from?" Sharon asks as she and Robert bring four Cokes from the kitchenette.

"Small town in North Carolina," Jim says.

Kim smiles, her face relaxing for the first time since she's entered the apartment. "We met at church."

"I came home on vacation from college and went to church with my parents," Jim says. "We had a visit from another church, and Kim was singing in the visiting choir. At the church social afterwards I asked her out right away."

"You didn't waste any time, did you?" Robert says.

Kim glances at her hands, then smiles. "We dated steadily from then on. As soon as I finished high school, we got married."

Jim puts his arm around Kim. "I wanted her at college with me. I didn't want to wait until I finished."

Sharon smiles back. "Robert and I met at a ..." – Robert's eyes signal her – "... college event. We disagreed with each other."

"And that's what attracted me to her," Robert says.

Sharon turns to Kim. "Robert and I went to a grocery store on Dixie Highway. I couldn't believe how few kinds of meat there were. I was trying to find lamb or even beef. I couldn't even find any brisket."

"What's brisket?"

"You've never heard of brisket?"

Kim shakes her head.

"It's a beef cut, sort of like shoulder roast, that you cook for a long time with potatoes."

"It's a popular Jewish dish," Robert adds.

"You're Jewish?" Jim asks.

As Robert nods his head, Sharon watches Kim look around the small living room, then her eyes return to her hands. "We've never been to the home of any Jews before," Kim says. "We didn't really know any back home."

Sharon's hands prickle. Are they staring at her and Robert to check for horns, the erroneous and pervasive myth dating back to Michelangelo? When Michelangelo carved his famous statue of Moses, he relied on the Vulgate Latin Bible mistranslation of the Hebrew word that could mean "ray of light" or "horn." Michelangelo erred by portraying Moses with horns protruding from his forehead rather than his face aglow with rays of light – the actual Hebrew Bible description. Michelangelo's mistaken portrayal of Moses with horns started the myth about Jews, causing ignorant people even today to sometimes ask Jews "Do you have horns?"

"There aren't any Jews in your town?" Robert asks.

"There may be, we just don't know any," Jim says. "I'm sure if we did, we'd like them."

Sharon sits immobilized, experiencing deja vu from her freshman lit course. A similar sentiment was said to her by a student of Lebanese descent from Detroit: "Now that I know you're Jewish I like Jews."

Robert cuts into the silence. "Listen, Sharon and Kim, I had an idea today when I realized how close we live to each other. I already discussed it with Jim. Suppose we carpooled? That way, Jim and I would drive together each day and you two would have a car. What do you think?"

Oh no! Sharon would be sharing a car for the nine weeks of AOB class with a stranger – a Christian Southerner! Kim seems nice, but will they have anything in common?

The alternatives – being without a car all day or driving back and forth twice a day to drop off and pick up Robert from the post – are also unappealing. Maybe she can try out the carpooling arrangement. If it doesn't work, she'll think of something to get out of it. "Sounds okay to me," she says.

Kim turns to her husband. "I already told Robert I thought it was a good idea," Jim tells her. "There's safety in numbers." Kim nods her head. "Just don't go to the ice cream parlor. It's in the troop area."

What ice cream parlor? And why can't they go there?

Before Sharon can ask, Robert says, "Let's start tomorrow. Jim can drive the two of us in the morning. After lunch Sharon can pick Kim up and the two of you can go to the PX together."

Sharon nods her agreement; she isn't going to disagree with him publicly. Has being on active duty for one day gone to Robert's head? He's already giving orders, dictating where she should go.

Jim says, "Remember Kim and Sharon will have to make plans the day before since we don't have a phone."

No phone? Robert gives Sharon a look that clearly says: Don't ask.

Robert claps his hands together. "And now that we've got that settled, do you guys play bridge?"

Kim and Jim shake their heads.

"We'll teach you."

The next day Sharon drives the couple of blocks to Kim and Jim's apartment, which is actually just behind her own complex and could be reached on foot across an open field. Large trees circle the small parking lot facing a single two-story apartment building.

Kim opens the door of her first-floor apartment. "Come on in," she says.

Sharon smiles at her, then shrieks. The white furry creature in Kim's hand jumps down and runs towards the back of the apartment.

Kim laughs, her short blond curls swirling around her face. "I didn't mean to scare you. That's just my pet white rat – Squeaky."

"A rat?" Sharon's eyes dart to the floor, checking for stray vermin.

"He's harmless. He was bred for laboratory tests and I rescued him. He keeps me company."

Kim motions for Sharon to sit down while she searches for Squeaky. When Kim brings him back, cradled in her hand again, Sharon asks, "Do you think you could put him in his cage – he does have a cage, doesn't he? – for now? I'm sort of afraid of animals."

Kim laughs again. "That means you don't want to pet him?"

"No, thanks."

While Kim puts Squeaky in the bedroom, Sharon looks around the front part of the apartment. This furnished apartment is basically no different than hers, and there aren't any personal signs of the individuals living here, just as there aren't in her apartment, except for some miniature figures set up on the floor near the coffee table. Metal soldiers in blue uniforms and other metal soldiers in grey uniforms face each other, cannons and horses lined up on both sides. Is it a reenactment of a Civil War battle?

Kim returns without Squeaky. "Would you like some Coca-Cola? It could be 7-up or Coke."

"I'd like a Coke. It certainly is hot out."

Kim brings out two Cokes and hands Sharon one.

Now what? Sharon thinks. What can they talk about?

Family. People always like to talk about their family.

"Did your parents object to your coming here with Jim?" Sharon asks.

A blush rises up Kim's neck. "I don't have any parents. I'm an orphan."

Yikes! Sharon has put her foot in her mouth already. When will she learn not to ask personal questions? "I'm sorry," she says.

"It was a long time ago. My sister and I were raised in foster homes, and the church was kind of our family. That's why I sang in the choir."

Oh, yes, Kim met Jim when she was singing in the choir. "You must have a beautiful voice."

Kim smiles. "It's passable. I was never a soloist."

Unsure of what else to talk about, Sharon asks, "Are you ready to go to the PX now? Do you have your ID?"

Kim nods, then says, "Something happened a couple of days ago. I'm not very comfortable going places here."

"What happened?"

Kim looks out the window, then back at Sharon. "I ... I went to that little store up the road to get some things. And ... and a soldier shot the clerk dead right in front of me."

A shiver runs up Sharon's spine. "How did it happen?"

Kim averts her face. "It just did."

Sharon hesitates to take Kim's hands to show sympathy – it may be too forward. Instead she says, "That's terrible! Yet it's obviously a freak thing – it's not going to happen again. We'll be okay at the PX."

Then she lightly touches Kim's hands.

Kim looks up, her eyes bright, and lets out her breath. "I'll go with you."

Now Kim walks towards the bedroom and comes back with her purse. "Are we dressed okay?"

Sharon nods. They both wear skirts and blouses, although Sharon's skirt ends considerably higher above her knees than Kim's. Certainly this is a long way from the required "to-the-knee or below" skirts of junior high, where the principal made Sharon kneel down in the library to prove her skirt touched the floor. Sharon wonders whether Kim's skirt length is modesty-inspired or just out-of-fashion.

They get into the Fiat. "Do you mind the top down?" Sharon says. "It's somewhat cooler."

Kim shakes her head, and Sharon backs the car out of the space.

"Your apartment is nice," Sharon says. "Did you have a hard time finding it?"

"It was the first one we saw."

"You don't know how lucky you are," Sharon says, then proceeds to describe the experiences she and Robert had.

"We really are lucky," Kim says when Sharon finishes.

They approach the entrance to Ft. Knox. Now that Robert has put the student status tag on the Fiat's bumper they are waved right through.

"What kind of game was that in your living room?" Sharon asks.

"It's a military strategy game," Kim says. "Jim likes to play these games, taking the part of both armies."

Does Jim approve of war, including the one in Vietnam? Is he anxious to fight over there to test out his military strategies? And is this part of the Southern military culture?

Sharon doesn't know Kim well enough to ask these questions – and she certainly doesn't want to put her foot in her mouth again. She also refrains from asking Kim why she and Jim have no phone and what Jim meant about the ice cream parlor. Right now her relationship with Kim is too fragile.

Sharon locates the PX, another one of the wooden frame buildings. At the top of the entrance steps a young black enlisted man in starched fatigues and shiny combat boots walks out of the door, sees them, and holds the door open. Sharon smiles at him as they pass.

They enter the PX and Kim turns to Sharon. "Did you see that? He was looking at us!"

"He was what?"

"Looking at us!" Kim hisses.

"He was just holding the door for us, being polite."

Kim's eyes flash her anger.

"Was the man black who shot the clerk?" Sharon asks.

"He was white. This has nothing to do with that." Kim strides off.

Sharon catches up with Kim in the towel department. Yves Saint Laurent towels in black and brown stripes and in blue and black stripes occupy a table. "These are terrific prices," Sharon says to Kim by way of making up. "The person who ordered these probably doesn't even know that Yves Saint Laurent is a famous designer."

Kim turns to her. "Have you ever been to the South?"

"No. Have you ever been to the North?"

"No." Kim fingers a towel. "We think of this as the North, Kentucky that is."

The North! That can't be! This is the South! Sharon opens her mouth to say something when she looks at Kim's serious face. Some things are better left unsaid.

Sharon picks up several towels with matching hand towels and washcloths in both color patterns. It still bothers Sharon that her mother didn't buy her towels and bed linen for a wedding trousseau. "You'll be moving around so much in the army. Wait until you're settled." Sharon still wonders whether this is disguised punishment for marrying a man just before he enters the army.

"I hope Robert likes these," she says to Kim. "We don't have many towels."

As Sharon walks to the checkout counter she tries to remember whether Kentucky was part of the Confederacy or did it stay with the Union? If only she remembered her high school American history course better. Because she would love to know whether at this moment she stands in the South or the North.

Robert arrives home that evening holding an envelope. "Believe it or not," he says, handing her the envelope, "there's an orientation coffee to welcome the wives of the AOB class. Typical army. After not even telling us you could come, there's actually an official function for the wives."

Sharon reads the paper inside. The typed invitation requests the pleasure of the company of the wives of the members of the AOB class at an orientation coffee in their honor the next day at Quarters One, Fifth Avenue – the home of the commanding general.

"Will you go?" Robert asks, putting his arms around her.

Regardless of her feelings about the army, Robert wants her to be a part of his new life. "It's Kim's turn to have the car tomorrow, so I'll go if she does."

"Then you'd better see if she'll go." He kisses her and releases her.

Since the Bentons don't have a phone, she has to drive over there now or walk over first thing in the morning. She isn't sure what her welcome will be. Kim was pleasant after the incident at the PX. Yet when Sharon dropped her off at her apartment afterwards, Kim didn't invite her in or make plans for tomorrow.

Sharon glances around the living room of the small apartment. She can't stage a sit-in, refusing to budge. And Sharon reminds herself of her liberal principles – not judging someone on one small incident.

"I'm not sure she wants to spend time with me," Sharon says.

Robert throws her a questioning look. Sharon hesitates before continuing, "In fact, I don't know if the carpool thing will work."

"Why not?" Robert sits down on the couch.

Sharon tells him what happened in the PX, then asks, "Why is she so upset about black men?"

"You're the one who's assuming it's about black men. Maybe it's all men. Maybe she thinks all men are always looking at all women." He smiles. "Which is probably true."

She picks up one of the sofa cushions and beans him with it. "You better not be!"

He holds up his arms to fend her off. "Not me of course. Other men, looking for – conquests."

Sharon sits down next to Robert. "I think it was only because he was black. Besides, it's obvious we're not single or we wouldn't be here."

Robert squeezes her. "Maybe for some men a married woman is more exciting – the lure of the forbidden."

70 injured in clash on Wall Street between construction workers and student anti-war demonstrators ...
May 8, 1970

KIM – III – May 14

"When you have received an invitation to a social function, acknowledge it within twenty-four hours."

Kim drops the mixing bowl into the sink. Two filled cake tins occupy the tiny oven, the thin batter transforming into a dense chocolate cake.

She came home from the PX with Sharon and immediately started to bake – a calming activity. She's not sure about this carpooling. She and Sharon are so different.

Last night as she and Jim drove home from Sharon and Robert's apartment, Jim said, "They seem nice, don't they?"

Kim didn't answer. She watched her husband's profile as he drove, aware of how much she wanted to fit into the role of an officer's wife. Had she said the right things? Or had she embarrassed him?

"Robert's idea to carpool is a good one," he said. "You'll have to spend a lot of time with Sharon but at least you won't be alone."

Kim knew what her husband wanted to hear – her having a personal escort wherever she went on the post was important to him – so she said: "We'll have a good time together."

Jim turned the car into their apartment complex. "You can hang out at the Officers Club. Just stay away from the other officers."

Kim's face burned. Why did Jim always have to warn her about other men? Didn't he know how much she loved him? That she would never look at another man in that way? She knew why he was suspicious of her ...

She got out of the car and walked beside her husband. Her husband. Such strength, such comfort in those two words. How could she ever live without him? Every night she prayed she wouldn't have to.

They walked into the apartment and Jim turned on the television. Kim didn't stay to watch the news. There was nothing she wanted to know from that box. Instead she headed to the bedroom and extracted her pet white rat from the closet.

Squeaky never failed to comfort her. Just watching his little nose quiver as he ran around the bedroom took her mind off "things." That was the word she used for what she wouldn't even permit herself to think about – the war her husband might have to fight in.

Now she removes the cake tins from the oven while she thinks again of Sharon Gold. Number one, she is a Northerner so she probably doesn't like Southerners. Number two, she comes from a large city so she will obviously be more sophisticated and make Kim feel like a country bumpkin. Number three, she is Jewish so she will ... be different than Kim. All in all, three good reasons not to like her.

Kim doesn't have a lot of experience with friends. Her foster parents hadn't encouraged her to invite friends over. And she would have been too embarrassed to go to a friend's house and never invite her back. She kept to herself in school and came straight home afterwards to her chores and homework.

Kim and her sister had done everything together, which meant not very much in a small town. Kim had been able to keep the money made from babysitting other people's children – caring for the foster parents' children was just one of her regular tasks – so she and her sister went to the movies sometimes. And they spent a lot of time in the library. It was a safe place with no one asking them to do any chores. Both of them read romance novels, dreaming of the day a pair of white knights would ride off with them, taking them away forever from their unhappy lives.

As a college man, two years older than she, Jim had seemed to be that white knight for her. Just like in the books he practically swept her off her feet. She had felt totally protected by his love.

When they married and lived in student housing, she didn't have a chance to meet any women friends. Then it was okay, because she was busy with her job in the college's biology department.

Here she has nothing to do. She doesn't want to be all alone day after day. Stuck without a car or a phone. Sharon seems nice. And Jim wants to carpool with her husband.

After all, it is only for nine weeks. Kim has put up with unhappy arrangements for a lot longer – almost her whole life.

Kim swishes chocolate icing over the two cake layers as a car stops right outside her first-floor apartment door. Kim puts down the icing knife and walks to the door to kiss her husband.

He follows her into the kitchenette. "Look at that cake," he says, sticking his finger into the bowl of icing and then licking his finger.

He gives her another kiss. "So what did you do today, hon?"

Kim continues to ice the cake as she speaks. "I went with Sharon to the PX. We saw some nice things there and it was good to get out."

Actually, she is relieved that Sharon forced her to leave the apartment even if the trip to the

PX didn't go that well. The shooting still bothers Kim. She doesn't want to mention her fears to Jim because she doesn't want Jim asking more questions – possibly finding out that the shooting happened because the soldier bothered her. Jim might think she started up with the soldier. Thank heavens the MPs haven't traced her and then come by to ask questions.

She follows Jim back to the bedroom, where he takes off his uniform. His high school football muscles still bulge underneath his undershirt. She didn't know him in high school even though their hometown has only one high school. Jim's parents sent him to military boarding school in a nearby town – they thought the discipline would be good – and those schools played football in a different league. The boarding school hooked him on military strategy games. He always had a game in progress in their married student housing apartment. Now it is the same here.

"Dinner's ready," she says, then goes back to the kitchenette, where Jim joins her.

"What's for dinner?"

"Fried chicken and homemade biscuits."

A parasitology major, Jim wrote his senior thesis on parasites in pigs. He became convinced that pigs were about the unhealthiest animals on this earth. Now he won't touch pork. They have fried chicken a whole lot.

She sets the plate of hot food down in front of him and puts another plate at her place. Then she sits down.

"Jews like blacks a whole lot, don't they?" she asks as Jim forks the first mouthful.

He chews before answering. "What do you mean?"

"Today at the PX, a black man held the door for us just so he could stare at us. I told Sharon that he was staring at us. She said he was just being polite holding the door open."

Jim swallows his milk. "Now look, Kim, it's not just Jews think that way. That's Northerners' thinking. They just don't know what we know, living with them the way we do."

Kim nods. It isn't just that Jim has a college degree and she doesn't. He hasn't been out of North Carolina, just as she hasn't, until they came here, yet he knows a lot about so many things.

For probably the millionth time she thanks her lucky stars that she has Jim. He is everything to her – father, mother, husband. He is also the reason she doesn't want children. Things are just perfect the way they are between the two of them. Children would somehow change that. And she can't risk losing this closeness.

The doorbell rings as she puts away the last of the washed supper dishes. Who could it be? The MPs? A stab of pain above her left eye punctuates her fear.

Jim gets up from the couch and opens the door. Sharon stands outside.

"Sorry to bother you," Sharon says. "I need to talk to Kim before tomorrow."

From the kitchenette Kim watches Jim motion Sharon to come in. What is she here for? To say she doesn't want their husbands to carpool anymore? That she doesn't want to share a car with Kim?

Kim walks into the living room. "Have a seat," she says, gesturing towards the couch. The small apartment smells of fried chicken – that's okay, Kim thinks, it isn't unpleasant. She watches Sharon glance around before sitting down. Probably checking for Squeaky.

"I just wanted to know," Sharon says, "if you're going to the orientation coffee for the AOB wives tomorrow. We could go together."

"See you, ladies," Jim says, walking towards the bedroom.

Kim sits down in the armchair facing the couch. "What coffee is that?" she asks.

"Didn't you get the invitation? It's for all the AOB wives who are here."

Kim shakes her head. Sharon glances towards the bedroom, then says, "Robert brought it home for me. Maybe Jim forgot to give it to you."

Kim stands. "That doesn't sound like Jim. Hold on while I go ask him."

Kim finds Jim sitting on the double bed reading from an army manual. Kim closes the door and comes up to him. She smiles. "Did you forget to give me an invitation?"

Jim closes the manual and stands up. "Honey, I'm sorry. I did forget. I have it right here." He reaches into his pants pocket and withdraws a folded white envelope. He gives her a quick kiss as he hands it to her.

Kim walks out of the bedroom before she realizes that Jim now wears the civilian clothes he changed into when he first got home. That means he transferred the invitation into those pants. Did he purposely not give it to her so she wouldn't know about the orientation coffee? Is he worried that his uneducated wife might embarrass him in front of the other officers' wives?

Her face feels hot as she shows Sharon the envelope. "Here it is. He did forget to give it to me." Kim sits down again, reaches inside the envelope and removes the invitation.

"Should we go?" Kim asks.

"It might be fun," Sharon says. "Besides we're probably expected to go."

"What should we wear?" Kim asks.

Between 75,000 to 100,000
young people demonstrate
peaceably in Washington against
the Cambodian incursion ...
May 9, 1970

SHARON – IV – May 15

"Certain social functions have an official aspect and should be considered obligatory."

As Kim drives, Sharon checks the map, then looks out the window. In the army, it appears, everything, even the houses, are by rank. Here in an area of officers' housing are four-family buildings – for the lieutenants on permanent assignment at Ft. Knox, then the semi-detached homes – for captains and majors, and finally the single-family homes starting with the colonels. When she and Kim reach the large house on a rise above a circular drive, there is no question who lives here.

Kim pulls into a space at the end of the parked cars. "Wait a minute," she says as she powders her near-perfect nose.

Sharon sighs. Her nose is near-perfect too, although it has been helped, the kind of help Kim probably can't even imagine.

"You look beautiful," Sharon says to Kim.

"You too," Kim says.

Both women wear sleeveless summer dresses, low heels, and nylons – in spite of the heat. Again, Sharon's dress ends higher above her knees than Kim's. They both carry purses, and in the purses, each has tucked a pair of white gloves.

"I can't believe you have gloves, too," Sharon said when they discussed this yesterday. "When I was growing up my mother always made me wear them for shopping on Michigan Avenue in downtown Chicago. I don't think most women wear gloves any more."

"Mine are for wearing to church," Kim said. "Do you think we should wear them to the coffee?"

"Let's take them in our purses and we can always put them on there. If we wear them and we're wrong, we'll feel ridiculous."

Now neither woman wears a hat. They talked about this, too. "The only hat I have is a red felt one that a sorority sister brought me from Florence – Italy," Sharon said. "I'd feel funny wearing it."

"I have a straw hat I wear to church," Kim said. "I won't wear it if you don't want to wear yours."

As they get out of Kim's car, Sharon says, "I hope we're not making a big mistake with our clothes."

Kim frowns. "How can they expect us to know what to wear? It's not as if they've told us a thing."

"Smile," Sharon says, "we're on Candid Camera."

At the door an attractive woman in her late twenties, several years older than Sharon and Kim and wearing a two-piece seersucker suit and a broad-brimmed hat, greets them. She wears gloves. Sharon and Kim look at each other.

"Welcome," the woman says. "Please leave your calling cards and pick up your nametags." She indicates the hall table supporting a silver tray and a pyramid of yellow nametags. "Mrs. Brisby, the commanding general's wife, is receiving inside."

Calling cards? Several white cards are stacked on the silver tray. Sharon shrugs as she picks up her nametag with MRS. GOLD written below the words "ARMOR – The Combat Arm of Decision" and SHARON written under MRS. GOLD. "Illinois" and "AOB" are written in the two corners above the word ARMOR.

Sharon and Kim stand in the hall pinning on their nametags. "Let's put our gloves on too," Kim whispers. "Good idea," Sharon says.

As they slide their hands into their gloves a thin man in his 50s wearing fatigues appears from the back of the house. Without even glancing at them he opens the hall closet and takes out a canvas bag, then ducks out the front door.

"Do you think that's the general himself?" Kim asks.

"He had one star on his fatigues," Sharon says.

They walk down the hall and enter a room overflowing with chintz-covered armchairs and couches. There are other older women scattered around among younger women who look to be Sharon and Kim's age. "The calling cards must be of the wives of officers stationed here at Ft. Knox," Sharon says to Kim. "The ones who have post housing," Kim says.

Sharon indicates the Japanese fans decorating one wall. "He must have done at least one tour in the Orient," Sharon whispers to Kim. There are also Hummel figurines from Germany lining the glass shelves of a cherry wood cabinet. Flowery perfumes and the scent of spring flowers whiff towards them accompanied by waves of chatter.

Sharon pictures herself back in the first round of sorority rush at MSU, entering house after house filled with strangers whose mandate is to look her over. The strangers must judge whether she is the right caliber for their "organization" while simultaneously she must decide whether she is interested in "joining." Only here at Ft. Knox she is a part of this group whether she wants to be – and still subject to inspection.

Another woman in her late twenties, this one wearing a purple linen suit, approaches them, glancing at their AOB nametags. "Welcome, Mrs. Gold and Mrs. Benton. I'm Mrs. McDermott.

Let me introduce you to Mrs. Brisby." She leads Sharon and Kim towards a gray-haired woman in a pink summer knit suit.

"Mrs. Brisby, I'd like to introduce Mrs. Gold and Mrs. Benton from the new AOB class."

Mrs. Brisby smiles. "Good afternoon, ladies. Welcome to Ft. Knox. I hope your stay here is pleasant."

Mrs. Brisby's voice matches her appearance – gracious and authoritative. Sharon imagines Mrs. Brisby herself commanding a battalion of tanks, ordering them to fire on the enemy.

"Thank you," Sharon says as Mrs. McDermott sweeps her and Kim towards the refreshment table, their moment of official greeting by the wife of the post commanding general over.

"Please help yourselves, ladies," Mrs. McDermott says. "The formal part of our program will start shortly." Then she leaves them, scurrying to new women entering the room.

Sharon and Kim survey the refreshments displayed on a rectangular linen-draped table. "The cookies look good," Kim says. "I think we take off our gloves to eat," Sharon says.

After removing their gloves and placing their cookie selection on china plates, they walk over to an unoccupied loveseat.

A young black woman sits on a wing-backed chair facing the loveseat. Sharon smiles at her and the woman smiles back. Even without looking at her nametag Sharon can tell the woman is the wife of an AOB class member – the woman's stiff posture telegraphs her uncertainty in this setting.

"I'm Sharon Gold and this is Kim Benton," Sharon says to her. "Is this your first time at one of these things?"

The woman smiles. "Yes, we just arrived a few days ago." Her voice is soft. She sounds Southern, like Kim.

The woman shifts her coffee cup from her right hand to her left, as if in preparation for shaking hands. Yet she doesn't extend her right hand. "I'm Wendy Johnson."

About to stick out her own hand, Sharon glances at Kim. What if Kim makes a scene about not shaking a black person's hand? Better not to create the situation.

"Your husband is in the new AOB class with our husbands," Sharon says.

"Where are you all from?" Wendy asks.

Kim swings her head around. Is it the use of the Southern phrase "you all" that has caught her attention?

"I'm from Chicago," Sharon says, pointing to the "Illinois" on her nametag.

Now it is Kim's turn. Nothing. Then, speaking to her hands clasped in her lap, Kim says, "I'm from a small town in North Carolina."

"North Carolina?" Wendy says. "I'm from South Carolina."

At the end of the living room furthest from the front door Mrs. McDermott raises a hand. "Ladies, may I have your attention?" she says. The room silences.

"Welcome, ladies. We're so happy to have a new Armor Officers Basic class here at Ft. Knox." Her smile travels the room.

"I promise you that you will look back upon your stay at Ft. Knox with fondness. The post has a great deal to offer, including the Officers Club, several swimming pools opening in a few weeks, a large PX and a well-stocked commissary.

"While here you will also have the opportunity to learn what is expected of you as the wife of an officer in the U.S. Army today. There are some rules and regulations that, once learned, make life easier for all of us. I recommend that you all buy the booklet at the PX entitled 'Mrs. Lieutenant' by Mary Preston Gross and study it carefully. It is an invaluable guide for an officer's wife."

Sharon glances around the room. Some of the older women must have heard this speech a thousand times. How many times will she have to hear it in the next two years?

"... and to help you prepare for your time as an officer's wife – whether it be only for a few years or as a career – we have planned several activities during your stay here."

Mrs. McDermott pauses as if to ensure that everyone is fully listening to her words.

"The final function for the wives will be an AOB graduation luncheon. It's going to have a Fourth of July theme and, as part of your training, you will be in charge of it. There will be four committees – refreshments, decorations, invitations, and entertainment. We need volunteers first to chair the committees, then each chair will choose her own committee."

Three AOB wives volunteer to chair the refreshments, decorations and invitations committees.

"Now for the entertainment committee," Mrs. McDermott says. "In past classes we have had a fashion show or an etiquette lesson or something similar. Who would like to be chair?"

Sharon's hand shoots up. Forget a boring fashion show or etiquette lesson! She wants to do something original, something creative, something that will show these people.

"Thank you, Mrs. Gold."

Now Mrs. McDermott smiles at everyone in the room. "This is the conclusion of the program for today. Please help yourselves to more refreshments. You are welcome to stay for a half hour longer. We look forward to seeing you all again at the next function."

Sharon turns to Kim. "We should be on a committee together. After all, we're sharing a car."

Kim nods.

Sharon hopes it isn't an urge to irritate Kim that makes her lean over and say to Wendy Johnson, "And you'll join us too." She doesn't even ask it as a question.

"Oh, I ...," Wendy says, "I'm not sure I ..."

"Of course you will," Sharon says.

Mrs. McDermott hasn't mentioned the number of women on each committee. Sharon thinks one more would be good. A few feet away a tall young woman with olive skin and dark hair stands alone.

Sharon approaches the woman, checking her nametag.

"I'm Sharon Gold. I see you're one of the wives of the AOB class."

The woman smiles and offers her hand. "Donna Lautenberg."

"Would you like to join the entertainment committee? We could use another person."

Donna laughs. "I'd like that."

"Then come meet the others so we can set a time to get together."

As Sharon introduces everyone, she realizes that Donna might be of Italian or Spanish origin. How ironic! A committee just like all those old World War II movies where the squad of men consists of one Jew, one Italian, one black, one WASP. No, wait, no black because blacks weren't allowed to fight in integrated units until the Korean War. Still, the entertainment committee smacks of being carefully chosen. Will anyone believe this wasn't planned?

"What did you think?" Sharon asks Kim as they drive away from the commander's home.

"It was nice seeing all those women dressed up."

Sharon glances at Kim, aware that it's also nice to have someone with whom to go places. Not to have to sit alone as both Wendy and Donna had to do when they got to the coffee. Perhaps Robert has done Sharon a big favor.

The road curves, and as they come around the bend the PX stands on their right. Kim turns the car into the PX parking lot. "Let's stop right now and buy that book they told us to get," Kim says. "Maybe we can find out exactly what to wear to what."

Sharon follows Kim out of the car and up the steps.

This time, thank heavens, no young black soldier holds the door open for them. Having Wendy Johnson join their entertainment committee has probably been enough shock for Kim for one day.

"Where can we find the booklet 'Mrs. Lieutenant'?" Sharon asks a clerk.

"Right over there," the clerk says, gesturing to a bookrack along one wall.

A tall woman stands facing the indicated bookrack. As Sharon and Kim approach, she turns around. It's Donna.

"Looks like you're buying the same thing we are," Sharon says.

Donna laughs and holds up "Mrs. Lieutenant" as Sharon and Kim each take a copy. Then Donna says, "I grew up an army brat, the daughter of an enlisted man. I've spent practically all my life on army posts. This is the first time I've been part of an officer's family. It's very different."

"Where's your own family originally from?" Sharon asks.

"Puerto Rico. The army was a chance to get off the island, a chance for a better life, and my parents took it."

"You have no accent," Sharon says as Kim asks, "What's Puerto Rico got to do with the United States? Why was your father in the American army?"

Donna looks at Kim. "Puerto Rico is a commonwealth of the United States. All men in Puerto Rico over the age of 18 are subject to the draft the same as in the U.S. My father was too young to be drafted in World War II. He joined the army as soon as he turned 18."

Do Southerners classify Puerto Ricans the same as blacks? Sharon doesn't want to find out just now. "Don't we have to go?" Sharon asks Kim.

"I do too," Donna says. "I'll see you both at the meeting tomorrow."

"Her English is so good," Kim whispers as Donna walks away.

"Maybe they didn't even speak Spanish at home when she was growing up," Sharon says. "Becoming 'real' Americans may have been the most important thing."

Oh for heaven sakes! How stupid can Sharon be! She said the word "real" with quotes in her mind, but Kim's not a mind reader. Has Sharon just reinforced another of Kim's stereotypes?

"He won't stay long," Robert says to Sharon that evening as he gets up from the couch to answer the doorbell.

Robert has already explained why he invited Len Tottenham. A Michigan farm boy, Len had been a college suitemate of Robert's before Len dropped out of school and enlisted. "I thought you didn't like him," Sharon said when Robert first told her that Len was coming over. In response Robert said, "This gives him a chance to get away from the barracks, and we can afford to be gracious."

In preparation for his visit Sharon had gotten out her crewelwork canvas – stretched over an embroidery frame – with its unfinished section of French knot flowers. "I'll work on my needlework while you entertain him."

"Hi, buddy," Robert says to a gangly man in rumpled fatigues with an enlisted rank – which one Sharon can't tell – sewn on both sleeves. "Come on in."

Len's shaved hair barely hints at its blondness above dark eyes and a prominent nose. He shakes Robert's extended hand and nods in Sharon's direction.

"Would you like something to drink?" Robert asks, motioning to the armchair.

"Beer, if ya have any."

Robert shakes his head. "How about some Coke?"

"It'll have to do."

He could have said thank you, that Coke would be just fine.

Sharon and Len sit without speaking until Robert returns with the Coke.

"Hey, Rob, couple of Jew boys in my unit."

She pricks her finger with the needle. Blood droplets sprinkle the white canvas.

"Now, Len, I taught you better than that," Robert says.

"Yeah, yeah."

Sharon has heard some of the things Len said about Jews when he and Robert first were suitemates. Then Robert "educated" him. In her book Len's attitude certainly would not have won him an invitation to their apartment.

"So what's going on?" Robert asks. "Thinking of making the army a career?"

Len shrugs. "What else I got to do, especially after getting my insides all busted up over in Nam."

Robert has already warned her not to mention Vietnam. As if she doesn't know not to.

Now Robert says, "That 20 year or 30 year pension sounds pretty good. There are a lot worse things."

Len's eyes darken and his mouth pulls down. Is he thinking about men he saw die in Vietnam?

Then his face relaxes. "Yeah."

"Have you heard from any of the other MSU guys?" Robert asks.

"Ol' Pete. Got himself some great big deer on a hunting trip..."

Sharon tunes Len out and leans over the crewelwork, wrapping the burnt orange thread into petite French knots. When she finishes this still life she'll have it framed in dark wood. Some day the picture will hang on the wall of a dining room furnished with a polished cherry wood table large enough for 12 and matching chairs upholstered in dark green brocade.

A half hour later Robert stands at the door shaking Len's hand. "Thanks for coming by," Robert says.

Sharon rises to be polite. The embroidery frame catches on her short skirt, pulling it up to her waist.

She grabs at her skirt as Len's eyes sweep up her thighs to her exposed undies-clad crotch.

"See ya around," he says, his eyes on her body.

She hopes not.

*448 colleges and
universities reportedly
closed or under strike
in response to Kent
State shootings …*
May 10, 1970

SHARON – V – May 18

"In military circles it is wrong to be 'fashionably late.'"

Sharon sets the plate of chocolate chip cookies baked this morning down on the Formica-topped coffee table. The oven has heated up the small apartment, and the air conditioner struggles unsuccessfully to cool the temperature. Yet she doesn't want to serve store-bought cookies – "home-baked is more hospitable" her mother always says.

Sharon is excited about her idea for the graduation luncheon entertainment. The proverbial light bulb exploded minutes after she returned to the apartment yesterday afternoon. Will the others like her idea?

The doorbell rings. Sharon re-tucks the hem of her white sleeveless blouse into the waistband of her blue cotton skirt and opens the door to Kim. Despite the heat and the walk around the block from her apartment, Kim looks cool in a sleeveless flower-print shift.

"Smells like cookies," Kim says.

Sharon smiles and motions Kim to the sofa. "How about some pop? You must be thirsty."

"That would be great."

Before Sharon can get the pop bottles out of the refrigerator, the doorbell rings again. Both Donna and Wendy stand outside.

"Did you come together?" Sharon asks.

"Just landed on your doorstep at the same time," Donna says.

Wendy, who wears pale green pants and a short-sleeved white blouse, takes a seat on the single armchair and pushes her short black hair out of her face. Donna, wearing a plaid short-sleeved dress, sits down next to Kim on the couch.

"This is a nice apartment complex," Wendy says. "We tried to rent a unit here."

"What happened?" Donna asks.

"The clerk at the housing office thought an apartment was still available. When we drove over here the manager told us it was already rented."

Sharon stands still with the pop bottles in her hands. Wendy has said this with no accusation in her voice.

Sharon flashes to the post housing office. The friendly housing clerk explains how she hadn't told

Robert and Sharon about this unit earlier in the day because she thought it had been taken.

Sharon leans over and places the bottles on the coffee table. Had the clerk sent Wendy and her husband to see this apartment not knowing that the shotgun-toting redneck manager wouldn't rent to them? Because that's what must have happened.

Sharon's stomach does a flip flop as she realizes that, because of racial discrimination, she and Robert got this apartment. Then she reminds herself that there was no way she and Robert could have known this at the time so she doesn't need to feel guilty.

"Please, everyone, help yourself to soda pop and cookies," she says. "And thanks for coming. I hope this is going to be fun."

Donna laughs, her black hair bouncing against her shoulders. "At least it will be something to do. There's not a lot going on around here."

"Where are you all from?" Wendy asks Donna.

Donna laughs again. "From an equally boring place. I was at Ft. Riley living with my parents – I'm an army brat – when I met my husband. Believe me, Kansas is not any more exciting than Kentucky."

"I know about Ft. Riley – my husband went to ROTC summer camp there," Sharon says. "You must have lived all over the world if your father was in the army."

Donna nods. "We lived in Germany, in Korea. When I was little we lived in Hawaii. And I've been to Puerto Rico to visit several times."

"I'd never been out of North Carolina before we came here," Kim says. "I can't believe all the places you've lived in."

Wendy rustles in her armchair. "I wasn't ever out of South Carolina before my parents sent me to college in Texas."

Kim stares at the glass in her hand. Then she looks straight at Wendy. "Whereabouts in South Carolina are you from?"

"Orangeburg. You probably never heard of it."

Kim shakes her head.

"It's a nice enough place. My papa's a doctor there."

Sharon, surprised herself, watches Kim's face.

Wendy doesn't wait for a response before adding, "He built his practice all by himself. First only black people were his patients; now whites go to him too."

Sharon glances quickly at Kim, then says, "Let me tell you my idea for the entertainment. It's not what the other women have in mind so I hope you'll like it."

"Out with it!" Donna says.

"I'll write a little play for us to perform. The play will be about the army – some of the funny things about AOB." She looks around at the others as she adds, "In keeping with the July 4th theme of the luncheon, the play will take place in 1776 when, I think, George Washington was at Valley Forge."

Donna nods. "Sounds like it might be cute. At least it will be different."

"It could be fun," Kim says. "I've never been in a play."

Sharon turns to Wendy. She smiles yes.

"Then let me show you what I've got so far," Sharon says.

"You already started?" Kim asks. "What if we hadn't agreed?"

"Then I would have wasted my time."

Sharon makes salmon patties for dinner. First she picks the little white bones out of the canned salmon and removes the grayish white outer skin clinging to the larger pieces. Next she mixes the salmon with an egg and bread crumbs before hand rolling the patties. Finally she fries the flattened patties in oil. She also heats canned peas and cuts up a salad of lettuce, carrots, celery and tomatoes.

She uses the "Betty Crocker's New Picture Cook Book" only for baking recipes. Otherwise she sticks to the few things she already knows how to cook. Robert and his two younger brothers grew up on meat meals three times a day. Since marrying Sharon,

Robert has been willing to cut down on what he'll accept as a meal. And out here in the boondocks he hasn't had much choice.

Robert opens the door to the apartment. She walks the two steps from the kitchenette to meet him.

"Hi, honey," he says, grabbing her around the waist. "How about a little something before dinner?"

"Let's have dinner first. I want to tell you about ..."

"Later," he says, his mouth clamping on hers while he pulls down her undies. It's a good thing she uses birth control pills, because there certainly isn't time for her to put in a diaphragm.

She smiles as Robert pushes her towards the bedroom. At least she turned the flame off under the salmon patties when she heard his key in the lock. She won't burn the dinner this time.

When they're done Robert's enthusiasm for lovemaking shows as a red flush all over his chest. She eyes the flush, then says, "The women were here today for the first entertainment committee meeting."

"How'd it go?"

Sharon ducks her head under the bed to look for her undies and bra. "I was worried about Kim and Wendy getting along, but it seemed to go fine."

"What were you worried about?"

"Wendy's black and Kim's a white Southerner. I was afraid Kim would say something, something derogatory about blacks."

"This is 1970. All that Southern white supremacy crap is over now. It's against the law."

Sharon shakes her head while hooking her bra. She doubts that this enlightened view of equality has taken hold among the Southern white population. Kim's reaction to the black soldier holding open the PX door is probably just the tip of the iceberg of Kim's Southern-inspired prejudices.

"Something kind of weird happened today," Robert says as he puts one foot through the leg hole of his jockey shorts. "We all got our pay vouchers for our uniform allowance."

"What's a uniform allowance?"

"Enlisted men are given their uniforms. Officers have to buy their own. When we first come on active duty we're given an amount of money to be used for buying the uniforms. I can't only have that one Class A uniform and fatigues from ROTC. I have to get more fatigues, another Class A uniform, suntans, and a dress blue uniform for formal affairs."

Robert pulls on casual pants and a shirt.

"Only thing is, my pay voucher wasn't there. Len Tottenham was the clerk handing out the checks and he couldn't figure out why mine was missing. He said he'd look into it right away."

"You think he did it on purpose? He's probably angry that you're an officer and he's an enlisted man."

"Len isn't like that. It's an accounting error, I'm sure. But I do need the money for more uniforms."

Robert follows her to the front of the apartment and sits down at the table. "I almost forgot to tell you. Some of us decided to get together tomorrow night at the Officers Club after dinner. There's a band from Louisville playing. Should be fun. I said we'd go."

Sharon pulls the Fiat into a parking space alongside the brick building and smiles at Kim. "Here we are," Sharon says. "The Officers Club."

"I'm glad you suggested we come today," Kim says. "It's a good idea to see it before tonight."

In the foyer there's an announcement board listing the activities of the day along with the menu at the snack bar.

"Let's eat at the snack bar," Sharon says. Robert had informed her last night that he and Jim wouldn't be home for lunch the next day.

At the back of the building they find a good-sized room with several tables and a snack bar counter. At the tables there are a few other women, all around their age, as well as several men in an assortment of uniforms from olive green fatigues to khaki suntans to olive green Class A uniforms.

They order hamburgers and fries at the counter, then sit at a table to await their order.

Kim whispers, "It's kind of funny to be here, don't you think?"

"What do you mean?" Sharon asks.

"Alone by ourselves, without our husbands."

Doesn't Kim go anywhere without her husband? Are women still chaperoned in the South?

Sharon purposely switches the subject. "Memorial Day weekend the pools will open. We can go to the one at the Officers Country Club; it's only for adults – no children allowed."

"I have to be careful not to tan. I'll have to bring suntan lotion," Kim says.

"Why don't you want a tan?" Sharon asks.

Kim wrinkles her mouth. "That's unladylike. Dark skins are for the ... I mean ..." She pauses for so long Sharon thinks Kim has forgotten the question. Finally Kim says, "I don't look good with a tan."

The employee behind the snack bar counter motions for them to come get their food. As they sit down again, Kim says, "We can't even go to our swimming hole anymore in my hometown."

"Why not?"

Kim's eyes fix on her plate. "Because the blacks go there now."

"Why can't you go?" Sharon asks.

"Because we can't."

A deep voice says, "Hello, Sharon. It's been a long time."

Sharon looks up into the face of an extremely good-looking young man wearing suntans. Mark Williamson!

"May I have this dance?" he says.

This time her stomach flip flops for a totally different reason. She and Mark Williamson have a history, one with a prologue in seventh grade. He attended the six weeks of dancing class she took then in preparation for the myriad Bar Mitzvah parties to which she would be invited. Never mind that with her teeth swathed in braces and pimples rearing their ugly blackheads – not to mention her perfectly straight hair that wouldn't rat no matter how many perms her mother gave her – Sharon didn't have much hope of being asked to dance by the Jewish boys who clustered in protective flocks at one end of the hotel ballrooms.

Mark wasn't Jewish – the class had been sponsored by a community recreation center – and she hadn't taken much notice of him. He first blipped on her radar when he fought with his older brother Roger over her hand for the last dance of the final class. Mark shoved Roger out of the way, even though Roger asked first, and she and Mark danced a slow waltz with Mark's right arm pressed tightly against her back. Then the class had been over and she hadn't seen him again until they attended the same high school. And that's when their history truly began.

She stands up. He towers above her. "What are you doing here?" she asks.

"I could ask you the same." He smiles.

Sharon glances at Kim; she's frowning. "My husband" – there, she has established this immediately – "is attending the Armor Officers Basic course here."

Mark laughs. "A green lieutenant! He hasn't been to Nam yet!"

How can he speak so openly about Vietnam?

She says, "What are you doing here?"

"I'm between assignments. Back from a tour of Nam – helicopter pilot – and I'm deciding whether to accept a commission. We're being offered the privilege of becoming officers and gentlemen, then they'll send us back to Nam."

He laughs again, and she can't tell whether he wants to go back or dreads it.

Another good-looking man stands behind Mark. "Williamson, are you going to introduce me to your friend?"

Sharon turns to the other man. "I'm not a friend. Just someone from the same hometown."

Both men laugh. "See you around," Mark says.

"Who's that?" Kim asks the moment the men leave the snack bar.

"Someone I was in dancing class with when we were in seventh grade. Later we went to the same high school."

"He's certainly good-looking."

Yes, he is.

☆ ☆ ☆

That evening Sharon and Robert park the Fiat at the Officers Club. She told Robert about going to the club for lunch, although she didn't mention running into Mark Williamson – the way Mark tossed off the words "helicopter pilot" and "Nam" – the goal to which Robert originally aspired until his hayfever got him involuntarily dropped from the ROTC flight program.

She didn't know what to wear tonight, even after consulting "Mrs. Lieutenant." In the end she put on a cotton dress with a jewel neckline and short sleeves, nothing too fancy, and took a sweater in case the club's air conditioning actually worked. She worried over jewelry; didn't want to wear too much and give people a chance to say Jews are flashy. Finally she chose tiny pearl studs for her pierced ears and a pearl necklace.

She's looking forward to meeting Wendy's and Donna's husbands. And she wants to see what the men in the class are like together. Have they formed friendships or is it just "business" relationships?

Robert holds open the front door at the Officers
Club for her and they step inside the foyer. A band
playing the Lovin' Spoonful's "Did You Ever Have To
Make Up Your Mind?" can be heard from the room
to their immediate right. They enter a swirling mass
of people and noise.

"Gold, Gold, over here, man. We're all over
here."

Robert leads her over to the others. Kim and
Jim sit at one end of two tables shoved together.
Next to them sit Donna and presumably her
husband, a slim guy with a regulation haircut
and an all-American look that contrasts with
Donna's dark hair and skin. Sharon waves at both
women.

Someone drags over two more chairs and makes
room for Sharon and Robert at the other end of the
two tables.

Bar glassware litters the tables. Beer mugs,
slender glasses holding liquor concoctions, and
small whiskey shot glasses jostle for space. "It's self
serve," someone yells. Robert flashes a question at
Sharon.

"My usual," she says into his ear.

When he gets up to place their orders, she feels
bereft. Or invisible. No one looks in her direction,
no one speaks to her. She watches the band play –
five boys all with long stringy hair and dirty clothes.
The hillbilly look.

Robert returns from the bar and hands her a Whiskey Sour.

The band's lead singer leans towards the mike and sings in a loud nasal tone:

In Louisville, Kentucky, all the hippies say
Come on back to beer

Sharon laughs.

"Pretty silly, heh?" asks the man sitting to her right. "Who hires these bands, do you think?"

She smiles at the man, not having noticed him before. Robert, to her left, talks to the man on his left.

"Your husband with this AOB class?" the man asks. She nods. "Not me. I'm back from Nam. Intelligence."

Robert turns towards the man as if a special antenna has picked up this broadcast in spite of the loud noise interfering with any transmission. "What did you do?" he asks the man.

"Phoenix program." The man looks at Robert. "Know what that is?"

"Yep." It is unlike Robert to be so abrupt.

The man watches her face as he says, "Your husband may not tell you – the Phoenix program arranges assassinations of Vietcong officials."

Sharon's hands tighten in her lap. Robert has once again, on the drive here, given her his speech about not revealing any opinions.

Robert says nothing, just lifts his glass to his lips for a swallow of beer. Then he says to Sharon, "Come on, honey, let's dance."

He leads her onto the dance floor and they try to make sense of the lopsided beat of the song. After a few minutes Robert pulls Sharon close. "Don't worry about what that guy said. He's probably drunk."

"You knew what he was talking about."

"Can't believe everything you've heard about the army in Vietnam."

On the dance floor, surrounded by other couples, Sharon's mind retreats to spring quarter of 1968 at Michigan State University:

Hell, no, we won't go!

The chant roars over the clanking manual typewriters and the shrilling telephones at the office of the "State News" – the daily college newspaper. Sharon Bloom, whose desk stands next to the open windows, leans out from the second floor as her fellow journalists rush to join her at the windows. The trees below sprout only a few new buds so there's a clear view of the action.

"Holy shit!" someone behind her shouts.

Striding across the campus are maybe 30 men and women, long hair swinging, posters held high.

Sharon studies the protesters. Who are these people and where are they headed? Can't be

Michigan State students. Too much hair, too hippy clothing, and too vocal.

One protester near the rear of the pack drops his poster. As he bends to pick it up, his torso twists towards the windows. Long hair halts right above "University of Michigan" on his misshapen maize-and-blue sweatshirt. The poster, now facing Sharon, says "KICK ROTC OFF CAMPUS!"

ROTC? Reserve Officers Training Corps! She scans the other journalists hanging out the windows. The news editor stands three people away.

"Lance," Sharon calls, slinging her purse's shoulder strap over her chest. "I'm going to check this story out."

Lance turns towards her. "Sharon, you're now the feature editor. One of my news reporters will go."

"Please, Lance. I want to do it."

Lance eyes her. He knows her politics. Knows how she feels. "Just be back in time so we don't hold up the press run."

Sharon grabs a large piece of cardboard from a bin near her desk. On it she scribbles "NO MORE WAR AT MSU."

No time now to worry whether it's a breach of journalistic standards to participate in the story you're assigned to impartially cover. There is no impartiality when it comes to the Vietnam War.

She runs down the stairs and out the door. The protesters have a block lead on her, aiming directly at the university's ROTC field. She runs, closing the distance. The excitement of something political finally happening on this apathetic campus spurs her feet.

On the field young men hup-two-three-four in razor-straight rows. The gold brass buttons on their olive green uniforms reflect the afternoon sun.

Closer to Sharon, young men and women walk to classes, the lettering on their green-and-white Michigan State sweatshirts partially obscured by armloads of textbooks and notebooks.

"Way to go!" one MSU student yells at the protesters.

"Get off our campus!" another screams.

The U of M students reach the field. *"Hell no, we won't go!"* hurtles towards the student soldiers.

"Charge!" yells the leader of the protesters. In unison they all raise their posters and rush across the field, their jeans, shirts and hair a kaleidoscope of mayhem.

The commander of the soldiers shouts: "Do not engage! Hold your positions!"

Sharon races towards the tangle of students all yelling "Kick ROTC off campus!"

The protesters reach the soldiers, and without mercy the protesters swing the wood poles of the posters smack against the soldiers' heads. Screams of pain and triumph can be heard.

The soldiers break ranks. The soldier in the lead yanks a poster from a protester and bashes the wild hair. The other soldiers follow, returning blow for blow, as disorganized in their counterattack as the protesters' original attack.

Now the protesters hold their arms over their heads, protecting themselves as they retreat. Their screams pierce the air louder than the wail of the approaching campus police sirens. Soldiers gallop down the field in pursuit of the fleeing protesters.

Sharon whirls away from the melee. Her foot catches and she stumbles. Above her head a student soldier raises a captured poster.

The attacker's blow misses her head. He's been pushed aside by another soldier.

"Come on," the second soldier says, yanking her to her feet. She hesitates. Her rescuer tugs her forward, away from the raging battle.

The police jump out of their cars. Shouts and swear words fly by as her rescuer steers her, aiming towards a clump of buildings. Other MSU students – attracted by the sirens and screams — rush past them, heading towards the action, their own voices ratcheting up the shouting.

"Up here," the soldier says. "We can take cover in a booth."

He tugs her up the stairs of the student union. Inside they collapse on the seats of an empty booth.

Her chest heaves, her sides hurt, she's afraid she'll puke.

"Thanks for saving me," she gasps, looking at him for the first time. He's lost his uniform hat – blood stains his exposed forehead.

"You're hurt," she says.

"The world's just swaying."

"Do you have a handkerchief or tissue?"

He shakes his head, the movement sluicing the blood sideways.

She searches her purse for a tissue to stop the bleeding. There is none. She hesitates, then yanks off her brand-new Villager heather mist cardigan sweater, the one she begged her parents for on their last trip to Philadelphia. She wads the sweater and presses it against the slash.

"I'll get blood all over the sweater," he says, trying to hand back the sweater. She presses harder against the wound. If the blood doesn't come out her mother will kill her.

"You're rather dressed up for a protest," he says as she holds the sweater against the wound.

"I came straight from the 'State News.' We have a dress code."

"Were you protesting or just covering the story?"

"I was protesting and covering the story."

She removes the sweater to check if the bleeding has stopped. It has, so she folds the sweater and places it next to her on the bench. Her senses have returned to normal, and she gags at the nauseating smell of burning meat on the student union grill.

She looks at the boy across from her. He'd be cute if he weren't in an army uniform. And he seems somewhat lost, unsure of what to do next.

"I'll go with you to the school clinic," she says.

"I don't need to go to the clinic. I should get back to the field – to my comrades."

"You should at least rest for a few minutes."

He smiles, a smile that would definitely be rated "beautiful" by her sorority sisters.

"I could use a cup of coffee," he says.

His blue eyes reflect the overhead light, his black wavy hair not that much shorter than standard MSU male length – slightly below the top of the ear.

"Let me get you a cup too."

About to say no, Sharon hesitates. There should be just enough time for a quick cup of coffee and then write the story before deadline. She'll call the campus police for a statement and to find out what she missed after this boy saved her.

She smiles at him. "My name's Sharon Bloom."

"I'm Robert Gold."

While he gets their coffee Sharon checks out the few students who sit at the Formica tabletops wedged between wooden benches whose backs form booths. The smell of other frying foods – onion rings, French fries – joins that of the cooking meat.

"You didn't even lose your pocketbook," he says as he slides back into the booth. "Some protester you are."

"It was slung across my chest." She hesitates. "Are you from New York?"

"Philadelphia. What made you think New York?"

"I have a friend who says pocketbook and she's from New York. I say purse."

"Where are you from?"

"Highland Park, a northern suburb of Chicago – near Lake Michigan."

She won't admit this to her parents – ever since that moment in sixth grade when her life changed forever she's kept her own counsel – but her decision to go to a college which wasn't a continuation of her high school crowd has been a mistake. Michigan State – as opposed to the liberal hotbed University of Michigan – is so apolitical. There are no marches or sit-ins or teach-ins. MSU's local chapter of SDS – Students for a Democratic Society – has almost no campus visibility. She hasn't even bothered to join.

A few weeks earlier, the head of the local SDS chapter had perched on her desk at the "State News" office wearing his starched – rumor said done by his mother; he is from Lansing – monogrammed dress shirt, a single chest hair poking up from the partially unbuttoned front. "Can you believe how MSU hasn't changed in the last few years?" he asked.

"It hasn't?" she said, then felt compelled to add, "Look at the changes in restrictions on women students – no more curfews. The dispensary now gives out birth control pills. We had that entire semester of guest lectures on sex topics sponsored by the university."

He got off her desk and left without replying.

Now Robert says, "MSU is certainly different than the East. I didn't know what I was getting myself into by coming out to the Midwest."

"Like ROTC?"

His eyes shift to his coffee cup, then back to her.

"I chose ROTC." Her face must be betraying her thoughts because he rushes on, "And ROTC has a right to be on campus just like every other campus organization."

"ROTC supports the war machine! Do you know how many boys your age may be getting killed right now in Vietnam as we sit here having coffee?"

"Serving their country."

"Getting killed for nothing."

They stare at each other as other students brush past their table, carrying trays loaded with fried substances.

Suddenly he leans towards her and recites:

The time you won your town the race
We chaired you through the market-place;

Man and boy stood cheering by,
And home we brought you shoulder-high.

To-day, the road all runners come,
Shoulder-high we bring you home,
And set you at your threshold down,
Townsman of a stiller town.

Smart lad, to slip betimes away
From fields where glory does not stay,
And early though the laurel grows
It withers quicker than the rose.

Sharon flushes. "That's the beginning of 'To An Athlete Dying Young.'"

Robert nods. "By the English poet A. E. Housman."

An ROTC cadet reciting poetry? "What's your major?" she asks.

"Political science. What's yours?"

"Journalism. I'm a junior."

"Senior," Robert says about himself. "I don't think I've seen you around before. If I had, I'm sure I would have remembered."

Sharon smiles. "It's a little hard to know all 40,000 people on campus."

"We must not travel in the same circles. Are you a Greek?"

"An AEPhi. I live in the house." No need to explain to him that pledging a sorority provided the only way she could live off campus after freshman year. MSU's *in loco parentis* policy is that women students who did not live in sorority houses had to either be a senior or 21 to not live in the dorms.

She checks her watch. Lance will be furious if she's late getting the story written. She's a fast typist but not a Wonder Woman.

She stands. "I've got a deadline."

He stands too. "And I've got to get back to the field. Maybe I'll see you around," he says.

Now Sharon follows Robert's lead on the dance floor of the Officers Club of Ft. Knox, Kentucky. Sometimes it's hard for her to reconstruct how that chance meeting at the ROTC protest has led her here – to being an army officer's wife.

Out of the corner of her eye Sharon spots Wendy and a man enter the room. He is of medium-build, on the stocky side, with a round face. They are the only two blacks in the room. Sharon stops dancing and leads Robert forward to meet them.

"Hi, Wendy," she says.

Wendy smiles. "Nelson, this is Sharon Gold. She's the head of the entertainment committee I'm on." Sharon and Nelson smile at each other.

"And Robert, this is Wendy Johnson," Sharon says.

Robert sticks out his hand to Wendy. He's making a point Sharon realizes. Then Nelson shakes Sharon's hand.

Sharon motions in the direction of the tables. "Come sit down. We'll get some more chairs."

The man in the Phoenix program has left the table, leaving his chair free. Robert gets one more chair and squeezes Wendy and Nelson next to Sharon.

Wendy turns to Nelson. "Would you get me a Whiskey Sour, please?"

"That's my drink too," Sharon says, then stands. "While Nelson's gone, let's go say hello to Kim and Donna."

"I'll just wait here for Nelson."

"No, no," Sharon says, pulling Wendy up. "Let's go say hello."

As Sharon and Wendy come up to the other two women, Jim stands and turns to Kim. "It's time to go home," he says.

"It is?" Kim asks. "We haven't been here that long."

"I said it's time to go, Kim." Jim pulls her chair back from the table and motions for her to get up.

"Good-bye," Kim says.

"See you tomorrow," Sharon says.

Donna motions for Sharon and Kim to take the vacated seats.

At this moment a man standing at the far end of the table from the women holds up his beer glass. "A toast," he says. "May we all get our chance to kill those little yellow bastards!"

☆ ☆ ☆

Sharon watches herself in the mirror as she brushes her teeth before going to bed. In the reflection she visualizes swarms of yellow jackets about to attack her.

At first she wonders why she should think this. Then she knows.

Yellow bastards – yellow jackets. The toast referred to the Vietcong, those "yellow" enemies.

Robert squeezes into the tiny bathroom, sees her expression in the mirror. "What's wrong?" he asks.

Sharon turns around to face him. "How could you stand there and drink to that awful toast?"

Robert puts his arms around her waist. "That's Geist. He's an idiot. Nobody pays any attention to him."

"You did."

"Honey, listen to me. The guy is the class moron. He's a high school graduate, Officers Candidate School, a 120-day wonder. The whole class thinks he's a jerk – even our Marine."

She tries to wriggle out of Robert's grip, but he keeps his arms around her.

"Most of the guys in class are all right," he says. "They're just like me. They want to do their two years nice and quietly, no heroics. There are some regular army types along with a bunch of warrant officers back from Vietnam – helicopter pilots."

Like Mark Williamson?

"What rank are warrant officers?"

"They're not really officers – they're a hybrid. Enlisted men who the army wants to promote but not make officers. They can go to the Officers Mess and the Officers Club. The army decided to commission these particular pilots as officers, so they have to take a branch officers course – this time the branch is armor. They're fuck-offs. All they do is strut around telling each other how tough they are, then figure out how to get out of every detail. Then there's Geist. Really, forget him."

"So why did you drink to the toast?"

"Didn't you see that look we all gave each other? You have to play the game."

She shakes her head. He slaps her rear. "Know what I mean, play the game?"

*Senate Foreign Relations
Committee approves Cooper-Church
amendment to cut off
funds for Cambodian military
operations ...*
May 11, 1970

KIM – IV – May 19

"When a woman attends a social function at night without her husband she should arrive and leave with another couple, seldom alone."

Kim lies on her back in the traditional missionary position. She shuts her eyes to block out her husband's face, cherry red from his exertions.

Usually she likes Jim so close. She feels protected, safe, loved. Tonight having sex just reminds her of what Jim fears she wants from other men.

There's a potential trap in almost every one of Jim's questions of her. "What did you do today?" can mean "Did you see any men today?"

She never responds, never rises to the bait. She knows why he is obsessed about this. He told her the night he proposed, before he made her swear on the Bible that she would never, never sleep with anyone else or she would rot in hell.

Jim rolls off her. It's over before it's really begun. For Jim sex is like shooting a pistol during target practice – you get off your round as quickly as possible, then tote up your points.

"Was it good?" he asks.

She smiles and snuggles closer. She doesn't tell him he's missed the target again. It's better to say nothing since she can't explain how to improve his performance. "So good," she says.

Earlier, when Jim came home for the day, Kim took the fatigue shirt and pants he handed her and hung them over a chair. Later she would press the creases sharp in the pants so that the pants could be worn one more time before being washed. She is good at ironing – another one of her many chores at the foster homes.

Jim had put on a pair of dark grey slacks and a white short-sleeved shirt to wear to the Officers Club. "What's for dinner?" he asked.

They sat at the small table in the nook of the living room. Kim served the meatloaf with slices of white bread and butter and glasses of milk.

"How was your day? Did you and Sharon do something together?"

She hesitated for only a moment before answering. "We had hamburgers at the Officers Club. It was nice there."

Jim looked up with his mouth full. He swallowed. "You didn't talk to any men there, did you?"

Kim lowered her eyes. "Of course not."

"Did any men talk to you?" He put his fork down.

"Not to me."

"Sharon?"

"A man from her hometown recognized her and came up to her. They were in the same dancing class in seventh grade. He just said a few words, then left."

"Is that all that happened?"

"Yes."

She clutched her hands together on her lap, hidden by the table. Please may he stop.

Jim persisted in his interrogation. "Was Sharon glad to see him? Do you think it was a planned meeting?"

At this Kim flushed. "Of course not. And she made it very clear immediately that she's married."

"What difference does that make?"

Kim said nothing, and he picked up his fork again to finish dinner.

Now in the dark bedroom she opens her eyes, stares at the ceiling. She wishes they could have stayed longer at the Officers Club tonight. Southern officers have a strong tradition in the army. So why does Jim appear uncomfortable around his fellow officers?

On the ceiling she spots a water stain with ragged edges that suddenly turns into the acid burn in the skirt of her old brown corduroy jumper. The Kruger boy threw the acid on her jumper in high school chemistry lab, then laughed as the material sizzled and burned. She didn't cry in front of him. Only later that night she cried when her foster mother found out and whacked her for it: "Look what you've gone and done! You only have two outfits and now you've ruined one!"

Kim forces her eyes away from the spot and the memory. Jim snores once and then flops over onto his stomach.

At least she didn't ruin her outfit tonight by spilling beer on it or dropping the greasy onion rings someone ordered for all of them. Sharon and Donna's outfits weren't any fancier than what Kim wore. Maybe Wendy's was nicer, but then her father's a doctor. A black doctor, but a doctor all the same.

Kim's fingers trace circles on the sheet that covers her and Jim. The bedroom air conditioner is actually working tonight so she's not too hot to sleep. Still she resists falling asleep, instead thinking about the last few days here at Ft. Knox.

It's nice having friends, friends who can share the strange world of what is expected of an officer's wife. Yet no matter how close she may feel to these women, she probably won't ever tell them anything about her family.

Her family. Kim's eyes seek the photo on the nightstand. Although it's too dark to see the faces, she can picture every line, every blemish that those faces have. Her parents were tenant farmers – probably white trash although no one ever said that in front of her and she hadn't been old enough to remember on her own.

She did remember the chicken coop perched behind the back porch. It had been her job to pluck the eggs from their nests under the hens, her younger sister Diane holding out the basket to receive each still-warm egg. Kim had been afraid of the hens at first, afraid they'd bite her on the hand or tug on her long braids. Her father taught her how to be patient gathering the eggs, how the chickens wouldn't hurt her, and her fear disappeared watching his calm movements.

She and Diane had been staying at neighbors while their parents made a trip into town for supplies. The two sisters waited on the neighbors' front porch until long after the sun set. Kim tried to be patient the way her father had taught her, telling Diane over and over that their parents would come soon, imagining them finally arriving just as the hens eventually gave up their eggs.

Their parents never returned.

That night, still unaware of the fatal car accident hours earlier, Kim and her sister bedded down with the neighbors' children. In the morning the nightmare began.

She squeezes her eyes shut. Don't think about that.

Her reopened eyes catch the glint off the gold metal of Jim's second lieutenant bars lying on top of the dresser. She squeezes her eyes shut again.

The next morning Kim has the car and she isn't picking up Sharon till after lunch, so Kim decides to visit Susanna. Normally she wouldn't drop in without calling. Except since Susanna visited her unannounced this must be considered okay conduct for an officer's wife.

Kim's not sure why she's moved to visit Susanna. Maybe it's because of Susanna's daughter Patty. Something about Patty strikes a chord within Kim.

Now Kim follows the route that Jim drove that first night. Once inside the housing area, she consults the map to find the right street. She parks the car in front of the house and walks towards the door.

"Stop that!" she hears Susanna yelling through the screen door. "Patty, stop that at once." Then she hears: Whack! Whack!

Kim hesitates. Should she go away or should she ring the doorbell? Which would be better for Patty? Kim rings the doorbell.

Susanna answers the door after a couple of minutes. Her hair neatly combed, she has on a clean cotton skirt and blouse although her face sports a reddish flush.

"Hello," Kim says. "I'm sorry if this is an inconvenient time to visit."

"Come in," Susanna says. "I'm just about to make some lemonade for the children."

Kim follows Susanna into the house. Billy Jr. waddles around a playpen in the living room gnawing on a red block. "He's teething," Susanna calls over her shoulder as she disappears into the kitchen.

Where's Patty?

"May I use your bathroom?" Kim calls through the open kitchen doorway.

"Down the hall."

Kim doesn't need a bathroom. It's an excuse to see about Patty.

As Kim passes a closed door there's snuffling on the other side. She pushes the door open and peeks inside. Patty sits on the uncarpeted floor between a bed and a crib. Her face lies buried in a raggedy teddy bear.

Kim walks into the room and touches the child on her shoulder. Patty looks up.

Kim says nothing; she doesn't want Susanna to hear. Instead Kim smiles and rubs Patty's shoulder. After a minute Patty stands up and holds the teddy bear out to Kim. Kim takes it in both hands, the way a treasure should be handled. "It's lovely," she says. Patty smiles at her.

Kim hands the bear back to Patty and motions her to follow. Down the hall they go and into the kitchen.

Susanna stands at the counter stirring the contents of a plastic pitcher.

"I opened the wrong door," Kim says, "and look who I found. Now we can all have lemonade together."

Susanna scowls. "Patty is bein' punished."

Susanna lifts the pitcher off the counter and places it on the table. She comes over to Patty and smacks her on the face, then points out the door. "Patty, go on back to your room till I tell ya to come out."

Kim turns her face to hide her own tears. The child's tears splatter the floor as Patty runs out of the kitchen.

As Kim pulls up to her apartment she spots two MPs standing outside her door. Oh, no, they found her! She stays seated in her car for a moment, then remembers Jim will be home soon for lunch. She must get this over with.

She gets out of the car. Without saying a word the MPs wait for her to unlock the door and follow her in.

The MPs sit on the couch and she takes the armchair. One MP explains how they tracked her down. They are here to "review" the shooting.

Twenty minutes later, only 10 minutes before Jim's expected home, they are still asking questions.

"Mrs. Benton, we still don't understand why you left the scene of the shooting without waiting for the MPs."

She twists her clenched hands. "My husband," she says.

"Yes?" the one named Skelly prompts.

"I can't explain."

"Jealous type, is he?" the other one, McCauley, asks.

She looks away.

"We're from the South," she says. "We do things differently back home."

Skelly nods. "Mind if we ask your husband a couple of questions about that night?"

"No, you can't! I mean, please don't. He'll be so furious."

"Why is that, Mrs. Benton?" McCauley asks.

She hesitates. "He just will."

"I see," McCauley says.

She has to get the men out of here before Jim gets home!

"I was wrong not to stay. I'm sorry. I really am. And I promise to come to the MP office if you need any more information. Please, please, don't stay here waiting for my husband. He just wouldn't understand."

McCauley stands. "We don't want to cause any trouble so we'll be going now. Just remember, never leave the scene of a shooting again."

Please God may she never again be at the scene of a shooting.

President Nixon tells labor
leaders that incursion into
Cambodia a huge success ...
May 12, 1970

WENDY – II – May 21

"There are no courtesies, customs, or privileges that apply ONLY to Regular Army officers and their wives."

Wendy checks herself in the tiny bathroom mirror. Her lipstick isn't smeared, her hair is combed, and – she smiles – she looks about as good as she's going to get. There's nothing else she can do around the trailer to put off going. Entertainment committee meetings don't fill all the time. She can't just sit around thinking about ... things. Things such as whether Nelson will be sent to Vietnam and whether she'll fit into the mold of an officer's wife.

She should go to this meeting. See if she can contribute.

The notice she spotted had been posted on the Officers Club announcement board: "Volunteers Needed to Help Out in Post Clinic." The notice invited interested wives to come to an introductory meeting at the post hospital at 1300 hours today.

Whenever Wendy sees time noted in military terms she feels as if she has wandered into the pages of a futuristic novel. The phrase 1300 hours connotes space ships blasting off, captains synchronizing their wrist communicators.

Wendy has read ever since she was little. Her mama encouraged her to travel through books. Once, at age 10, she asked her mama, "Why are all the girls white in the books? Aren't there any little black girls who have adventures?" Her mama said, "Sure, honey, but they just don't get written about." Then her mama added, "Just pretend the little girls are black."

Wendy still wonders why she can't read about black women having adventures the way white women do. It's getting harder and harder to pretend the heroines are black.

As she starts the car, she remembers there will be black patients in the clinic because lots of black enlisted men are stationed here at Ft. Knox. It's just in the officers' ranks that black men are not very prevalent. There's one other black man in Nelson's AOB class. His wife's home having a baby and Wendy hasn't met him.

Yesterday evening, feeling lonely for other blacks, Wendy suggested to Nelson that, when the post pools open on Memorial Day, they swim at the pool where children are allowed – the one that families of both officers and enlisted men go to – so that she might meet some black women. Nelson said no. "I'm an officer and I want to be with my fellow officers."

Wendy parks her car in the lot outside the post hospital. Why hasn't she told Nelson where she's going? He might discourage her, perhaps say, "You think a bunch of whites want your help?"

Determined to do something herself, she whispers "I think I can, I think I can" from the children's book "The Little Engine That Could." Then she walks into the hospital.

Next to the door marked "clinic" a taped sign announces the volunteer meeting in the multipurpose room down the hall. Wendy hesitates outside the room, stalling before confronting a room of strangers, white strangers. She reminds herself she went to the coffee for new AOB wives. Yet she was rightfully there. Here she may not be wanted.

"I think I can, I think I can."

She enters a room where six white women sit around a long table. An older white woman standing near the table approaches Wendy.

"Good afternoon. I'm Mrs. Donovan." For perhaps the first time in her life Wendy is relieved not to hear a Southern drawl but a clipped New England accent. Aren't Northerners less prejudiced? "Have you come about the volunteer meeting?"

"Yes, I have." She hesitates. "I'm Wendy Johnson."

"Welcome, Mrs. Johnson. Please be seated. We'll just wait another moment to see if anyone else comes."

Wendy sits down in a chair two away from the nearest woman. All the women wear suits. Following the dress code in "Mrs. Lieutenant," Wendy has worn a navy blue cotton suit. She puts her purse down on the table. Has she sat in the wrong place?

Wendy has never ridden a bus. Her mama or papa drove her anywhere she wanted to go and she walked to school. At college everything was close enough to walk to or she would take a taxi to shop in the nearby stores. She knows that in the South blacks sat at the back of buses for decades. In school she learned about Rosa Parks' refusal to give up her bus seat to a white man in Montgomery, Alabama, in 1955, resulting in a black boycott of the buses and ultimately the desegregation of those buses. Yet now Wendy feels as uneasy as a black dropped in from Mars might feel sitting down in the front section of any Southern segregated bus and then noticing the white sea of hostile faces.

Mrs. Donovan takes the chair at the far end of the table. "Let's start." She welcomes them all again, then asks everyone to say her own name and her husband's assignment at Ft. Knox.

Everyone makes a point to state her husband's rank. All the husbands are officers. Perhaps there was no notice posted at the enlisted men's club.

Wendy explains that her husband is here for Armor Officers Basic.

"You'll only be here a short time, isn't that right?" Mrs. Donovan asks. Mrs. Donovan's husband has the highest rank of the husbands of the women here. Is that what makes Mrs. Donovan in charge of this meeting?

Wendy nods. "I'd like to help out. I really would."

A dark-haired woman in a lime green linen suit asks, "How do you think you can help, Mrs. Johnson?"

"My papa is a doctor" – she feels, actually feels, the surprise of the other women – "and I've watched him do simple procedures. I could ..."

"Your father is a doctor?" the same woman asks.

"He's an internist in South Carolina."

"I'll be," the woman says, turning to the person next to her.

Tiny droplets of moisture prick Wendy's hands. See, Nelson would say, you asked for this, going to a meeting where you don't belong.

Mrs. Donovan stares down the table at the whispering woman. "Please, ladies, let's have no extraneous talking."

She turns to Wendy. "That's wonderful, my dear. I'm sure we can find something for you to help out with."

Relief washes over her. Mrs. Donovan has included her, made her feel welcome.

A half hour later Mrs. Donovan ends the meeting after explaining the workings of the clinic and the opportunities for volunteers. Then she passes around a sign-up sheet. Wendy records her name, address and phone number. In the column marked "preferred assignment" she writes "whatever will help most."

Mrs. Donovan stands at the door saying good-bye to each woman. As Wendy comes up to her, she smiles and says, "We very much appreciate your offer. I will call you in a few days. I have something specific in mind for you."

In her mind's eye Wendy sees herself on her knees, scrubbing the clinic floors. Stop it! she tells herself. She'll just have to wait for Mrs. Donovan's call.

If there is a call.

Later that day Wendy sits at the minuscule kitchen table in the trailer and opens a letter from her best friend in college. Assigned as roommates in their first year, Regina and Wendy also roomed together during the following three years. Regina remains at school, now doing graduate work in literature.

"Dear Wendy," the letter reads. "I miss you terribly and hope that you are having a good time in Kentucky. Ginny and I have been getting along rather well this year in our graduate dorm suite. Tim sends his best and hopes that you'll be able to come to our wedding in December in Chicago."

Wendy rereads the words "our wedding," then peers at her formal wedding photo in its silver frame propped on the coffee table. She purposely placed the photo in the middle of the small trailer to remind her of better times.

Her parents saw to it that her wedding day was truly magnificent. Chantilly lace completely covered her dress of ivory satin, and she had a matching Chantilly lace mantilla. The dress' train stretched for several yards behind her, and two little girls in ivory satin dresses held it up.

The ceremony took place in her family's neighborhood church with the reception in the church hall. Huge flower bouquets transformed a drab chapel and reception hall into a tropical paradise.

Only blacks attended the wedding. Her papa had white patients, and her parents knew many of the whites in the town, but her parents didn't want to chance any trouble at their only child's wedding. Peace and serenity were the reigning attributes of the day. And much joy.

Afterwards she and Nelson drove to a hunting lodge loaned to them by a white friend of her papa's. They were welcome to the place for two weeks, with one condition: they couldn't tell anyone except her parents whose place they used.

In the bathroom Wendy took off her going-away outfit – a checked sleeveless dress with matching coat – and slid her new silk nightgown over her excited body.

She could feel Nelson's tension as she slipped into the double bed. Wendy had been brought up that respectable women didn't sleep with men before marriage. So here she and Nelson were – about to make love for the first time. A wave of nervousness rocked her stomach. Then Nelson put his arms around her and kissed her.

The knock on the trailer door startles Wendy.

At the door stands a thin woman perhaps in her late forties holding a plastic tumbler. "Hi, I wondered if I could borrow a cup of ..." The woman stops in mid-sentence.

She's realizing that I'm black Wendy thinks. She'll probably decide she doesn't need to borrow anything.

"... sugar." The woman holds up the tumbler. "I ... I brought my own container."

Wendy lets out her breath and smiles. Maybe the woman's hesitancy came from nervousness over asking a favor of a stranger. "Come on in," Wendy says. She opens the trailer's screen door and motions the woman inside.

A white neighbor has entered her home for the first time. Wait till she tells Nelson.

✵ ✵ ✵

Two days later Wendy sits in the passenger seat as Nelson drives their Mustang. It's a graduation gift from her parents, a gift they made plain they hope her husband Nelson will live to enjoy.

Every time she thinks of her parents and their adamant views against the Vietnam War she shivers.

"We shouldn't be fighting that war for those people who don't even appreciate our sacrifices," her mother would say if a friend happened to mention Vietnam. "We should be spending our money and efforts here at home. There's plenty to fix in the United States."

And her father would add, "It's not the same as World War II. We're not fighting to save the world from fascism."

Neither one understands why Nelson would want to serve in the U.S. Army. They seem to have forgotten knowing that all male students at Wendy and Nelson's college were required to take two years of ROTC. And once in ROTC Nelson became convinced that he should serve.

Wendy watches Nelson drive, seeing him as she did the first time, singing a solo in the college glee club, his round face glowing, his voice echoing throughout the practice hall. She joined the glee club her second semester at college; she didn't have the confidence to join first semester. As her homesickness intensified, she wanted to recreate the joy that filled her whenever she sang in her church choir. As she watched Nelson perform, a thrill ran through her.

She didn't have the courage to introduce herself. He came up to her.

At this moment Nelson signals for a right-hand turn, and they pull into a parking lot in front of an industrial building.

They need to get the most out of Nelson's one-time $300 uniform allowance. Obviously the lower the price paid for each uniform, the further the allowance will stretch. So here they are, at a warehouse in Louisville reputed to sell officer uniforms for better prices than on the army post.

The building's door opens into a huge room where ceiling fans churn the humid air. A mothball-and-lint aroma floats up from the endless rows of uniforms hanging from rods stretched vertically away from the door. Glass cases off to their right showcase brass insignia and other accessories. The colors of the rows make clear the location of the different uniforms. Cardboard signs indicate the sizes.

"I'm going to get my dress blues first, then see how much money I have left for everything else."

Nelson leads her over to the far right wall of blue and finds the section marked 42 regular. He takes out a set of navy blue pants with a yellow stripe down each leg and a lighter blue jacket.

Within 30 minutes Nelson buys all the uniforms he needs along with the accessories, including a bowtie and shoulder epaulets for the dress blues.

"We need gas," Nelson says when they are back in the car. "I don't want to cut it too close."

Wendy buckles her seat belt and rolls her window down, hoping for a little limp breeze. "There's a station on the next corner," she says.

They pull up to a pump as an older man in a plaid shirt and blue jeans appears at the driver's side of the car. Wendy smells sweat and tobacco smoke as he peers in at them, then checks out the stack of uniforms laid neatly across the back seat with the dress blues on top.

"Hey, boy, what ya doin' with that officer uniform?"

Nelson's hands grip the steering wheel. "I just bought it for Armor Officers Basic training at Ft. Knox. I'm an officer."

"Ya, boy? Niggers ain't officers. Niggers a' cannon fodder. That's what we'a fighting that war far. Rid us of some niggers."

Nelson guns the engine and races out of the gas station. The man's laughter follows them.

"I should have known better than to get gas up here," he says. "We have enough to make it back to the post."

She's nauseous and afraid of the answer, but she has to ask. "Nelson, what did that man mean about blacks as cannon fodder?"

Nelson shifts the car into third gear. "He's just an ignoramus."

She's heard this word before. It's Nelson's favorite for explaining away the insults directed at blacks.

"Nelson, you're trying to protect me – just like my parents – but I'd really like to know what that man meant."

Nelson honks at a pickup truck cutting in front of them, then says "Statistics."

"What?"

"Statistics. How many blacks getting killed in Vietnam compared to how many whites."

She swats at a fly buzzing around her face. "What about the statistics?"

"Some people think they're skewed. More blacks than whites proportionately in line units."

"Line units?"

"Combat units."

Wendy's stomach protests as she remembers the Bible story about King David. He sent Uriah the Hittite into the front lines to be killed so that David could marry Uriah's beautiful wife Bathsheba.

Was that horrid gas station man saying that whites send blacks into battle in the front lines to get rid of them?

"Nelson? Can I ask another question?"

"Honey, can it wait? I want to concentrate on the traffic. Let's listen to some music."

Nelson snaps the radio on. Steam sings "Na Na Hey Hey Kiss Him Goodbye." Wendy chokes back the tears.

The next day Nelson asks "Why did you have to say yes to Sharon?" as Wendy places the hotdogs wrapped in cellophane into a straw basket.

"Why shouldn't I have said yes? It was nice of Sharon to organize for the whole class a bring-your-own barbecue."

Nelson stands up from the kitchen table. "It wasn't so nice at the Officers Club. It was noisy and crowded and hardly anyone spoke to us."

Wendy closes the top of the straw basket, hooking the latch into the leather slot. "No one hardly spoke to you because you didn't speak to anyone. And besides, the music was too loud to hear anyone say much of anything."

She takes the basket in one hand and his hand in the other, then leads him out of the trailer and into the car.

Nelson says he wants to be with his fellow officers – won't let her go to the family pool when it opens in a week. But now he doesn't want to go to this picnic with his class members.

It isn't just being with all the whites that makes him uncomfortable, she knows; he's also self-conscious about his lack of social skills. He didn't have the same opportunities she did. Large family gatherings with aunts, uncles, and little cousins running around constitute his idea of "getting together" with other people.

Her parents warned her when she announced her intention to marry him: "Honey, Nelson's a nice enough young man, but he doesn't have any class, he's not very 'presentable.'" She didn't listen. He appealed to her in a way that the other boys her parents introduced her to back home didn't. Perhaps the appeal was that Nelson needed her and the others didn't.

Nelson starts the car. "I just hope no one says anything about 'niggers.' It could really ruin my appetite."

Armed Forces Day observances
at 23 military bases
canceled due to planned
anti-war demonstrations …
May 16, 1970

SHARON – VI – May 24

"Protocol is simply good manners."

Sharon places the beef hotdogs and buns on a paper plate and adds a paper towel on top to keep off the flies. All the other hotdogs will probably be pork. And while she and Robert don't keep kosher, she doesn't eat pork. She'll have to keep a close eye on her beef hotdogs while they cook on the communal grill.

This AOB class barbecue will be a chance to get together where there isn't a band so loud you can't hear yourself think let alone talk. Hansen's Apartments has an area with barbecue pits and picnic tables. Perfect for this.

"Hurry up," she says to Robert. "We don't want to be late to our own party."

"One minute, honey. I'm just filling out a withdrawal slip for our savings account."

"Why are you doing that?"

Robert looks up from the kitchen table. "I need the money to buy more uniforms. I told you I haven't gotten my uniform pay voucher yet. The paperwork apparently keeps getting lost."

"Don't you think that's odd?"

"It's routine for the army to mess up."

Sharon hesitates before speaking. "Robert, we agreed not to spend any of our wedding money."

"I promise to replace it just as soon as my pay voucher comes through."

A car enters Hansen's parking lot. With these thin windows and walls you can hear everything from inside the apartment. Sharon peers out the living room window as Wendy and Nelson get out of their car.

Sharon hopes there won't be any trouble at the party. There's no telling what someone might say about blacks.

Sharon well remembers the day at college when an edict was announced to the editorial staff of the "State News": "From now on the correct description in our pages for Negro is 'black.' It will be used lower case. The word 'Negro' will no longer be used." And henceforth and forevermore no one used the word "Negro" in the pages of the college newspaper. One of her colleagues even wrote an editorial about the mandate. The editorial had been an eloquent plea to adapt one's speech to the written word.

"I'm ready," Robert says now.

Sharon hands him two bags of potato chips and a large bottle of Coke, then picks up the plate of hotdogs and a stack of paper cups. "I hope no one's going to get drunk," she says.

Robert holds open the front door for her. "An officer is a gentleman. We have nothing to worry about."

"And the officers' wives?" Sharon asks.

✶ ✶ ✶

"South Carolina is hot, too," Wendy says, swatting away a fly hovering over the apple pie. "You get used to it."

The women sit at the picnic tables talking and watching over the desserts. In a few minutes Sharon will call the men back to the tables.

They have already cooked and eaten their hotdogs. Then the men separated, moving off towards a still-hot barbecue grill. During dinner, food talk was the focus. Now the men will discuss more serious things: their AOB class, their army commitment, maybe even Vietnam.

Sharon wonders why the women aren't discussing their husbands' time in the army, their fears of a Vietnam tour. Is something not real if you don't talk about it? Or is it because it is only their husbands' decision – they have been brought up to support such choices regardless of their own feelings?

In a letter last week to her mother she wrote: "In many respects one could think we were on a huge college campus, but the war hangs over everything. The career men's wives don't seem as worried about it as the wives of other second lieutenants who want to serve their time and get out. Of course, the career women could be putting on a front because they have to."

Sharon watches Wendy, Kim, Donna and the others chatting about the food in the commissary and the bargains at the PX. How many of these women believe the war in Vietnam is right? How many feel it is the duty of their husbands to fight?

The truth is, she is relieved the women don't talk about their feelings because undoubtedly they would expect her to reciprocate. She doesn't want to share with these other women her opinions and fears. Ever since ... ever since sixth grade she has chosen not to reveal her innermost thoughts. There are things even Robert does not know.

She blinks away the moisture in her eyes and walks towards the men to see if they're ready for dessert.

As she approaches she hears Jim talking, gesturing with his hands. "The South has a long history of military tradition," he says. "At my college graduation the Confederate flag was bigger than the American flag."

Sharon's breath catches. How can this be? Then she remembers Anne's words when they visited Elizabeth – "These Southerners are in love with the 'noble duty' of the army." And in psychological terms, doesn't it seem reasonable that the descendants of the losers would continually strive to prove that Confederacy soldiers are as good as the Union ones?

Sharon reaches a spot behind Robert just as a man with a shaved head laughs. He's in cutoff jeans and an olive green sweatshirt cut out at the armholes.

"You guys don't know shit about what you're talking about." He grins and looks at the other men. "Now you should see the dinks fight. That's something to see."

Sharon leans close to Robert to whisper in his ear. "What does he mean by dinks?" Robert turns his head to look at her, then places a hand on her arm and leads her away from the group.

"Don't listen to that guy. He and his warrant officer pals are the helicopter pilots in our class I told you about. They're a little rough."

Sharon glances back at the man. "I still want to know what he meant by dinks."

Robert hesitates. "It's a derogatory term for the Vietnamese." He pats her arm and returns to the men.

Sharon's face flares hot. She sinks down on a picnic table bench as Kim walks towards her.

"Sharon, this is a great idea. I'm so glad you thought of it," Kim says.

Donna stands behind Kim. "And it was so nice of you to invite the entire class. Not everyone would have."

Sharon smiles, picturing herself in the dining hall of her sorority house. They'd come downstairs in their pajamas, hair wrapped around jumbo rollers, bunny or puppy slippers on their feet, after taking off the cocktail dresses worn for this final stage of sorority rush. Time to vote on which potential pledges to offer places to in the sorority. Who would be living in their house next year, learning the secret handshake and password, wearing the special jeweled pin?

Several girls were voted in with minimal discussion. Then they got to Amanda. Not the most attractive potential pledge – Amanda could have a better haircut and her clothes could be more fashionable. On top of this, she came from a small Midwestern town instead of an affluent suburb of Detroit or Chicago.

Only one blackball vote would keep Amanda out of the sorority. From the way the discussion progressed it looked like she'd get more than one blackball. At that moment Sharon, surprising herself, burst into tears and said: "We shouldn't exclude people just because they are a little different. There's nothing wrong with Amanda except that she's not so attractive!"

The outburst had been so unexpected – Sharon not known for histrionics – that the naysayers had withdrawn their potential blackballs. Amanda was voted a member of AEPhi.

"Sharon, thank you so much for the invitation," Wendy says, standing next to Donna. "This is terrific."

Sharon looks at Wendy. There were no blacks in her sorority. Of course the Jewish sororities were first organized because Jewish girls couldn't join the non-Jewish sororities. Sharon shakes her head at the memory of that terrible first stage of sorority rush at MSU when potential pledges had to visit all the houses on campus. At the Kappa Kappa Gamma – *I'm so glad that I am a ...* – house Sharon felt as if she had fallen through Alice's rabbit hole into a world populated by blond-haired and blue-eyed giants. She had been as anxious to exit the elegant, two-storied house as they had probably been anxious for her to leave.

She smiles at Wendy, Kim and Donna. "Let's get the men. It's time for dessert."

Sharon lies in bed that evening while Robert brushes his teeth. All in all, everyone seemed to have a good time and no one got noticeably drunk.

Yet for Sharon the barbecue's light mood was overshadowed by that helicopter pilot's derogatory term for the Viet Cong. Because regardless of what you called the Viet Cong, their soldiers could kill your husband.

Sharon fingers the bedspread. She stares around the bleak bedroom.

After the ROTC protest that day she met Robert, Sharon resolved to better understand why young men would willingly enroll in ROTC. She told herself this was simply an academic interest on her part with no connection to the young man she'd let bleed on her Villager sweater.

Ten minutes before the end of class Sharon slipped into Wesley Fishel's classroom. As "State News" feature editor she'd assigned herself a feature piece on Professor Fishel's current views on the Vietnam War. One of the U.S.'s first civilian advisors in Vietnam, Fishel was blamed by some for encouraging the U.S. to become more involved in the ensuing conflict. He'd written books on Vietnam, and of course he'd previously been interviewed by "State News" reporters. Sharon had read those old articles and then convinced herself the paper needed an update from him.

Sitting in the back, she spotted Robert sitting two rows from the front. Her stomach lurched, her palms perspired. Then she realized it made sense for an ROTC guy to take this course – to hear Fishel explain his beliefs why the war couldn't be won the way the U.S. was fighting it – the military not being allowed to bomb North Vietnam into submission.

"That's all for now," Fishel said to the class. "I'll see you on Monday."

Sharon inched up towards the front of the classroom. Turn around and see me, she thought. Robert did not turn around.

"Hi, Robert," she said, coming up alongside him.

He turned around. "Sharon!"

She pointed at Fishel, talking to another student. "I've come to interview him."

"He's a fascinating guy."

"You can read my story in the 'State News.'"

He smiled. "Why don't you tell me in person? A friend of mine is having a party tomorrow night. I could come by the sorority house at 8."

She hesitated. Shouldn't she stop this right now?

"That'll be great" came out of her mouth as if someone else said it. Before she could snatch back the words Fischel said, "Miss Bloom, I'm ready for our interview."

"See you tomorrow night," Robert said.

Fishel waved her to a classroom seat. She took her reporter's steno notepad and a pen out of her purse.

"I'm not sure there's anything I can add to my previous interviews," Fishel said. "The real question is whether – given the fact that the United States has assumed the responsibilities of leadership in the defense of Southeast Asia since 1954 – we can now, in Munich-like fashion, consign the Vietnamese, the Lao and their neighbors to the limbo of Chinese domination for generations to come."

Fishel's familiar responsibility refrain. Sharon's pen dashed across the lined pages of her notebook, capturing his remarks with a combination of handwriting and shorthand symbols.

"What about our responsibility to the Americans who are dying over there for a war that can't be won?" she asked.

The professor swiped his arm across his eyes. "The stakes are simply too great for anyone to leave South Vietnam alone."

The perspiration drips down his face, oozing into his eyes and sliding over his mouth. He swipes at the beads dripping from his nose with the arm of his filthy fatigue shirt. "This heat is unbearable," the armor officer says to the 19-year-old enlisted man quivering beside him inside the tank. "How do the Vietnamese survive?"

The officer pops the hatch, standing upright in the commander's seat to check the terrain. The enemy hides somewhere nearby.

The explosion lifts his body up into the air, twisting it around before dumping it on top of the tank, his sweat-stained face turned downward as if searching for the softest place to land.

The 19-year-old screams.

DONNA – II – May 25

*"When your husband returns to civilian life, his military
record will be his only recommendation and reference for the
past two years."*

Five o'clock. The first bars of a bugle blowing
retreat over the loudspeaker system. As required even
for civilians, Donna stops her Buick at the side of the
road, gets out, and stands at attention. The bugle
sounding retreat always bring memories of other
posts, of a small girl clinging to her mother's hand,
of feeling special, as if she too, for the moments the
bugle played, was a real American.

Donna thinks about her father, an army supply
sergeant, and the places they lived throughout the
U.S. and in Germany and the Orient. In Korea they
lived in an apartment so cold they only took baths
once a week. In Germany her father's rank didn't
entitle them to army housing, so they lived "on the

economy." They overcame the prejudices of their German neighbors and were greeted on the street in the same formal way Germans greet each other. In the U.S. they lived in small towns and on large bases. At each post she and her family learned to adjust, working hard to be accepted in the enlisted men's community and by their neighbors.

A tremor shakes Donna. Although her father is now stationed at Ft. Riley, Kansas, her brother, her only brother, is a forward artillery observer in Vietnam. For him it's the price of going to OCS, of becoming an officer. Donna knew, without her brother telling her, that forward observers spend their first six months in Vietnam living in trees, positioned ahead of the rest of the troops, peering into the jungle praying to spot the enemy before the enemy spots them.

Whenever she thinks about her brother her entire body trembles. She hasn't always felt this way about Vietnam. That was before …

This morning she reread her brother's last letter, trying to gauge between the lines his mental state. No clues in the few scribbled words. She felt compelled to write him today even though she could mail him a letter next week that could get to him before the one she mailed today. Writing was almost like saying Hail Marys when she was a child. If she just wrote enough, if she just believed enough, her prayers would be answered.

Retreat ends. The sudden silence causes Donna to look around herself, the wooden buildings of Ft. Knox pulling her back to the present. She gets back in the car and drives the few remaining yards to where she will pick up Jerry.

Because she doesn't carpool with anyone the way Kim and Sharon do, if she wants the car for the day she has to drive Jerry both ways. In the morning she doesn't always have time to dress and she'll wear a robe just to drive. This doesn't seem to bother Jerry although she's gotten looks from some of the other men as she's pulled up to drop off Jerry.

Now she parks her car and waits.

Last night Donna lay next to Jerry after they had sex. "Did you have a good time?" she asked.

"Yes." He leaned over to bite her shoulder, then put his arm around her and drew her closer. Within seconds he fell asleep.

Donna watched his chest rise and fall, his blond hair almost invisible against his pale skin. A strand of her dark hair fell across her eyes and she brushed it away. How unlikely that the two of them had married.

Jerry's parents hadn't been overjoyed when he brought her home to St. Louis to meet them. They expected an all-American wife for their all-American son. Instead they got a Puerto Rican and a ...

Donna pushed the thought out of her mind. Instead she pictured Jerry's father displaying Jerry's high school tennis trophies. She had to laugh. Tennis was not high on the required skills list for the daughter of an enlisted man – bowling at the PX alleys more her speed. She'd been suitably impressed.

His mother took her up to the attic to show off Jerry's school papers. In a corner of the attic stood a small filing cabinet along with a bookcase of photo albums.

In the filing cabinet the elementary, junior high and high school report cards had a special file of their own. "See all the As and Bs Jerry got," his mother said. "And all the teacher comments are so wonderful. We didn't reward him with a $1 for each A – not like some parents did. He did well just for himself." And for you, too, Donna thought.

Donna flipped through the other files, one for each school year. At the file marked "School Year 1965-66" she stopped and pulled it out of the file drawer. Jerry had once told her about a paper he did senior year of high school. She wanted to see it for herself.

And here it was: "The Future for Diverse Ethnic Groups in the United States by Jerry Lautenberg." While his mother watched, Donna skimmed the paper. She already knew it offered an optimistic thesis, fueled by Jerry's belief that the civil rights movement began a nationwide acceptance of people different from the white majority. Although Jerry still believed in his premise first proposed four and a half years ago, Donna thought this envisioned utopia seemed unlikely to be achieved in the near future.

"Come on, dear," his mother said, rustling at her side. "I have some other things I want to show you." Donna put the file back as his mother lifted the first photo album off the shelf.

"These are Jerry's own souvenir albums. The family albums – with the good photos – are downstairs; you've already seen those. These are the ones Jerry made of his souvenirs from trips and other things he did. He even saved the stubs from all the movies he saw and labeled each movie."

Now Donna watches the first few men of the AOB class exit their classroom building. Jerry isn't among this first group.

Donna thinks about how, when Jerry asked Donna to marry him, she hadn't considered saying no because of his ROTC commitment. "It's this way or be drafted as an enlisted man," he told her. "I'd rather be giving orders than receiving them."

Whenever Donna thinks of her fear – the fear that Jerry will ... – she distracts herself by thinking of what they did the night before, what they will do tonight, and tomorrow night – together.

The entertainment committee is a welcome activity, a good excuse to get out. In her apartment building there's nothing to do and no one to talk to. Elderly couples occupy the other units in the building. At night they probably put glasses up to their adjoining walls to listen to what she and Jerry are up to. One old woman always passes her on the stairs with a penetrating stare.

Jerry tells her to ignore the other occupants, to enjoy herself. After their weeks here they'll move on to Ft. Holabird. In Baltimore they can take advantage of the big city, get a little culture. Here she should just soak up the sun, work on her tan. "I'm already dark enough," she tells him. He laughs and kisses her. "I like women with swimsuit marks. It's sexy."

Donna laughs at the thought as Jerry walks towards the car, his smile for her lighting up his face. He could have had his pick of apple-pie American girls. Instead he chose her! She prays that Jerry won't have to serve in Vietnam. Hasn't her family done enough?

The next day Donna dumps the potato chips into a black lacquer bowl and sets the bowl on the imitation wood coffee table. She volunteered to host the meeting of the entertainment committee today – Sharon asked if they wanted to take turns having the meetings.

Donna would like to serve a Puerto Rican favorite, fried green bananas, but she can't get the right bananas around here. She'll have to wait until her mother comes to visit her and brings the bananas. Then she can show these women a true Puerto Rican treat.

Glancing around the living room, Donna thinks that the apartment isn't so bad. The few personal items they brought with them make it seem cozier.

Her eyes land on the black lacquer bowl. She looks away. She told Jerry it comes from when her family lived in the Orient. This isn't the truth. And even though the truth is painful, she can't bring herself to give the bowl away or even not use it.

The doorbell rings. Wendy stands outside.

"Hi," Wendy says, holding up a slim booklet. "I brought my copy of 'Mrs. Lieutenant' like Sharon asked us."

Donna smiles. Sharon thinks they might enjoy reading some of the rules and regulations together. Donna herself studied the booklet from cover to cover the moment she got it. Being part of an enlisted man's family is totally different from being an officer's wife. She wants to avoid making obvious blunders. Yet the instructions in "Mrs. Lieutenant" are so detailed and lengthy for each type of occasion that the booklet makes her more nervous.

Before Donna can offer Wendy something cool to drink the doorbell rings again. Sharon and Kim have arrived. They don't look anything alike, but since they go everywhere together, Donna thinks of them as "the twins." It's better that than "the couple."

Donna puts the bottles of Coke and 7-Up on the coffee table, and Sharon reaches for some chips. "That's a beautiful bowl. Did you get it in the Orient?"

Donna nods; she doesn't trust her voice. What did she expect? That no one would notice the bowl? Hasn't she put it out to be noticed?

Donna turns to Kim. "Did you bring your copy of 'Mrs. Lieutenant'?"

Kim laughs. "Do you think Sharon would let me forget it?"

Donna asks, "Sharon, do you want to begin?"

"Why not?" Sharon opens her booklet and reads: "This book is written for 'Mrs. Lieutenant' and other Army wives who would like a direct answer to the many questions pertaining to military life." She takes a sip of Coke before continuing:

"It has been said that when a man acquires a commission, the government has gained not one, but two – the officer and his wife. If the wife is well-informed as to what is expected of her, the probability is greater that the officer will have an easier and more successful career."

Sharon laughs. "That's supposing we want our husbands to have a 'successful career.' I'm already counting the days until Robert's two years are up."

Donna looks at Sharon – what she said is rather revealing. Then Donna inclines her head as if in agreement, although her own fears prevent her from thinking much beyond each day.

"Wendy, you continue," Sharon says.

"Social customs are cultivated through man's efforts to make his companions comfortable and happy," Wendy reads. "Rules may be learned, but graciousness is developed by living with kind thoughts and consideration for others."

Donna waves her hand to stop Wendy. "Why don't we skip a few pages? This introduction is too much for me. I like the part on dress." She reads aloud: "Fashion and style change, but the Army wife lives by a few proven rules: her own good judgment and her aptness of applying good taste.

"Slacks and shorts on the tennis court, or about the house, are fine on a cute slim figure ..." Donna pauses. "Don't you love it? 'Cute slim figure'!" Then she goes on, "...but are out of place and usually forbidden at the commissary, post exchange, theater, and public places. Since today's fashions stress women in pants, try to be discreet as to where and when you wear them."

Donna glances at the others. Kim wears a light blue cotton shift with no sleeves. Sharon has on a flower-print cotton skirt and a white short-sleeve blouse. Wendy wears a stylish two-piece pants outfit.

Donna herself has on shorts and a top, but she is in her own apartment.

Kim takes over: "Sunbathing should be done in your own secluded yard." She turns to Sharon. "Are we going to be in trouble for going to the Officers Club pool?"

"Trouble with who?" Sharon says.

Kim smiles, then continues: "Hair curlers belong in the beauty parlor or your own bedroom. Other fads that degrade your position as a lady, and the wife of an Army officer, should be avoided. You are your husband's 'lady,' and are expected to attain the same respect that he does."

Sharon laughs. "Husband's 'lady.' I love it!"

"It's kind of nice," Wendy says. "Especially the part about respect."

"Enough!" Donna says, holding up her hand. "All this makes me really nervous. I'm not sure I can do all this stuff."

"What stuff do you mean?" Sharon asks.

Donna clasps her hands in her lap. How to explain? "I just can't think like an officer's wife all the time. If I want to wear slacks to the commissary, I'm going to wear them. I can't always worry whether I'm doing everything right – it will drive me crazy."

Wendy puts her booklet down on the coffee table. "There aren't so many things for us to do," Wendy says. "It just seems that way when we read all the rules together. One at a time there's not that much. I'm sure you can do it."

Donna walks to the living room picture window. Outside the trees droop, their branches pointing downward as if divining for water. Here inside the room the air conditioner makes the heat bearable.

Puerto Rico is hot too. There at lunchtime people rest inside thick walls that block out the heat. Here at lunchtime people race around in the sun attending luncheons, teas, reviews – wearing gloves and hats and "appropriate" dress.

She turns to the others. "I was part of an enlisted man's family for so long. All this seems overwhelming."

Wendy nods. "We just have to think about it as any other place that has its rules," she says. "In school we had to follow the rules even if we didn't agree with them. If we didn't, we got in trouble. Here, the trouble we might get into could make it harder for our husbands. We have to help them out."

Kim's eyes stare into Donna's. "I spent my whole life following other people's rules. I never had a choice. Now for the first time I can actually choose to do these. I want to feel a part of this. I'm so tired of feeling different, of being an outsider."

These words surprise Donna. Kim, with her blond hair and rosy complexion, looks like the all-American girl. What is she talking about?

Sharon jumps into the silence. "I'm sure it's occurred to all of you how different the four of us are," she says, looking from one to the other of them.

"I expected everyone in the army to be alike." Is that a flush spreading across Sharon's face Donna wonders? "Like hillbillies or something. I was wrong."

Wendy takes Donna's arm and leads her back to her chair. "My papa warned me the night before Nelson and I left for Ft. Knox. He said we might have a hard time in the army because … of who we are. Yet so far it's been okay, at least the official army part. Maybe these rules help that."

Sharon nods. "We all benefit from the recommendation to have 'kind thoughts' and 'consideration for others.'"

Donna feels the tension leaving her body. "You guys are terrific," she says.

She pauses to take a sip of Coke, then says: "And now I've got a question I've been wanting to ask. Who's using birth control?"

Wendy's expression gives nothing away; Sharon smiles; Kim looks horrified. Donna holds up a hand as if to halt what she's said. "What I really mean is – who's planning to start a family soon?"

Wendy says, "I want to wait until we're back home. I just wouldn't feel right being away from my family at such an important time."

Donna looks at Sharon next. "I'm waiting until Robert is out of the army. I don't want to be left alone with small children." Donna knows that Sharon might be referring to being left alone stateside while Robert serves an unaccompanied tour, although she probably means being left a widow. That is something even Sharon wouldn't dare say aloud, maybe not even to herself.

Donna turns to Kim. "What about you, Kim?"

"I'm ... I'm not sure when I want children."

Donna smiles. "I'm ready now but Jerry isn't. He wants to wait a couple of years."

She passes the chips around to the others who sit silently as if waiting for her to end this conversation. "I'm lucky that I've lived all over the place so I know about birth control. You know Maria Perez? The Puerto Rican wife who only speaks Spanish? I asked her about birth control. She doesn't even know what I mean – she's married three months and pregnant already. That's what living among all Catholics does to you."

No one still says anything. Donna places the bowl back on the table. "Why don't we get down to entertainment committee business?" she says.

"Wait till you see what I now have planned," Sharon says.

Wendy laughs. "I just hope it's not going to get any of us in trouble."

Later that day Donna pushes her shopping cart through the commissary aisles overflowing with cereal boxes, baby food and juice. As a child the post commissaries seemed to her like fairylands. So many different kinds of food, so much of each kind, so many long, long aisles to roll the cart down. She could have spent hours among the boxes and bottles and jars and cans.

Up ahead a woman stares at Donna as they approach each other in the aisle. "Donna, Donna Garcia?" the woman asks.

The wheels of Donna's cart clank to a stop. The woman used her maiden name! Donna stares at the woman in a starched white blouse and pleated navy skirt. An officer's wife Donna thinks, then reminds herself that she's an officer's wife too.

"I'm Donna Garcia – or I used to be. Donna Lautenberg now." She smiles at the woman. "I don't recognize you."

"Sylvia Obermeyer – now I'm Mrs. George Warren – my husband is a sergeant in the 194th. You sat next to me in sixth grade."

Sixth grade? Donna tries to remember what post that was. Ft. Sill in Oklahoma? She can't remember her class, or her teacher, or anything else about that year. She isn't surprised. The posts where she was happy she can remember quite well; the periods when she felt most like an outsider are black holes.

"That was a long time ago," Donna says.

"Is your husband stationed here? Or are you visiting your parents?" the woman asks.

"My husband is here at Armor Officers Basic."

The woman stares at Donna, then says, "Your husband is an officer?"

"Yes, he is."

The woman grips her cart and turns it away from Donna. "That's certainly a step up for you." A flush spreads across the woman's face. "Excuse me, I've got to hurry." And with that she disappears down the row of laundry detergents and bathroom tissue.

Donna grabs her own cart and heads in the opposite direction. She has just remembered Sylvia Obermeyer, also the daughter of an enlisted man – the two of them bullied all year by Jennifer Turner, the daughter of a major. Jennifer would open a magazine and point to a picture of white girls. "Donna," she would say, "none of these girls looks like you. They all have light skin." Or Jennifer would say to her and Sylvia, "It's too bad you both have to walk home all the way to the enlisted men's area. The officers' quarters are so much closer." Whether Jennifer learned her bullying at home or came to it naturally Donna never decided.

Now Donna laughs aloud. Donna being married to an officer would upset Jennifer's vision of the world, a world in which military rank passes down from generation to generation. Once in a caste always in the same caste.

Too bad Sylvia hurried away. They could have had lunch together at the Officers Club.

The cart wheels squeaking on the linoleum seem to ask a question. Donna could take an enlisted man's wife to the Officers Club, couldn't she?

SHARON – VII – May 26

"For a formal invitation written in the third person your answer should be handwritten on plain white note paper in the third person, the same manner in which it was extended."

Sharon turns over the two rib steaks sizzling in the broiler. The steaks are part of the treasure trove of kosher meat she and Robert bought in Louisville, and she doesn't want to burn them.

The lit broiler adds to the heat, which, as usual, the living room air conditioner can't alleviate. She doesn't care. For a change they will have a good dinner.

Grease splatters her hand as she closes the broiler. She retreats to a chair in the living room in front of the air conditioner.

With its minimal furniture this apartment seems like a student apartment at MSU. It was to just such an apartment that Robert took her on their first date.

"You're just like all the girls I know back home in the East," Robert said as he led her into his friend's apartment. Was he insulting her?

"I mean it as a compliment," he said. "You know, sophisticated. You don't seem like a Midwesterner."

He couldn't know that her secret ambition was not to be a backwater Midwesterner. And she hoped she didn't look like a Midwesterner either. She wore another of her Villager sweater and skirt sets, this one in a pink blend. Classic and comfortable.

Robert looked good in jeans, a white turtleneck and tweed sport coat. He took a bottle of rum from his back pocket. "I'll mix us rum and Cokes."

The room's furniture had been shoved aside to provide dancing space for the crush of people barely visible in the dim light. Cigarette smoke and liquor smells flushed the air.

"Duke of Earl" sung by Gene Chandler spun on the 45 record player. Robert handed her a drink and pulled her down next to him on a battered couch.

"I'm going to Vietnam," he said.

She couldn't believe he said this to her just like that! "How can you fight in such an immoral war?" she said.

"My father fought in Europe in World War II. His father served in the Jewish Legion in World War I. It's what I have to do."

Sharon's eyes darted around the room. No one was close enough to overhear them. "To prove yourself a man to your father?" she said. And without letting him answer, she continued, "How can you support the war machine?"

"I'm not 'supporting the war machine' – I'm not even saying the war is right. I'm simply doing my patriotic duty for my country."

The tantalizing smell of broiling steak yanks her back to the present. She could discuss her fears with Kim, yet she won't. That sharing of innermost feelings with friends, that vulnerability, stopped a long time ago. She realized this the summer after seventh grade, one year after her life changed. At the concluding campfire of overnight camp she stood dry eyed as the other girls cried. One boy, a chubby specimen of adolescent insecurity, said, "Sharon's not crying. She's taking it like a man." She didn't tell him she'd already shed a lifetime of tears.

Robert's key in the lock startles her. "I've got some important news," he says as he comes through the door. Then he swivels towards the kitchenette.

"Hey, smells like steak," he says. "Let me change first and sit down for dinner. We'll talk while we're eating."

Robert strides out of the room before she can say anything. What can the news be? Is it about going to Vietnam?

Her hands shake as she lifts the steaks out of the broiler, places one onto each plate, and sets the two plates on the table to join the waiting bowls of salad and green beans. Sharon sits down across from Robert as he returns from the bedroom.

"How would you like to live in Europe for a year?" he says.

Europe?

"Can you believe it?" Robert forks a bite of steak into his mouth. Sharon wants to swipe the piece out of his mouth.

"What are you talking about?"

He swallows. "It's called voluntary indefinite – vol indef. We agree to sign up for a minimum of at least a third year of active duty, and we're promised to first go to Europe for a year on an accompanied tour – we can take our wives – before they send us on a 'short' tour."

"A 'short' tour?"

"Vietnam."

Three years minimum rather than the now-required two years of active duty! "And you'll still go to Vietnam!"

"Hear me out," he says, putting down his fork. "First, it's a great opportunity to see Europe. ROTC guys usually don't get a European assignment because an accompanied tour to Europe is supposed to be for three years – it's for career guys. Second, Nixon has to end the war before the elections in '72 or he won't get reelected. This year in Europe buys us time – the war may be declared over before I have to go."

Sharon fingers her fork, then looks up at Robert. "You were gung ho on going to Vietnam – just not in infantry. And your branch transfer to military intelligence took care of that."

"I was gung ho on being in the army, being as brave as my father, as patriotic. The more time I spend in the army the more I realize I don't have to get myself killed to prove I'm a man. If I serve in Europe I'll still have done my duty."

There has to be a catch. "Why is the army so generous?"

"They need more officers. An extra year of active duty from each ROTC guy goes a long way towards helping meet that manpower requirement."

Robert hands her a sheet of paper. "And we're invited to attend a meeting – separate meetings for the MI and armor guys – wives too – to hear more about this. Some MI major's flying here from Washington to talk to the MI guys and an armor major's coming too for the armor guys."

"Where in Europe would we go?" Sharon asks.

Robert switches his eyes to the steak. "There are a few small units in Belgium and Italy. The main army posts are in Germany."

"Germany!"

Robert looks up. "Now, Sharon, the war's been over for 25 years. We won't see Nazis standing on every corner."

"Germany!" Sharon shrieks again. "We're going to live in Germany!"

The next day Sharon tugs down the skirt of her black-and-white seersucker two-piece suit – is it too short? – and enters the designated post building. The voluntary indefinite meeting for the Armor Officers Basic men commissioned in military intelligence will begin in five minutes.

Germany! Since last night she's been haunted by goose-stepping Nazi soldiers snapping off their "Heil Hitler" salutes. Then she pictures Jewish men, women and children crammed into sealed boxcars traveling across Europe with no air, no water, no food, and no toilet facilities for days and days – eternity – before reaching the death camps. A rabbi once told her it took the Greek Jews 10 days to reach the death camps in Poland. "The lucky ones died before," he said.

Robert waves as she enters the room. She walks over to join him where he sits next to Donna and Jerry, an MI officer like Robert. The meeting for the armor guys will be tomorrow. Robert and Jim have arranged their carpooling schedule so each wife would have her own car to drive to the respective meetings. Wendy and Nelson, an armor officer like Jim, will be at tomorrow's meeting with Kim and Jim.

"Looks like a college lecture hall," Sharon says to Donna. "The same varnished seats and pull-up writing arms." Yet at school they never waited to hear a lecture on a potential life-or-death decision they had to make.

"Here he comes," Donna says, squeezing Sharon's hand.

The major who walks to the front of the room has a face that invites confidences. Does it also encourage men to do what's not in their best interests?

"It's a pleasure to meet with all of you today, especially the ladies," he begins, then launches into his pitch.

There is option A: the Intelligence Officers Basic Course – the QV course he calls it – and then a "short" tour – he doesn't say to where. Robert whispers to her that "QV stands for Quick to Vietnam." Or option B: voluntary indefinite. "You have to remember," the major says, "there are no guarantees. The needs of the service come first."

He smiles, gesturing at the American flag in a corner of the room along with the flag of the U.S. Army Armor School. Sharon envisions animals who eat their young.

"You must make your decision by July 6th," the major says. "After that the option is no longer available."

July 6th! Sharon calculates in her head – that's a little less than six weeks away. Six weeks to make a decision that can change your whole life and affect whether your husband lives or dies.

The major looks around the room. "Anyone with questions or special circumstances can come up and speak to me individually. Thank you, that's all." He remains at the podium.

"What do you think?" Sharon asks Donna as their husbands huddle with some of the other men.

"I'll be right back," Donna says and walks up to the major. What question can she be asking him? Sharon wonders.

Sharon looks around. How many of these men – and their wives – will decide to opt for at least another year of active duty in order to postpone Vietnam? How many others will want it over with as soon as possible, not wanting the fear hanging over their heads for longer?

Donna returns to Sharon's side, her face lit up by a huge smile. "Jerry probably won't have to serve in Vietnam! He'll be exempt ..."

Does Jerry have a physical problem that prevents him from serving in a combat zone? Sharon thinks.

"... *because my first husband was killed in Vietnam.*"

Sharon can't breathe. Her oxygen tank has just been depleted and she doesn't have enough air to make it back to the surface. Schools of fish swim in front of her eyes. A shark comes alongside, poised to attack.

She chokes out, "You ... you were married before?"

"A boy I knew from Puerto Rico. We were married right out of high school. He enlisted after our wedding."

There's a little more oxygen in the reserve tank. Sharon inhales. "Why? Why did he enlist?"

"He didn't want to wait to be drafted, same as all these men here," Donna says, waving her arm around the room. "He just wasn't an officer."

Sharon's knees shake – divers get the bends when they come up too fast. Yet she has to know. "What happened?"

"He went to Vietnam. With an infantry unit. When the first telegram came saying he was wounded, I wasn't worried. I was sure everything would be okay. Then the next telegram came saying he was in critical condition. I still wasn't that worried – it didn't seem real."

Sharon braces herself for what will come next.

"Then the third telegram came. He was dead."

Sharon tells herself to conserve the remaining oxygen. Not to panic. "And then?"

"My father was in Vietnam at the same time. He got compassionate leave to bring my husband's body home. Miguel was buried at Arlington National Cemetery. And I ... I became a war widow."

PART II – DECISIVE WEEKS

*State Department informs
Senator Fulbright that it
has agreed to a Cambodian
request for $7.5 million
in military aid ...*
May 22, 1970

DONNA – III – May 27

"Calling cards should not be printed, but engraved in black on white parchment or Bristol board."

Donna follows Jerry down the stairs of the building after the voluntary indefinite meeting. The major's response to her question has made her jumpy with excitement. Yet she isn't yet ready to share the information with her husband. Jerry may not be as thrilled – he doesn't like asking for favors.

"Nice guy, wasn't he?" Jerry says.

"Yes, yes, he seemed nice."

"And his presentation was done very well."

"He was quite interesting."

Why did she tell Sharon about Miguel? Was it the excitement of the moment – or the same compulsion that makes her use the Oriental bowl? His last gift to her, the one that arrived after his death.

Her mother tried to keep the unopened brown-paper package away from her. "Some things are better left unknown," she said. Did her mother fear the box contained a lace negligee, never to be worn to please the sender, or something else equally intimate? Donna pleaded, "Mama, **por favor**, I must see it. Miguel sent it to me. He wanted me to have it!" Her mother handed her the box with tears in her own eyes.

Donna removed the outer wrapping, then the wads of cushioning newspaper. She lifted up the gift – so small and alone.

Like Miguel the day she kissed him good-by. Praying that he would once again hold her, make love to her.

"See you in Hawaii for R & R," he said.

He never made it to Hawaii.

Donna feels nauseous. It's probably just tension. She has to tell Jerry what she found out from the major and then ask Jerry ... beg him ... to apply for the exemption. And she has to do it before Sharon tells Robert and he says something to Jerry.

At home in the bathroom she runs cold water into a glass. The mirror reflects tangled hair, shadows under her eyes, cheeks tinged with grey, her mouth drooping from the pull in her stomach.

She looked worse after the third telegram – after the official notification that she was a widow at the age of 19. In her mind Donna sees the scenes of that day:

Donna and her mother have been out shopping that day, buying the green bananas to make the delicacy that Donna so loves. They and her three younger siblings have returned to Puerto Rico to wait out the Vietnam duty tours of Donna's father and husband. Donna does not want to go shopping that day. She wants to wait, wait for a telegram that she is sure will say that Miguel is out of danger, that the doctors have been successful. "**Por favor**, Mama," she says. "Please let me stay home." Her mother insists that Donna go shopping with her.

Absorbed in the sights and sounds of the marketplace, Donna doesn't think about what might await her at home. She and her mother wander among the open stalls in the old part of San Juan, searching for the best fruits and vegetables. The flowers that hang from every balcony smell extra sweet that day, as if promising all is well with the world. She and her mother see no one they know, no one to ask Donna how both her husband and her father are doing, no one to remind them of reality.

As they shop she thinks of her childhood – the visits to Puerto Rico that were such a welcome change from the "white" world of the army posts. On those posts, whether in the U.S. or overseas, everything seemed to conspire to remind her that she was different, no matter how unaccented her

English and how careful her parents were to speak only English in front of others. She was not "white," and the other children didn't let her forget it. They called her a "Mexican," not even knowing the difference between Mexicans and Puerto Ricans.

Then comes the moment she and her mother have to return home from shopping. The younger children will be arriving from school and will worry if Donna and her mother aren't there to greet them.

Donna climbs the outside stone steps and approaches the apartment door. A yellow envelope sticks out from the mailbox.

"It's here, the news that Miguel is okay! He's going to be fine!" She rushes forward, dropping the bag filled with bananas.

She tears the envelope open and reads the brief message. She reads it a second time, and a third. Only then does she collapse onto the balcony floor and scream and scream and scream.

After that she only vaguely remembers her mother holding her as her brother and sisters rush up the outside steps. They get her into the apartment before the neighbors arrive, before the commotion and noise become overwhelming.

Miguel's family lives nearby. His married sisters come with their babies, the babies and the women wailing together. The noise turns into guns in battle, firing and firing and firing. No trees, nothing to hide behind. The ammunition and mines explode all around her. Why is she not hit?

An unknown man leans over her. "I will give you a shot to let you sleep." She floats into blessed silence.

Miguel stands at the end of a long white corridor. He wears a spotless white suit – his wedding suit. He beckons to her to come towards him. He smiles.

When she reaches the end of the corridor, he has vanished. She runs around the corner, following the long white hall to where it leads outside to the garden. And there she finds him.

He lies in a shallow furrow, his white suit wrinkled and covered with mud. His eyes are closed. He no longer smiles

When she bends lower, she sees the blood. And she screams and screams.

Donna gulps the water she poured into the glass and again looks into the bathroom mirror.

How can she convince Jerry to take the exemption? He wants "to do his patriotic duty" – that's why he joined the army. And he might want to prove that he is as brave as Miguel.

She gags over the bathroom sink.

✧ ✧ ✧

The next morning Jerry moans and rolls onto his side. The bed springs jiggle. "I love you," he whispers.

Donna kisses his ear. "I love you too," she says, snuggling into the curves of his nude body. For a few minutes the two of them remain like that, saying nothing.

He is so wonderful! So gentle and caring. So open-minded. From the moment they met, their obvious differences never meant anything to him.

In Puerto Rico, the remaining months of her father's Vietnam tour after he brought home her husband's body, she ate, slept and answered simple questions when someone spoke to her. Other times she curled up in an armchair facing the living room window. There she awaited the sun's shadow passing across the sky each day, the moon slipping into the sun's place each night.

When her father returned from his own tour – alive! – she would agree to leave the apartment, although only briefly each time. "Mama," she would say, "I'm keeping us all safe by staying home."

Her father's next assignment was Ft. Riley, Kansas. Once there and her younger siblings in school, her parents decided a job could be her path back to living. A nearby college had an open secretarial position in the economics department.

"Excuse me, miss," the student said. She hadn't seen him come in. The typewriter ribbon had unspooled and she was struggling with it, the red and black ink tattooing her hands. She looked up into a smile.

"I'm Jerry Lautenberg. I'm a junior and I need to check on my requirements for graduation. Can you help me?"

She held up her hands and said, "Let me wash first before I look at your records."

He came around the desk without an invitation. "Are you having problems with that ribbon? Let me try."

His breath brushed her check as he wrestled the ribbon back into place. "There," he said. "Now we can wash our hands together." And, for the first time since the yellow message of the third telegram, she laughed.

She helped him with his records, told him her name when asked, and accepted his thanks as he walked out of the office. She smiled as she resumed her typing.

The next day he returned. "Would you consider going out with me?" he said, offering a single red rose. "That is, if no one else has captured your heart."

Surprise, flattery, confusion flooded her. Was it too soon after Miguel ... too soon to go out with someone? And an Anglo at that. What would her parents say? And what a strange expression – "capture your heart." She blurted out: "I'm not a college girl. I'm ... a widow. I wouldn't want to mislead you."

He hesitated, then said, "You didn't have to tell me that now. You could have waited until I was so caught I wouldn't care. You know what? I'm caught now. Would tonight at 8 be okay?"

They had gone out that night, and the next night, and the night after that.

Jerry had been polite and friendly with her parents, making them feel less self-conscious about an Anglo dating their daughter. Eventually her parents became so comfortable that they sometimes lapsed into Spanish in front of him. When they did, he didn't get upset. He just smiled and reminded them he didn't understand. They would smile too, and apologize, and switch back to English.

Her parents had been happy for her. Pleased that she could start over again, to overcome the setback that had befallen her at such a young age.

Jerry's parents were a different matter.

When Jerry proposed to her, she hadn't yet met his parents. For all she knew, he hadn't even told them about her. He was their only child, his father a high school teacher, his mother a housewife.

The father didn't serve in World War II because of a physical disability Jerry had explained. "Perhaps that's why my parents are unhappy about my decision to join ROTC. They don't understand where I'm coming from," he said. Now he would be delivering a double whammy: marrying a Puerto Rican and a widow.

"I can't say yes until I meet your parents," she said. "I have to see for myself if they'll accept me."

"Great idea," he said. "We'll go to St. Louis for a weekend to visit them."

Her parents gave their consent to the trip.

Only as she and Jerry approached the front door of the brick two-story house in a quiet neighborhood did Jerry admit he hadn't told his parents anything about her beyond her first name. "I want them to form their own impressions, not have preconceived notions."

As he rang the doorbell she trembled with fear, afraid that his parents would betray their prejudice the moment they saw her. Yet all his mother said was, "So you're the one our son's in love with." And then his father had ushered her into the house.

She would be lying if she said it wasn't somewhat uncomfortable. Jerry's parents hadn't been prepared for her. Yet they were gracious.

At the end of the two-day visit, she told Jerry, "I may never be close to your parents. Yet if they can continue to be this polite to me, I'll marry you."

Jerry hugged her. "I already told my parents you said yes. And my mom gave me my grandmother's ring for you." Out of his pants pocket he pulled a ring with a garnet stone surrounded by pearls. He slipped it on her ring finger as tears sluiced down her cheeks.

She isn't giving up this happiness – ever. Not if she can help it.

She'll speak to him now.

"Jerry," she says, rubbing her hands across his chest. "I talked to the major from Washington right afterwards – while you were talking with Robert and some other men – about ... about Miguel."

Jerry stiffens under her hands. "Why would you do that?"

"I wanted to know ... to know if what happened to him could keep you from serving in Vietnam."

"What?" Jerry sits up in bed.

She sits up too. Do not cry, she tells herself. The tears don't listen – they drop onto her bare breasts.

Jerry wraps his arms around her. "Darling, darling," he says.

"I can't ... lose you," she says, sobs interrupting her words. "I've made ... one sacrifice. You can get ... an exemption ... because of him."

Jerry tightens his arms around her body – she can read his answer in his eyes before he speaks.

"Darling, I can't use that exemption. I'd never be able to look myself in the mirror again without seeing a coward."

"You wouldn't ... be a coward! You'd be doing ... it for me. For our love."

He kisses her tears. "Please forgive me. I have to take my chances like everyone else."

She can't stop sobbing.

He strokes her face. Then says, "Maybe we should consider this vol indef option. Robert thinks it could keep us out of going to Vietnam because Nixon wants to be re-elected."

SHARON – VIII – May 29

"On your husband's card the service should be designated as 'United States Army' but indication of the branch is optional."

Two days after the voluntary indefinite meeting, Sharon puts on her black-and-white seersucker two-piece suit in preparation for following up on something she saw at the commissary – a notice for a meeting of the Jewish Wives' Club. The concept seems a little funny in the middle of hicksville Kentucky, but she's not going to pass up the chance to possibly make new friends.

Sharon has nothing in common with her neighbors Anne and Elizabeth. Sharon can't stand going over to watch their "programs" with them. When invited, Sharon always gives the same excuse – she and Kim have plans – which is usually true anyway.

And Sharon enjoys getting together with her entertainment committee. Yet something is missing. She longs to be among others more like herself. Today she hopes to do that.

Sharon checks herself in the bedroom mirror. She's wearing the same outfit she wore to the voluntary indefinite meeting. She thinks again of Robert walking her to the car after the meeting. He asked what she thought of the major's talk. She gave a noncommittal answer, too agitated by Donna's "announcement" to say anything more.

As Robert walked back to class, Sharon sat in the car, her hands clasping the steering wheel, not turning on the engine, fixating on an image of Donna's first husband dying in Vietnam. And then Sharon's mind switched to another imagined mental picture – the death of Robert's friend Kenneth in Vietnam. Sharon could recall quite clearly when she heard the news.

It was only a few weeks after her first date with Robert during which he had told her he was going to Vietnam – a first date followed by other dates in spite of Sharon's better judgment that a relationship with a Jewish boy headed for Vietnam was not for her. Something very appealing about Robert in spite of this major drawback made Sharon hesitate to call off seeing him.

During those weeks of their first dates the "State News" carried several articles related to the war in Vietnam:

On April 5th a news analysis headlined "Johnson bows out, but not too far" began: "President Johnson's announcement Sunday that he will not seek re-nomination certainly will be considered one of the most startling political moves of the century."

On April 8th an article headlined "U.N. official shows war, racial optimism" reported: "His Excellency C.V. Narasimhan, Under-Secretary-General for General Assembly Affairs of the United Nations, indicated Friday that President Johnson's decision to de-escalate the war in Vietnam and seek meetings about an eventual case-fire is viewed as an 'extremely hopeful development' at the United Nations."

On April 11th an analysis headlined "Asians fear U.S. withdrawal from Vietnam" began: "While public support for President Johnson is on the rise in the United States following his announcement of de-escalation in Vietnam, the government of that country, and countries in the area, probably view it as an abandonment of the American commitment in Southeast Asia."

And then on April 23rd an article headlined "Current Vietnam stand result of policy change" detailed author David Schoenbrun's appearance at MSU, including: "In a speech in Wells Hall, punctuated by frequent plugs for his just-published book and digs at MSU professor of political science Wesley Fishel, Schoenbrun traced the history of the conflict and called for negotiations, a cease-fire and free elections in Vietnam, accompanied by a U.S. troop withdrawal."

Sharon had read this entire article in a fury at the U.S.'s sending soldiers to fight in Vietnam, especially when she got to the paragraph that said Schoenbrun "received his biggest hand during the speech when he said, 'Anything I can do to help any young man avoid fighting in this immoral, illegal and cruel war, I will do.'"

With this article clutched in her hand she entered the student union for a pre-arranged coffee date with Robert. The intended rant against the Vietnam War died in her throat the moment she saw the bleak expression on Robert' face.

"What is it?" she asked as she slid into the booth opposite him.

He looked up. "It's Kenneth."

"Kenneth?"

"My best friend in high school. An infantry officer in Vietnam."

Sharon pressed her two hands together under the Formica table top. "What about him?"

"Dead. Killed in an ambush near his firebase."

Her stomach lurched. She grabbed for Robert's hands across the table. He pulled out of her reach.

"When?"

"I'm not sure. His parents called my parents last night. They called me."

Robert's voice almost inaudible: "He was so gung-ho. Enlisted, went to Officers Candidate School, thrilled to be assigned infantry. He wanted to fight for his country. And he died for it!"

Sharon said nothing.

Robert recited:

Do not weep, maiden, for war is kind.
Because your lover threw wild hands toward the sky
And the affrighted steed ran on alone,
Do not weep.
War is kind.

Hoarse, booming drums of the regiment,
Little souls who thirst for fight,
These men were born to drill and die.
The unexplained glory flies above them,
Great is the battle-god, great, and his kingdom –
A field where a thousand corpses lie.

Do not weep, babe, for war is kind.
Because your father tumbled in the yellow trenches,
Raged at his breast, gulped and died,
Do not weep.
War is kind.

Swift blazing flag of the regiment,
Eagle with crest of red and gold,
These men were born to drill and die.

Point for them the virtue of slaughter,
Make plain to them the excellence of killing
And a field where a thousand corpses lie.

Mother whose heart hung humble as a button
On the bright splendid shroud of your son,
Do not weep.
War is kind.

When Robert finished reciting he said nothing more.

"Who wrote that?" Sharon asked. "I don't know it."

"It's Stephen Crane's 'War Is Kind.'"

Sharon dropped the clutched newspaper article onto the tabletop and ran into the women's restroom.

There she stared at herself in the three-way mirror. Was he referring to Kenneth? Or was Robert warning her about getting involved with him? The ultimate risk – loving someone about to go off to war? And here Sharon's anger flared – especially going off to an "immoral, illegal and cruel war" according to David Schoenbrun.

The perspiration drips down his face, oozing into his eyes and sliding over his mouth. He swipes at the beads dripping from his nose with the arm of his filthy fatigue shirt. "This heat is unbearable," the armor officer says to the 19-year-old enlisted man quivering beside him inside the tank. "How do the Vietnamese survive?"

The officer pops the hatch, standing upright in the commander's seat to check the terrain. The enemy hides somewhere nearby.

The explosion lifts his body up into the air, twisting it around before dumping it on top of the tank, his sweat-stained face turned downward as if searching for the softest place to land.

The 19-year-old screams.

In the student union restroom Sharon splashed water on her face. She had made a decision – she was resolved never to see Robert again.

As she approached the booth she saw that his fingers drummed the article she had dropped. Yet when she sat down again he made no mention of the article. Instead he said, "I have one other poem I want to share with you."

She nodded, not yet ready to say anything.

"You'll have to read this one yourself."

"Why?"

He looked down at his hands as he pulled a folded sheet of paper from his shirt pocket. "I'm embarrassed. I wrote it for you after we went out Saturday night." He handed her the paper. Under the title "Morning" she reads:

> *After waking from a dream*
> *When the memory is sweet –*
> *The smell of yellow jasmine,*
> *The taste of scented oil –*

Returning to it
Breaking away from the arms of light
And penetrating the cloudy screen
That keeps the dreams confined –

Cannot be done.
Only snatches
Only dips into the haze,
Glimpses for wishing

Her tears baptized the paper.

For one second she held out, held out against a future that frightened her. Then she looked up at him and said, "Will you be my date for the sorority formal?"

"Do I have to wear a tux?" he said.

"It's a 'uniform' – not much different from your ROTC uniform," she said.

They both laughed, and he reached for her hands.

Still sitting in the car following Donna's revelation about her first husband, Sharon was gripped with the desire to drive over to Kim's, to tell her what Donna revealed, to share the pain and shock. Just this once Sharon could make an exception – she could share her fears and innermost feelings. Tracy would understand.

Sharon wears the three-quarter-sleeve blue spring coat they bought together, a coat now splattered with droplets

– tears, not rain. The rabbi's graveside service finished, the workers lower the four coffins into the ground.

Sharon grips the shovel's handle, dumping the dirt on the lid of Tracy's coffin. The dirt clumps thud onto the wood. The thuds mask Sharon's whisper: "I promise, Tracy. No one will ever replace you. You'll always be my best girlfriend."

Sharing with Kim wouldn't be replacing Tracy. It would just be ...

Sharon fingered the steering wheel, still not turning on the ignition.

Kim was an orphan. Jim was everything to her. How could Sharon be so selfish? To give Kim even more to worry about than she already had?

Sharon shook her head. She wouldn't drive over to Kim's. It was for Donna to tell Kim and Wendy. With that decision Sharon had finally turned on the ignition and driven home from the vol indef meeting.

Now Sharon shakes her head at herself in the bedroom mirror. That was two days ago. Unwilling to again experience the emotions generated by Donna, Sharon still hasn't told Robert.

Sharon glances at her watch. She's going to be late to this meeting of the Jewish Wives' Club. Quickly she grabs the car keys off the dresser and heads out the door.

It doesn't take her long to reach the housing area and find the right house. The sign next to the door reads "Captain Fred Weinstein."

Sharon smooths the wrinkles in her skirt and again checks her watch. Only a few minutes late. She rings the doorbell.

A short, dark-haired woman wearing beige slacks and a white sleeveless blouse exposing pale arms opens the door. "I'm Janice Baum," she says, gesturing Sharon to enter. "Judy's inside getting refreshments."

The woman has a New York accent. Probably Brooklyn.

Sharon steps into a small foyer. A wooden coat rack holds yellow rain slickers in small sizes. Umbrellas stick up from a gold-painted metal milk can perched on the polished wood floor. The house smells of cookies and floor wax. Sharon follows Janice Baum through an arch into a small living room. Above the hum of the air conditioner Sharon can hear children's shouts and laughter coming from somewhere nearby.

Three women sit on a sofa underneath a picture window. A fourth woman – Judy Weinstein? – stands in front of the sofa placing a tray of glasses on the coffee table. All four women smile as Janice and Sharon enter the room.

Sharon notices that one woman, wearing a rose-patterned shift over a bulging stomach, is quite pregnant. The other two seated women wear pants with matching tops and the fourth woman has on slim forest green pants and a white scooped-neck blouse.

Sharon is overdressed. Apparently this meeting of the Jewish Wives' Club does not fall into the required dress parameters of an official army officers' wives' meeting.

Sharon also notices that the living room furniture appears not to be army issue. The sofa features a blue-toned flame-stitch pattern. The armchairs in pale blue satin have high backs shaped into what Sharon thinks of as Dumbo ears. The navy-cloth director's chair seems out of place. It's probably been pulled in from outdoors to provide extra seating. Extra seating for her, the odd one out.

The standing woman, heralded by the unmistakable scent of Shalimar, comes towards Sharon. "I'm Judy Weinstein. So glad you could join our little group. Please sit down." Judy waves Sharon to the director's chair.

The others say their first names quickly. The pregnant one is Nancy; the other two are Millie and Elaine.

"Where are you from?" Elaine asks. Her dark brown hair hangs straight down from a center part and her eyes, set wide apart, anchor a nose that tilts upwards.

"I'm from Chicago," Sharon says.

"South Side?" Nancy's auburn hair pulled back in a pony tail emphasizes the puffiness of her face.

"North Side."

"I'm from the South Side," Nancy says. "Where's your husband from?"

"Philadelphia."

"Mine's from New York."

Nancy is the game show host, Sharon thinks, in a game of 20 questions.

"Is he a doctor?" Millie asks.

A doctor? Her parents only wish.

"He's here for Armor Officers Basic before going on to Ft. Holabird for military intelligence training."

"And then where?" Janice cuts in.

"We don't know. It could be … anywhere." Sharon looks around the room. The others don't meet her eyes.

"All our husbands are doctors, except Janice's. He's a medical technician assigned to the hospital here," Nancy says.

Janice blushes. She says quickly, "Kenny was in the Navy. But being on a ship for six months at a time was too hard on the children. So he transferred to the army."

"Judy got us together in an informal group," Millie says. "She's the organizer among us." Millie has short black curly hair and a wide freckled face.

"Please have some oatmeal cookies," Judy offers. A tortoise shell plastic headband holds her medium-length fine blond hair in place and her thin face matches an equally thin body. Sharon wonders how many children Judy has and whether she has always been this thin or whether running after children accomplished this.

"Let's begin," Judy says, "before we're interrupted by the kids."

Elaine says, "The first order of business is to plan for the family picnic two weeks from Sunday. It's from 11 to 2." She turns to Sharon. "You and your husband are welcome." She turns back to the rest of the women. "Is everyone able to come?"

"My husband may be on call, but I'll be there," Millie says.

"I'm two centimeters dilated already," Nancy says, "so I'm not sure I'll be around."

What does two centimeters dilated mean? Sharon doesn't want to ask.

Judy laughs. "With my first my mother came to stay two weeks before the baby was due. Eight weeks later the baby finally arrived. The doctor was off by a whole month, and then the baby was two weeks late."

"I may have a Caesarean," Nancy says. "It's a breech baby right now."

What's breech?

"Oh, no, Nancy. You'll be so sore afterwards," Janice says. "I had a Caesarean with my second. Kenny was at sea and a neighbor took care of my first son while I was in the hospital. I really had it hard when I came home."

"My husband is getting me a nurse," Nancy says. "He asked around at the hospital and found someone who does private duty."

"I'll have to keep it in mind in eight months," Elaine says.

"You're pregnant!" Millie says. "That's terrific! I was going to wait to tell all of you at the next meeting – I am too."

Everyone except Sharon breaks out in a babble of happy congratulations. She's the only one here who doesn't know anything about pregnancy and childbirth. It's so unfair! These women's husbands are all safely ensconced at Ft. Knox. It's okay to be a doctor in the army, but a second lieutenant in military intelligence possibly slated for a tour of Vietnam?

Tears moisten her eyelids and she flashes to an earlier time when she also felt the odd-man out.

It's the evening of the AEPhi formal at MSU and Sharon wears her high school prom dress – a simple white cotton brocade Lanz, junior size 7. Robert wears a blue tux jacket and tux black pants rented from a store on Grand River Avenue. They've arranged to double date with a sorority sister. Frieda and Larry are pinned – he's a ZBT, the best Jewish fraternity on campus.

"Robert," Larry says as they walk into the Lansing hotel location of the formal, "you should come by the house, join us in a TGIF beer night."

"I usually study on Friday nights," Robert says. "With working 20 hours a week and my ROTC commitment, I don't have much time to study."

"A Jewish boy in ROTC? You've got to be kidding."

To prevent Robert's reply Sharon stumbles against Larry. "I'm so sorry," she says. "My ankle twisted."

"Come on, man," Larry continues to Robert. "Why do you want to be in ROTC?"

"Patriotic duty. Someone has to defend our country."

Patriotic duty. How many times must she hear those words?

At this moment Judy says "Sharon."

Sharon yanks her attention back to the moment. "Yes?"

"You don't have any children, do you?"

"We've only been married a few months."

"Newlyweds," Janice says. "I can dimly remember those days."

Millie turns to Judy before Sharon can respond. "How's your quilt coming? Are you finished yet?"

Judy reaches into a wicker basket on the floor next to her chair. She holds up a quilt of crocheted pale blue and darker blue squares. "I've just got the fringes to add and I'm done."

"You work fast," Elaine says.

Judy laughs and turns to Sharon. "It's the one thing I can do while watching my children that they can't destroy."

"She has four children under the age of five," Nancy says to Sharon. "I don't know how she does it. I'm worried about taking care of one."

"I let them play in the backyard all day," Judy says. "That's why I get a lot of crocheting done."

Elaine flutters her hands in everyone's direction. "Let's get back to the picnic plans. Who's going to bring what?"

Sharon watches the women talk, their hands moving to emphasize their points. She certainly doesn't fit in with these women sitting here today the way she hoped she would, their concerns and hers so totally different. All mothers or mothers-to-be, they have husbands who work in a hospital, albeit an army rather than a civilian one. They're barely in the army with its emphasis on infantry, artillery, armor – war.

The central concern of Sharon's universe – will Robert be sent to Vietnam? And the corollary, should he go vol indef to put off Vietnam for one year? And secondarily, how does she fit in as an officer's wife?

Sharon thinks about Kim and Wendy and Donna, all facing the same concerns as she.

Can it be that Sharon is looking for friends in all the wrong places?

✡ ✡ ✡

That evening Peter, Paul and Mary's album "Blowin' in the Wind" plays on Sharon's stereo reacquired today. As she makes coffee for Robert and her brother Howard – just arrived from Chicago, her tears splash onto the Faberware coffeepot as the trio sings Bob Dylan's words to the title song:

How many deaths will it take till he knows
That too many people have died?
The answer my friend is blowin' in the wind
The answer is blowin' in the wind.

Maybe she shouldn't have asked her parents to send her stereo with her brother. Some of her favorite songs too closely mirror her current situation.

Robert and Howard sit on the couch talking while she's preparing dinner. Howard took the train from U of I Thursday night to Chicago to get their father's car and her stuff. Then today Howard drove straight through from Chicago. After dinner he will drive up to Louisville to spend the night at their grandparents and drive back to Chicago tomorrow to return the car. Then he'll take the train back to school from Chicago on Sunday.

"Dinner's ready," she tells them now as she shuts off the stereo.

"Roast beef. Nice going," Howard says as he and Robert sit down at the table.

"Had to import it from Louisville."

Sharon passes Howard the roast beef platter. "It's just so great to see you. I haven't seen anyone with really long sideburns since we left Chicago."

Howard laughs and lifts a forkful of roast beef to his mouth. "They are pretty long, aren't they?"

"You want to see the post?" Robert asks.

"Hell, no. I'm not setting foot on any military installation – ever, if I can help it."

Should she ask ... ask Howard if he will go to Canada if he's drafted? She can't do it. She doesn't want to know.

"It looks more like a resort in the Catskills than anything else," Robert says.

Howard brushes his long hair out of his eyes. "I'm still not interested."

"What will you do if you're drafted?" Robert asks.

Sharon gasps.

Her brother looks at her. "I've decided not to worry about the draft until I get my notice. Then I'll worry."

Now she must ask. "You wouldn't ... you wouldn't go to Canada, would you?"

Howard puts his fork down. "This war is wrong, totally wrong. Yet I'm not sure it's right to run away from my country. I'd first try for a medical deferment."

"Any particular ailment?" Robert says.

"Allergies. The sinus headaches I get can be horrendous; sometimes I have to stop studying and lie down. That would certainly interfere with being a good soldier."

"Allergies? Allergies!" Robert pushes away from the table and strides outside.

"What's the matter with him?" Howard asks Sharon. "Just because I said the war is wrong?"

"It's not that." How to explain it to Howard? "It's probably what you said about allergies. Robert has such bad allergies he had to be hospitalized at ROTC summer camp for pneumonia. But he didn't get kicked out of the program because his training officer said the army needed smart people too."

Howard laughs, then says, "Is Robert a good soldier?"

She doesn't answer, instead getting up to refill the applesauce bowl.

Is Robert a good soldier? She ticks off a mental list: hair cut the regulation length, brass and shoes shined to a high gloss, fatigues always starched and pressed by the laundry up the road, and follows all the instructions given in class. Yet isn't a good soldier by definition a soldier who's good in battle?

Robert's father always bragged how good a
soldier he was fighting in Europe during WWII.
During a Friday night brisket dinner or a lox-and-
bagel Sunday brunch he'd retell his war stories for
the hundredth time. Neither he nor Robert's mother
ever mention that the war separated them for years
soon after they married.

"My unit saw so much action," he'd say, "that
when the war in Europe ended, the army decided
to award my unit by not sending us to the Pacific.
The irony is that the European units sent back to
the States en route to the Pacific got released in the
U.S. as soon as the war with Japan was over. And my
unit got stuck in Europe another year cleaning up
the mess."

Sharon would help Robert's mother serve the
meal while Robert's father talked about being a
good soldier. All this recounting of his dangerous
exploits – how could Robert not feel obligated to
equal his macho father?

Yet in all the times his father talked, she never
heard him express his opinion of Robert's ROTC
commitment. He talked only of the past, not of the
future.

Regardless of what Robert's father thinks, Sharon
prays that Robert won't have the opportunity to find
out whether he is a good soldier in combat. She can
live her whole life without ever knowing the answer
to Howard's question.

✣ ✣ ✣

"Yes, Mother. And thanks again for sending everything down with Howard," Sharon says the next morning.

Sharon hangs up the phone as Robert comes up behind her and hugs her. "You know what?" Robert asks. "After breakfast, let's go over to Kim and Jim's for a few minutes."

"They might be at the PX. Why?"

"Because I have to qualify on a pistol, and I'm not very good at it. Jim has his own pistol at home – he keeps it next to the bed – and I want to practice holding it and aiming it."

Sharon pulls out of Robert's arms. "I'm not going. I don't want you to practice with a loaded gun."

"Honey, it's not loaded. No one keeps a loaded gun next to his bed."

White House announces U.S. prepared to continue air cover if needed for South Vietnamese forces expected to remain in Cambodia after U.S. troops withdrawn …

May 22, 1970

KIM – V – May 30 (Memorial Day)

"An officer leaves one card for each adult member of the family (and house guest) and a lady leaves one card for each adult lady (over 18 years of age), but neither leaves more than three."

Kim answers the knock on the door to find Sharon and Robert outside.

"Is Jim here?" Robert asks. "I need to ask him something."

"Come on in," she says, then goes towards the bedroom to get Jim.

"Hi," Jim says as he follows Kim back into the living room. "What can I do you for?"

"Could I practice a little with your pistol – just getting the feel of it – to help me qualify?" Robert says.

"Just a sec," Jim says. "I'll unload it."

"Unload it! You keep it loaded!" Sharon says.

"Of course it's loaded," Jim says. "What good would it do otherwise?"

Kim looks at Sharon's face. "Would you like to sit down?" Kim says.

"No thanks. I'll stand."

Jim comes back out of the bedroom and hands the gun, handle first, to Robert. Robert points the gun at the base of the ugly ceramic green table lamp, pulls the trigger a few times, then hands the gun back to Jim. "Appreciate it."

"That's it?" Sharon asks him. Robert nods.

"Would you like some Coke?" Kim asks.

"No, thanks, we have to go," Sharon says.

Outside the door Kim hears Sharon say, "I told you so!"

Jim goes into the bedroom once more to return the gun, then comes back into the living room. He sits down cross-legged on the floor next to his military strategy game.

Kim sighs. Jim will be occupied for hours. She might as well write to her sister now.

Thinking of her sister Diane brings a throb to Kim's temples. Kim had done well in school. She had tried hard, grasping at anything as a possible means of escape from their miserable lives. Diane, two years younger, found school harder. She needed as much help as Kim could give her: "Please, Kimmie, please help. Pretty please with sugar on top." Sometimes

Kim wished she and Diane had been sent to separate homes so she wouldn't always feel so responsible. Yet they had never been separated until now.

Come on, Kim tells herself, she left town and went off to live at college with Jim when they married. Yet they had been only an hour away from Diane and they saw her almost every weekend. She came to visit or they went back to stay with Jim's parents and saw her then.

Diane's letters describe the customers at the grocery store where she works full-time now that she's finished high school. At 18 she moved out of the last foster home into a tiny one-bedroom apartment. "It's a relief," Diane wrote, "not to have to do any ironing except for myself." Yet Kim can tell her sister's also lonely, so lonely.

What could Kim do even if she were home now? Have Diane live with them? Kim wonders what Jim would say to that. Try to find young men to introduce to Diane?

Kim closes her eyes and imagines herself and Jim living in a pretty white-frame house on a quiet street. She pictures her sister married and living a few blocks away in an equally pretty house on an equally nice street.

She opens her eyes. Is it so wrong to want this?

She picks up the pen.

✳ ✳ ✳

"It's sort of spooky here," Kim says two days later. She stares out the window of Sharon's car as they drive the winding back road to Louisville. They're taking the Fiat to be checked by a mechanic who works on foreign cars. Sharon hasn't been able to find anyone around the post who knows anything about a Fiat, so Kim offered to drive with her to Louisville. Sharon wanted to avoid driving Dixie Highway so they're on this back road.

The scenery outside the windows looks as remote and inhospitable as the backwoods of the South. Blackened junked-out cars and trucks surround the crumbling houses. Scrawny dogs bark at the car from the edge of the road. The scents of wild flowers mix with smoke from small bonfires. Few cars pass them on the road.

"Why is the car jerking so much?" Kim says.

"I'm sorry," Sharon says. "I wanted to see something."

"What?"

"There's a car behind us. The driver seems to be keeping pace with us. Whenever I speed up, he does. And when I slow down, he does."

Kim twists her head to see behind her. All she can see is a cap on the driver's head. "He can't pass you on this road, so he has to keep pace. You're just imagining things."

Sharon frowns. "You're the one who said it's spooky out here."

"We should have brought the gun."

Sharon gasps. "I wouldn't have let you. It's too dangerous."

Kim knows from first-hand experience that guns are dangerous. She still wakes up nights dreaming about the pool of Marvin's blood growing larger and larger. Yet while the soldier used his gun to kill a poor soul who wouldn't have harmed anyone, Kim wants Jim's gun for self-defense.

Kim looks out the window as they pass more dismal little houses, so like the one with the peeling yellow paint she lived in with her sister and parents before ... How can you ever depend on someone's love?

"What are you so scared about?" Sharon asks, breaking into Kim's thoughts.

Kim twitches in her seat. She looks at Sharon, unclear to what Sharon is referring

"The loaded gun next to your bed and everything?" Sharon says.

"Rape."

"Rape?"

Kim nods, her eyes glued to the road ahead. "If I were ever raped, I'd kill myself."

"Even if you had children to take care of?" Sharon asks.

"I wouldn't want to live anymore," Kim says. "It would be too shameful."

Sharon pushes her sunglasses further up her nose. "Why are you Southerners obsessed with rape?"

Southerners! Surely all women are terrified and horrified of being raped, of being violated! "Obsessed? We're not obsessed. We just know what's right and wrong."

Sharon doesn't turn to look at her; her eyes straight ahead on the winding road. "Then you're obsessed with sex. Always seeing sexual motives lurking behind every tree – or door."

Kim clasps her hands together. "I was just trying to explain about rape – that's why I wanted the gun with us."

"I don't understand living in fear all the time," Sharon says.

Kim doesn't reply. Can Northerners really be so unconcerned about the terrible things that can happen to women?

A mile further down the road Sharon says, "Kim, when did you first learn about sex?"

Again Kim says nothing.

"My mother bought a book for me," Sharon says. "Something about not being taken advantage of by men. She told me not to read the book until I was ready. So I didn't read it."

Sharon pauses. "Then one day I was at a girlfriend's house with another friend – either 9th or 10th grade. The girl whose house we were at had a book she found on her parents' bookshelves. The three of us walked over to a nearby park and read the book together. We were so surprised."

Kim nods in agreement. "I ... I was surprised too when I read about it in a book."

Sharon laughs. "I was still so naive. When I was a freshman in college I went to this foreign film – Swedish I think. After the couple had sex the woman used a towel to wipe her legs. I didn't understand why. Another freshman girl explained to me about the semen dripping down the woman's legs afterwards." Sharon hesitates, then says, "If the man had been using a condom, the towel wouldn't have been necessary."

"Is that what you and Robert use?" Kim asks.

Sharon shakes her head, her eyes on the road. "I take birth control pills. My brother Howard always lectures me on the dangers."

"I take them too."

Kim smiles. They're back on safe ground again.

That evening Kim and Jim enter the Officers Club and head for the tables occupied by the AOB class members. They find two chairs at the end of one table and Kim sits down while Jim stands over her.

"Would you like something to drink?" he asks.

"No, thanks, I'll wait."

The band hits the opening chords of the Foundations' "Build Me Up Buttercup" as Sharon and Robert walk in. Kim waves them over to the table. Jim is talking to some single officers off to one side of the room, so Kim gives Jim's chair to Sharon while Robert goes off to join Jim.

"Lots of people here," Kim says. "Some have been dancing."

"I love to dance."

A good-looking guy across the room looks familiar. "Sharon," Kim whispers, "there's Mark Williamson. He's heading straight towards us."

"Hello, ladies," he says as he comes up to them. Then he bows at the waist and says to Sharon, "May I have this dance?"

Sharon hesitates. Kim can't believe this! Kim wouldn't hesitate. She'd know to say no. But Sharon stands up, following Mark onto the dance floor.

The band plays Neil Diamond's "Sweet Caroline." It's a fast dance so Mark isn't touching Sharon. Kim glances at Robert but he has his back to Sharon talking to another man.

The song comes to an end and the band switches to a slow dance, the Lettermen's version of "Goin' Out Of My Head." Mark sweeps Sharon into a tight embrace and dances with his body pressed against hers. Mark leans his head down and says something in Sharon's ear.

Kim looks over at Jim. If he sees Sharon dancing with Mark like this he might think Sharon a bad influence on Kim and not let her be with Sharon anymore. Thank heavens Jim stands at the bar getting a drink, his back to the dance floor.

The song ends. Sharon steps out of Mark's arms, curtsies, and walks back by herself to the table.

"I love dancing," Sharon says as she sits down again, her face flushed. She pushes a strand of damp hair out of her eyes.

Before Kim can ask wasn't Sharon ashamed to dance that close with another man, Jim and Robert return from the bar with their drinks and stand behind the two women.

In unison the AOB men raise their glasses and shout to the theme song for the Mickey Mouse Club:

Mickey Mouse, AOB!
Forever let us hold our banner high!

Oh, no! How can the men be so reckless? They'll be lucky not to be arrested for conduct unbecoming an officer. And if they are arrested, Kim is sure their punishment won't be "Mickey Mouse."

Laotian government troops
open drive to counter Pathet
Lao and North Vietnamese
military gains ...
May 24, 1970

WENDY – III – June 2

"Do not call an older woman or senior officer's wife by her first name until she has invited you to do so."

"We're doing pretty well, aren't we?" Nelson says, his fingers circling Wendy's erect nipples. "I'm accepted by the men in my class. Robert Gold even maneuvered to be on my tank for the night training exercise. Said he wanted to be with someone competent."

Wendy wiggles her toes underneath the top sheet. She and Nelson have just made love and she feels terrific – but not just because of the good sex.

Today Mrs. Donovan actually called! "We would like to extend an invitation, Mrs. Johnson, for you to be a volunteer visitor at the hospital. So many young soldiers are at Ft. Knox by themselves," Mrs. Donovan said, "and no one visits them when they are in the hospital. The volunteer group is organizing regular visiting days. Could you take Monday afternoons?"

Wendy has been ecstatic since the phone call.

Won't Nelson be impressed that she is on a visitors rotation just like everyone else – like all the white women. Her offer of help has been accepted! She waited till now, the right moment, to tell him the news.

"Guess what?"

"You're pregnant?"

"No, Nelson, you know that's ..." She blushes and pulls away from him, hiking the sheet over her breasts.

"Joke, joke."

She smiles. "Remember that meeting I told you about after I attended – the one about volunteering at the hospital?"

"You didn't know if you'd get to do anything?"

"Mrs. Donovan – the head of the committee – called me today. She wants me to be a hospital visitor!"

Nelson leans over and kisses her. "That's the good part about the army," he says. "They may not like us but they're good soldiers – the wives, too. And the orders are: all second lieutenants are created equal – equally low. Except for the RA guys. They're more equal."

He looks down at the sheet, then up at her again. "In five weeks we have to give our answer about going vol indef. I've been thinking ... about going Regular Army – making the army a career."

Pain jabs between her breasts. Regular Army!

"What do you think?" Nelson asks.

"Why?" She inhales. Tries to force the pain away. "Why would you do that?"

"It could be a good opportunity," Nelson says. "I could do pretty well as an officer, be treated fairer than outside the army."

Spend the next 20 or 30 years as an officer's wife? Mrs. Donovan called, but that doesn't mean other women would. Wendy says: "I want to go home after two years, not move from post to post all around the world."

Nelson laughs. "Our phone bills would be pretty big with you always calling your mama."

She throws her arms around him. "Nelson, I do not want to be an officer's wife any longer than I have to. I do not want to worry our whole life together about unaccompanied tours. I want to go home!"

Nelson pulls her down so they lay side by side. "I want to make you proud – this might be a way to do it. But if you're so against it, then maybe it's not right."

She leans her head on his chest. She loves him so much. "Thank you, thank you, Nelson."

✡ ✡ ✡

The next day Wendy parks her car in the hospital lot and walks towards the main hospital door. Nervousness and excitement fight each other.

This morning at breakfast Nelson hugged her. "I'm proud of you." And grabbing her breasts and giving them a squeeze, he said, "Aren't all those soldiers lucky? I'm just glad they're in bed and can't get any ideas." She laughed and kissed him.

Now she enters the lobby and follows Mrs. Donovan's directions to the nurses' station. "Hello," she says to the woman sitting behind the reception counter. "I'm Mrs. Johnson. Mrs. Donovan arranged for me to visit soldiers this afternoon."

The woman doesn't look up. Her pen slashes across a medical chart on the counter. Wendy's knees wobble. Has Mrs. Donovan sent her here only to be insulted?

The woman clicks her pen shut and smiles. "Welcome aboard. I'll show you around in just a sec."

Relief floods through Wendy.

Two hours later she returns to her car, exhausted and pleased. The soldiers were friendly, happy to have a visitor hand them water cups, straighten their pillows, joke with them. "Won't your husband be jealous?" they said.

Of course these soldiers are only sick, not wounded. She doesn't think she could do this for soldiers missing limbs, soldiers swathed in bandages.

Soldiers who might make her realize what could happen to Nelson.

And if Nelson goes Regular Army ...

Wendy turns on her engine and pulls out of the parking lot. She won't think of this now. It is five weeks before the commitment must be made. Anything can happen in that time.

✶ ✶ ✶

Three days later Donna says "We thought you weren't coming," as Wendy walks across the grass towards the other women standing in front of a Ft. Knox building. "Maybe you had better things to do."

"Not likely," Wendy says. She wouldn't miss this officers' wives' tour of Ft. Knox for anything. Nelson doesn't talk much about what he does. Maybe seeing things for herself will help with some of her fears.

"I like your outfit," Sharon says.

Wendy smiles her thanks. The distributed Disposition Form for the "Visit of Ladies to US Army Armor School" had included dress options:

"1. A tour through the Armor School for ladies of student and Staff and Faculty officers is scheduled for Saturday, 6 June 1970.

"2. A copy of the itinerary is attached as enclosure 1. Ladies will assemble in Gaffey Hall Auditorium (Bldg 2369), at 0810 hours, with activities commencing at 0815 hours. Ladies attending are encouraged to wear low-heel shoes; slacks may also be worn.

"3. To assist in planning for this tour, students are requested to complete the attached questionnaire and deliver it to your class leader by 29 May 1970.

"4. Staff and Faculty wives desiring to attend are requested to notify Guest Speaker Branch by telephone, extension 4-7445, NLT 29 May 1970."

The form had been signed by the Armor lieutenant colonel who was the deputy director of instruction. And the distribution list read like an induction into a secret society:

DISTRIBUTION:
1 - Ofc of DA/Secy
1 - Ofc of D/I
1 - Ea Married Student
  AOAC-3
  AOB-21 & 22
  OMO-14
1 - Armor School Bookstore
5 - Ea OP Off
  AMM Dept
  Autmv Dept
  Comm Dept
  Wpns Dept
  CO, Sch Bde

Wendy had chosen a navy blue pair of slacks that set off her thin waist and a white short-sleeved blouse along with navy low-heeled pumps.

Now Donna indicates a woman raising her hand to get their attention. "She's one of the older women from the coffee at the general's quarters," Donna says.

"Come, come, ladies," the woman says, motioning them all to enter the building. "Please take a seat in the room on your left."

When Wendy was growing up, blacks had to enter movie theaters from a different entrance than whites and sit in the balcony. Her parents convinced her that those balcony seats were actually the better ones – you could see clearer. Only when the separate entrances had been eliminated and blacks could sit wherever they wanted did her parents admit their "little white lie." And now she sits in the first row of this audience with her white friends!

An officer in suntans stands in front of them. "I'm Major Polens and I'll be your tour guide." He turns his head from side to side so they can all see his smile. "Today you're in for a real treat – a chance to climb inside a M60A1 tank, a certified killing machine."

Certified killing machine! How can he say such a thing? Isn't this what they are all scared of?

The major continues, "It's not the easiest thing to get up into. Young soldiers hop aboard; older officers use the little toe hook on the front slope and haul themselves up. For your convenience we've arranged a set of steps.

"Once on the deck you climb up on the turret, where you can look down into the tank through the commander's or the loader's hatch. The commander's is bigger. Sit on the edge and swing your feet inside, then lower yourself to the seat."

The major grins. "We've got a lot to see today, so let's begin our tour. First stop is the enlisted men's mess hall. I'm sure you're curious how we feed all these men."

They file out behind the major. "Certified killing machine," Sharon mutters to Wendy as they walk across the grass towards the mess hall. "Why did he have to say that?"

"Just what I wondered."

In the immense kitchen the major points out extraordinarily large ovens, mix masters, pots and pans, and recites statistics on how many meals a day are prepared.

"I bet our husbands are pleased they don't have to eat here," Sharon says. "Robert thinks it's funny they can eat in the Armor School cafeteria, go to the Officers Club or Country Club, or come home for lunch every day."

Wendy smiles. "Nelson told me we can even pack them a dinner when they go on that night training exercise."

"What night training exercise?" Kim asks Sharon.

Is it Wendy's imagination or does Kim never direct a question or statement to her?

"The men are going to practice firing live ammunition off the tanks at night," Sharon says.

Wendy sees Kim clench her hands. "Jim didn't say anything about this."

"Our men will be fine," Wendy says to Kim as they all follow the major out of the mess hall and across more grass. "It's not really that dangerous."

"I hope our husbands are all on good teams," Donna says, coming up on Wendy's other side. "I'd hate for them to be with any imbeciles. I don't want my husband shot at by accident."

Wendy doesn't look at Kim's face to see whether she's heard Donna's comment.

Two minutes later the women reach their next destination: an olive green tank sitting outside another low-slung building. "Here it is!" the major says.

Close-up the tank hovers over them like a huge Frankenstein. The top of the treads are level with Wendy's chin and the long main gun points at her head.

Wendy touches the tank. "I thought it would feel like a big heavy truck, metal, but hollow inside. Put your hands on it," she tells the others.

"It doesn't feel like there's anything inside it," Sharon says. "It's like a rock!"

"Ladies," Major Polens says. "Here's your chance to see the inside of a tank. Who wants to climb in?"

Several women indicate they will try, and Wendy gets in line with them. Sharon stands behind her, while Kim and Donna step to one side to watch.

Wendy flashes to standing in line at the county fair. She is five years old, waiting for a ride on the Ferris wheel. Her mama holds her hand, her papa stands on her other side. She eats pink cotton candy and her mama tells her to "hurry, finish it up" before they get to the head of the line. Wendy licks her fingers of the last wisps of cotton candy before it's their turn.

There is no ride. When they reach the ticket taker – an old man in baggy pants with a smelly cigar – he says something to her papa. Then her papa takes her hand and leads her out of the line. She cries and her mama offers her an ice cream cone. She stops sniffling and accepts the ice cream cone. That night she dreams of riding the Ferris wheel, of going up, up, up so high in the sky and coming down, down, down so fast. The ice cream cone was a poor consolation prize.

This time when Wendy gets to the head of the line she is motioned forward. She uses the steps to mount the tank, swings her legs over the rim of the open hatch, and lowers herself. Then she's sitting on a stool, with handles and dials and knobs all around her.

Wendy gulps, her breath catches. Perspiration drenches her face. It's so tiny inside!

She's hiding in a hole. The dogs are above, sniffing out one more runaway slave. She's not going to make it!

Wendy flings her hands over her head and pulls herself halfway out of the hatch. The major grasps her under the arms, pulls her legs out, and helps her down the steps.

"Wendy, are you okay?" Sharon asks.

Wendy nods as Sharon climbs up the steps for her turn.

Then Wendy sinks onto the grass. Kim and Donna bend over her.

"What's wrong?" Donna asks. "Are you sick?"

"I ... I just got frightened. It's so small inside." Like a hole where a runaway slave hides.

Her high school education hadn't spent much time on the civil rights movement – that subject was too close to the students' segregated lives. But time had been spent on "safer" black subjects of a 100 years ago – the stories of those slaves who braved death or brutal beatings to make a dash for the North and freedom.

Wendy looks up at Kim and Donna. They are not here to capture her – she's safe – at least for now.

✵ ✵ ✵

Two days later Wendy picks up Nelson's dirty fatigues piled on the couch. She'll drop them off at the laundry on her way to Sharon's for the committee meeting.

As she reaches for the car keys, Wendy thinks about when she learned that Nelson had a two-year commitment to the U.S. Army – an army fighting a guerilla war in the jungles of Vietnam, wherever that was, with men being killed by "soldiers" as young as 10 and 12.

It wasn't the first time she and Nelson spoke – when he came up to her after choral practice during her freshman year and introduced himself. It was the next choral practice. He asked to walk her back to her dorm.

Leafless trees arched overhead as they walked along the path towards the school dorms. At first they talked about their majors. Wendy said she chose sociology "because I'm not sure what I want to do after college and sociology offers a broad background." Nelson said he was studying history – "even if it is white history."

He stopped at a fork in the path and took her hands. "Only by studying the past can we learn how to improve the future," he said. "Martin Luther King, Jr. is showing us the way, but we can't expect him to do it all for us. We have to do our share."

Then Nelson dropped her hands and told her about his father, who had been decorated in World

War II for bravery in combat in an all-black unit in Italy. "He came home a war hero – to discover that the only job he could get was a porter for the railroad."

Wendy didn't say anything. She waited to hear what else Nelson would say.

"I'm the oldest of five children. My mama comes home exhausted every day from cleaning white folks' houses. Sometimes she brings home the leftovers – of food, clothes, and toys. We are appropriately grateful for this 'bounty.'"

"How did you get to come to college?" she asked.

"Scholarship. My parents are proud that I'm getting to better myself. And they didn't say anything when I told them that two years of ROTC are required here."

"ROTC?"

"Reserve Officers Training Corps." He paused. "Now I've decided I'll stay in the program after the two years. Told my parents that being an officer was a whole lot better than being an enlisted man. My father agreed. 'More respect. Less KP.'"

Wendy stood on the path next to Nelson trying to take everything in. There was so much – his parents, his siblings, his fervor – that the ROTC part got submerged. She only understood that he would be an officer and that this would be good for his future.

After that night, as they spent more and more time together, she didn't discuss ROTC or the army with him except in the vaguest way. And she avoided seeing him on campus on the days he wore his uniform.

She did resent the times he went on overnight exercises with his ROTC unit. She hated being left in the dorm on a Friday or Saturday night while the other girls were out with their boyfriends, going to parties, seeing movies. "Nelson's busy; tons of school work," she'd say if asked.

Only the morning they left for Ft. Knox, the morning after her papa's big speech, did she really believe that her husband was to serve in the U.S. Army for two years. Even so, she visualized two years of living somewhere in the U.S. while Nelson had a regular job, just one requiring an olive green uniform.

Vietnam was halfway around the world. Surely he wouldn't be sent there.

The next morning Nelson says "There's still time to change your mind" as she clears the breakfast dishes. "You can drive me to the post so you'll have the car."

She shakes her head. What would she do with the car? She went to the commissary yesterday, she doesn't have a committee meeting today, and it isn't her day to visit the hospitalized soldiers. Sharon asked her to come swimming at the Country Club now that the pool is open, but Wendy isn't sure she'd be comfortable there.

What she says to Nelson is, "I have letters to write today. I'll be fine at home."

To keep her company she has Nelson's framed photo of Martin Luther King, Jr. His eyes stare at her as she turns on the radio. A commercial praises air conditioning units at a store in Elizabethtown.

"Now back to music," the announcer says, "with the song 'He Was My Brother' from Simon and Garfunkel's first album – 'Wednesday Morning, 3 a.m.'"

Wendy stops piling the breakfast dishes in the sink. She may have been sheltered from experiencing much of racial discrimination, but the song's image of a Freedom Rider being killed for his beliefs always brings tears to her eyes:

> *He was singin' on his knees*
> *An angry mob trailed along*
> *They shot my brother dead*
> *Because he hated what was wrong …*

As the song finishes she clicks off the radio and wipes her eyes with a tissue. Then she picks up a dish scrubber and takes out her anger on the crusted frying pan.

She doesn't know very much about the white Freedom Riders who came down to the South to register black voters in the early 60s. There hadn't been any in her hometown and she was too busy as a self-absorbed teenager to notice what her parents kept from her anyway.

Yet one night, a month after she had said yes to Nelson's marriage proposal, she and Nelson took a walk around campus. The moon crowned the trees, moonlight sparkling their path. The bell struck as they passed the campanile.

Nelson stopped below the tower. She stood in silence with him until the bell struck the ninth and final time, then they walked on.

Nelson waited until they had gone quite a distance further before he finally spoke.

"That bell reminds me of when I heard that the three white civil rights workers had been murdered over in Philadelphia, Mississippi," he said. "I felt so bad, so useless that I wasn't there too, that I ran over to our church and pealed the bells for them."

"What could you have done in Mississippi?"

"Maybe nothing."

The next day he met her after classes holding a record album. "This is a gift for you. Listen to the song 'He Was My Brother.' I don't know if it's about those three people in Mississippi or some other Freedom Riders. Yet every time I hear it ... I relive their deaths."

Nelson didn't have much money. The song had to be really special for Nelson to have bought the album. She took it back to her dorm room and played it on the stereo her father sent with her to college.

And that was the first time she cried when she heard the words, cried for the "brother" who'd been killed trying to help blacks, and for Nelson, who believed he failed in some way.

She places the last of the washed dishes onto the dish drying rack. Now what? There's always the television. Yet even looking at it turned off makes her uncomfortable, reminding her of the story told her by Marylou Williams, the daughter of the white man who loaned his hunting lodge for Wendy and Nelson's honeymoon.

Wendy didn't know much about Marylou, who was a few years older, except that Marylou married an army officer. Marylou – who was back home visiting her parents at the time of Wendy and Nelson's wedding – called Wendy before the wedding with instructions about using the lodge. "Make sure you turn the hot water heater on two hours before you need it or you'll be taking cold showers." Wendy thanked her for the advice.

"As long as I'm on the phone," Marylou said, "is there anything I can tell you about the army, one officer's wife to another?"

One officer's wife to another?

Wendy asked *the* question. "Has your husband been to Vietnam?"

"Yes," Marylou said, "yes he has. But he's back now."

"What did you do while he was gone?"

"I worked. Went out with my friends. I saved my money and bought him the biggest motorcycle and television I could find as coming home presents." Marylou paused. "Then the son of a bitch called to tell me to meet him in Hawaii for a week. He wasn't finished with his mission and he was extending his Vietnam tour another six months. I sold the brand-new motorcycle and television – I was so furious!"

What did the woman mean by "his mission"? What could he have been doing in Vietnam so important that he had to finish it rather than letting someone else take over? And not come home to his wife when he could?

Later she asked Nelson about Marylou's story. "What could be so important that a man would risk his life for six more months while his wife waits for him?"

"Honey," Nelson said, "you just don't understand. It's a man's duty. People's lives depended on him."

A man's duty? Little boys played with toy guns, threatening to blow off their mama's head when called in for dinner. Grown-up boys played at real war, getting to blow someone's head off when called upon to do so.

Guns. Wendy's papa offered her and Nelson his gun when they were packing to come to Ft. Knox. "You never know when you might need it," he said. Nelson shook his head no.

"I'd feel better if you took it," her papa said. "I can always get another one."

They insisted they wouldn't need it. This was 1970 and Nelson was a commissioned officer in the U.S. Army. They assured her parents they would be fine.

Guns kill.

They left without the gun.

SHARON – IX – June 9

*"The thoughtful wife will keep a record of courtesies
extended to her and her husband and make some kind of
repayment."*

The sun slants across their backs as Sharon and
Kim settle down for another afternoon by the pool
at the Country Club. Since Memorial Day they have
taken advantage of the open pool each afternoon.
Sharon now sports a beautiful tan although Kim's
skin remains pale thanks to the generous slathering
of suntan oil.

Sharon looks around the pool at the other
women and some men. How many of them truly
want to be here and how many simply accept army
service as a temporary way station on their life's
journey?

Sharon flashes on what she learned when last
Friday night she and Robert attended the post's

religious services for Jewish personnel. She and
Robert had arrived a few minutes late at the army
chapel, a frame building whose interior barrenness
trumpeted its use for the services of different
denominations. The Friday night service to greet the
start of Shabbat – the Jewish Sabbath – had already
begun.

"They obviously start on military time, not Jewish
time," Robert said.

They took two small prayer books from a stack
of books – "Look, Robert, an official army Jewish
prayer book." On his head Robert placed one of the
provided black satin **yarmulkes**.

"I'm the only woman here," Sharon whispered to
Robert as they sat down.

Sharon had a decent Jewish religion background.
She attended Sunday School from kindergarten
age, started Hebrew School in third grade, had a
Bat Mitzvah at age 13 (a Friday night chanting of
the week's Haftorah followed by an Oneg Shabbat
dessert kiddish; not the Saturday morning Torah
reading service followed by a sit-down luncheon that
her brother had), and continued religious school
education through Confirmation in 10th grade.
She could read along in the Hebrew although she
couldn't translate what she read.

During the brief army Friday night service,
shorter than the Friday night service to which
Sharon was accustomed, all but the most important

prayers were recited in English rather than Hebrew. Most of the men wore fatigues and their olive drab uniform "baseball caps." A few wore suntans and their uniform green garrison caps. Robert was the only one in civilian clothes and the satin **yarmulke**.

The Jewish army chaplain, a young rabbi in suntans with a blue-and-white crocheted **yarmulke** on his head, said a few words on the Bible portion of the week. At the conclusion of the service he invited everyone into the social hall for cookies and soda pop.

The chaplain came up to them. "I'm Chaplain Daniel Levin." Robert shook his hand while Sharon smiled. "Lieutenant Robert Gold and my wife Sharon."

"Welcome," Chaplain Levin said. "Please join us for refreshments."

The chaplain turned towards the social hall. Sharon touched his arm. "Excuse me, but why are there no women here?"

"You mean why aren't there any wives?" He smiled. "Ft. Knox is a basic training post. We have a lot of Jewish draftees here."

"Jewish draftees!" Robert said. "I never expected so many."

The chaplain nodded. "They're mostly National Guard and Reserves. And even if they never go to synagogue at home, they come here."

"Why?"

"Because for enlisted men it's an approved way to get out of their units for a couple of hours. You know, get out of cleaning the latrines or some other distasteful task. And it's an opportunity to be with other Jews."

Sharon could certainly relate to that.

"The few Jewish officers – the ones who have their wives here – they're mostly doctors and they don't come. On Friday nights they're home with their wives or at the Officers Club."

"Chaplain," Robert said, "if there's ever any problem, just let me know. I'll do whatever I can."

"That's what I'm here for, Lieutenant. I know every drill instructor and basic training company commander on the post. Besides, you'll be gone in how many weeks?"

She and Robert probably won't go back to services at Ft. Knox. It's bad enough to feel out of place being Jewish in a non-Jewish environment. It's altogether another thing to feel out of place in a Jewish environment.

Two days later on Sunday on the way to have lunch with her grandparents she had said to Robert, "You were right. You made the right decision."

Robert didn't take his eyes from the road. "Right about what?"

"It is better to be an officer."

"What are you talking about?"

"When we went to services – all those enlisted men."

"Jewish trainees." Robert shook his head. "When I was at ROTC summer camp, there was only one other Jew in my platoon. Nobody ever said anything specific to us, but I'm sure that we were singled out for some extra harassment. And we were officer cadets. I can't imagine what would happen to a Jewish basic trainee."

Sharon nodded, flipping her hair out of her eyes. With the Fiat's top down the humid air blew through the car. "I really appreciate your going to lunch again at my grandparents' apartment."

Robert laughed. "You didn't think I'd go again after once sitting in a tiny sweltering hot kitchen at high noon in front of the hot oven having hot chicken soup, hot brisket and hot apple pie?"

Sharon laughed too. "That's what I meant."

"Where did your grandmother learn to cook?"

Sharon pictured her step-grandmother as she often described herself playing with the black children in the cotton fields of Mississippi. "She grew up poor. Maybe these big hot meals mean she's made it, or maybe her first husband liked to eat this way."

"It could have been what killed him."

They passed the small houses and cluttered yards she'd seen on this back road before with Kim. At one place a little boy clutching a rope swing with one hand waved to Sharon with the other. She waved back.

"Do you want to see the movie 'Patton' at the post theater?" she asked.

"Patton's nephew is an armor officer stationed at Ft. Knox right now." Robert smiled. "It's neat that we'll be seeing this movie about Patton while I'm training on tanks and his nephew is also here."

Neat? Seeing a movie about tank battles in World War II while Robert trained on tanks for the Vietnam War? Why did the military hold such fascination for some people?

The first time she attended a military function flashes in her mind. A few weeks after her momentous decision at the student union, she attended the 1968 ROTC Commissioning Parade for both the U.S. Air Force and the U.S. Army at Demonstration Hall Field at "four-ten o'clock" per the formal invitation from the colonel who was the professor of military science and the lieutenant colonel who was the professor of aerospace studies. Robert in his dress green uniform escorted her to the ceremony.

Sharon felt odd being alongside a man in uniform. She had seen the old black-and-white photos of her father in his World War II army uniform and her mother in her student nurse's uniform standing next to him. Yet then the U.S. fought a just war to save the world from fascist tyranny. The Vietnam War ....

As they approached the field, another army cadet greeted Robert, who stopped to introduce Sharon to Walter and his girlfriend Beth, who were to be married at the end of spring quarter. As the four of them continued walking towards the field, Robert and Walter talked to each other about the overnight training the following week – the rations they'd eat, the gear they'd pack.

Sharon asked Beth, "Aren't you worried about marrying a man right before he goes on active duty?"

Beth smiled. "Any time we can have together before he gets assigned an unaccompanied tour ..."

Sharon persisted. "Don't you think this war is wrong?"

Again Beth smiled, as if she understood Sharon. "It's not really important what I think about the war. I love Walter – and I admire him for his commitment to something he believes in, serving his country. It's a better goal than most boys here at college have. They seem more interested in getting drunk."

As if these patriotic boys could really stop the Communist juggernaut from rolling over the Republic of South Vietnam Sharon thought.

At the ceremony the commissioning address had been given by Major General Alden Kingsland Sibley, but Sharon had barely listened, her mind distracted by what Beth had said to her. And Sharon had only glanced at the commissioning program listing into which branch each army ROTC cadet was being commissioned, so she had not really absorbed that Robert was one of the few being commissioned in infantry.

Instead, by the end of the commissioning address, Sharon had accepted that, although she was adamantly against the Vietnam War and thus the U.S. Army by extension, she had to admire Robert for committing to something for which he felt passionate, something bigger than his own juvenile desires. And Sharon realized that love isn't controlled by political considerations. It's much more irrational than adding up the pros and cons of the U.S. in Vietnam and then deciding to be anti-war.

The night of the AEPhi formal Sharon and Robert had "parked" in his Corvair on a back road near the sorority house. Since the start of the fall quarter of 1967 the university curfew for women of 11:30 p.m. on weekdays and 1:00 a.m. on Fridays and Saturdays had been abolished, so Sharon did not have to fear breaking curfew.

Sharon and Robert kissed – long kisses that excited the blood.

Robert reached under the Corvair's front seat and removed a small gift-wrapped box. "This is for you," he said.

Sharon slipped off the wrapping paper. The box from the student bookstore held a tiny American flag pin lying on top of a note.

Can you understand my commitment to serving our country? Robert.

She stared at the flag pin, then reached towards Robert's tux bowtie.

"Don't."

"Why not?"

"I can't tie it again. Had to have someone tie it for me."

Sharon placed her hand on the bowtie. "What if it's not tied?"

"It won't look right when I go back to the dorm."

Sharon dropped her hand to the top button underneath the tie. "I can start lower."

Robert's honking at a stray dog alongside the winding road brought Sharon back to the rural Kentucky scenery. And 30 minutes later they pulled up to the two-storey red-brick apartment building where her grandparents had a first-floor apartment. Goldenrod, Kentucky's state flower, scented the air.

Her grandparents met them at the door, her grandfather clasping a brass-headed cane in his right hand. The hot air from inside pushed against the drenching humidity from outside.

"Dinner's not quite ready," her step-grandmother said.

"Maybe we could take Grandpa for a walk," Sharon said. The heat outside had to be better than the heat inside. Outside there might be a faint breeze.

The old man shook his head. "I can't walk that far."

"Of course you can, Grandpa. We'll just go around the block."

She held his left arm. In slow motion he moved first one foot, then the other foot, his cane tapping out his snail-pace progress from the building's front door to the street sidewalk.

"What's new, Grandpa?" Sharon asked.

The old man didn't answer. He concentrated on shuffling his feet.

Sharon glanced at Robert, his short haircut a constant reminder – even when not in uniform – of his army status.

She looked back at her grandfather.

He was born in a different century, didn't have indoor plumbing as a child or any of the other conveniences she considered necessities. Two things were still the same: 1) the need for a country to have an army and 2) residents of that country who refuse to fight. Her grandfather had told her about this in his Yiddish-accented English.

"My father – his name was Velvel – was drafted and served six years in the czar's army on the Turkish border. He came one time for a furlough in six years. My mother Chaye Shifra had to go out and peddle dress goods among the rich people, the ones who had money, and my Aunt Rivka – she was divorced – was a dressmaker. She took care of the babies, her daughter and my oldest brother, while my mother sold the goods."

Although Velvel was rewarded for his six years of baking for the czar's army – granted the rare privilege of a Jew in Russia being allowed to own land, he did not let his sons serve. As each son came of military age, Velvel sent that son to America. No son of his would fall into the czar's clutches!

Ship after ship at the turn of the century brought escaping immigrants to America – "Give me your tired, your poor, your huddled masses yearning to be free." The immigrants fled harsh governments and years of required military service. Was this so different today when long-haired draft protesters waved their "Make love, not war" placards and burned their draft cards in demonstrations across the country? They protested what to them seemed a harsh government and they yearned to be free of the quagmire of the Vietnam War.

Sharon shifted her hold on her grandfather's arm. "Did you go over to the Jewish Community Center this week?" she said.

"It's too far."

"Grandpa, it's a block away! How could it be too far?"

The man stopped. "I'm sick," he said. "Real sick. My doctor, he doesn't believe me." Tears rolled down his cheeks.

"Grandpa!" She'd never seen him cry.

Sharon put her arm around his shoulders. Robert supported him on the other side. "Let's go back to the house. We'll take care of it."

Now at the Country Club pool as the sun shines on Sharon's suntanned back she reaches into her straw bag and pulls out the book she started last night.

Opening a magazine, Kim asks, "What are you reading?"

"'While 6 Million Died' by Arthur D. Morse about the Holocaust."

"What's the Holocaust?"

Sharon hesitates. Does Kim not know about it?

"When the Nazis – the Germans – during World War II killed six million Jews."

Kim sits up. "What do you mean the Germans killed six million Jews?"

Sharon sits up too. "Did you have American history in high school?"

"Senior year."

"Did you study World War II?"

Kim looks at the magazine in her lap, then up at Sharon. "We didn't get that far in the book. We spent most of our time on the Civil War. We just got up to World War I when school ended."

Sharon will have to explain.

"You've heard about Hitler, right?"

"Yeees."

"Hitler, the leader of the Nazis during World War II, was obsessed with getting rid of people whom he considered **untermenschen** – subhumans. He set up concentration camps to exterminate – kill – all these people." Sharon pauses to take a breath, keep her voice even. "Besides the six million Jewish men, women and children killed solely because they were Jews – the Nazis also killed millions of others, including Gypsies, religious dissenters, political prisoners, mentally and physically deficient people, and homosexuals. The book is about how the U.S. did nothing to stop the killing."

Kim's face flushes. "What could the U.S. have done?"

"For one thing, bomb the train lines used to bring the Jews and others to the death camps. For another, make it clear that there would be severe retribution against people who were involved in the killings after the war was won by the Americans and our allies. What's more, right-wing groups in the U.S. prevented Jews trying to escape Hitler from entering the U.S. Even children were turned away."

Kim peers down at her magazine. "I want to read this article. I'll ask Jim about the Germans tonight."

Sharon lies back down. There's no purpose in continuing a conversation that makes Kim uncomfortable. You can only change people's thinking if they're open to change. If you push too hard, their minds close, perhaps permanently.

Sharon stares at the book's open pages. All her known relatives and all Robert's known relatives left Russia at the turn of the century. Years before Hitler they had sailed steerage across the Atlantic to not only escape service in the czar's army but to escape the pogroms – murderous attacks on Jews by mobs led by Cossacks or incensed by rabble-rousers.

One day, after her grandfather bought her cherry strudel at a Jewish bakery in Chicago, he told her about his trip to America in the bowels of a ship: "On the boat they gave us herring, black bread and beer. We were eating the herring and black bread and drinking beer like all the rest of them were doing. There was a real religious man there and he was about to die – he wouldn't eat any of the food because it wasn't kosher. There was also a sister and brother – their mother packed them all kinds of kosher food with whiskey and wine in a big basket. We begged them to sell us some food so we could give it to this real religious man but the brother wouldn't do it.

"And when he went up on deck with his sister we turned the basket over and we took a knife and cut the bottom off – a sailor sold us a needle for a dime and gave us a string so we could fix the hole – and we took out whiskey and some of the food and some of the cookies. We hid the food and fed that old man and we kept him all right. And we brought that man with us to Chicago."

Now the wrong food has almost killed her grandfather. Sharon's mother flew down to Louisville Monday morning after Sharon called her. On the way to the doctor's office in the taxi her grandfather explained his symptoms to her mother. The cabbie turned around and said, "He's got sugar." Thirty minutes later her mother asked the doctor one question: "Have you tested him for maturity-onset diabetes?"

The young, inexperienced doctor admitted, "I thought the old man's complaints were just old age." Only after the diabetes test showed her grandfather had high levels of sugar did the doctor realize the old man was truly ill.

With a diagnosis and a medication plan, her grandfather would soon feel better.

If only everything could be fixed so easily.

*U.S. jets bomb anti-aircraft
sites 90 miles north of
demilitarized zone ...*
May 25, 1970

WENDY – IV – June 10

*"Courtesy and cordiality are never influenced by rank or
position – you should never be reluctant to speak to a senior
representative."*

The knock on the trailer's door startles Wendy.
She walks to the door but doesn't open it. "Who's
there?" she asks.

"Your mama and papa!" her papa says.

Oh, no, they're here to take her home! They'll
never let her stay when they see the inside of this
trailer!

She grabs her purse, opens the door and pulls it
shut behind her. "Mama, Papa," she says as she hugs
them both. "What a surprise!"

"Honey, aren't you going to invite us in? We came
all this way to see your home," her mama says.

Wendy stands with her back pressed against the
trailer's door. "I ... I was just cleaning and it's still
a mess. Let's go to the post first for something to

eat." She takes her mama's arm. "We can go to the Officers Country Club."

Wendy brushes her hair out of her eyes as she climbs into the backseat of her parents' car. "Where did you come from?" she asks.

"We came from home. Drove most of the way yesterday and stayed overnight in a small motel. Then drove the rest of the way here this morning," her papa says.

"Why didn't you call?"

"Wanted to surprise you."

"Let me tell you what's new at home," her mama begins.

Wendy doesn't ask *why* they've come – she knows. And all the way to the club, as her mama talks about this person and that person, Wendy imagines her parents throwing her clothes into a suitcase, forcing her to come home with them.

"Welcome to the Officers County Club," she says, leading her parents into the snack bar. The more formal dining room would be better for impressing them, but it would mean three black people surrounded by white officers and their ladies. Easier to blend in with the fast-food crowd.

Wendy spots an unoccupied table alongside one wall and steers her parents towards the table.

"Here, Mama, sit down with Papa. I'll get us all hamburgers and Coke."

Wendy takes the $10 bill her papa stuffs into her hand and goes to the counter. As she turns from ordering, she faces Sharon and Kim approaching the counter.

"Here by yourself?" Sharon asks. "Come sit with us."

"I'm ... I'm here with my parents."

"Your parents? You didn't say they were coming," Sharon says.

"They just surprised me. I've brought them here for lunch." Wendy waves in the direction of her parents.

"Why don't we all eat together?" Sharon asks. "Can we join you?"

Kim says, "We shouldn't intrude."

Sharon glances at Kim, then smiles encouragement at Wendy.

Should Wendy say yes to Sharon's offer? Kim probably won't be comfortable. Yet if Wendy can show her parents that she's accepted by these white women, maybe her parents won't drag her home.

"That would be lovely," Wendy says.

Wendy waits while Sharon and Kim order, then leads them back to her table. "Mama, Papa, this is Sharon Gold and this is Kim Benton. Both their husbands are officers in class with Nelson and we're all on the entertainment committee I told you about."

"Where you all from?" her mama asks as Sharon and Kim pull up chairs from a nearby table.

"I'm from Chicago," Sharon says.

Kim glances down at the table, then looks up. "I'm from North Carolina," she says.

Her mama beams. "We're from South Carolina."

Kim nods.

Now what are they going to talk about for the rest of lunch? Wendy wonders.

"Is this your first time in Kentucky?" Sharon says. "I still can't get over how Kim and Wendy call it the North."

"I went to medical school in Chicago," her papa says. "Wendy was born there."

Sharon laughs and turns to Wendy. "You're from Chicago too. You never told me that."

Wendy laughs too. "We came back to the South when I was just two years old."

"I'm certainly outnumbered here," Sharon says, "with all you Southerners."

Wendy smiles. How kind of Sharon to make her parents feel more comfortable – four Southerners to one Northerner instead of three blacks to a room full of whites. Maybe her parents will let her stay.

"Where do you live here?" her mama asks Sharon and Kim.

"So you see, Mama and Papa, all the student officers have to make do with temporary housing. The housing office gave us a list and this was on it."

All the way back from the post Wendy tries to prepare her parents. "It's just like Sharon said at lunch. The wives being here makes all the difference to our husbands." Her parents don't respond, just listen to her chatter about the wives' tour – "The tank was so big from the outside, although inside it seemed so small." – and the upcoming graduation luncheon.

Now they stand in front of the trailer and she can't stall any longer. She unlocks the door and leads the way. Her parents come in behind her and say nothing.

Then, "You said it needed cleaning, honey. It looks clean to me," her mama says, sitting down on the couch. "And it's certainly passable."

Wendy sinks into a kitchen chair, lightheaded with relief.

Her papa sits down next to her mama and laughs. "You should have seen the one-room apartment – and I don't mean one-bedroom apartment – we all three lived in when I was in medical school. We were thrilled to have the one-room with a tiny kitchen and bathroom."

"Yes, dear," her mama says. "Before we got that apartment we had a room above a laundry with kitchen privileges and a bathroom down the hall.

With expecting you we thought we should at least have our own kitchen."

Wendy hesitates. Her parents always avoid talking about the "problem." She has to show them she's an adult now, capable of facing anything on her own – or at least with Nelson.

"Did you live like that because that's all blacks could get then?"

"It's all there was after the war," her mama says. "Whites lived the same way too. All the young men were just back from the war like your papa and trying to go to school on the GI Bill and support a family. There wasn't much housing available with everyone coming home, and nobody had much money."

Wendy mashes her hands together. Has she been so insensitive that she thinks her parents care only about material things? Just because her father has done well doesn't mean her parents expect the same from her and Nelson immediately.

She kisses both her parents. "Thanks for coming," she says.

Three hours later her mama's frying her special chicken recipe. The sizzling oil permeates the small trailer. Wendy and her papa sit on the couch waiting for Nelson to come home.

Her papa says, "We've been talking all afternoon, yet you still haven't told us what your plans are for after the army. If Nelson wants to go to graduate school, I'll be glad to pay for it – and your living expenses too. And, of course, Nelson will have the GI Bill."

Her mama waves the spatula at Wendy. "And maybe you could even choose a graduate school close to home," her mama says from the stove. "We'd like you to be nearer, especially if any children come along."

Wendy nods, then rolls her hands across the waistband of her cotton skirt. She wants children, she does, although she isn't sure she's ready for all the responsibility. And what if she and Nelson don't come home in two years? What if Nelson goes Regular Army?

"Papa, how come when I was growing up you never talked about the hardships blacks had in the South? Nelson's always on me about how naive I am. You didn't tell me anything."

Her papa looks up at her mama behind her, then reaches out and takes hold of one of her hands. "Sugar," her father says to Wendy, "how come you're asking about this now when you've never asked before? Have white folks been saying things to you?"

Wendy thinks of her experience at the volunteers meeting for the hospital. Maybe the initial reception from the women was just a natural reluctance to accept newcomers – whether they're white or black – and Mrs. Donovan did include her. "Everyone's been very nice to us."

Her papa stands up. "I knew it. Wendy marrying someone going into the army was a mistake."

Before Wendy can protest, her mama comes around the couch and pulls her papa back down. "Nothing's going to happen to Wendy," she says.

"To me?" Wendy asks. "Don't you mean Nelson? What are you talking about?"

Her mama looks at her papa. He nods his head slowly. Her mama releases him and goes back to the stove.

"Wendy," she says, "why don't you and your papa go for a walk? It's real hot in here with all this frying going on. You all might as well be cool."

Outside the hot air billows in their faces. It isn't any cooler out here. Is this the equivalent of going into her father's office for one of their talks?

She waits for him to begin as they walk towards the road.

"Wendy," he says, "we've always told you that you were our only child. And while that was true for your entire lifetime, it wasn't true before you were born."

Before she was born?

"We had another child before you, a boy we called Arthur Henry. We were so proud of him. It was as if we were the first people ever to have a baby."

A brother. She had an older brother.

"It was a hot day ..."

Her papa pauses. They reach the road and she follows him to the left.

He begins again: "It was a hot day. There was a swimming hole outside of town that few people went to because there was a bigger one closer to town. Even at this smaller one, where there weren't any signs that said 'no coloreds,' we knew we weren't welcome."

The "no coloreds" signs. The ones her parents had kept her from seeing.

"I ... I wanted to take the baby there, thought the baby would like to play in the cool water. I told your mama there was no reason we couldn't go. She begged me not to – 'it isn't our place' – so I said I wouldn't. I'd just take Arthur Henry for a ride."

He increases his stride as if trying to escape from his own story. "I drove out to the swimming hole anyway. Wanted to show your mama she was wrong, that we didn't have to put up with the white folks' rules. I had just gotten out of the army and I was feeling very good about myself.

"At the swimming hole I undressed down to my boxer shorts and took the clothes off the baby. Then I sat in the shallow water splashing him."

Wendy is having a hard time keeping up with her papa and hearing his words. He's slightly ahead of her at the moment so she can't see his face.

285

"After a while two white men came swimming. Started saying nasty things. Said they didn't want 'no niggers stinking up' the swimming hole.

"I started yelling back at the men. I became so caught up in the name calling that I ... I forgot about the baby. When the other two men finally left rather than swim with a 'nigger,' I remembered the baby.

"It was too late."

Wendy wants to shout to her papa to stop – she doesn't want to hear this story! Her mouth doesn't open and her papa's does.

"Arthur Henry had drowned."

No breath. She collapses on the ground. Her papa, still ahead, doesn't notice.

His words come from over his shoulder. "Somehow he got turned upside down in the sand in the shallow water and couldn't right himself."

Then her papa stops, sees she's not with him, and in two long steps his arms encircle her.

"Sugar, sugar," he says as he brushes hair out of her eyes. "I didn't tell you this now to upset you. I just wanted to explain why we kept you so protected all these years, why we're so worried about you in the white world of the army."

She says nothing as her tears dribble into her open mouth.

"I had been punished for the sin of hubris – for thinking I could ignore the rules of the white world.

My arrogance had cost our baby's life." He rubs one hand over his eyes.

"It was a terrible time. I thought your mama could never forgive me and that I could never forgive myself. Our friends at church helped us to understand God's belief in forgiveness. And your mama and I resolved we would never, ever again forget who we were."

Her papa takes a deep breath, then goes on: "I was left with a burning need to do something, to make a difference with my life, to prove to myself and your mama I wasn't the lowest person on earth. I decided to go to medical school on the GI Bill. To learn to save other people even though I hadn't been able to save my own son."

Off in the distance a bird warbles, the notes floating towards them on the waves of humidity. Her father glances in the direction of the sounds.

"When I went to medical school in Chicago we knew things would be better in the North. Even there we kept to ourselves, not wanting to get used to any kind of white acceptance. Because no matter what we thought about our treatment in the South, your mama and I both wanted to return home. And when you came along, it was even more of a miracle than the first time. We were being given a second chance."

"And that's why," she snuffles, "you never let me go places where you thought I might not be accepted?" And why her parents had shown no interest in the civil rights movement. Even without Nelson's "educating" her she had thought that strange. "You were afraid of what might happen if you dared to question the white world's rules?"

Once again she recalls the little girl standing in front of the Ferris wheel with her parents, the little girl bribed with an ice cream cone so she won't make a scene. In her childish mind she's angry at her parents for leaving the line without protesting. Now she knows why they complied so quickly. Out of fear for her safety.

"We'd been given a second chance," he says again. "We weren't going to blow that."

She stares into his face. "And now I'm grown up and married and you can't protect me all the time anymore. It must be terribly hard on you."

Her papa buries his head on her shoulder. A patch of moisture spreads across her blouse.

She won't tell him now that Nelson has talked about going Regular Army.

*Cambodian leader Sihanouk
arrives in Hanoi and urges
people of Indochina to unite in
fight against foreign intervention …*
May 26, 1970

SHARON – X – June 12

*"Junior officers and their wives are not expected, nor
encouraged, to extend themselves beyond their financial
capabilities."*

Robert breezes in the front door. "What's for
lunch?"

"Tuna fish."

He grabs her around the waist. "I've got a better
idea," he says as he pulls her towards the bedroom.

He leans her against the bed so her back and
head lie on the bed and her legs dangle over the
edge. He pulls his starched green fatigue pants and
jockey shorts down to his ankles – "I can't take my
boots off, they take too long to re-lace" – yanks her
undies off, and stands next to the bed thrusting into
her.

She wipes herself off in the bathroom and puts
on her undies. Do the men in Robert's AOB class

talk about sex? Do they brag to each other how often and how good? She would never consider talking to Kim or Wendy or Donna about sex with Robert. It's too private.

She walks into the kitchen and puts their tuna fish sandwiches on the table. Robert eats his in large bites.

The sex reminds her of Mark Williamson and what she and he did and didn't do in high school when their paths converged for a second time. She pictures the two of them dancing at the Officers Club. He'd held her close but not close enough that her husband could have objected.

She wonders whether Mark had a lot of experience dancing quite close to those Vietnamese women she's heard about, their thick black hair hanging straight down their backs, their native costumes – Sharon isn't quite sure what these look like so she pictures the revealing garment worn by the young lieutenant's Polynesian girlfriend in the film version of "South Pacific" – leaving bare shoulders exposed and no undergarments underneath.

Will Robert be dancing with those sexy Vietnamese women soon?

"Have you decided about vol indef?" she asks. "Are you going to sign up for the third year?"

"That year buys us valuable time."

It's time to tell him – the information has been burning inside of her for over two weeks. She doesn't know herself why she hasn't told him before. "Robert?"

He looks up in mid-bite.

"Donna told me that Jerry could probably get an exemption from going to Vietnam."

"I didn't know he had a medical problem."

"He doesn't."

"Then what does he have?"

She stares down at her plate. "Donna ... Donna was married before. Her first husband ... was killed in Vietnam."

Robert's expression doesn't change.

"Jerry never said a thing."

He wouldn't have. Admitting you are the second husband at the age of 22 probably isn't something a man would relish.

Sharon looks at Robert. He's eating as if all she's said is "please pass the milk."

"Kim and Wendy don't know. Donna only told me and I didn't tell them."

"I won't say anything."

"That's not the point." She hesitates. "Apparently it entitles him to an exemption from Vietnam."

"Is he going to use it?"

"Donna told me the moment she found out he was eligible. He didn't even know at that point."

Robert gestures with his sandwich. "I'll bet he isn't going to use it. He's pretty patriotic. There's another guy who's going to use the sole surviving

son exemption – the sole support for his parents'
old age. Jerry doesn't think much of the guy. Ol'
Jerry is pretty gung ho on doing his duty."

Duty. Robert's friend Kenneth did "his duty,"
Donna's first husband did "his duty." And what did
it get them?

Death.

✥ ✥ ✥

"Are you sure you really want to go to this?"
Robert asks her two days later on Sunday as he heads
the Fiat out of the apartment parking lot. "We don't
really know anyone."

For response Sharon clutches the grocery
bag on her lap filled with three different kinds of
chips. True, she isn't enthusiastic about this picnic
sponsored by the Jewish Wives Club. She has already
learned at Judy Weinstein's house that she doesn't
have much in common with these women. Yet the
picnic is something to do, a distraction from her
concerns.

A "Whiter Shade of Pale" sung by Procul Harum
fills the Fiat. Waves of heat press down on Sharon as
they drive past trees whose leaves look desperate for
a cool drink. Even the heat here is different – the
humidity worse than in Chicago.

The concept of being different keeps recurring
to her. Growing up, she lived in an area with a

large number of Jews. She was part of an imagined, if not actual, majority. She attended Jewish summer camps, took after-school classes in ballet, swimming, and tennis with other Jewish kids, and, after a bumpy start at college, belonged to a Jewish sorority and socialized with the college newspaper's editorial staff, a large percentage of whom were Jews.

Until the first day of college, when she met her assigned roommates, only one other time in her life she could remember feeling like an outsider – the summer when she'd been 12 and hurt herself in a bike race with Howard. She'd run into a tree, so intent had she been on winning, and cut her left knee wide open. The cautious orthopedic surgeon decreed: "You'll have to be on crutches for a week. We want to ensure that nothing more serious develops."

Unfortunately, that week Sharon and her family had reservations at Fidelman's resort in Michigan. She spent the entire vacation on crutches – no swimming – although she participated as fully as possible in other resort activities.

One afternoon she signed up to go horseback riding, a perfect activity she figured since she'd be seated. The mother of some other children saw Sharon preparing to go. The woman came over to Sharon and said, "How can you go riding? You're a cripple, honey."

Rage coursed through her body. Rage at being made to feel diminished, less than other humans. On top of it the woman was wrong. That afternoon Sharon rode as well as any other novice.

"Here we are," Robert says as he swings off the highway. Although there are "No Parking" signs along the edge of the grass, all the other cars have parked there. Robert pulls alongside. "These guys must know something we don't," he says.

Sharon and Robert walk across the ground towards the men and women. Children play with balls nearby. All the women at the meeting at Judy's are here – obviously Nancy hasn't had her baby yet, plus a couple others. The men, of course, she has never seen.

"We just started cooking the hamburgers," Elaine says by way of greeting, then she introduces Sharon and Robert to the others.

Sharon can't remember all the new names. She does catch that the dark-haired man supervising the hamburgers is Judy Weinstein's husband Fred.

A muscular man in shorts and a plaid shirt asks Robert what he's doing at Ft. Knox.

"Armor Officers Basic school."

"How'd you do that?"

"ROTC."

The man shakes his head. "Why join ROTC?"

Before Robert can reply Fred asks, "How could you sanction this war by voluntarily joining the army?"

Sharon's palms tingle as Fred doesn't give Robert a chance to answer. "It's one thing for us to take the army's money," Fred continues, "so we could afford to go to med school – and hell, these people deserve good medical care too – but to volunteer to be part of the war machinery!"

Robert fixes his eyes on Fred. "All Americans have a duty to serve their country," Robert says, his hands hanging straight at his side, "regardless of whether the country is engaged in a 'righteous cause.' How many Americans weren't in favor of going to war against Hitler? They still served."

"Hey, guys!" someone shouts from behind them.

They all turn towards another man in shorts standing in front of the parked cars. An MP stands next to the Fiat writing something.

Robert leads the way across the grass. As they all reach the car, the man who shouted asks the MP, "Why are you only writing up the Fiat and not any of the other cars?"

"The rest of the cars have officer tags, sir," the MP says.

Fred steps forward. "This car also belongs to an officer." He gestures at Robert. "It just doesn't have officer tags because he's a student here, not yet permanently stationed."

The MP turns to Robert. "May I see your ID, sir?"

Robert fishes his wallet out of his back pocket and extracts his official army ID card.

"Sorry, sir," the MP says. "Please obey the 'No Parking' signs in the future."

Fred waves a hand in the departing MP's direction. "He was going to give an enlisted man a ticket but not an officer for parking in a 'No Parking' zone. What a place!"

Sharon passes her hand across her perspiring forehead, the heat pressing in on her.

Rank may have its privileges but rank won't save Robert from being killed in Vietnam. Before the branch transfer to military intelligence came through, Robert had the shortest life expectancy in Vietnam – as a second lieutenant in infantry.

✡ ✡ ✡

The next night Robert hands Sharon a drink as he joins her at an Officers Club table occupied by some of the AOB class members and their wives.

"Hey, Gold!" someone from the other end of the table yells. "Let's drink to long life!" The man holds up his beer glass.

"I'll drink to that," Robert shouts back.

"You should," the man says. "You came awfully close to buying it today!"

Sharon's heart flutters. "Robert," she says, tugging on his arm to get his attention. "What's buying it mean?"

"Nothing."

On her other side a man who looks familiar says, "He was damn lucky today on the firing range. Some idiot pointed in the wrong direction and missed your husband by inches."

"It's not real ammunition, is it?"

"What else would we use?" the second man says. His laughter almost muffles his words. "That's why Gold almost bought the farm – a little piece of earth!"

Robert was almost killed today!

"Lay off, Geist," Robert says to the man.

Geist again!

Robert then turns to Sharon. "Accidents like this happen in shooting practice."

Geist's face twists into a sneer. "Good thing it wasn't a fragging. Then you probably would have bought it."

She's drowning but she has to know. "What's a fragging?"

"Hey, guys, little lady here wants to know what a fragging is!" Geist yells up the table.

"Come on, Sharon, let's dance." Robert pulls her to her feet.

Geist takes hold of her other arm. "It's a slang term – officers getting killed by their own men – on purpose."

She collapses back into her chair. "I don't understand."

Now Robert faces her. "Fragging is when an enlisted man purposely kills his officer – usually by tossing a grenade at him."

"Happens a lot in Vietnam," Geist says.

The bile rises in her throat. She staggers up out of the chair and rushes from the room. She stumbles out the front door of the club and slams her right foot against the curb. The stabs of pain slow her down.

Robert catches up to her. "Sharon!"

She collapses onto the ground and fights to catch her breath.

"Robert, it's horrible enough to be killed by a heartless enemy. To be killed by your own men – on purpose!"

He crouches beside her. "It doesn't happen that much. Reports are highly exaggerated. Geist should have kept his mouth shut."

"Why do they kill their officers?"

Robert offers her his hand to pull her up. She doesn't take it.

"The men are drafted. They don't want to fight in a war that makes no sense to them. There's lots of drugs. They hate their officers who risk getting them killed. So they get rid of their officers. The next ones may be better."

Her knees shake. She can barely stand. She wraps her arms around her chest. "I want to go home."

"I'll drive you back now."

"Home to Chicago."

Robert puts his own arms around her, then shakes his head.

"You're an officer's wife now – for better or worse."

The tears drip down her nose.

*Senate approves, 82-11,
the preamble to proposed
legislative curb to the
President's war-making
powers in Cambodia ...*
May 26, 1970

DONNA – IV – June 18

*"To repay an elaborate dinner with a hamburger
cookout, minus apologies, is quite appropriate and your
thoughtfulness will be appreciated."*

Donna staggers through the door of Wendy's
trailer. "Where's the bathroom?"

Wendy points and Donna runs. She heaves into
the toilet.

When she emerges, water drops clinging to her
face, Wendy asks, "What's wrong? Are you sick?"

Donna sinks onto the couch. "It must be
something I ate."

Wendy sits next to her and studies Donna's face.
"How long has this been going on?" Wendy asks.

"A couple of weeks."

"A couple of weeks! You need to see a doctor.
Promise me you'll go to the clinic tomorrow
morning."

Donna nods. "I'll go. I'm awfully tired of feeling so sick."

There's a knock at the door. "It must be Kim and Sharon," Wendy says.

"Please don't say anything to them," Donna says.

The next morning Donna drops Jerry off without telling him where she's going. She's been assuring him for days that she's fine, just indigestion. She isn't about to let him know it could be something more.

At the post clinic there's already a line this early in the morning. She stands behind a young black woman holding the hand of a little boy in a white t-shirt and blue shorts.

A medicinal odor floats towards the line. Donna gags. What is the matter with her?

Ahead of her the boy whimpers. The woman gives him a piece of bread, then turns to Donna. "He's hungry again. We left Louisville real early this morning to get here."

"Why do you live all the way in Louisville?" Donna asks. "Don't you live in housing around here?"

"Louisville is the closest we could afford," the woman says. "We just come here for the free medical care."

The stab of nausea isn't from whatever is causing Donna to stand in this line. This woman's husband must be an enlisted man in Vietnam. That's why she doesn't live on the post or right near it.

"Is your ... is your husband ..."

"Dead. Killed in Vietnam when I was eight months pregnant with him." The woman points to the little boy.

Donna steps off the high dive and falls, falls towards the water below.

"I went berserk, out of my mind," the woman says. "When the baby came I didn't know what I'd do." The woman glances at the boy. "Then I had to take care of him, feed him, change him. I had to get in control. And most days I'm okay ..."

The boy tugs on his mother's hand. "Mama, more bread."

Donna sinks onto the floor.

✡ ✡ ✡

Donna opens her eyes. A man in a white coat leans over her. She's lying on an examining table, her skirt bunched around her waist. His hands move over her body.

"You're going to be fine, Mrs. Lautenberg," the doctor says, writing on a piece of paper. "You just fainted. Which is nothing unusual for someone in your condition. You're pregnant. No reason you shouldn't have a normal pregnancy and delivery."

Pregnant! What will Jerry say? He knows how much she wants a child. He'll think she did this on purpose.

"How can that be? I've been using a diaphragm every time. Checking carefully to make sure it's positioned correctly."

The doctor looks up. "Diaphragms get holes, the rubber gets old and cracks. You lose weight and it doesn't fit anymore. There are numerous ways."

A few hours later Donna sits in the car waiting to pick up Jerry after class for the day is over. She's trying to decide how best to tell him about the baby. For distraction she rereads the letter received today from her brother in Vietnam. It has been written three weeks before.

The short letter in English says: "Thanks so much for your letters. I got six from you all at once. I'm back at a base for supplies. Tonight I had a hot meal for the first time in weeks. Say hello to Jerry for me."

Donna refolds the letter. Maybe her brother is lucky that he doesn't have a wife at home waiting for his safe return. Or a baby who might never know him.

What if Jerry never knows his child? What if she becomes like the woman in line at the clinic? Going through the motions with her child but not really there.

At least that woman has something of her husband. There's nothing of Miguel.

Donna pats her still flat stomach. There will be something of Jerry.

She'll tell him tonight.

What she can't answer even though she's been thinking about it for hours is this: When she fainted this morning at the clinic, was it because of the pregnancy? Or was it the memory of the third telegram triggered by what the woman in line said? The first morning in the apartment here she had fainted when the Western Union man delivered that telegram by mistake. She was probably already pregnant then.

Telegrams and hospitals jostle in her mind.

Miguel lived three days – or almost three days. She can't be sure all three telegrams reached her in the same amount of time. So the army's medical personnel must have helped him. They must have thought he could be saved.

She knows what the word triage means. Heard her father explaining it one night to her mother after Miguel died when her parents thought she was asleep. "The medical personnel in Vietnam practice triage – giving priority to those who have the best chance for survival," he said in Spanish.

She had crept closer to the open kitchen door.

"When an evacuation helicopter sets down at a field hospital, the medics run with their litters. A doctor or a nurse or even an orderly has seconds to make these decisions."

Hidden by the kitchen door she was enraged by the unfairness! Each of those soldiers had been fighting for his country; they all deserved an equal chance!

Her mother asked the question on Donna's mind. "Why must they decide such things? Can't they try to help everyone?"

"There's not enough medical personnel when so many wounded come in at the same time," her father said. "Someone has to decide."

She bit her lips to keep from screaming as her father continued: "I'll tell you what an army nurse told me. For the hopelessly wounded all they can do is hold the soldier's hand so he doesn't die alone. Sometimes they don't have enough personnel to do that."

Donna crashed onto the floor with a shriek that brought her parents rushing from the kitchen and the other children from their bedrooms. Led back to bed, she prayed, prayed that Miguel hadn't died alone.

Please may someone have held his hand, told him it was going to be all right. Even though it wasn't. Even though it never would be.

Now, just before going to sleep for the night, the moment of truth has come – she'll tell Jerry about the baby as soon as he finishes brushing his teeth.

"I'm coming," Jerry calls from the bathroom.

Moments later Jerry asks "How do you feel?" as he slides into bed.

It's the same question he asked after the first time they made love, the night they got back from their trip to St. Louis. She didn't ask if he meant was it "as good" as with Miguel. All she said then was "wonderful."

Now she feels wonderful too. If only Jerry can understand.

"I went to the clinic today."

"What did the doctor say?" Jerry strokes her breasts.

"He said ... he said I'm pregnant."

"What?" Jerry's hands stop.

"He said we're expecting a baby."

Jerry sits upright in bed. "How can that be?" He looks at her with eyes that say betrayed. "Didn't you use your diaphragm?"

She sits up too. Nausea stabs her. Is the baby reacting to Jerry's response? Or is it her own anxiety?

"The doctor says it can happen. There's a tiny hole, or the rubber cracks, or something."

Anger sweeps through her. He's the one who doesn't want to use the Vietnam exemption. He should realize what this baby means to her. That no matter what happens, there'll be something of him to love.

"Jerry," she says, taking his hands in both of hers. "I've never talked to you about Miguel after the first time I told you about him – I wanted only to talk about us." His hands tighten in hers. "And I don't really want to talk about him now." The hands don't relax. "I didn't try to get pregnant – you must believe me. Yet I'm so happy to be having your child."

"Darling," he says, releasing his hands and gathering her in his arms.

She says into his shoulder, "I won't try to make you use the exemption. I just want this baby! I want a part of you so that ... if anything ..." Tears choke her voice.

Jerry lays her back down on the bed and kisses her.

"Is it okay to make love? We won't hurt the baby, will we?"

The next morning, Saturday, Donna first searches under the bed, then finds her purse under the kitchen table. She isn't thinking clearly.

Last night Jerry's response to her news was such a relief. His lovemaking so gentle, so sweet that he must be pleased about the baby. This morning, the passion of lovemaking over, she worried he would accuse her, demand an abortion.

He didn't. He got out of bed, bent down to kiss her, and said, "Take good care of my baby today."

Yet something troubles her. She shakes her head. It isn't telling her parents. They'll be thrilled. And it will be great news to write her brother. Something hopeful, something ... to make it home for.

What then? Telling the other women? After she proclaimed how she and Jerry were waiting? People are entitled to change their minds. Anyway, does she have to tell them now? Maybe she won't begin showing until after they leave Ft. Knox. She can just be pregnant at the next post, where only Sharon will be. Wendy and Kim will be at other posts.

Her glance falls on the Oriental bowl. Miguel. She's pretty sure Sharon hasn't told Kim and Wendy. They haven't looked at her strangely, anxiously, as if silently showing their sympathy – or horror. If she tells the other women about the baby maybe she'll have to tell them about Miguel, too. About the emptiness that never left her even when the tears stopped, when his sisters packed up their own babies – the babies she would never have with Miguel! – and went back to their own apartments, their own lives.

She'll write the sisters. They'll be happy for her, as they were when she remarried. They will also be sad for themselves, for their only brother Miguel, whose children would never play with their children, who would never again return to the streets of San Juan.

Enough! She doesn't want to see Miguel in his white wedding suit beckoning to her every time she thinks of the baby. This is Jerry's child she's carrying. Miguel was her past; Jerry and the baby are her future.

Jerry comes into the apartment – he's been out getting gas for the car. "I feel like a drive," Jerry says.

"Where to?"

"Let's see where the road takes us."

The air breezing into the open car windows blows hot, although not as sticky as the standing air. The road offers a menu of smells as they pass from the countryside into more built-up areas around Louisville. At a stoplight the escaping steam from a laundrymat mingles with whiffs of frying hamburgers from a roadside shack.

Then they are in downtown Louisville and Jerry turns the car into a parking lot next to a building whose sign announces HOLLY'S BABY STORE. "Surprise!" he says. "We can do a little sightseeing."

"You're wonderful!" she says, kissing him before unbuckling her seat belt.

The store brims with cribs, highchairs, and strollers. Other expecting couples and couples with babies walk up and down the aisles admiring or disregarding the available merchandise.

"It doesn't make sense to get anything now and have it shipped," Jerry says. "We can just have a good time looking."

She squeezes his hand as they wander among the baby equipment. "There's so much to get," Jerry says. "Babies need a lot of things."

She's too happy to answer, just keeps holding his hand as they walk, eyeing all the combinations of changing tables and dressers and rocking chairs. "I like white painted furniture. It's good for both boys and girls," she says.

After 30 minutes she has seen enough. "Can we go have something to eat?" she says.

Two blocks away they find a diner. As she enters, greeted by fat-frying smells, an older black man comes towards her with a take-out order. Jerry holds the door open for him, then follows her inside.

The counter man leans towards them. "Hey, fella, ya always hold doors open far niggers? Mebbe it's 'coz ya girl is a Spic."

Jerry jumps the counter and pulls the man's arm tight behind his back. "Say you're sorry to the lady. Or you won't be cooking for a long time."

The man remains silent. Jerry yanks the man's arm higher and the man squeaks out "Sorry, mam."

Jerry jumps back over the counter and leads her out through the door. "Come on, honey," he says. "We don't want to eat with white trash."

Jerry drives in silence for 20 minutes. Then he speaks. "You know we discussed going vol indef?"

Donna says nothing.

"Would you mind living in Europe when the baby comes? We'd be pretty far from your parents."

She would like to be close to her parents after the baby's born. And her father won't be eligible for a transfer from Ft. Riley until the end of their year in Europe, so she can't even hope that he'll be stationed in Europe at the same time.

As a young child stationed with her family in Germany, she hadn't lived in army housing on the **kaserne**. At that time her father's rank wasn't high enough to entitle him to army housing, so they had lived "on the economy." Yet her family shopped only in the army commissary – grocery store – and the PX, which carried gift items from all the countries in Europe. "Look at these lovely teak salad bowls from Denmark and the miniature wooden shoes from Holland," her mother would say as they chose gifts representing countries they hadn't visited.

The Germans seemed so different, their language incomprehensible, that her parents didn't attempt to travel anywhere else in Europe. They weren't even willing to go to Spain – "Perhaps our Puerto Rican Spanish won't be understood." Now with Jerry she could experience another culture. Maybe even study German.

The baby complicates this decision. "What do you think?" she asks.

"I'd like to go to Europe. See the museums and churches, the famous sights like the Eiffel Tower and Big Ben. And the opportunities in MI are pretty good in Europe. Here in the U.S. I'd probably just do document research and analysis. In Europe you can interview real people, people who sometimes risk their lives to bring out information from behind the Iron Curtain. I'd be doing something meaningful."

And it would postpone Vietnam, at least for a year, Donna thinks as she looks at his hands on the steering wheel. He'll get to hold the baby – have his picture taken with his child even if ...

"Let's do it. My parents will just have to come to Europe to see their first grandchild."

Jerry smiles. "I know you'll be happy."

Only one thing will make her happy – and no one can guarantee that.

KIM – VI – June 21

*"The following day it is a nice gesture to write a brief note
thanking your hostess for including you at the party and
extending a few complimentary remarks about its success."*

For a regular churchgoer, Jim hasn't shown any
interest in attending church here at Ft. Knox.
"Bunch of Northerners probably," he said when
Kim suggested going their first Sunday at Ft. Knox.
Yet there wasn't much he could say when Bill and
Susanna Norris asked them to a church picnic.

"How's it going?" Bill asks now as Kim and Jim
walk across the grass behind the church building.
Bill crouches on both legs, his rear end inches from
the ground, watching Billy Jr. run around in circles.
He stands to shake hands with Jim.

"Learned that little trick in Nam," Bill says. "The Vietnamese can sit for hours like that. Came in handy during monsoon season, not sitting on the wet ground."

Kim shudders as Susanna calls hello from the picnic table, where she's finishing braiding Patty's pigtails.

"Now off you go to play," Susanna says.

Patty remains where she is. Kim smiles at the child.

"Patty!" Susanna yells. "I told you to get goin'!"

Patty smiles at Kim, then walks towards the swing set, where two other children have claimed the two swings. Kim watches as Patty stands to one side, her eyes following the other children as they swing back and forth.

Kim sits next to Susanna on the picnic table bench. After swatting a fly off the table, Kim sets down her bag.

"What did you brin' for lunch?" Susanna asks.

"Cold fried chicken."

"I brought ham hocks. Want to share?"

Kim drops her eyes to her hands, then looks up. "Jim doesn't eat pork."

"He doesn't eat pork! What kind of Southerner is he?"

"He ... he has a food allergy to it."

Susanna lays her hand on Kim's arm. "How terrible! What do you cook?"

"I ..."

"Honey, come over here!" Bill calls to Susanna. "See what Billy Jr. is doing."

Kim fishes her food out of the bag and arranges it on the table. She's not sure why she fibbed, especially at a church picnic. She didn't want to explain Jim's peculiarities to Susanna.

Off to one side Kim sees a man who must be the minister shaking hands with some of the picnic people. It would be polite to go over and greet him – even though she'll be embarrassed if he asks why she hasn't been at church.

She glances towards the swing set. The other two children have left. Patty just sits on one idle swing. Doesn't she know how to pump her legs?

"Want me to push you?" Kim says as she walks over to the child.

Patty smiles.

Kim shoves the swing, sending the child high up into the air.

Patty shrieks! A shriek of terror, not enjoyment! Kim grabs the metal chains and stops the swing.

Susanna runs over. She hauls Patty off the swing and whacks her across the face. Pain jabs above Kim's eyes as Patty's smacked skin springs up into a red welt.

"What do you think you're doin', Missy? Screamin' like that? You could have scared someone real bad."

Kim looks over at the men; they're occupied watching Billy Jr. toddle around.

Susanna shakes Patty. "Answer me!"

Kim catches Susanna's hand as it again swings towards Patty's face. "It was ... it was my fault. I swung her too hard and frightened her. I'm sorry to have upset her – and you. Please don't punish her."

Susanna snaps her hand out of Kim's hold. "Then I'm sorry too. I want my children to behave. I don't want any kids of mine yellin' like little niggas."

An aura of rainbow colors blinds Kim. Why does Susanna have to say such a thing? Wendy is one of the gentlest people Kim has ever met. Kim's sure if Wendy had children they would be well behaved.

"Now be quiet and do what you're told," Susanna says to Patty. "I'm goin' to go fetch Billy Jr. and then we'll all eat."

Kim smiles at Patty, then follows Susanna. Ten feet away Kim turns back to wave to Patty, the slap mark bright on the child's face.

The Christian expression "turn the other cheek" occurs to Kim. What about "Christian charity"?

✵ ✵ ✵

"Food for us," Sharon says as she arrives at Kim's apartment the next evening and hands Kim the Coke and potato chips. "And speaking of food, I packed so much for Robert! He could go on a three-day trip instead of this one night training exercise."

"I did the same for Jim."

Sharon points to Jim's military figures marching across the floor. "How's the game coming?"

Kim can feel her face flush. Just because Jim is hooked on these games doesn't mean he's gung ho army, does it?

Not waiting for an answer, Sharon goes on to her next question. "When do you think the fireworks will start?"

Fireworks! Doesn't Sharon realize it can be dangerous?

Sharon plops down on the couch. "Robert said it would be loud and not to worry. Tank firing sounds worse than it actually is."

Surely Sharon has to know what happens if a tank takes a direct hit – the explosion, the burning ... the deaths. Maybe Sharon is purposely pretending it's no big thing.

"Do you want the Coke now?" Kim says.

Sharon nods and opens the bag of potato chips. "What have you and Jim decided about going voluntary indefinite?"

Kim pours the Coke into two glasses. "Jim hasn't told me what he wants."

"We're leaning towards doing it," Sharon says. "Nixon will have to end the war to be reelected. There's too much anti-war feeling not to."

"What does that mean?"

"The primaries are in spring of 1972. By fall of 1971 Nixon will have to announce he's ending the war. That's why we figure going vol indef – buying a year to 18 months in Europe – will improve Robert's chances of not going to Vietnam."

Isn't Sharon embarrassed to say Robert doesn't want to go to Vietnam? Even if Jim didn't want to go, he would never say it to anyone – that's unpatriotic. And he certainly wouldn't want her to tell anyone if he said it to her. If he had. Which he hadn't

"If Jim goes to Vietnam I want him to make out a will," Kim says.

"Why?" Sharon asks. "Everything you have together would be yours, wouldn't it?"

Kim shakes her head. "Without a will Jim's parents might take everything, leave me nothing."

"Why would they do that?"

"He's been theirs for a lot longer than he's been mine. They might say I don't deserve anything."

Kim can see from Sharon's puzzled expression that she doesn't understand. Since Kim can't explain any better, she holds up a crocheted square of light green wool. "I'm making an afghan for my sister for Christmas. What do you give your family for Christmas?"

Sharon brushes hair off her face. "We don't celebrate Christmas."

"Everyone celebrates Christmas."

"Christmas is a Christian holiday; Jews don't celebrate it. We have our own holidays."

"Jews don't celebrate Christmas?" Kim says.

"It's not a Jewish holiday."

"It's an American holiday," Kim says. She drops the crocheted square onto the table.

"It's not an American holiday like the Fourth of July or Thanksgiving," Sharon says. "It just seems like an American holiday because everything is closed on Christmas Day and all the stores are decorated and there are Christmas carols everywhere. It's really a religious Christian holiday."

Kim pictures herself on Christmas Day in the church choir, singing about the birth of the little baby Jesus in the manger.

"Jesus Christ was Jewish," Sharon says.

"He was not!"

Kim learned in Sunday School class that Jesus lived in the land of the Jews. If he were Jewish surely she would have learned that too.

"His name was Yehoshuah in Hebrew, or Joshua in English." Sharon says.

"I would have known if he had a different name."

"Jesus is the Greek translation of Yehoshuah. Jesus, Yehoshuah, Joshua are all the same name, only in different languages."

The BOOM makes them jump, the first thunder followed by another and another.

Sharon says, "Are those the tanks firing?"

Kim's head throbs. *The pool of blood grows larger and larger. The clerk slumps against the counter.*

"Put on the radio," Sharon says. "Let's try to drown those sounds out."

Kim yanks at the radio knob. "People Got to Be Free" by the Rascals blares out of the box.

"What an appropriate song," Sharon says.

"What do you mean?"

"Our husbands are training to go off to war to free the Vietnamese from Communism."

If only Jim didn't have to be one of the Crusaders!

✡ ✡ ✡

The night training exercise is successfully over. Thank heavens! Sharon and Kim are relaxing at the Officers County Club pool the next day. Sharon reads that book again.

"I told Jim about your book," Kim says to Sharon. "He says I don't have to believe it."

"You don't have to believe the Germans killed six million Jews?" Sharon asks.

Kim stares down at the blanket they share. "He said I didn't have to believe any of those things."

Sharon opens her mouth, shuts it, stands up. "I'm going in the water," she says.

Why is Sharon so angry? Jim said Kim didn't have to believe the book and he's educated. Why would he lie?

Sharon stands at the edge of the pool, her arms positioned for a racing dive. Then she turns back to Kim.

"You're just repeating what Jim told you – I shouldn't be angry at you." Sharon drops back onto the blanket and shades her eyes with a hand. "Let me tell you a story that illustrates what I think about the South."

"At the beginning of World War II Robert's father, an enlisted man, trained at an army post in Alabama. Robert's mother, a schoolteacher in New York, came down for summer vacation to be close to her husband. At the end of the summer she went into a general store for wrapping paper to protect a glass coffee pot."

Kim draws her knees up and clasps her arms around them, squishing herself into a protective shell. Something is about to happen in a store!

"The store owner came on to her, backing her into a corner. She cried out, 'Why are you doing this?' He replied, ''Coz ya teach niggas up there, don't ya, so I figure ya easy.'"

Heat flushes through Kim's body.

"Robert's mother ran from the store."

"That was a long time ago," Kim says, trying to think of that Alabama incident and not the one up the road from her apartment here in Kentucky.

"Are things any different now?" Sharon asks, then without waiting for an answer she strides to the edge of the pool and this time does dive in.

At least no one got killed in the Alabama store Kim thinks. Although that started out the same – a man coming on to a married woman.

Sex – the root of so much. Growing up Kim didn't know anything about sex. Certainly the foster parents never said anything to her and school health class didn't discuss the topic.

One day at age 16 she cleaned the living room of a foster home, taking out and dusting each book in the bookcase. A thin book hid behind larger books. The book's title – something like "The Facts of Life" – meant nothing to her. She opened the cover. The things explained inside shocked her, and her innocence vanished. She knew about sex.

If Jim went to Vietnam would he sleep with any of the women there? An AOB warrant officer classmate had announced to the table one night at the Officers Club: "A guy feels horny after killing!" Would Jim feel it his right to find release wherever he could?

Sharon had told Kim about finding letters from Robert's father fighting in Europe during World War II. "He wrote his wife about his sexual tension as well as his decision not to sleep with any other women." Then Sharon laughed. "Robert was born nine months and three days after his father returned from Europe."

Now Kim watches Sharon breaststroke the length of the pool.

Here at Ft. Knox sex isn't the only thing Kim has to worry about. Although Kim wouldn't admit it to Sharon, she had been a little nervous about going over to Wendy's for the committee meeting – the first time she'd ever been inside a black's home. Kim still remembers what one foster mother yelled when Kim's cleaning hadn't met the woman's perfection standard: "Ya clean just like a nigga!"

Now perhaps for the first time Kim thinks about Wendy, about a black person, growing up in the South, being treated like scum, the way many of the foster parents treated Kim. It was terrible, just terrible, to be treated like that – no matter what your skin color.

Kim couldn't credit herself for helping others less fortunate than herself. Growing up she didn't know anyone less fortunate than herself and her sister. Only once had Kim been able to help someone else feel better about herself.

In third grade Kim's reading partner had been a girl named Linda, an exceedingly lucky girl in Kim's eyes as she lived with her parents and younger brother. Yet one day the teacher had asked to speak to Kim after school. The teacher said that Linda's brother had "mental problems" and that Linda wanted to make up to her parents for this by being called Tom. When Kim hadn't understood what this meant, the teacher had explained that Linda wished to be the boy her parents wanted. The teacher said that the principal felt Linda's request couldn't be granted, but perhaps Linda could be called Lynn, a name that could be either for a girl or a boy.

Would Kim help this name change happen by being the first one to call Linda by the name Lynn? Kim had said yes, surprised that a child living with her parents could feel unwanted.

Now Kim thought about Patty. The little girl lived with her parents and younger brother. Yet she seemed unhappy – always out of step with what her mother wanted. Was there anything Kim could do for Patty? Or was Patty destined to be another lost soul? Forever feeling inadequate and unloved. Or at least until she married.

*President Nixon claims allied
drive into Cambodia "the most
successful operation of this
long and difficult war" ...*
June 3, 1970

SHARON – XI – June 23

*"You may use your cards to accompany gifts (but never
Christmas gifts), to issue invitations, to answer invitations,
and for messages of thanks or farewell."*

"Three diamonds," Robert says, winning the bid.

"I'm dummy again," Sharon says. "Anyone want anything?" Robert, Kim and Jim shake their heads, intent on the bridge hand.

Sharon opens the refrigerator, letting the cold air blow on her body. Before Kim and Jim arrived, Robert watched the news about the War of Attrition in Israel. The question of American Jews' loyalty to Israel had come up in the background check on Robert necessary for a security clearance for his MI branch transfer request.

Robert's high school friend Charles had told Robert about when FBI agents doing Robert's background check questioned Charles' mother, a social-register Southerner. "Would Robert put loyalty to Israel above loyalty to the U.S.?" they asked. Robert's friend didn't know what answer his mother gave – it must have been all right, though, because Robert got the branch transfer. Yet how dare the FBI agents ask such a question? American Jews are Americans first!

Although Sharon's grandfather had escaped the czar, he still faced anti-Semitism in America. His junk business had first been in a Southern Indiana small town with only two or three other Jewish families. The Klu Klux Klan burned a cross on one family's lawn sometime between the two world wars. The message: No Jews wanted. Her grandparents stayed for a few more years, then moved to another small town 50 miles away. And there her mother as a teenager had an early curfew because, as one of two Jewish families in town and the only one with children, her parents didn't want anyone to think that Jews had a "loose" daughter.

And Robert's mother in New York City in the early 1940s had a hard time getting an entry-level job because she was Jewish. Sometimes she was told: "We've already hired our one Jew." Other times she was told: "We don't hire Jews."

While Robert plays out the bridge hand, Sharon replays in her head the phone conversation she had earlier this evening with her parents.

"What's new, Sharon?" her mother asked.

Sharon had glanced over at Robert reading on the couch. "We're trying to make up our mind whether we're going to go voluntary indefinite."

"What's this 'we' business?'" her father on the extension line said. "You're not in the army, only Robert is."

Sharon doesn't answer. Instead she explains the third year commitment required in order to go to Europe first. "Mom, it will postpone Robert going to Vietnam for at least a year. And we really think the war may be over by then."

"Europe is so far away!"

Not as far as Vietnam.

After hanging up the phone, Sharon sat on the couch, recalling how a month after the ROTC Commissioning Parade, Sharon had broken it to her parents that she had fallen in love with someone committed to serving on active army duty.

"Robert's coming to visit later this summer," Sharon said after a family dinner. She was home for quarter break before going back to MSU for the summer quarter to take a full-time course load besides working full-time at the "State News" as feature editor. This was a plan that would require considerable time manipulation to pull off. But after unexpectedly gaining a whole quarter's credits by taking two poetry courses at Harvard Summer School the previous summer, she had decided she wanted to graduate a year early.

The moment had come to tell her parents after Howard had gone out with friends. She first told her parents that she would come home from school for the weekend to be here when he visited. They knew Robert only as the boy she had casually introduced at the sorority house when her parents helped her move her stuff to the apartment she had sublet with other "State News" staffers for the summer. She had said only that she and Robert had become "good friends" in the past few months.

She hadn't told her parents much about Robert before because ... because she hadn't been ready to hear their objections. Yet when she spoke to Robert last night on the phone, right before he left Philadelphia for army officers' basic training summer camp at Ft. Riley, Kansas, she had impulsively invited him to visit as he passed through Chicago on his way back to MSU. That left her no choice but to tell her parents.

As briefly as possible she had explained that he would be at Ft. Riley for the next few weeks before coming through Chicago en route to MSU where he would complete a master's in communications in one year thanks to being dually enrolled his last undergraduate quarter at MSU – and also thanks to a one-year deferment from active duty in the army.

"Active duty in the army!" her mother said.

"What kind of thing is that for a nice Jewish boy?" her father asked. "And what are Robert's long-term career goals?" her mother added.

She could read in their eyes "Can't you find a nice Jewish doctor to marry?"

How to explain Robert's army commitment to her parents, especially since Sharon herself was adamantly against the war in Vietnam? On the high school debate team she argued the topic: "How can you sacrifice Americans to save a country for democracy that doesn't have democracy now and may never have it?" Her parents attended the debates where she argued the rightness of this position and they agreed with her points.

They also were patriotic – her father served in World War II, having been called up after he finished two years of junior college. But he saw no fighting – he spent his entire army service fueling airplanes at a base in Florida. And her parents certainly understood the desire to escape repressive regimes. Except that Vietnam was halfway around the world and had seemingly so little connection to the lives of most Americans.

Once as a young child Sharon had begged to be taken to Riverview amusement park during the month of August, a time when prudent mothers would not allow their children to go. August had been the major polio-new-case month and, until Salk polio vaccine became available when Sharon was in elementary school, Riverview earned the distinction of a prime place to contract the virus. Her mother explained the dangers inherent in insisting on fun over safety. Now Sharon realized that falling in love with an army officer during the Vietnam War could be as dangerous a thrill as going to Riverview during polio season.

"Sharon! You didn't answer my question about Robert's long-term plans."

"I'm not sure what they are. Why don't you ask him when he's here?"

But before the weekend that she met Robert back in Chicago, there were several weeks at the sublet in E. Lansing. And Robert had used the sublet's address for his forwarding address while he attended Ft. Riley.

One early evening upon Sharon's return from the "State News" office she had found in the mail a regular letter-size envelope with the return address of Robert's college apartment. The addressee: LT Kenneth Rogers, APO New York.

Scrawled across the envelope: *Return to Sender. Addressee Deceased.*

The flash flood of sobs produced a runoff that soaked her blouse collar. Robert's last letter to Kenneth – it didn't reach him in time! Robert must never know.

She flew into the kitchen of the sublet house and reached for the matchbox on the sink counter. She ignited the envelope, then dropped the burning letter into the sink.

"What's that smell of smoke?" one of the housemates called down from the second floor of the house.

"I'm burning something."

"Be careful, Sharon."

Be careful. You could live your whole life being careful and then be run over by a car on a visit to St. Louis in your old age like her great-grandmother. Or you could volunteer for Vietnam and be killed before your 23rd birthday like Kenneth.

Or before your 12th.

✧ ✧ ✧

Last night Sharon had not told Robert the content of her phone conversation with her parents. She had just said everything was fine in Chicago.

Now at the club Sharon turns over onto her stomach as Kim slathers on more suntan lotion. It's close to 5 p.m. and the swimming crowd has thinned. Robert and Jim will be coming home late tonight, so she and Kim are staying at the club longer than usual.

Here she is suntanning next to a Southern Baptist who until a few weeks ago didn't even know one Jew and whose ideas on blacks are positively primitive.

Sharon flashes to the spring of 1968. In her sorority house bedroom Sharon surveys herself in the full-length mirror, checking her sleeveless lime green gabardine dress and black t-strap heels. Twenty prospective pledges will be here for the sorority rush formal dress event and she's hurrying to be downstairs.

As she fastens a pearl stud earring she hums along with the radio playing the Seekers' "Georgy Girl." They are singing the words "so fancy free" as an announcer breaks in:

"We interrupt this program with a news bulletin. The Reverend Martin Luther King Jr. has been shot and killed today in Memphis as he ...."

Martin Luther King killed! Sharon freezes, the second pearl stud halfway to her ear.

The loudspeaker cackles. "Everyone downstairs immediately. We're opening the door to our guests."

Sharon snaps off the radio, shoves in the second earring, and runs down the stairs. She wills herself to concentrate on the evening, to give these potential pledges her full attention. Then afterwards she glues herself to the sorority's single television set, both hands wadding the moist tissues.

What did Kim as a white Southerner think when she heard about Martin Luther King? Did she clap, the way some white Southerners reportedly did, or didn't she pay any attention to his death? Sharon doesn't dare ask – they have stayed off controversial topics since Kim reported Jim's reaction to the book "While Six Million Died."

"Can we get you both a drink?" a voice above Sharon says.

Mark Williamson stands there in a tight-fitting bathing suit, water dripping down his legs. *Water dripping down his legs.* Sharon last saw Mark at the end of the summer after senior year of high school. He stood on the raft in the middle of the quarry, water dripping down his legs, as she said good-bye and dove into the water to swim to shore. She hadn't looked back.

When she doesn't answer Mark says, "This is Wayne Sawyer," gesturing to his friend also in a wet bathing suit.

The man smiles at Sharon. "Who's your friend?"

"We're busy," Sharon says. At her side Kim stiffens.

The men pull up chairs. "It turns out we're stuck here longer than we expected," Mark says, stretching out his legs. "Haven't seen you at the club at night recently."

"Our husbands have been busy studying," Sharon says. "We've been home with them."

The other man says "Your husbands." He looks up. "Might these two be they?"

Robert and Jim are walking towards them! Robert smiles. Jim's face flushes purple.

Kim rushes towards him as Mark and his pal quickly evacuate their chairs and head in the opposite direction.

"Jim," she says, "Jim ..."

Jim spins away from Kim and strides towards the club building. "I'll see you at home tonight," he says over his shoulder.

Sharon exhales, steps closer to Robert. "What are you doing here?"

"We were given a break before the next class. Jim and I came over to grab something to eat."

Sharon says, "Kim and I will go home right now. Talk to Jim. Tell him he's got it all wrong. Mark came over to say hello to me. Kim didn't even say a word to either man."

"Who's Mark?"

"A guy from my hometown."

"I'll see what I can do," Robert says, then follows after Jim.

Kim shoves suntan lotion, magazines, towels into their swim bags.

Suddenly Mark's friend is standing next to them again. The friend leans over Kim. "Honey," he says, "is your husband always this friendly?"

Kim doesn't look up. Sharon notices Kim's hands tremble although her eyes remain dry.

The man bends closer to Kim, his face inches from hers.

"Good thing your husband didn't have a gun with him."

✡ ✡ ✡

The next morning Sharon stands in her kitchenette. If only Kim had a phone! She and Kim didn't make plans for today and Sharon suspects Kim is hiding in her apartment, unwilling to go anywhere.

Last night when Robert came home Sharon met him at the door. "What happened? Did Jim calm down? What did he say?"

"He wouldn't talk about it and he wouldn't let me talk about it."

Now Sharon grabs the apartment key and heads across the overgrown field behind her building.

The weeds and long grass snap against her bare legs. The pollens tingle her eyes and nose. Please may Kim be okay, please may Kim be okay.

At the apartment door Sharon knocks.

No answer.

"Kim! Kim! Are you there? It's Sharon."

The door opens. Kim stands in the doorway, dressed in a cotton bathrobe.

Sharon says, "I came over to" – make sure you're alive? make sure you're all in one piece? – "to ask you for some sugar. I just ran out."

Kim gestures for Sharon to enter the apartment. "I don't think I can go anywhere today," Kim says. "I ... I don't feel so well."

Sharon sits down on the couch. What can she do?

Before Sharon can figure out what to say, Kim says, "Do you swear not to tell anyone what I'm about to tell you?"

Sharon nods.

"You have to swear."

"I swear."

"I've never told anyone this." Kim swats a fly off her arm. "Before we met Jim had an affair with a married woman. Now do you see?"

Regardless of what Sharon may think of this, she knows that many people wouldn't consider Jim's affair such a big deal. Sharon asks, "What does that have to do with you if it was before you and Jim met?"

Kim clasps her hands in her lap. "Jim is terribly afraid that I'll have an affair with someone."

"Why would he think you'd have an affair just because he once had one? It's obvious how much you love him. The other woman must not have loved her husband."

"He ... he thinks women are weak. That a woman will just fall for any man who wants her."

"Does he think that because he started the affair with the married woman?" Sharon asks.

Kim brushes tangled curls out of her eyes and swats at the fly again. "He says the woman started it. She was a waitress at a drive-in. She asked him to meet her after work. He knew she was married – her husband worked the night shift at the nearby factory."

"I still don't understand," Sharon says.

Kim stands up. "Could you wait a minute? I'd like to show you something."

Sharon puzzles the significance of Kim's story while Kim walks towards the bedroom. What is Kim really saying?

Minutes later Kim returns wearing navy blue slacks and a flower-print blouse, her hair combed. She holds a frame out to Sharon.

Sharon takes the cheap metal frame in her hands. There is no glass over the picture.

"These were my parents."

Sharon knows that Kim's farmer parents were killed in a car accident, knows that the only family Kim has is a younger sister back home. That's all she knows.

What can she say? Looking at a picture of a man and woman who would not live to see their children grow up, who would not know whether their farm would ever provide a decent living, who would not know the name of the elected president every four years since they died. Who would not know about the Vietnam War.

"There's a family resemblance," Sharon says. "Do you have a photo of your sister too?"

Kim takes back the frame and leaves the room again, returning with an unframed school photo. "This is her senior year picture. We do look alike."

"She's as pretty as you are." Two spots of pink dab Kim's cheeks.

Sharon hands the picture back. "Thanks for showing me these pictures."

Tears trickle down Kim's cheeks as she sits next to Sharon. "I haven't ever shown anyone that photo of my parents except for Jim. I don't talk about my parents. I ... I don't want people to feel sorry for me."

"Why did you decide to show it to me now?"

Kim wipes away the tears with her hands. "I wanted you to understand why Jim is so important to me – no matter what he does. He is the only one I have. I mean, I've always taken care of my sister, she's never really helped me. Jim is the only person who takes care of me, who truly loves me for me. I have to understand his anger, why he's so ... suspicious of me having ... sex with someone else."

Say nothing, Sharon tells herself. Jim, as Kim has just pointed out, is all she has. Sharon has no right to say that Jim's obsessive behavior is abnormal. Sharon says, "What can I do to help?"

Kim shakes her head. "He'll calm down. Maybe I shouldn't go with you to the pool."

"It's so hot!"

"Right now I don't want to do anything that will upset him."

Sharon stands up. "Let's go use the phone at my apartment. I want to call Wendy and Donna and see if they'll meet us at the bowling alley. It should be air conditioned and there's safety in numbers."

Kim stands up too. "Do you still need the sugar?" she says.

✡ ✡ ✡

An hour later all four of them place their rented bowling balls in the ball holder in their lane as Donna says, "I have some good news."

Oh, oh. Is Donna going to tell the others about her husband's Vietnam exemption? "What is it?" Sharon asks.

"I'm pregnant."

"How wonderful! Terrific!" Kim and Wendy say.

Sharon hesitates. Donna's awfully good at coming out with shocking statements. Yet there's no comparing the announcement of the death of her first husband with the announcement of being pregnant by her second husband.

"That's so exciting!" Sharon says. "When are you due?"

"January."

"What does Jerry think?" Kim asks.

"He's pleased."

Wendy hugs Donna. "I'm so happy for you. Have you thought about names yet?"

Is that pain in Donna's eyes? Is she thinking of her first husband?

"No, we haven't," Donna says.

Sharon says, "Who wants to bowl first?"

Donna goes first, followed by Kim, Wendy and Sharon. Kim is a good bowler, and Wendy and Donna are pretty good too. Sharon is lousy, although that's to be expected. She's only bowled perhaps three other times in her life.

They finish a game and decide to bowl another one. Donna heads towards the restrooms, and Wendy and Kim follow her. Sharon walks towards the rental counter to buy a Coke.

The tap on her shoulder spins her around. It's Mark Williamson, again.

"Are you following me?" she says.

"Hey, there're only so many places to go on this post when you're killing time. When the sun gets too hot at the pool, this is a good place to hang out."

Mark waves his hand in the direction of the restrooms as Sharon hands money to the clerk.

"You've brought reinforcements today. Do you need that much protection from me?"

Sharon looks at Mark. Instead of the man in front of her now she sees the boy to whom she once said good-bye.

"Sharon," he says, then hesitates.

Out of the corner of her eye she spots the other women exiting the restrooms. She has to get away from Mark before Kim spots him.

"I have to go," she says, and flees back to the bowling lane.

KIM – VII – June 28

"Remember, a gentleman calls on all adult members of a household, but a lady never calls on a man, so, she is calling only on the female members of the family."

"Hurry up, we're going to be late," Jim yells as Kim packs their picnic food into the grocery bag.

Pain stabs above her left eye – his voice still echoes his anger from the pool four days ago.

She doesn't recall the drive back to her apartment from the club or whether she said anything to Sharon. She only remembers standing in the living room reliving those horrible seconds.

What did that man Wayne say about Jim? "*Good thing your husband didn't have a gun with him.*"

The gun.

She had run into the bedroom and yanked open the drawer. It crashed onto the floor, tipping the unsteady night table and sending the photo frame skittering over the edge. The glass shattered when the frame hit the floor.

She grabbed the gun, looked around. What should she do? Where should she hide it?

He'd check. He did every night. Even if he didn't go for it the moment he got home, he'd know soon enough she'd done something with it.

Take the bullets out. That's it! If he checked, the gun would be there. If he squeezed the trigger ...

She stared at the gun, seeing in her mind's eye a man, surely her father, sitting at a kitchen table cleaning a gun. He holds it out to her, saying she can never touch it without him, it can kill her. "Guns can be darn dangerous," he says. "Never treat 'em lightly."

A gun hadn't killed her father – a car had. Yet she believed her father's words. A gun could kill her. She took the bullets out.

She hadn't been so anxious, so fearful that something terrible was going to happen, since ... yes, since that night she and her sister waited – and waited and waited.

Headlights appeared in the living room window. Then the car door slammed, the apartment door clicked open.

Jim threw his army gear on the floor and walked towards her.

Seated at the table, she flinched.

"Thought you'd be asleep. Had a busy day, didn't you?" he said.

"I always wait up for you."

He was inches from her. "Not because you don't trust me. You can always trust me. It's you who can't be trusted."

How could he think this? Kim's hands, already clasped together, squeezed tighter.

"Jim, ask Sharon. Just ask Sharon what really happened."

"It's a little late to go calling. And besides, she'll stick up for you."

He strode towards the bedroom. Pain jabbed above her eyes; she made herself follow him.

He jerked open the replaced drawer. Rainbow colors blurred her vision.

He lifted the gun out of the drawer, twisted towards her ...

Then he grabbed a pillow and the blanket off the bed. "I'll sleep on the couch tonight."

In the morning she didn't come out of the bedroom until Sharon knocked on the door.

Then that evening Jim gave her the silent treatment. Even when he returned to their bed, he slept with his back to her. This continued for two more days with all meals eaten in silence.

Now this morning he spoke only to remind her of the AOB class picnic. A classmate had an uncle with a farm nearby. The entire class and their wives had agreed to meet there.

In the car Jim listens to the Beach Boys sing "Sloop John B." Heat pricks her skin, her hair clumps to her forehead. Jim turns down a back road as bleak as the one she and Sharon drove to Louisville. The one on which she wished she'd brought the gun.

The gun. This morning, when Jim brushed his teeth in the bathroom, she checked the night table drawer.

The gun was back. Still no bullets. Hadn't Jim noticed the missing bullets? Or did he notice but not trust himself with a loaded gun?

"Everyone will be talking about going vol indef," Jim says to the windshield. "That's probably the whole purpose of this darn picnic. And I sure as hell don't want to discuss my plans with a bunch of men I hardly know."

Kim doesn't risk answering him. Instead she fans herself with a paper napkin from the picnic supplies. Fans were all they had in their first apartment, not even an unreliable air conditioner like here at Ft. Knox. They'd been lucky to get the apartment on campus. Jim had known someone who'd known someone and their name miraculously moved to the top of the list of married housing. She and Jim set up housekeeping there right after their small church wedding – a brief ceremony followed by cake and a bottle of inexpensive champagne for the toasts. Jim's parents weren't going to pay for anything more elaborate and she had no one on her side to even offer.

Ahead cars line both sides of the dirt road. Jim wedges their car in between a Corvair and a Chevy.

Wrinkles crumple her pink cotton dress thanks to the heat and the pressure of the bag on her lap. She smooths the wrinkles with one hand while wrapping her other arm around the picnic food.

The bag escapes her grasp and slumps to the ground.

Red strawberries spill out – *the pool of blood widening on the store's checkout counter.* She freezes.

Jim stuffs the strawberries back into the bag and thrusts the bag into her arms. Her breath comes in short gasps.

Several yards away long metal tables have been set up under oak trees whose abundant leaves offer shade. The scent of honeysuckle beckons from shrubs edging the tables.

As a young child Kim loved honeysuckle with its bright scarlet trumpet-shaped flowers. She and her sister would pluck and twist the flowering vines into crowns. They imagined themselves modern-day Cinderellas whose princes had carried them off to beautiful castles set high atop enchanted mountains where servants fulfilled their every wish – and where they never had to iron or clean house for anyone else ever again.

Then one day honeysuckle betrays Kim. Lulled into such wonderful visions, she doesn't see the Kruger boy sneaking up on the other side of the shrubs. He reaches his arms through the shrubs and pulls her panties down around her ankles.

Red splotches cover her panties! This surprises even the Kruger boy, who races off screaming, "Kim made blood! Kim made blood!" Kim pulls up her panties and flees with her sister to their foster home.

The foster mother explains to Kim, "You're not dying. It's natural to start at your age."

Since then the bright red honeysuckle flowers always remind her of the red splotches. One whiff of the sweet blooms floods her with shame.

Robert waves from where he stands with the other men around a keg of beer, and Jim joins Robert. Kim holds the bag with both arms and reaches the tables where the women watch over the food.

"What are the men talking about?" Kim asks Sharon.

Sharon shrugs. "Whether to go vol indef."

Jim's probably boiling right now, annoyed and angry about all the talking. "I joined ROTC to do my part," he said when he first told her about his commitment. "A Southerner has a military tradition to uphold." She had been tearful, afraid of everything connected with the army. "It's only for two years," he said, taking her into his arms. "We'll be entitled to officer housing, and, with careful planning, we should be able to even save a little money."

Kim moves towards her husband. Perhaps she can distract him, prevent him from getting upset about the men's discussion.

She has almost reached Jim when she hears Nelson say: "I'm thinking of going RA."

Regular Army!

"It's a good opportunity for me. A guaranteed job and built-in career advancement."

Kim glances at Jim. His face dark, as if he can't believe what he's heard, as if someone has told him a whopper.

"Maybe the army doesn't want you," Jim says. "The officer corps is mainly Southern whites. We're the ones who've got a tradition to uphold. You ... blacks sure don't."

Kim's stomach flip flops. How could Jim be so cruel?

Before Nelson can answer, Robert slings an arm around him.

"I'd take this guy any time," Robert says to Jim. "He's one of the best in our class."

Jerry and some of the others nod.

Jim strides away from the men; he hasn't seen her. She turns to follow him.

Wendy stands a couple of feet away, her hands clenched at her sides, her body as stiff as a shirt left out to dry too long. She has heard what Jim said!

Poor Wendy! First Nelson's announcement about going Regular Army – did she even know about that? – then Jim's terrible words.

Kim's legs carry her to Wendy. "Come taste my corn bread," Kim says. "It's the Southern dish I make best."

Wendy stares at her. Then she blinks. "I'd like that."

Kim doesn't take Wendy's arm – she's not comfortable doing that. Instead she smiles encouragement, leading the way over to the picnic things. She hands Wendy a piece of corn bread.

Sharon stops chatting with Donna to ask Kim, "Did you eavesdrop? I'm dying to know what they're saying."

Dying. Isn't that what they are all considering? Whether going voluntary indefinite will reduce the men's chances of dying in Vietnam?

PART III – COMMITMENT

In St. Louis an estimated 40,000 workers and veteran groups members march in support of administration's Vietnam policies ...
June 7, 1970

WENDY– V – June 28

"Cards for first and second lieutenants are the same, 'Lieutenant' being correct for both of them."

"Honey, I'm sorry to ask you not to do the play. You do see my point, don't you?" Nelson says as they undress for bed in the trailer that night after the picnic. "It could be held against me that you're in a play poking fun at the army."

"Nelson, this is the American army. It's not the South. Things are different here."

He slides into bed. "This is important to me – even if I don't go Regular Army."

Regular Army! She presses her fingers against her chest. A week from tomorrow the men must declare their intentions. And ever since the picnic earlier today she has wanted to get up the courage to ask Nelson about what he said to the other men. Perhaps she heard him wrong.

Now he has said it to her.

She faces him, her nipples pushing out the thin cotton of her nightgown. "Nelson, you said if I was against it, you wouldn't consider going Regular Army."

Nelson wraps his arms around her, pressing his nude body into hers. "Sugar, I'm just trying to do what's best for us." His lips clamp onto hers, his tongue probing for an opening.

He seals shut her mouth with a passionate kiss, ending the discussion before it's begun.

The next morning Wendy parks her car in front of Kim's apartment. Her hands twitch as she drops the car keys into her purse. She has the prepared speech as memorized as her lines for the play – the lines she won't be reciting. Will the women understand?

She has to trust her husband – she owes it to her parents. The evening of her parents' visit to the trailer her mama and papa said good-bye after the fried chicken dinner. Her papa hugged her, then whispered in her ear, "We will never, ever understand why our son was taken from us. We don't want to lose another son. Take care of Nelson."

Kim opens the door to Wendy's knock. "Sharon and Donna are already here."

Wendy isn't surprised. She dawdled, straightening things in the small trailer, things that didn't need straightening because there's no room to put anything except back in its place.

"We have a lot to practice." Sharon says.

Wendy stays in the center of the room. She inhales. "I ... I can't."

"You can't practice today?" Sharon asks. "Do you have a doctor's appointment or something?"

"I can't ... be in the play at all." There, she's said it.

"What do you mean?" Donna asks.

Wendy swivels her wedding ring around her finger. What did she and Nelson rehearse?

She says, "Nelson is afraid he can get in trouble for it."

The others stare.

"He thinks ... Nelson's thinking about going Regular Army." Their expressions don't change. Maybe Kim told them what she overheard. "He has to be accepted into the program so he's been trying to do really well here. Because he's black, I mean we're black, this play could be held against him. It makes fun of the army."

"The army in 1776," Sharon says.

"It's really the army now."

Wendy sinks into the armchair. "I don't know how to explain this. I understood when Nelson explained it to me. I just can't seem to explain it now."

Donna pats her hand. "I understand. Now that I'm married to an Anglo I don't feel so vulnerable. When I was growing up, the only Puerto Rican kid in my classes at the army post schools, I felt I had to do everything right. If I missed the volleyball, they would think Puerto Rican kids weren't good at sports. If I couldn't do well on a spelling test, they would think all Puerto Ricans couldn't speak English."

Donna does understand! "And Nelson feels that if the army gets angry at this play, they won't punish your husbands. They'll use him, the black, as a scapegoat. And he doesn't want this to hurt his time in the army, whether he goes RA or not. He's trying to prove he's as good as the ... whites."

Sharon nods. "Wendy, I'm truly sorry to have put you in this position. We can give up the play and do something about fashion or etiquette or ...."

"I want you to do the play," Wendy says. "It's funny and different and everyone will like it. I just can't be in it."

Sharon looks at Kim and Donna. "What do you think?"

"I want to go on with the play," Donna says. "There will only be women there, no men, and I don't think even the senior women will be upset. If they are, don't army regulations require them to be gracious even when they disapprove?"

Wendy laughs with the others. All those silly rules in "Mrs. Lieutenant" – they could use some in their own favor.

Sharon turns to Kim. "Are you comfortable going on with the play?"

Kim nods.

"We'll go on as planned," Sharon says. "I'll just change things around so that we can do it with three people."

Wendy stands. "I'm sorry again. And I'll be leaving."

Sharon reaches an arm towards her. "Oh, no. I'm going to make the changes right now. At the luncheon you can be a guest. For now we're going to put you to work as our prompter."

✻ ✻ ✻

When Wendy gets back to the trailer after the rehearsal, she leafs through her copy of "Mrs. Lieutenant," looking for answers to her present problems.

On one page she reads: "Your husband's job should never be discussed. Don't relay tales of business personalities to your friends. If your husband is fortunate enough to have a wife with whom he can air his problems, be sure that you don't betray his trust by discussing his affairs with others."

Should she have withdrawn from the play without saying why? Did she need to tell the others about Nelson's fears?

It's easier to tell the truth than say nothing. This way it's Nelson who forced her to stop, not she herself. She hasn't abandoned her friends. They understand that loyalty to her husband has to come first.

"Mrs. Lieutenant" is so strange! Two paragraphs after this serious instruction comes the following: "Restrict your telephone calls to five minutes. Make your appointments over the phone and do your real chatting in person. Having long conversations on the telephone is a bad and hard to break habit, but your accomplishments will certainly be greater if you can overcome it."

Wendy turns to the last page: "Be gracious to and understanding of your friends as they too learn and mature. People more often need help than criticism."

Wendy relates to this advice – it's something her parents have taught her.

"To a truly gracious person, there will be many times when she feels the proper thing to do will be the incorrect one. Rely upon her judgment and be gracious yourself by accepting her ways when her manner of doing things is different from yours."

And then the final paragraph: "Sometimes it is better to do the wrong thing graciously than the proper thing rudely."

Maybe she did the wrong thing graciously instead of the proper thing rudely. If Nelson is upset by what she said, she could show him this page.

She stares at the booklet. If Nelson goes RA she'll have to live by these rules for the next 20 or 30 years. Will it be any harder than living by white folks' rules?

Senate subcommittee discloses
U.S. has paid Thailand $50
million annually since 1966
to send troops to South
Vietnam ...
June 7, 1970

KIM – VIII – July 1

"If a soldier salutes you after recognizing your military car
tag, smile and thank him for the courtesy."

Kim sets the table for dinner after she drops
Sharon off. The Beatles singing "Day Tripper" keep
her company. Since the picnic two days ago Jim has
been speaking to her, and she's trying very hard not
to do anything that could upset him again.

Earlier she and Sharon drove through the troop
area to borrow an MP helmet from Robert's school
friend Ken Tottenham. Sharon promised that she
would run into the building for only a minute. Then
they stopped at the hospital clinic to borrow a white
doctor's coat thanks to Sharon's friend Dr. Fred
Weinstein. Even here Kim stayed in the car.

Yet she hadn't stayed in the car at their next two
stops. As they approached Ft. Knox Sharon had said,
"Getting the props should take no time at all. Then
we'll have the rest of the afternoon. Why don't we

drive over to Donna's apartment and wish her good luck on her pregnancy – show we're really happy for her? Then on the way back we can stop at Wendy's trailer and show her we don't have any hard feelings about her dropping out of the play."

Kim shook her head. "Jim may not approve of my paying a social visit to Wendy. It's not the same as going to a committee meeting there."

"You're probably uncomfortable doing this for the first time," Sharon said. "If I were feeling lonely, I'd sure want someone to show support for me."

And Sharon had been right. Donna and Wendy had both been pleased to see them.

Donna chatted about plans for the baby. "My mama's making maternity clothes. Then she'll start on clothes for the baby."

"How will she know what kind of clothes to make?" Kim asked.

"She'll make newborn clothes that can be worn by a girl or boy. Then once the baby's born she'll make more clothes."

Kim clenched her hands together. Donna had a mother who could sew maternity and baby clothes, who would be excited to hold her infant grandchild, who had always been present in her daughter's life! Something an orphan could never have.

Kim felt relief when Sharon said to Donna, "We have to go. We're stopping by Wendy's on the way home."

When Wendy saw them on her doorstep her face lit up like a Christmas tree. "Come in, come in," she said.

With less than a week before the men had to decide, the conversation naturally turned to the question of voluntary indefinite. "I told my parents about going vol indef," Sharon said. "Europe sounds so far away to them."

Kim's parents – the two people in her broken picture frame.

Her parents didn't own a camera, of course. One day a traveling salesman knocked on their farmhouse door. Her parents said there was nothing they needed. Only later did she realize there was probably nothing they could afford. The man offered to take a family photograph in exchange for a meal. "We don't need no photograph," her mother said, "but you're more 'n welcome to stay for supper."

When the man left, she and Diane tagged along behind him to the yard gate. Her parents stood together in front of the house. At the gate the man turned around and snapped a photo. Her parents had been surprised, didn't pose or smile into the camera. When the photograph unexpectedly arrived in the mail they laughed at their expressions.

Her mother said she hoped she didn't look that bad. Her father said it was foolishness. Kim stared at the photo. In her parents' faces she could see pieces of herself and her sister. She had her father's eyes, her sister had her mother's. And there was something else in the faces, something that as an adult Kim has considered over and over – hopelessness, resignation. As if, as the photo was snapped, her parents foresaw their brief future.

"Can I have this picture? Can I?" she had asked. Her mother walked over to the cabinet where she kept the family papers. From a small drawer she pulled out a metal picture frame displaying the Lord's Prayer. "Got this in Bible class," her mother said. "This here photo should fit in it." And she placed the photo on top of the prayer, saying, "The prayer's still here too in case you ever have need of it."

Her sister cried. She wanted a picture too. Her mother said, "There'll be time for more pictures." There hadn't been time.

The doorbell rings. Kim opens it to Susanna and her children.

"We had to come this way to run an errand. Thought we'd say hello."

Kim hasn't seen the Norrises since the church picnic. The red welt on Patty's cheek that day still haunts Kim. For the little girl's sake she'll be civil to Susanna now.

Kim offers Cokes all around and Susanna accepts a Coke for herself and one for Patty – "Billy Jr.'s too young."

"Are you settlin' into army life?" Susanna asks.

Patty jumps up from the couch to take her Coke bottle from her mother. The movement knocks her mother's bottle out of her mother's hand, spilling part of the Coke.

"Patty, look what you've done!" Susanna smacks the child across her back.

Pain stabs Kim's eye. Patty's expression doesn't change.

"It was an accident," Kim says. "I'll just get a rag to wipe up."

"I swear," Susanna says, "this child only responds when I yell at her or hit her. I end up havin' to hit her all the time."

Does Kim's face betray her horror? She can remember all the smacks she got from foster parents when she wasn't quick enough or when she spilled something or when they were just feeling downright ornery. She once tried to protect her sister from a punishment that by rights should have been Kim's. All Kim got for her attempt at heroism was both of them sent to bed without dinner. Her sister cried that night that "it would be better to be smacked. The pain goes away pretty quick. Hunger doesn't."

Kim motions Patty to follow her. Susanna doesn't say anything as she's busy getting Billy Jr.'s bottle out of the diaper bag. The little girl has tears in her eyes as she follows Kim into the kitchen.

"I'll get you a cookie," Kim says. She picks up the metal cookie canister and tries to pry the lid off.

The canister slips from her hands and crashes to the linoleum floor, the noise so unexpected she jumps. Patty doesn't move.

Kim looks at Patty. She considers the times Patty responds and the times she doesn't.

"Patty," she says in her normal voice, "do you want a cookie?"

The little girl doesn't answer.

"Patty," she says in a very loud voice, "do you want a cookie?"

"ooie," Patty says.

"Susanna," Kim says, pulling Patty out of the kitchen. "This child is deaf."

"That can't be."

Kim describes the canister and her experiment. Susanna only shakes her head.

Kim walks to the front door. "Patty, come here."

The child doesn't move.

"See, she's just willful," Susanna says.

Kim leads Patty to the door, facing her away from it. She points at the far wall so that Patty will keep her eyes there.

Then, behind Patty, Kim opens the door and slams it shut.

Patty does not react.

"She should have jumped," Kim says. "She didn't even turn around to see what happened."

For a moment Susanna doesn't respond. Then she sets Billy Jr. on the floor and kneels down in front of Patty and hugs her. "You're deaf. My child is deaf."

Tears wet Susanna's cheeks. "All those times I hit her to get her to listen. She couldn't hear me. Oh, God, forgive me."

Now tears well up in Kim's eyes. She runs into the kitchen for tissues, then bends down over Susanna and Patty. "The important thing is to get her help now."

"ooie?" Patty asks.

Kim nods at Patty to show she understands. Then turns back to Susanna. "And the way her speech sounds, her hearing problem has affected her speech ability. She needs help for both."

Susanna wipes her eyes with her hands and picks up Billy Jr. "I'm goin' to drive over to the clinic right now and see what can be done." She grabs the diaper bag and her purse and motions Patty to follow her.

At the door she turns back to Kim. "Thank you. Thank you very much." And they are out the door.

What a wonderful feeling! Kim may not have been able to help her sister and herself when they were young, but she has helped this little child.

The promised cookie! She runs out the door with the canister, handing Patty a cookie through the open car window.

Patty waves good-bye, the cookie crumbling down her dress.

Poor Patty. She may always be different.

Being different. That's what Kim hates most. Every year in elementary school when they made presents for Mother's Day and Father's Day – painted rocks for paperweights and decorated orange juice cans for pencil holders – Kim pretended to be making these gifts for her parents. She couldn't bear telling the other kids that she was an orphan, different, even if they knew. Each year she wrapped her handiwork in color tissue paper – and dumped the gifts in a trash bin.

She could have given the gifts to her sister – Diane would have been thrilled at any gift, no matter how ugly and misshapen – but Kim couldn't stand seeing the gifts around. They would be constant reminders of the horrible truth about Kim and Diane – orphans, orphans, forever orphans.

Kim checks her watch. Jim will be home soon. Tomorrow morning she'll bake a pie. She's good at pies – always made at least one for every church social. All the ladies at church complimented her.

At church they always pray for the widows and orphans. Kim has already been one of these at an early age; she doesn't want to be the other.

✡ ✡ ✡

An hour later their car stops outside the apartment.

The door bangs open as she reaches for the doorknob. One look at Jim's face tells her that he knows about the trip to the troop area. How? They were at the MP's office for less than two minutes. Just enough time for Sharon to take the helmet and say thank you.

"You were with Sharon today, weren't you?" he says, his hands clenched at his sides.

She nods.

"Robert said Sharon was going to pick up an MP's helmet in the troop area. You went with, didn't you?"

Should she lie? Robert may not have known she was going. Jim's probably guessing.

"Didn't you?" he repeats.

Her shoulders sag. She's tired of being afraid. Afraid of not being loved. Afraid of being abandoned. Like Patty.

Unlike Patty, she's old enough to stand up for herself.

She raises her head. "I went with Sharon. She ran into the MP office for less than one minute while I stayed in the car. No one came near the car, no one spoke to me, and I did not call or wave out the window at a passing soldier."

He strides towards their bedroom. The gun! He's getting the gun!

The toilet flushes, the water gurgling.

Jim comes back, his hands empty.

"Let's have dinner now. We're going to the club to meet some of the others."

They eat in silence again.

✿ ✿ ✿

The music blares as they enter the Country Club. Jim walks towards the bar where Robert stands. Kim accepts the chair Sharon offers. Wendy and Donna sit at the next table.

"Isn't this nice the men wanted to get together tonight?" Sharon says.

"Is there a reason?"

"They're celebrating a reprieve."

Kim looks around the room. "A reprieve? From what?"

"Somebody – they don't know who – cheated on a test they took today. Robert says it was probably one of the helicopter pilots; they're always pulling stunts like that. The instructor threatened to give them all weekend duty, then relented."

There's shouting at the bar. It's Jim's voice.

"I know who cheated, even if he won't admit it." Jim swings around from the bar and faces the tables, pointing at Nelson. "It's the nigger."

Kim sees Jerry spring up from his seat and stand alongside Robert next to Jim.

Robert says, "We all know who probably did it – one of the guys who always goofs off. Nelson takes everything seriously; he's one of the best guys in our class."

"And your language is inappropriate, Jim," Jerry says.

Jim strides up to Nelson with Robert and Jerry right behind him. Nelson stands with his hands clenched at his side.

"I'm telling you the nigger did it. Wanted to show he knows more than anyone."

Kim wants to go to Jim, tell him to stop this right now! Her feet don't move.

"Come on, nigger. Don't you want to fight me?"

"Let's go outside and cool down," Jerry says, twisting Jim's arm behind his back.

Robert grabs Jim's other arm, then says "Wait a minute" to Jerry. Robert reaches into Jim's pocket and takes out the car keys, tossing them to Sharon. He says, "Go home with Kim now. I'll bring Jim home after he's cooled off."

Sharon stands, snatching her purse off the table.

Kim is about to follow Sharon when instead Kim says, "I have to do something first."

Now Kim's feet move. She walks up to Wendy standing with Donna's arm around her. "I wish I could take it all back," Kim says.

Tears stream down Wendy's face. Kim feels tears on her own face.

"I'm sorry," Kim says, then follows Sharon out of the room.

✼ ✼ ✼

In bed Kim hugs the blanket pulled up to her neck. She and Sharon did not speak on the drive home. Now she waits for Jim.

His voice reaches her in the dark as he enters the bedroom.

"I'm not going vol indef so they'll be sending me to Vietnam after a couple of months of troop duty. I'm not waiting. I'm going to volunteer for combat duty."

"You're ... you're going to Vietnam? Why? Why?" The pain in her head jabs, the colors zig zag across her vision.

"We Southerners have a military tradition to uphold," he says. "Can't let these kikes and niggers and Yankees do our jobs for us. Have to show them that the South should have won the war. We're not pussies."

Kim uses the pillow to stifle her sobs.

✼ ✼ ✼

The next morning Kim begs off going to the pool when Sharon comes by, using menstrual cramps as an excuse. Kim says nothing about the night before at the Officers Club nor does Sharon.

Although Kim feels terrible about Wendy and Nelson, about what Jim said, the tears today are for herself. Her husband going to Vietnam. How will she survive?

Even with the tears she tries to be productive today. Starts one letter after another to her sister, then rips up each attempt. Some too honest, some too dishonest.

She takes out the afghan she's crocheting for Diane. If she can't write to her, at least she can do something for her. The hook becomes tangled in the yellow yarn every other stitch.

Now she has dinner ready. Jim's favorite. Fried chicken and homemade biscuits. But a favorite dinner can't change Jim's mind – he believes he's always right. Jim grew up in a home that revolved around him. Jim got straight A's! Jim scored the winning touchdown! Kim pictures the conversations around the family dinner table. His younger sister's accomplishments relegated to the expected, Jim's elevated to the extraordinary.

Kim twists the crochet yarn in her hands. She knows that, even if she doesn't believe everything he does is right, he would still expect her to go along with his Vietnam decision. She's been brought up to believe that husbands know best no matter how wrong those husbands might actually be. Certainly she, uneducated and without any family of her own, can't hope to go against his decision.

She imagines her papa appearing at the apartment door, gun in hand, demanding that Jim not go to Vietnam. "I didn't let my little girl marry you so she could become a widow." And if only her mama could send Jim home-cooked Southern treats, enticing him to come on home.

Being an orphan doesn't just mean being an "orphan" – a name to cry yourself to sleep with every night in a foster home, but being a person without family for all time.

The sound of the car engine being turned off announces Jim's arrival. She stands up, brushes her tears with the backs of her hands, then walks to the door.

Jim bangs it open. "Where the hell were you today?"

Her mouth opens. Nothing comes out. Where has she been? Home crying. "I was ... I was home all day. I have bad cramps."

"Is that your story? Can't you come up with a better one?"

What is he talking about?

"Don't you have anything to say for yourself?" His angry face is inches away from her.

"What should I say?"

"Why weren't you with Sharon today at the club? Who were you off with?"

"Who was I with?"

"That's what I asked."

"I wasn't with anyone. I was home all day. I ... I worked on the afghan for my sister."

"Don't lie to me. I know you were with a man."

Jim's face flushes with the ugliest shade of purple she's ever seen. His eyes will pop out of his face any minute, landing at her feet and rolling away, becoming marbles for Squeaky to chase.

She sinks to the floor as her knees fold under her. "I swear, Jim, I swear on my sister's life, that I was home all day alone. That I was not with another man today, or ever before, or ever in the future." The tears plop onto her hands.

He strides down the hall. In a moment he's back.

He has the gun!

"I'll kill you if you're ever with another man. I promise you, Kim, I'll kill you."

President Nixon receives
optimistic report from
11-person commission he
sent to study Cambodian and
South Vietnamese war zones …
June 10, 1970

SHARON – XII – July 3

"If you accompany your husband to a unit party where soldiers are present, you should arrive a little late and stay only a short while."

Sharon locks the apartment door behind her. The cars parked below sizzle on an asphalt frying pan.

Kim isn't due to pick her up for another half hour. At least Sharon expects Kim to pick her up at the usual time. Even though yesterday Kim begged off going to the pool when Sharon came by to pick Kim up, she didn't say anything about canceling today.

Even this early in the day the apartment feels like a blast furnace. Outside there might be a breeze. She'll walk at a slow pace to Kim's apartment and get there before Kim leaves.

How did people get along before telephones? Of course, in all Sharon's favorite English novels people find somebody, a servant or a street urchin, with whom to send a handwritten note. Sharon has neither at her disposal.

Telephones, though, are not the primary invention that Sharon would miss most. That convenience is indoor plumbing – flush toilets! She hated Girl Scout camp, hated the outdoor latrines with the putrid smell. She would run down the path, do her business at lightning speed, and race back up the path to sweet-smelling civilization.

Americans take flush toilets as part of their national right. Yet what about Donna's brother, perched in a tree where even the slightest movement betraying his forward position could bring a fatal bullet? How does he go to the bathroom? War movies, the ones where the good buddies save each other against overwhelming odds, never show these things. If they did, perhaps fewer little boys would dream of going off to war to prove they are men.

Sharon tramps through the field. A patch of bluebells reminds her of the imitation bluebells on the large Marshall Field's box that Bonnie Morgen, the daughter of Sharon's mother's best friend, opened at her bridal shower Sharon attended the same weekend she had told her parents about Robert first coming to visit.

"Look, Mother," Bonnie had said, "aren't these towels beautiful!"

Farther down the restaurant banquet table Sharon twisted around to whisper to her own mother. "For heaven's sake, the way she carries on you'd think Bonnie was the first girl to ever get married," Sharon said.

Sharon's mother leaned closer. "Just because you don't approve of things like wedding showers doesn't mean you have to be rude."

"How bourgeois," Sharon mumbled, not quite loud enough for her mother to hear, then turned back to watch Bonnie unwrap more gifts.

Bonnie Morgen. Sharon's long-standing competitor in the "my daughter is the best" contest that Bonnie's mother and Sharon's mother have engaged in since the two girls were young children and the Morgen and Bloom families first became good friends.

Rainbow lights darted from the large pear-shape diamond on Bonnie's left hand as she tore into yet another package. Sharon could visualize the night Bonnie announced her engagement to her AEPhi sorority house at U of I. The same type of ceremony took place regularly at Sharon's AEPhi sorority house at MSU.

The house mother announces on the loud speaker, "Everyone come to the dining room now. There's a candle ceremony."

They all rush down the stairs dressed in their pajamas or robes, hair set in curlers, barefoot or with slippers, and stand in a circle alongside the dining room tables. Then the electric lights are turned off and a single candle lit. The sorority president passes the candle to the girl on her left and around the circle the candle goes once for good luck. Then if it stops before making a complete second circle, the girl who blows out the candle is announcing she's pinned. If the candle is on its third trip around when the lucky girl blows it out, she's engaged!

Bonnie blows the candle out on the third circuit. Everyone exclaims and hugs her. She takes her engagement ring out of her bathrobe pocket and slips it on her finger for all to admire.

Sharon could puke, particularly since Bonnie's intended is Neil Rosen, already attending law school at Northwestern. Bonnie has definitely won this contest – becoming engaged before Sharon. That's really hitting the jackpot for Mrs. Morgen.

Yet a few weeks later, now with brown hair 12 inches shorter than her dyed blond hair of last quarter, she met Robert's plane at O'Hare Airport on his way back from Ft. Riley.

At the gate the deplaning exodus included mothers with small babies, soldiers in uniform, old people, young people. Out of the corner of her eye she spotted a young man in a short-sleeve shirt and jeans, his head practically shaved.

"Robert!"

"Sharon!"

Two steps take her to him.

"I didn't recognize you with such short hair," she said.

"I didn't recognize you. What did you do to your hair?"

They walk to the luggage carousel to claim his meager army luggage.

"I really appreciate how you wrote every day – it kept me going," he said. "I'm sorry I couldn't write more. There was no time."

He wrote her four short letters in his six weeks at Ft. Riley. He did call twice, once on each weekend he'd gotten leave, when he and some other guys piled into an air-conditioned motel room and slept for two days.

At home when she brings Robert into the house her parents and Howard are gracious to him. They sit down for dinner and no one even obliquely refers to military training or the war. Until her father stands and says, "The news is on."

Robert nods his head at her father, then turns to her mother. "Thank you, Mrs. Bloom. Delicious dinner."

"Let's go out on the patio," Sharon says.

She grabs his hand. Finally a closed door separates them from her parents and Howard.

Robert recites:

Shall I compare thee to a summer's day?

Thou art more lovely and more temperate:

Sharon laughs. "You're quoting Shakespeare?"

"I've had six weeks to think," he said.

"About what?" How wrong the war is? How he wants out of his military commitment?

He took her hand. "Sharon, will you marry me?"

She hadn't expected this.

"We've only known each other a short time."

"I know what I want," Robert said.

"I love you – I really do," she said. "I just can't marry you now."

"It's Vietnam, isn't it?"

"You're a second lieutenant commissioned in infantry. Those are the men with the shortest life expectancy in Vietnam."

"Sharon ..."

She disengaged her hand. "There are flies out here. Let's go back inside."

As she now approaches the parking lot of Kim's apartment building, Sharon wipes an arm across her sweat-beaded face. Maybe staying in the apartment would have been a better idea.

Sharon spots Kim's car in front of her apartment, heat waves shimmering off it the same as all the other cars. Sharon knocks on the apartment door.

Kim doesn't answer. Sharon waits. Calls out "Kim." Then knocks again.

Not even an "I'm in the bathroom; I'll be right out" which would be heard across the small apartment and through the flimsy door.

Sharon's hands itch and her armpits clutch. Is Kim ill? Is she too sick to walk to the front door or lift her head and call out?

The laundry room! Sharon runs over to the separate building. Empty.

Sharon dashes back to the apartment and twists the doorknob. Locked. The curtains across the living room window block the view. She runs around the apartment building to the back side of Kim's apartment. Like hers, these apartment units have no back doors.

Curtains stretch across the bedroom window, but the bathroom window stands open. "Kim, Kim!" Nothing.

Firewood logs lean against the side of a tool shed. Sharon scoops some logs up and piles them at the foot of the window. She drops her purse into her swim bag and throws the bag through the window. Then she removes her sandals – useless for climbing – and throws them through the window.

She steps up carefully onto the logs so as not to get splinters in her feet, grabs hold of the window sill, and pulls herself up, her bare feet bracing against the outer wall. She swings one leg over the sill, assesses the drop zone, then swings the other leg over.

She drops into the bathroom.

On the floor an open medicine bottle tilts against the sink base. It's empty! Her hands shake.

Kim. Where's Kim?

Sharon turns left out of the bathroom and into the bedroom. She stumbles against something in the dark room.

Sharon flicks on the light switch. Kim lies on the floor, one arm stretched towards Squeaky in his cage, the other arm cradling her head.

"Kim, Kim!" Sharon shakes Kim by the shoulders. Her head rolls forward.

First aid! What has she learned in high school first aid class? Feel for a pulse. Kim's wrist – no pulse! The spot on the neck – something! Please may she be alive.

Sharon dashes into the kitchen, fills a glass with water, and runs back to the bedroom. Splashes the water on Kim's face. A slight reflex!

Hospital. Call an ambulance. No, wait.

Kim would die of embarrassment if people knew what she's done. The apartment complex might look deserted. Yet the moment Muldraugh residents hear an ambulance, they'll scurry outside. Better to keep this quiet. AND KIM DOESN'T HAVE A PHONE!

If Sharon can somehow get Kim into the car, she can drive to a hospital as fast as waiting for an ambulance. Which hospital? The only one Sharon knows is the post hospital. This might go on Jim's army record. Jim would be furious.

Fred. Dr. Fred Weinstein. He could help. How to find him? Call Judy. Ask her to reach her husband. KIM DOESN'T HAVE A PHONE!

First things first. Sharon can't lift Kim. Maybe she can drag her. Sharon runs into the bathroom and slaps on her sandals, shoves the empty pill bottle into her swim bag and hooks it over her arm. Then she runs back and places her hands under Kim's armpits.

Two good things. One, Kim wears street clothes, not a nightgown. Two, Squeaky isn't a bull dog who will devour Sharon.

Sweat pelts down Sharon's face, back, arms and legs as she tugs Kim across the living room floor. At the apartment door she remembers. NO CAR. She runs back into the bedroom. The car keys lie on the bureau top, in the same spot Robert keeps his keys.

Sharon opens the apartment front door and pulls Kim out. She props Kim against the apartment door while she opens the car door on the passenger side. Please may no one decide to come outside right now.

She drags Kim across the asphalt to the car door. Kim's slacks should protect her legs from the blazing pavement.

How to lift Kim up into the seat? People are supposed to have Herculean strength in life-threatening circumstances. Sharon doesn't. "Kim, Kim," she says. "Please, please, wake up."

Sharon slaps Kim across the face. She has seen this in a movie. Maybe it will work. One eye opens. Sharon slaps Kim again. The other eye opens.

"Kim." Sharon shakes her. "You have to help me. Please help me get you in the car."

No response. Sharon places her hands under Kim's armpits. She's not as heavy as before. Perhaps the slight consciousness makes Kim less of a deadweight.

Sharon pushes and pushes. Kim's upper body rolls onto the seat, her head sliding beneath the steering wheel. Sharon straightens Kim into an upright position and slings her legs in front of her. Sharon fastens the lap belt around Kim's waist and rolls down the window on her side. The car feels like a fondue pot of bubbling oil.

Sharon slides into the driver's side, fastens her lap belt, and rolls down her window. The steering wheel burns her fingers. She grabs the towel out of her swim bag to hold the wheel.

She drives out of the parking lot, then around the block to her complex. In front of her apartment she jumps out of the car and dashes up the outer stairs. Inside her apartment she grabs the phone. With all those children Judy should be home at this time in the morning. The number appears on a list with other Ft. Knox numbers next to the phone.

A young child answers. "May I please speak to your mother?" The receiver bangs against the wall as the child calls "Mommy, Mommy."

"Yes?" Judy says.

Sharon gulps tears back into her throat, then tells Judy what has happened and why she doesn't want to take Kim to the army hospital. "It could affect her husband's career and he'd be furious."

"Call me back in two minutes," Judy says. "I'll try to reach Fred at the hospital and ask if he can come home for a 'family emergency.' Then you can bring her here."

Sharon runs outside and leans over the railing. Kim sits upright in the car. Please may all the other wives be inside watching their favorite television programs.

" ... 119, 120." She redials Judy's number.

"My husband will meet you here in 10 minutes," Judy says. "Drive carefully but hurry!"

✡ ✡ ✡

Forewarned that Kim has swallowed a bottle of pills, Judy's husband Fred prepares to pump Kim's stomach. "Watch the children while I help Fred with the procedure," Judy says.

The four children catapult around the backyard, fight over the sandbox toys, chase each other up and down the slide. The four-ring circus keeps itself amused until the youngest falls off the swing.

"You're fine," Sharon says. The child ignores her and climbs back up on the offending swing.

Judy appears in the backyard. "Go speak with Fred. I'll watch the children."

Fred meets Sharon in the hall outside the bedroom. "She's going to make it," he says, then adds, "You should have called the post ambulance, had her taken to the post hospital."

"You don't understand about her husband."

He shakes his head, then asks, "Do you know why she took the pills? Was she trying to kill herself?"

"She was dressed to go out," Sharon says.

Fred twists the clasp on his doctor's bag. "She may not have wanted to be found in her nightgown."

"How is she?"

"She'll be very tired. Can you take her home by yourself and stay with her?"

Sharon nods. The apartment key resides on the ring with the car key – Sharon tried the wrong key first in the ignition – so she will be able to get back in the apartment. Then what? How to help Kim and what to tell Jim? She'll ask to use Judy's phone – call Wendy and Donna.

"Try to talk to her – see how you can help," Fred says. "Next time she might not be as lucky."

Yes, Fred is right Sharon thinks. Next time Kim might use the gun.

☆ ☆ ☆

Thirty minutes later Sharon lets Donna into Kim's apartment. "Thanks for coming," she tells Donna.

"I called Wendy – she'll be here soon." Donna sits down on the couch. "Now tell me what's going on with Kim."

"I walked over to Kim's because it was so hot in my apartment. Then I climbed in the bathroom window when Kim didn't answer the door."

"You what?" Donna bends forward, as if she is about to spring up and inspect the bathroom window, check if Sharon can fit through the space.

"I climbed through the window ... and found Kim lying unconscious in her bedroom."

Donna's mouth sags around her disbelief.

Sharon paces away from Donna, then turns back to her. "I knew she was alive because I found a pulse. I tried to revive her, but couldn't."

Donna jumps up. "She's okay now, isn't she? You didn't call me over to figure out what to do about a ..."

"She's resting in the bedroom. I need your help to talk to her about what happened and figure out what to say to Jim."

Donna sits down and motions for Sharon to sit back down too. As Sharon moves towards the couch the doorbell rings again. Sharon opens the door to Wendy.

"What's going on?" Wendy says. "What's wrong?"

"Sit down," Donna says.

Sharon repeats what she has told Donna. "I can't believe it, I can't believe it!" Wendy says.

How much help are these two going to be? Sharon thinks, then says that Kim's stomach was pumped. "She took ... she took almost a whole bottle of pills."

"Why?" Wendy asks.

"I haven't asked and she hasn't said."

Donna takes Sharon's hands. "We're here."

Sharon gulps back a sob. "Help me fix it, especially the part about not calling an ambulance."

"You didn't call an ambulance? How did you get Kim's stomach pumped?" Wendy asks.

Now Sharon tells the rest of the story. The mad dash to the Weinsteins' house. Afterwards the talk with Fred.

"Did I do the right thing?" Sharon says. "Kim could have died! It would have been my fault!" *Again.*

Donna says, "You have to believe that nothing here is your fault. Another person makes a decision – to enlist, to leave his family, to whatever. And if something happens after that, if you react to the consequences of that action a certain way, it's not your fault. You did your best at that particular moment."

Sharon looks at Donna. She's talking about herself as much as Kim, about herself and her first husband.

"What should we do now?" Sharon asks.

"Let's talk to Kim together," Wendy says. "Show her she has friends."

Senate rejects, 52-47,
proposal to affirm
President's authority
to retain troops in
Cambodia if he considers
it necessary for protection
of U.S. troops in South
Vietnam ...
June 11, 1970

KIM – IX – JULY 3

"... as a military wife, never insist that a friend tell you about
her husband."

Kim lies on the bed staring at the ceiling.

On the drive home Kim had been aware of what was going on, but she said nothing to Sharon. Kim's clothes stuck to the back of the car seat as the heat pressed against her. She thought of the World War II movie she'd once seen. The one – was it "The Bridge on the River Kwai"? – where the British officer is imprisoned in a solid metal cage as punishment by the Japanese. Afterwards Kim had been haunted by the image of the officer crammed in the small dark cage, the blazing furnace of heat pressing against him.

She imagined herself trapped like that. No air to breathe. No way out.

Kim knew Sharon wanted to ask "Why?" Did Sharon say nothing because she was being polite or did she dread hearing the answer?

Kim couldn't even answer herself. Did she mean to take all those pills? She could remember an intense headache, a headache that sent pain flashing through her entire body. She walked into the kitchen for a glass of water, then into the bathroom. She sat on the closed toilet seat, opening the cap, then what?

When they reached Kim's apartment Sharon stopped the car. "We're home," Sharon said.

The nausea flashed through Kim's body, more powerful than the headache pain. Home! They weren't home, they weren't even close to home.

Her head throbbed as Sharon opened the passenger car door for her. She accepted Sharon's offer of an arm to lean on.

"I'd like to lie down," Kim said as they stepped into an apartment almost as broiling as the car.

Sharon guided her onto the bed, then stooped to take off Kim's shoes and swing her legs up. Sharon closed the bedroom door behind her.

Kim heard the doorbell ring in the living room. Her stomach twisted. It was too early for Jim to come home, wasn't it?

A few minutes later Kim heard the doorbell ring again.

Now Kim waits for whatever will happen next. She can't think about who might be here and what Sharon may be doing. Kim has to save all her energy and worry for when Jim gets home. He'll never be able to understand, to forgive her weakness. Maybe he will finish what she started.

The door to the bedroom squeaks open and Sharon comes in, followed by Donna and Wendy. So Sharon called for reinforcements. An entire army can't overrun Jim's anger.

"Mind if we sit on the bed?" Sharon asks. Kim shakes her head.

Sharon glances at her watch, then says, "We have a few hours before the men get home. We can work this all out among ourselves and the men need never know."

Not tell Jim? He'll know. He'll see it in her face.

"Can you tell us about it?" Donna says. "Tell us why you took all those pills?"

Why she took all those pills? Kim looks at the picture of her parents, the frame without the glass. The photo as unprotected as she has been all her life. Yet that's going too far back.

"Jim's volunteering for Vietnam."

All three women gasp. "Vietnam!" Sharon says.

"I want to go home," Kim says. "I just want to go home."

Wendy picks up one of Kim's hands. Kim thinks to pull back her own hand – a black touching her in such a familiar way. Then she stops herself. Wendy is her friend. Friends touch each other.

"I know how you feel," Wendy says. "I miss home all the time." She turns to the others. "Living in the South is different. It's more ... something. I feel protected there. Safe."

Protected. Kim nods that Wendy understands. At home Kim is accepted for who she is. Even if she comes from white trash, at least she knows who she is and what's expected of her.

"Has Jim officially volunteered or has he just made up his mind?" Sharon asks.

Kim says, "I think he's just decided."

There is silence. Then Kim understands. "You think I did this to get him to change his mind?" She shakes her head. "I really don't know why I did this. I certainly didn't think it would change his mind. Nothing will."

Tears form. She shakes her head again. She will not cry now. It can't help.

"What about postponing his decision?" Donna asks. "Why not just go on to your first permanent assignment? Let Jim see the real army before he volunteers to go to Vietnam?"

Kim hesitates. "He's punishing me. He thinks I'm looking at other men."

The three faces can't have been more shocked. Maybe Sharon's is less shocked, because she knows about the ... jealousy.

Wendy says, "That doesn't make sense. If he's in Vietnam you'll have ample opportunity to be with other men."

Kim says, "He only sees that he's punishing me with the one thing I dread the most."

Sharon says, "Maybe we can convince him that you only have eyes for him."

Kim shakes her head. Sharon doesn't know Jim.

Supreme Court rules, 5-3,
a person is entitled to
conscientious objector
status if he sincerely
objects to all wars ...
June 15, 1970

SHARON – XIII – July 3

"An afternoon tea is one of women's greatest pleasures and should be well planned with details given great thought."

"Bonnie's pregnant," Sharon says that evening after Robert has changed out of his uniform. "My mother said Mrs. Morgen called all excited. Bonnie's due in January – around the same time as Donna."

Sharon thinks about Bonnie's wedding last June, a year after she became engaged. When the baby is born, Bonnie and Neil will be married a year and a half, only three months more than Sharon and Robert.

"Very nice," Robert says. He doesn't look up from the "New Yorker" magazine he's picked up off the imitation-wood coffee table.

"Robert, when I talk to you, I want you to look at me," Sharon says.

Robert comes over to her. "What's wrong? You seem jumpy tonight."

"Jumpy? Why would I be jumpy?"

"Is it your time of the month?"

"You mean my period. No, it is not."

"Then what's wrong?"

"Nothing besides you're an officer in the U.S. Army and there's a bloody war going on halfway around the world in some country most people can't even locate on a map!"

Robert hugs her. "I've told you everything is going to be all right."

"What makes you so sure?"

"It's Bonnie's pregnancy, isn't it? You're jealous, right?"

Sharon pulls away. "I AM NOT JEALOUS. It's just ... it's just that I want the option of having a baby now. Instead my life is dictated by the army!"

Robert shrugs. "Donna's having a baby and her life is dictated by the army too. The army doesn't stop you from having a baby."

"The war does! Donna knows that Jerry can get out of going to Vietnam. You don't have an exemption!"

She runs into the bedroom and throws herself on the hideous brown cotton bedspread. Robert lies down beside her and recites:

Let me not to the marriage of true minds
Admit impediments. Love is not love
Which alters when it alteration finds,
Or bends with the remover to remove:

"You're quoting Shakespeare again."
"Sonnet 116."

O, no! it is an ever-fixed mark
That looks on tempests and is never shaken;
It is the star to every wandering bark,
Whose worth's unknown, although his height be
taken.
Love's not Time's fool, though rosy lips and cheeks
Within his bending sickle's compass come;
Love alters not with his brief hours and weeks,
But bears it out even to the edge of doom.
If this be error, and upon me proved,
I never writ, nor no man ever loved.

Robert reaches for her undies.

Minutes later, his chest rosy, Robert traces the outline of her breasts.

"We talked about our decisions today," Robert says. "You know, what we're going to officially respond on Monday."

"And what did everyone say?"

Robert laughs. "Remember loud-mouth Geist." He pauses, waits for her nod. "Always shooting off his mouth about how Southern officers are the best soldiers, the most patriotic, the stars." His fingers brush around her nipples.

"Today he announces he's going to go vol indef. Says he wants the chance to see Paris before serving in Vietnam. Truth is, he's no more eager to get his butt shot off than the rest of us. He's all talk."

"What did Nelson, Jerry .... and Jim say?"

"Jerry's taking vol indef. He wants to go to Europe."

"Maybe they'll be stationed with us," Sharon says. "You did tell him you were going vol indef, didn't you?"

"Of course."

"Nelson?"

"He wants to apply Regular Army so I'm not sure how that works with vol indef."

Sharon's fingers twist the sheets. "And Jim?"

"Not going vol indef. Says he has no interest in living in Europe with all those foreigners. Wants to do his two years and return to his hometown."

Sharon waits for Robert to say Jim plans to volunteer for Vietnam. When Robert says nothing, Sharon climbs out of bed. Perhaps Jim hasn't said anything.

"I have to get ready," Sharon says. "Kim and Jim will be here after dinner."

An hour later, Sharon stacks the playing cards on the table. The evening has been carefully orchestrated, and Robert will be as unwitting an actor as Jim. "*All the world's a stage and ...*"

The doorbell rings. Butterflies circle inside her stomach as if on opening night of a Broadway play.

Jim says hello and Kim nods. "I'm glad Sharon asked you over tonight," Robert says. "Now let's play bridge."

Robert shuffles the cards and Kim cuts to him, her face pale. Did she manage to get through supper without letting Jim see how upset she is?

Sharon, Donna, and Wendy talked and talked to calm Kim down. Then they formed a plan. It has a chance of working, with a little finesse.

Sharon waits until the second hand, the first being won by her on a bid of three spades. "I'm getting excited about living in Europe," she says, laying down a three of clubs. "Robert says we'll probably be sent to Germany. He knows some German, so that should be good."

Jim turns to Robert. "You've definitely decided to go vol indef?"

Robert lays down his five of clubs. "It makes the most sense at this time."

Neither Jim nor Kim says anything.

After another time around the table Sharon asks, "What have you guys decided?" She doesn't look at Robert. Is he wondering why she's asking Jim if Robert has already told her Jim's decision?

Kim studies the dummy's cards. Jim tosses a card down and says, "I'm going to volunteer for Vietnam."

"Vietnam!" Robert says. "You can't be serious."

Thank you, Robert. We thought that's what you'd say. Yet Robert's shock had to be sincere; they couldn't risk coaching him.

"This is a chance to do something for my country," Jim says.

Sharon hesitates; her words can't seem rehearsed in any way. "Do you have to make the decision now?" she says. "Or can you wait until you're at your first assignment and see what you think then?"

Robert nods. "That makes more sense," he says. "At least you'll get a feel for the real army, not just the student army."

"What makes you think I'll change my mind?"

"Look, pal, it's your funeral," Robert says.

Sharon glances at Kim. Her expression doesn't change.

"I don't see why you can't wait," Robert continues. "It won't make any difference at your first assignment."

"Kim, what do you think?" Sharon asks.

Kim's voice can hardly be heard. "Whatever Jim wants. He's the head of the family and he makes the decisions. I just want to be with him."

Not too much, just right.

Sharon doesn't look at Jim. She says, "It sounds like the two of you have a strong foundation together. If you wait to make your decision until your first permanent duty station, then you'll be better informed."

Jim throws his cards down. "I don't need anyone's advice!"

✯ ✯ ✯

Sharon trembles after Jim and Kim leave the apartment. How can Jim be so pigheaded?

Robert kisses her. "Has Jim's decision bothered you that much?"

Sharon wants to share with him, she really does. Yet she's worried that Robert might let something slip to Jim. Instead she says, "I was up for a pleasant evening. How about going to the Officers Club for coffee or something?"

Robert checks his watch. "We can go over for a little while."

Nancy Sinatra sings "These Boots Are Made For Walkin'" as Robert drives towards the post. Sharon fingers her purse strap. If Jim wants to volunteer for Vietnam, Kim will have to accept his decision. She'll have to wait for his return. And pray.

Sharon herself doesn't know anyone who's been to Vietnam. Her sorority sister Debra told her that two Jewish men from her small Illinois town served in Vietnam. One was newly married. The entire year his wife would come with his parents to Friday night services at the synagogue to pray for him. And as a radio operator he could sometimes connect with ham operators around the world who would arrange for him to talk to his wife. At least for those moments she knew he was alive.

The other Vietnam soldier was his cousin, a twin. "While one twin served as a medic in Vietnam, his brother served a hellish time in Bolivia in the Peace Corps, never sure when he went to bed at night if he would wake up in the morning," Debra said. "At least the brother in Vietnam knew who the enemy was. His brother in Bolivia didn't; he slept with his gun the whole time. And he didn't tell his mother until he was safely home."

Then Debra went on to say, "The twin in Vietnam did a heroic act. He had finished his tour. He was safe. Just before he left his firebase an urgent call came for a medvac. There was no medic available. He volunteered to go out one more time. And came back alive."

Would Jim come back alive?

As they approach the entrance to Ft. Knox, the MP motions for Robert to stop the car. This surprises Sharon. Since Robert attached the student sticker on his car, neither she nor he has been stopped at the entrance.

The MP approaches Robert's side of the car. "Step out of the car and open your trunk."

Robert obeys.

She sits in the car, her palms twitching, the minutes forever. Then Robert returns to his side of the car and slides in.

The MP leans in at the window and salutes him. "Sorry, sir."

Robert starts the car.

"What happened?"

"Earlier tonight a whole load of rifles was stolen from a warehouse on the post. The MPs are stopping cars and checking for the rifles."

Sharon laughs. "How would rifles fit in the Fiat's tiny trunk? And why did he apologize to you?"

"Because," Robert says as he drives towards the Officers Club, "they are stopping only enlisted men, not officers."

"Only enlisted men would steal the rifles?"

"Officers are gentlemen."

Sharon stares at Robert.

"Because of my student sticker the MP didn't realize I was an officer – just like at the picnic. If he had, he wouldn't have stopped me. That's why he was apologizing."

How outrageous! More evidence of the army's rigid division of officers and enlisted men into a class system. It's the same as those college campuses where not being in a sorority or fraternity means you are forever and ever on the outside. **Untermenschen**. And treated as such.

"Robert," she says, then stops. Tonight she wants to pretend all is right with the world.

*Vice President Agnew calls
8 anti-war critics, including
Democratic senators Kennedy,
Fulbright, and McGovern,
"advocates of surrender" ...*
June 20, 1970

KIM – X – July 3

*"Do not attempt to give a tea unless you have a lovely cloth
for the table and a tea service."*

Kim brushes her hair in the bathroom after returning from Sharon and Robert's apartment. The curls flatten as she snags the brush through them, then spring up as she releases the bristles.

While Robert and Jerry go to Ft. Holabird next for MI training, Nelson's assignment is Ft. Hood in Texas and Jim's is Ft. Jackson in South Carolina. Once back in the South, if Jim hasn't already committed to Vietnam, her friends, *yes, her friends,* think he might change his mind. Besides, they said, in time he would get over his jealousy.

Kim trembles. Even if by some miracle Jim doesn't volunteer for Vietnam now, he is likely to be assigned a Vietnam tour during his two-year commitment.

At the Officers Club one night Kim overheard a pilot talking to one of his buddies. "I met this lieutenant on an in-country R and R on an island off Nam. One night his platoon takes fire from a friendly village. The next morning he goes into the village and complains to the head guy. The head guy said it's not happening. The second night the lieutenant loses a couple of men and two others have to be medvaced out. He goes back to the village and the head guy says no again. The third night two more men are wounded by fire coming from the village. The next day he goes into the village and kills everyone – men, women and children."

She wasn't thinking of that story when she took the pills. Nor had she been thinking of the story about American POWs she'd heard once at church choir practice before she'd met Jim. "Hell, the Vietcong don't even follow the Geneva convention," the man said. "They torture 'em, then kill 'em."

Maybe all these stories are in her head, demanding to be noticed. And acted upon?

"Kim!" Jim calls from the bedroom. "Are you coming to bed?"

He's in the mood – she's expected to be responsive.

She lays her brush down. Maybe he should think about being without her at some firebase in Vietnam. Without her responsiveness. He can rub up next to his rifle.

✫ ✫ ✫

It is the next morning. A Saturday. Jim is home.

"We need some things at the commissary. Want to come with?" she asks him as they finish breakfast.

"Can't you go by yourself? No one's going to shoot a clerk in front of you there."

Kim gasps. She hasn't said anything to Jim about the shooting since the night at the store. Why would he bring it up now?

"I ... I ..."

Jim walks by her towards the bedroom. "I'll take you."

Kim picks her purse off the couch.

He comes back into the living room. In his left hand he has the gun. With his right hand he places bullets in the chamber.

Pain stabs above her left eye. "Why ... why are you taking that with?"

"I'm going to go over to the range and practice while you're at the commissary. That way the trip won't be a total waste of time."

In the car the humid air plasters her curls to her forehead and her dress to her back and thighs. The Turtles sing "Happy Together" on the radio.

Did she ever go anywhere special with her parents? She doesn't remember any trips farther than their nearest neighbors or the church. She closes her eyes. If she concentrates hard enough she might recall a trip to a swimming hole or some other fun place. She opens her eyes. How childish – there was never such a trip. Her parents clawed a living from their farm. They didn't have time for foolishness.

At the entrance to the post the MP motions for Jim to stop the car. "What the hell does he want?" Jim says. "Can't he see my sticker?"

The MP says to Jim, "Please step out of the car and open your trunk."

Jim gets out of the car. The stabs in Kim's head escalate, an aura of colors skips across her vision.

A second MP, a young black man, peers through her open window. "Sorry, mam, for bothering you," he says. "I just have to check the interior."

"Hey, you, get away from my wife!" Jim screams from the other side of the car. He jerks his car door open and yanks the gun from under the seat.

Oh no. Oh no.

Jim balances the gun on the car roof and screams again, "Get away from my wife!"

"Put the gun down, sir." The MP steps away from Kim's window, one hand pointing at Jim, the other reaching for the flap on his holster.

The pain blinds her. She doesn't need to see to know what's going to happen. *Her parents' car skids towards the telephone pole.*

"Jim," she says.

"Get away from my wife."

"Jim, please Jim."

"Put the gun down."

From behind Jim the first MP yells, "Put the gun down now!"

Jim turns towards the first MP, then back to the MP near Kim. His gun still in his hand.

A single shot.

Her screams detonate, ricocheting inside the car as if they themselves are bullets. She waits for the young soldier to fall, his pool of blood billowing towards her.

Jim slumps to the ground.

✫ ✫ ✫

A nurse gives Kim a sedative and draws the curtain around the clinic bed.

It's like the killing at the store. A mistake. A terrible mistake. And both because of her!

On the curtain, like a home movie screen, first Marvin, then Jim, slump over, their pools of blood ballooning.

Through the open window the smell of honeysuckle pervades the air. Red splotches dot her dress. The Kruger boy shouts over the honeysuckle hedge: "Kim made blood! Kim made blood!"

She has made all this blood – Marvin's and Jim's. And, unlike her menstrual period, this isn't natural. They have both died.

A spider crawls up the curtain.

The itsy bitsy spider went up the waterspout.
Down...

She's washed out, her life over. She'll go back to her hometown and stay with her sister, get a job, and never marry again.

She brings death to everyone she loves.

Despite Senate's repeal, 81-10,
of the 1964 Gulf of Tonkin
Resolution, President Nixon
says he still has the
constitutional right for U.S.
participation in Vietnam War ...
June 24, 1970

DONNA – V – July 4

"To be asked to pour at a tea is a great compliment."

Donna sits on the front steps of the apartment building. No mail today because it's a national holiday.

She believes no news is good news, still she worries. Worries the way she didn't worry about her husband, in the days when she was naive, when she believed men came back to their wives and families as if they had only been off on a men-only camping trip.

Of course there were men who came back to their families – in pieces. Would she have wanted Miguel to come home in a wheelchair, never to have walked or danced again? It could have been a slow death for both of them. Or would they have overcome his handicap and lived happily ever after?

Now she knows no one lives happily ever after.

She goes inside the apartment for a Coke. Perhaps they'll go to the post tonight for the July 4th fireworks. It seems appropriate to celebrate the founding of the nation if your husband, brother and father are serving in the armed forces that protect that country.

She reaches to open the refrigerator and shooting pain flashes through her. She staggers to the bathroom toilet. Her abdominal muscles cramp, blood spurts down her legs.

Is this a spontaneous abortion? Is she losing the baby?

The hospital. Save the baby. Jerry's at the PX with the car! Wendy lives nearby.

Donna calls Wendy.

She'll come right over with Nelson.

Donna puts on two sanitary napkins, writes a note for Jerry, and grabs her purse.

Please, please, let the baby be okay.

Nelson helps Donna into a folding chair in the clinic's waiting room. "We'll go speak to the receptionist," Wendy says.

The door to the clinic pushes open with a swing that cracks the door against the wall. Sharon storms into the room, followed by Robert. How could they know so soon?

Sharon rushes over to Donna. "Where is she? Is she okay?"

"Who?"

"Kim."

"Kim?"

Sharon stares at Donna. "What are you doing here? Aren't you here because of Kim?"

Wendy comes alongside them. "What's going on?" she asks.

"You tell me," Sharon says.

"I'm bleeding," Donna says. "I may be losing the baby. Jerry's not home so I called Wendy to bring me here."

"Oh, God," Sharon gasps.

"Why are you here?"

"I ... I can't tell you right now."

"Can't or won't?" Wendy asks.

Sharon bends over Donna and takes her hands. "Jim was killed today ..."

Donna falls, falls. Beside her Wendy moans.

"... by an MP in front of Kim. She's here and the doctor called me to come be with her."

The hole so big and so black that Donna falls and falls and there is no bottom.

Sharon straightens up. "I have to find Kim. I hope ... I hope the baby can be saved. I'll come back to see you as soon as I can."

Wendy grasps Donna around the shoulders. "The receptionist said they'll try to see you as soon as possible. Just hang on."

Donna closes her eyes. From the end of a long white corridor Miguel beckons. She follows him through a maze of halls, twisting right, left, left, right. He pushes against a concealed door and they enter an enclosed garden. Water spouts from the mouth of a stone nymph. Wind chimes moan as a breeze brushes her face.

Miguel points to a tiny mound of dug-out earth – a grave for a baby.

"No!" she screams.

"What's wrong?" Wendy asks. "Is the pain bad?"

Donna looks up at Wendy. Miguel and the garden have disappeared.

The clinic door swings open again. Jerry rushes in.

He kneels beside her. "I love you, Donna."

"I think I've lost the baby."

"We'll make more. Everything will be okay."

She sobs. "No, it won't."

Jerry whispers in her ear. "Darling, I'll take the exemption. I won't go to Vietnam."

The sobs tear her apart.

Corporate Executives Committee
for Peace – 100 leaders of
major corporations – calls
for an end to Vietnam War
by December 31, 1970 ...
June 24, 1970

SHARON – XIV – July 4

"The pourer should not leave the table until she is relieved by the next pourer."

Sharon sits by the bed as Kim sleeps. Hospital personnel moved Kim from the clinic to this hospital room, where she will stay for observation until tomorrow.

Sharon sits alone; Robert stays out in the hall – "It's better for only you to be with her," he said. Tears slide down Sharon's cheeks.

Is she crying for Kim, for herself, for Donna, or for Wendy? Maybe she's crying for all of them, for their similar and dissimilar reasons: Kim's dead husband, Donna's dead first husband and probable miscarriage, Wendy's husband going Regular Army, and the threat of a Vietnam tour hanging over Jerry, Nelson and Robert.

Now Jim is out of that. Kim won't have to worry about receiving a telegram announcing he's been killed. Her husband was killed in front of her own eyes, the news telegraphed in less than a second.

Bile rises in Sharon's throat. She gags.

At age 10 she and Howard stand in the carpeted hallway of a Jewish funeral home in Chicago waiting for her paternal grandfather's funeral to begin. The rabbi from their synagogue comes up to them. "Let's go down the block to the Jewish book store. You don't need to be here now," he says.

It is only later, during **shiva**, the traditional week of mourning, that Sharon asks her father, "Why did the rabbi have Howard and me leave the chapel until the service began?" Her father glances over at his mother sitting on a low stool talking in Yiddish to one of her sisters.

"Your grandmother is superstitious. She insisted on an open coffin even though it's not Jewish custom," her father says. "The rabbi didn't want you to look into the open coffin so he took you down the street."

And five years later, when this superstitious grandmother herself dies and her father makes the decisions, there is no open coffin.

Now Sharon wonders if there will be an open coffin for Jim. Is this a Southern Baptist tradition? Or maybe his wound can't be covered up enough and the coffin will be closed regardless of the tradition.

She brushes her eyes, her head throbs. Her mother had a first cousin who at seven years of age was struck in the head by a baseball bat. He lay in bed for several weeks before he died. When Sharon's grandmother visited her nephew, the boy whimpered, "Aunt Fannie, it hurts so much."

That's how Sharon feels – it hurts so much. Jim's death, Donna's probable miscarriage. Kim needed Jim so much and Donna needed this baby in case, in case ...

Sharon strides across the room and pulls the room door open. Robert jumps off the hall bench.

"Is she asleep?" Robert reaches out his arms to Sharon.

She pummels his chest with both fists. "It's all your fault! It's all your fault!"

Robert grabs her hands and holds them at her side. "Be quiet or we'll upset the other patients. The staff might even call the MPs."

Sharon shudders, gulps air, and allows him to pull her down onto the bench. He wraps his arms around her.

"It is your fault," she sobs into his chest. "You and your adolescent dreams of being a war hero, proving to your dad you are as good as he. Why are all you men so hung up on playing war, proving how macho you are? Shooting toy guns when you're little, then real guns when you're older?

Robert rocks her back and forth. He says:

The time you won your town the race
We chaired you through the market-place;
Man and boy stood cheering by,
And home we brought you shoulder-high.

To-day, the road all runners come,
Shoulder-high we bring you home,
And set you at your threshold down,
Townsman of a stiller town.

Smart lad, to slip betimes away
From fields where glory does not stay,
And early though the laurel grows
It withers quicker than the rose.

She sobs. The beginning of A.E. Housman's poem "To An Athlete Dying Young." Robert recited it when they first met, minutes after they escaped the ROTC protest.

Men and war games. She thinks of the times she played cowboys and Indians with Howard when they were little; the fort they built with a blanket over a card table; the time he tied her to a tree so that he could pretend to ride up and rescue her; his collection of metal soldiers that their mother melted down on moral grounds. The movies, the television shows, the books – all glorifying men who go out to fight, their guns strapped to their sides, to protect their womenfolk and their homesteads.

Robert holds her chin in his hand and looks in her eyes. "I know now it's not a game. It's serious and people get killed. I can't take back what I've committed to, but I can be as careful as possible."

His chest heaves. "And I pray to God I don't have to go to Vietnam. I don't know whether I believe this war is right. I just don't want to shoot another person, to choose between his life and mine."

Sharon pulls Robert's face down to hers. She presses her lips against his. Please may she not lose him. She already knows too many widows.

✡ ✡ ✡

Sharon has brushed her hair and put on some lipstick in the hospital bathroom. Kim still sleeps.

"Let's go visit Donna now," Sharon says.

"Are you up for this?" Robert asks.

She nods. She has to see Donna, who's also being kept overnight for observation.

"She's one floor down," Robert says. The soles of their shoes squeak on the wooden stairs.

On the lower floor Wendy and Nelson sit on a bench halfway down the hall talking to Jerry. Wendy runs to Sharon and flings her arms around her. "Is Kim okay?" she asks.

"For now."

"What really happened?" Nelson says as he and Jerry come up beside Wendy.

Robert shakes his head. "Apparently Jim pulled a gun on an MP and another MP shot Jim."

"Jim pulled his gun on a black MP," Nelson says. "That's what I heard."

"Why did he do that?" Wendy asks.

All three of them look at Sharon. "He ... he was obsessed. He thought men were looking at Kim. He must have thought ..."

"He needed help," Robert says. "After what he said at the club about Nelson I should have known he was coming unglued. I'm the one who spent the most time with him. I failed him."

Jerry puts his arm around Robert. "It's as much my fault. I was at the club too. I should have realized his reaction was way out of line from his usual behavior. I'm supposed to be sensitive to others' feelings – I didn't realize what was going on."

Jerry's eyes blink. "And now Donna has lost the baby. It was a spontaneous abortion. Doctor told her it happens often."

"She can still have children, can't she?" Sharon asks.

Wendy nods. "It's just that she wanted this baby so that if ... if ..."

Jerry puts his hand on Wendy's arm. "There will be no if. I'm going to use the Vietnam exemption I'm entitled to."

"What exemption?" Nelson asks.

Oh, no, Wendy doesn't know.

"Donna's first husband was killed in Vietnam. That gives me ..."

Wendy slumps to the floor. Her body sags against the wall, her head on one side. "Wendy, Wendy," Nelson yells.

Sharon bends over Wendy, holding Wendy's head down between her knees. "Take it easy," she says.

Nelson crouches next to Wendy and strokes her head.

Jerry looks at Sharon. "I thought you all knew."

"Robert and I do. I didn't tell Kim or Wendy."

Jerry leans over Wendy. "I'm sorry, Wendy. This has been a terrible day for you."

Wendy raises her head. Tears plop onto her lap. "And Nelson's insisting on going Regular Army!"

"Honey!" Nelson puts his arms around her. "I've explained it to you. Regular Army is a great opportunity for us. I'll have the same chances for promotion as everyone else."

"Not if you're dead."

✳ ✳ ✳

Sharon stands behind Wendy, who sits in the only visitor's chair in Donna's room. Both Kim and Donna have single rooms, aren't forced to share with cheerful or depressing roommates.

"I'm sorry you had to find out this way," Donna says. "I thought Sharon would tell you."

Sharon shrugs. "I didn't know whether you wanted me to. And I thought Kim especially would be upset. I didn't want her more worried than she already was."

The three of them look at each other. No one says the obvious: Kim needn't have worried about Vietnam. Jim didn't even make it through AOB training.

"Jerry's going to take the exemption," Donna says. "He told you, right?"

Sharon nods.

"We're still going to sign up for vol indef. He wants to go to Europe."

Sharon smiles. "Robert told me. Maybe we'll be stationed near each other. And, Wendy, you'll have a European tour if Nelson goes Regular Army."

"If he survives Vietnam," Wendy says, crushing tissues between her hands. "He'll probably go in a couple of months."

Sharon hugs her. "I don't have a crystal ball, but I'm betting on Nelson. Robert says he's a terrific soldier."

Secretary of State Laird
affirms U.S. plans to continue
bombing raids inside Cambodia
after June 30 ...
June 26, 1970

SHARON – XV – July 5

"Unless she can be positive that her pocketbook will not slide from her lap, the pourer should place her bag under the skirt of the table or under her chair, making sure that the other guests will not trip over it."

Sharon answers the phone the next morning.

"It's Nelson. Do you know where Wendy is?"

"No. Why?"

"She's not here. She doesn't have the car and she's never gone away when I've been home. I was just up the road for a few minutes getting milk."

"Maybe she went for a walk."

"In this heat?"

"What about the hospital? Maybe she went to see Donna and Kim."

"How would she have gotten there?"

"Good point," Sharon says.

"I'm sorry I bothered you."

"Call me when she gets in so I won't worry."

Robert comes out of the bedroom. "Who was that on the phone?"

"Nelson. Wendy's not home and he's worried."

Sharon glances at the pancake mix ready to be poured onto the griddle. "Do you mind if we don't eat right now? I just want to drive around Muldraugh. See if I spot Wendy."

Sharon pulls out of the lot. How silly. Wendy will be home any minute. Maybe she's at a neighbor's, borrowing a cup of sugar.

Sharon drives up the main street of Muldraugh and parks the Fiat in front of the post office. Behind the building lies a small park Wendy sometimes visits. It's better Sharon come here than Nelson in case Wendy's walking back into the trailer right now.

Across the mowed grass a flower-edged path leads to a small pond. Scum floats on the still water.

Wendy sits on a bench, her knees pulled up to her chest and her head bent over. Sharon sits down next to her. Wendy doesn't look up.

Wendy clutches a newspaper in her arms. Sharon pries the paper from Wendy.

"New Vietcong Offensive Claims Many American Lives." The headline screams its news across the whole front page. Wet blotches dot the story.

Lower down on the front page another headline reads: "Bomb Explodes in ROTC Building on University Campus."

"Wendy," Sharon says.

Wendy raises her head. She stares at Sharon.

"What's going on?"

Wendy shakes her head.

"Nelson's worried. He called me."

Wendy's eyes flash. "Let him find out what it's like," she says. "Worrying about the person you love."

Sharon wraps her arms around Wendy.

Wendy pulls herself away from Sharon. "I want to go home."

Sharon squeezes Wendy's hands. "You would never leave Nelson."

"I am. I'm leaving Nelson."

"Now?"

Wendy tosses her head. "You know how I'm driving home with Kim?"

They worked this out together after they all offered to drive back with Kim. Wendy's the obvious choice. Her parents live not that far from Kim's sister. They will come get Wendy and take her to the airport near their home so she can fly back to Louisville.

"I'm not coming back."

Sharon waits as Wendy stares at the pond scum.

"I love Nelson. I just can't stand to be with him until right before he goes to Vietnam. I wouldn't know how to say good-bye."

"Have you told Nelson?"

Wendy shakes her head.

"When are you going to tell him?"

"I'll write him a letter as soon as I get home."

Sharon stares at Wendy, then glances at the newspaper with its ominous headlines.

In her mind Sharon sees Bonnie Morgen in her wedding gown pause at the top of the red carpet so that she can be admired by the 300 wedding guests. On her left Sharon's parents smile. Are they imagining Sharon in Bonnie's place? On her right Robert sits erect, his eyes straight ahead. He has been quiet ever since they took their seats in the ballroom of the Ambassador Hotel.

This whole past school year he has not repeated his offer of marriage. It's almost as if he has decided not to ask her to make such a tremendous commitment. And after several months he still has heard nothing from the army about his request for a branch transfer from infantry to MI – a transfer request based on the army correspondence course in psychological warfare he took and his master's degree in communications to be awarded this month.

The rabbi recites the marriage ceremony as Bonnie and Neil stand together under the **chupah,** the marriage canopy. The white satin gown's train trails down the red carpet, a road leading to marriage.

Sharon reaches over and takes Robert's hand. Is he thinking that Kenneth never had the chance to marry? To pledge himself to another for life no matter how long – or how short – that life is?

Sharon feels her heart flutter. Is she being selfish in refusing to marry Robert before he goes into the army? Couldn't marriage help Robert through this difficult duty he's convinced he must do? And, if he goes to Vietnam, wouldn't marriage give him something to stay alive for: his wife waiting for him back home. Would having a wife back home have helped Kenneth to survive?

Now Bonnie turns to face Neil as he recites the ancient marriage formula while placing a ring on her left pointer finger: "*Harai at mekudeshet lee, b'ta-ba-at zu, k'dat Mosheh v'Yisrael.*" Bonnie repeats the words in English: "Be sanctified to me with this ring in accordance with the law of Moses and Israel."

In accordance with the law of Moses and Israel, Sharon repeats to herself.

Jews faced death from so many people over hundreds of years – the Crusaders, the Inquisition, Cossack-led pogroms, the Nazis' gas chambers – with rituals that affirmed the celebration of life – continuing to marry and have children in the face of the most terrible survival odds. Aren't Robert's odds somewhat better?

Sharon's hand in Robert's shakes as she whispers in his ear: "Robert, I'll marry you now if you still want me to. Before you go into the army."

Sharon turns to face Wendy. "None of us ever talk about Vietnam to each other. It's as if we all believe that if we don't talk about it then the war doesn't exist."

Wendy nods.

"Let me tell you something. I wasn't going to marry Robert until after he finished his time in the army. I was against the war – still am. I didn't want to be connected even by marriage to the war machine. And, if I'm truthful, I didn't want to face being a widow."

"What changed your mind?"

"Partly Robert's friend Kenneth. He ... he was killed in Vietnam." Sharon chokes back a sob. "I eventually realized how selfish I was. If I loved Robert, then I should treasure every day with him. My politics – and my own fears – were not as important as my love for Robert. Finally I said yes."

Sharon looks at Wendy.

"Do you understand what I'm saying? You owe it to Nelson and yourself to have every day you can together. And, God forbid anything happens, you'll be the survivor. You'll have to live with yourself. You don't want to have deserted your husband when he needed you most."

Wendy's tears irrigate their clasped hands. "I'll come back," she says.

✵ ✵ ✵

Thirty minutes later Sharon turns off the engine in her apartment parking lot after driving Wendy home. Sharon feels queasy. It's an awesome responsibility to give people advice on life and death issues.

She remembers, before the wedding ceremony, the rabbi in the privacy of the synagogue building's lounge instructing Robert to lift her veil. As Robert raises the short piece of tulle attached to Sharon's bridal headdress, uncovering her face, the rabbi says, "You have now had the opportunity to ensure that the bride is the one you intended." Sharon and Robert both smile.

"This custom comes from the story in the Bible where Jacob thought he was marrying Rachel and instead was given her older sister Leah," the rabbi says. "Now we let the groom check that he has the right wife."

The rabbi lowers the veil back in place. "Sharon," he says, "why don't you wait here for a few minutes? I'll get everyone in their places and then someone will come for you."

Robert squeezes her hand and follows the rabbi out of the room. She is all alone.

Except for the memorial plaques on the room's walls. The English and Hebrew names of the deceased synagogue members commemorated on these metal plaques. Sharon's finger traces the raised lettering of one name.

The two little girls play bride dress-up with their mothers' old white tablecloths. "I'll be your maid of honor and you'll be mine," Sharon lisps between two missing front teeth. She twirls around to glimpse her make-believe dress train in the full-length mirror.

"Silly," her playmate says. "One of us will have to be the matron of honor. We can't both be maids of honor."

KIM – XI – July 6

*"Receptions are commonplace in the Army and need not be
thought of as a bore, but anticipated with pleasure if you
are self-assured and know what to do."*

Two days later Kim places the picture frame in
her suitcase, the glass not yet replaced. Perhaps it
never will be.

This last suitcase she adds to the packed car.
Then she sits in the empty apartment with Squeaky
in his cage at her feet. She's ready.

It's wonderful of Wendy to drive home to North
Carolina with her. Sharon and Donna also offered to
come, but one is enough. And it makes sense for that
one to be Wendy. Her parents live nearby and she
can visit with them before returning to Louisville.

At first Kim worried about Jim's parents' reaction to Wendy. Then she realized she is free to do what she wants. No foster parents, no jealous husband.

She may still not like all blacks, Puerto Ricans, and Jews, but she likes Wendy, Donna, and Sharon. They are her friends.

Sharon worked so hard not to bring Kim to the hospital when she swallowed the pills. Sharon didn't want to blemish Jim's army career. Now Jim has no career and Kim ended up at the hospital anyway.

Sharon has told Kim over and over again that what happened is not her fault. "Kim, you didn't cause Jim's death. A flaw in Jim's personality killed him."

By running away from the convenience store Kim avoided the questions of the MPs. This time she couldn't run away. Flanked by Sharon and Robert, Kim answered their questions. "Why did your husband have a gun with him? Why did he threaten the black MP?"

Robert arranged for Jim's body to be shipped back home. He also worked with army officials on the paperwork for Kim's widow benefits. If Jim's parents give her nothing because there's no will, she won't be penniless. Robert disposed of Jim's army uniforms and offered to pack the rest of Jim's stuff. She wanted to do that herself – something she could do for Jim.

Susanna and Bill and the children stopped by the apartment to offer their condolences. Bill stood in her living room holding Billy. "I'm terribly sorry about your husband," he said. "You should be all right with your army dependent benefits."

How many letters had he written home for men killed under his command in Vietnam? How many times had he told parents or wives that their son or husband died defending their country? And how many times here in the States had he been the one sent to deliver in person the terrible news, the news that no one could ever take back?

Bill couldn't offer her the comforting words that Jim died for his country. Except, of course, in a strange way he had.

She didn't cry because Susanna cried for both of them. Between sobs Susanna burst out the information that the army would provide a hearing aid for Patty. Under the army's rules for medical benefits for dependents, Patty wasn't entitled to speech therapy until she started school at age five!

"We have to wait two more years, two more years of Patty not speakin' right! I feel so terrible. She could have had a hearin' aid sooner and she probably would be talkin' better right now."

Kim hugged the little girl good-bye. Poor Patty – a child who had both parents and yet had been treated no better than an orphan.

As Kim watches through the living room window, the three women drive into the parking lot. It's a momentous day for them – today Robert and Jerry declare going voluntary indefinite; Nelson will not as he will apply for a Regular Army post. Jim also would not have declared voluntary indefinite. He would have ...

Kim forces herself to go out the door to meet the others – Sharon in the lead, Wendy with a small suitcase in one hand, and Donna back to her old self.

Kim couldn't hang on to her husband – she knew it was a fragile relationship – yet for the first time in her life she has friends. Real friends who care about her.

"I'm sorry I won't be here for the play," Kim says to Sharon as she reaches the women.

Sharon eyes Squeaky in his cage in Kim's hand. "I'm thinking of calling off the whole thing. There're only two of us. And I'm not sure it's such a good idea."

"Don't call it off," Kim says. "We worked so hard. Ask someone else to help out."

"I don't know who to ask."

Wendy shifts her suitcase from one hand to the other. "How about I reconsider – and take Kim's part? I'll be back in time for the luncheon."

"I don't want to get you in trouble with Nelson," Sharon says.

Wendy smiles. "Leave Nelson to me."

Sharon places her hand on Kim's arm. "Before you go," she says, "I have a confession to make to all of you."

Sharon looks at Wendy and Donna, then her eyes return to Kim. "I seem confident, sure of who I am. It's true that on the outside I've probably had an easier life growing up than any of you. Yet we all have our secrets."

She glances down at her feet, then her eyes return to Kim's face. "When I was 12 years old I vowed that I would no longer share my secret thoughts with anyone."

"What made you do such a thing?" Donna asks.

"It was my penance for something terrible I did – I caused the deaths of four people."

"How!" Wendy gasps.

Sharon hesitates. "Tracy Fein was my best friend. We had a secret club – just two members. Every Sunday afternoon we met at my house. One Sunday Tracy didn't want to meet. She called me on the phone."

"My family is going shopping for new living room furniture, Sharon. I want to go with them."

"And miss our meeting?"

"Just this once."

"We took an oath. We pledged that we'd meet every Sunday afternoon. Besides, we have new business to discuss.

My parents gave me some extra record money and we have to decide which record to buy. You have to come over."

"I'll ask my parents to drop me off on their way to the furniture store."

"Tracy's family drove out of their way that day to drop her off. On their detour to my house ... the brakes on a five-ton truck failed and the truck slammed into them. Their car didn't have seat belts. They were all killed – her parents, her younger brother, Tracy."

Tears stream down Sharon's face. "If I hadn't insisted – demanded – that Tracy come over, she and her family would be alive."

Kim wraps her arms around Sharon. Wendy and Donna move closer.

Sharon pulls away. "That's when I resolved not to replace Tracy's friendship. I've had friends since then, but I've never shared the closeness I had with Tracy." She uses the back of her hands to wipe her eyes.

"I just wanted you all to know what you mean to me. I'm trusting you with my deepest secret."

Kim wipes the tears out of her own eyes. How can she tell Sharon what it means to her, a defenseless orphan, that someone as strong and self-confident as Sharon should also be vulnerable? She hugs Sharon. "Thank you" is all Kim says.

Donna and Wendy also hug Sharon. "You weren't responsible for their deaths," Wendy says. "They could have all been killed on the direct way to the furniture store. If it was their time to go …"

Sharon shakes her head, staring at the ground. "That's too easy an out."

"Sharon," Donna says. Sharon raises her head. "I've told you before, you can't blame yourself for things in the past you can't change. You have to move on."

Sharon smiles. "And now I have, thanks to you guys."

"I have one piece of good news," Donna says. "My brother was just rotated to the rear. He'll spend his second six months in Saigon. It's not the safest place, but it's better than being a forward observer."

Sharon leans closer to Kim on the side away from Squeaky. "I got you a little gift."

Sharon lifts a rectangular package wrapped in cobalt blue paper out of her purse. "Don't open it until you're on the road."

Lines zig zag across Kim's vision. This saying good-bye is harder than she imagined. And now a gift.

She hugs both Sharon and Donna. "Thank you, thank you for everything. I'll never forget you."

Wendy hugs Sharon and Donna too, then disengages the car keys from Kim's hand. Wendy mashes her suitcase into the filled backseat of Kim's car. Then Wendy slides in behind the wheel, motioning Kim with Squeaky to get into the passenger seat.

Kim waves to Sharon and Donna. She doesn't look at the apartment.

Kim sits with the package in her lap, staring straight ahead. She doesn't allow herself to think of her arrival here with Jim.

Her fingers rub the package. A gift for her! Growing up, the only gift she received each year was from the church's orphan Christmas gift drive. When she was little she hoped for a doll, then when she was older a necklace or bracelet or even some records. What she got, wrapped in green and red or gold and silver paper, were socks or religious books or hair ribbons.

Once, when she was 16, she received a pink angora cardigan. "Somebody's cast-off!" the foster mother said. Kim didn't care. The sweater so soft and pretty, and all hers. She didn't even let Diane wear it.

Kim slips her finger into the taped opening of the wrapping paper and lifts the paper off. That same foster mother insisted that wrapping paper be removed carefully so that it could be reused. Now Kim smooths the paper on her lap and then opens the plain white rectangular box.

A silver picture frame – the same size as her broken frame. Kim's hands shake as she reaches for the card taped to the glass.

Kim – May you use this gift to preserve a photo from your past or to display a photo of your future. I'll miss you. With love, Sharon

Kim's tears splash onto the paper, causing whitish streaks on the cobalt blue. Wendy keeps her eyes on the road, saying nothing.

Kim stares at herself in the reflection from the new piece of glass, her cheeks blotched with red and her eyelids puffy above watery eyes. One curl strand sticks to her damp forehead. She remembers the children's rhyme from kindergarten – a favorite of her teacher Miss Jefferson:

> *There once was a girl with a curl*
> *Right in the middle of her forehead.*
> *When she was good she was very very good,*
> *But when she was bad she was horrid.*

If Kim had been good would this have happened to her?

Senate adopts, 58-37, the
Cooper-Church amendment to
limit U.S. troop involvement
in Cambodia, the first such
limitation on a President's
powers as commander-in-chief
during a war situation ...
June 30, 1970

WENDY – VI – July 6

"Your dress will be determined by the time of day."

After hours of driving Wendy and Kim arrive at Kim's sister's apartment. Diane clasps Kim, holding her close, then turns to Wendy. "Come on in," Diane says.

Wendy searches Diane's face for any surprise about seeing a black person with Kim. There is none. Kim must have warned her.

"I'll call my parents and they can come get me tonight rather than tomorrow," Wendy offers. "That's if my staying for the funeral is a problem."

"I want you to stay," Kim says. Diane smiles her agreement.

They carry Kim and Jim's possessions into the apartment. Kim places the gift from Sharon on the coffee table.

They sit around the kitchen table, drinking iced tea. It's obvious to Wendy that Diane and Kim, with their similar coloring and facial features, are sisters.

"How did it happen? You didn't say on the phone," Diane says.

"A training accident," Kim says, staring down at Squeaky in his cage on the floor.

Wendy glances briefly at Kim's face. Yes, it's better this way. There's no need to tell the truth when the truth will cause more anguish.

After dinner Wendy calls Nelson collect to tell him they arrived. Then she drives with Kim and Diane to the funeral home.

Cars fill the small lot to the side of a large white frame building. It looks like an antebellum manor house surrounded by magnolia trees whose branches beckon them forward.

A carpeted hall leads past the viewing rooms. Diane stops outside a door halfway down the hall. Then the three women walk through the open door.

Inside Wendy looks at the circle of white faces. Are they whispering about her or about Jim's death?

Jim's coffin lid is closed. "It's probably not open because he doesn't look so good," Diane whispers to Wendy as everyone hugs on Kim.

"This is my friend from the army, Wendy Johnson," Kim tells a middle-age woman in a black dress and a middle-age man in a black suit standing next to her. "Wendy, these are Jim's parents, Mr. and Mrs. Benton." Neither Benton offers a hand.

Wendy and Diane stand at Kim's side for the better part of an hour, listening to the Bentons' friends murmur at Kim. When Kim turns to Diane and says, "Please, let's go home," they leave.

Kim gets ready for bed while Wendy and Diane sit together in the living room. Diane looks at her watch and says, "We'd better go to bed too. We have to get up early. I'll get the sheets for the couch."

Wendy stretches a white sheet across the couch as Diane heads towards the bedroom to share the double bed with Kim.

At the bedroom door Diane turns around. "Thanks for helping Kim. I know she appreciates it."

✵ ✵ ✵

In the morning they eat breakfast before driving to the church. "It's not too hot yet," Wendy says.

"In another hour it'll be hot enough to fry an egg on the sidewalk," Diane says.

Kim slides her eggs around her plate. She looks up. "I wish Sharon and Donna were here too. I'm sorry I told them not to come." There's a catch in her voice.

"Their thoughts will be with you today," Wendy says, visualizing the four of them standing together. Just what this small Southern town needs. A black, a Jew and a Puerto Rican alongside one of their own.

"It's time to go," Diane says.

Outside the church more people hug on Kim. Wendy stays a few steps behind, letting Diane guide Kim through the throng of people.

A car engine sliding to a stop on the gravel road causes Wendy to turn around. Surely the yellow Fiat is a mirage brought on by the heat and dust.

Sharon and Donna climb out of the car.

Wendy touches Kim on the sleeve, and Kim turns in the direction Wendy indicates. Kim pulls away from Diane and runs back towards the churchyard gate. Screams and sobs trail her.

Sharon and Donna wrap their arms around Kim who buries her head in their embrace.

"How come you're here?" Wendy says as she joins them.

"We had to come," Sharon says.

"Kim, we have to go in," Diane says, tugging on her sister's arm.

As Wendy walks back up the path behind the others, she glances at Jim's parents waiting outside the church door. Wendy would swear Jim's parents are surprised that Kim has such good friends, friends who would drive all the way here to be with her today. Even if they are a black, a Jew and a Puerto Rican.

Inside the church Kim sits in the front pew with the Bentons and Diane while Wendy, Sharon and Donna sit in the pew right behind Kim. Even inside the humidity causes perspiration pools around Wendy's neck. Sharon and Donna sit on either side of her. Is this the first time Sharon has been in a church?

At least the stares at their row can't only be for her; some of the curiosity must be for Sharon and Donna too.

Into the humid air the preacher talks of the sacrifice of young men during wartime. "Jim Benton is one more fine American who gave up his life in the service of his country."

Wendy imagines Nelson lying in Jim's coffin, then shuts her eyes to banish the mental picture.

"I knew this young man well," the preacher continues. "He came to church regularly. And when he married, his wife Kim also became active in our church. We will all miss him."

At the end of the service Sharon leans over the front seat. "Kim, may I ask the minister permission to speak at the cemetery?"

"If you want," Kim says. Her sister leads her out into the sunlight.

"He's called a preacher, not a minister," Wendy whispers to Sharon.

Sharon steps over to speak to him.

At the cemetery Diane and Wendy stand on either side of Kim, their arms linked through hers.

Sharon and Donna stand behind them. The sun explodes needles of heat as the preacher recites the 23rd Psalm:

Yea, though I walk through the valley of the shadow of death,

I will fear no evil...

As the preacher recites these words, Wendy visualizes a Vietnamese jungle valley between two low mountains, the tranquility of green grass below blue sky. Then the scene cracks apart with rifle fire and mortars and men screaming.

With her free arm Wendy wipes her eyes with a handkerchief. Donna has the comfort that her first husband died a hero for his country. Kim doesn't have that comfort. Jim died because of his own weaknesses – jealousy and prejudice.

The preacher motions Sharon forward.

Sharon nods at the preacher. "Thank you for allowing me to speak."

She next nods at the mourners. "I drove from Ft. Knox to be here today," she says, then pauses.

"I don't know how many of you men have ever served in the armed forces – or you women have been married to a man who is serving. If you haven't personally experienced military life, it's hard to imagine the pressures and expectations."

Sharon's gaze circles her audience. "Jim was an officer, with all the additional obligations that brings. He voluntarily made a commitment to fight for his country. And, if necessary, he was willing to give his life to do that. This makes him a hero."

Wendy looks at Donna to see her reaction to Sharon's words. Listening to Sharon, Wendy can almost believe Jim is a hero.

"There are also obligations that come with being an officer's wife. In fact, the army is fond of saying that it just doesn't get one person with a married officer, it gets two people – the officer and his wife.

"Kim Benton is an officer's wife. She supported her husband 100 percent. She accepted her husband's commitment and fulfilled her obligations in her new role."

Sharon hesitates. "There is such a thing as quiet heroism. The kind that doesn't bring attention to itself. The kind that just does a good job. That's Kim Benton – a true hero."

The others look at Kim now as Sharon steps back. Wendy's eyes sweep Jim's parents' faces. What do they think of Kim being called a hero?

Is Kim a hero? If so, are they all heroes – Sharon, Donna, and Wendy herself – for supporting their husbands' commitment to serve their country, no matter what they as wives feel about the army or the war?

The preacher motions to Kim. She leans forward and throws a handful of dirt onto Jim's coffin. "I'm sorry, Jim. So sorry," she whispers.

Afterwards they drive to Jim's parents' house, a frame structure pinched in the middle of a quiet block. The humidity hangs in the air as they walk towards the front door.

Inside the room air conditioner can't cool the cramped living room. Jim's mother offers around iced tea as visitors perch on chairs fanning themselves.

Wendy stands next to Donna. "Why did you bring the Fiat instead of your bigger car? Then I could have gone back with you two."

"We didn't want your parents to be disappointed at not spending time with you."

Wendy nods as Sharon comes over to them.

"Sharon, did you really mean what you said about Kim being a hero?" Wendy asks. "Or did you only say it to make Kim feel better?"

Sharon looks around the room. Then she says, "It is a kind of heroism for the wives of officers – and enlisted men – to just get through each day without dwelling on what can happen. If we thought about everything that could happen, we'd never leave our houses or do anything except take care of our basic needs."

Diane comes up to Wendy. "There are two … people just sitting outside in a car – a man and a woman. Must be your parents."

Wendy looks out the window, then goes over to Kim. Together they walk outside, followed by Sharon and Donna. Wendy carries her suitcase she's brought from Diane's apartment. As she comes down the sidewalk, her parents get out of the car.

Her parents smile at all of them and don't seem surprised to see Sharon and Donna. Wendy's mama takes Kim's hands. "I'm so sorry, my dear."

Her papa says, "May God watch over you."

Wendy hugs Kim, tears flowing down both their faces. "Take care," Wendy says.

"Thank you for everything," Kim says.

Wendy waves good-bye as Kim stands between the other two women. Sharon and Donna will drive back in time to pick up Wendy at the Louisville airport tomorrow.

In the car, as soon as the women fade from sight, Wendy's mother says, "Have you heard anything about Nelson having to go to ... to Vietnam?"

"No, Mama," she says, "we haven't heard anything." Which is true as far as it goes.

She can't bring herself to tell them that Nelson is going Regular Army. She's promised Sharon that she'll return and she doesn't want anything to weaken her resolve now.

At home that evening after dinner Wendy's mama cleans up the kitchen. Wendy finds her father in his study. "Papa, do you have any pictures of Arthur Henry?"

Her papa unlocks the desk drawer that she has never before seen open. He lifts up a black cardboard-cover album and places it on his desk. Then he opens the cover.

A baby lies in the arms of her younger mama, smiling out at the camera. Her younger papa has his arms around both mother and baby. Wendy searches the baby's face for any similarities to hers.

He was my brother
Tears can't bring him back to me
He was my brother

*Defense Department announces
need for 10,000 men in August,
lowest since December 1969 ...*
July 1, 1970

SHARON – XVI – July 9

*"In the afternoon, or before retreat, a suit or dress with hat
and gloves will be considered appropriate."*

Back from the funeral, Sharon remains without
wheels again if she doesn't drive Robert to the post.

"Mrs. Lieutenant" might be a silly book with silly
rules. Yet these are rules she'll have to live by if she
doesn't want to embarrass herself or her husband at
their first permanent duty station.

Following the advice of the booklet, she keeps the
car today and drives to a print shop to order calling
cards. Robert's cards read "Lieutenant Robert Gold."
Her cards read "Mrs. Robert Gold."

Robert's are 3 1/4 x 1 1/4 inches in shaded
Roman engraving and hers are in the larger 3 1/4 x 2
1/4 in the recommended matching black engraving
on white parchment. Why are the women's cards
larger? Sharon has no idea. Perhaps because men
leave more cards than women when making an
official call.

Sharon visualizes handing her card and her husband's to the head of MSU's SDS chapter. "These go with your monogrammed shirt," she tells him.

She isn't selling out. She now realizes that appearing correct – "strac" as Robert calls it in army jargon – can help them get through this time. "It's the image they care about. Look the part and they'll leave us alone," Robert says.

Later the same day she goes to the post transportation office and arranges for their belongings – "household goods" – to be sent to Ft. Holabird. They'll take the most important possessions with them on the drive north; the things Howard brought will be sent.

On the way back from the transportation office Sharon turns off the main road and drives through the troop area to the ice cream parlor. She sings a song by The Shirelles popular when she was in 8th grade, when Vietnam was a Southeast Asian country she'd never heard of:

Soldier boy
Oh, my little soldier boy
I'll be true to you

Here in the troop area she sees no soldier boys – no enlisted men. They are all on duty, training for war.

She pulls into the parking lot of the ice cream parlor, the place that Jim wouldn't allow her and Kim to go. Inside it's empty except for two women with their kids. Sharon orders a banana split with one scoop each of chocolate, vanilla and strawberry ice cream topped with hot fudge sauce and whipped cream. The works.

She raises the spoon before taking the first bite. "Kim, this is for what we didn't get to do together."

Then to complete the day she drives to the Officers Country Club to swim. She eats a hamburger and fries at the snack bar, then walks towards the door leading to the pool. The man in suntans placing his order at the counter turns around.

It's Mark Williamson!

He's still wearing his warrant officer insignia on his uniform. What does this mean in connection with his decision? Her eyes ask the question.

"I accepted the commission," he says. "I'm going back to Nam."

He's volunteering to risk his life again! Does being an officer mean that much to him?

"Where's your sidekick?" he asks when she doesn't reply. "I've never seen you apart."

"Kim. She's ..."

She can't tell Mark without breaking into tears.

Mark says, "I ... I want to ask you a question." He hesitates. "Would you have married me if I'd asked you?"

This shocks Sharon. "We had just graduated from high school when we broke up," she says.

"When you broke up with me," he says.

"I was going away to college; you were staying home and going to community college."

He stares into her eyes. "If I'd asked you then to marry me after college, would you have said yes?"

A fly lands on Sharon's arm. She swats it away.

What should she say that won't make him feel badly? She can't say she didn't love him enough to marry him. She could say she wouldn't marry a non-Jew. Or that from her perspective he wasn't going places – Vietnam excluded, of course.

"I don't really know what that person I was at age 18 would have said then. Why do you ask?"

Mark shifts from foot to foot. "I wanted to ask you that day at the quarry. My mother had pressured me not to."

"Because I'm Jewish."

He nods.

"Your mother gave you good advice," Sharon says.

"If you had said yes, you'd be here with me now instead of with your husband."

She smiles. "Does this mean I was destined to come to Ft. Knox?"

Mark smiles too, the tense moment past.

She holds out her hand to him. "I wish you the best of luck as an officer."

They shake hands.

The next day Sharon dons a two-piece linen suit for the graduation luncheon. It's show time.

Thirty minutes later Sharon enters the Officers Club carrying a bag with the props for the skit. She stashes her bag behind the divider the entertainment committee requested for scene changes before she mingles with the other wives sipping vile sherry.

"Why is sherry the protocol pre-luncheon drink?" Sharon says to Donna.

"I hear the refreshment committee wanted something else," Donna says. "They were told, 'The general's wife likes sherry.' End discussion."

The women take their assigned seats for chicken slathered with sauce. On the luncheon tables miniature American flags stick up from oatmeal cylinders decorated with colored paper to represent regimental drums. One senior woman across from Sharon says, "The decorations committee has outdone itself this time."

Now, during the dessert course of ice cream also decorated with miniature American flags, Sharon, Donna, and Wendy exchange their dresses for their husbands' starched and pressed fatigues. They roll the shirts' long sleeves up and push the blouson pant legs into their husbands' second pair of combat boots, their faces reflecting in the boots' black shine.

A senior officer's wife in a pale blue dress and matching blue hat walks up to the microphone. "And

now I would like to introduce Mrs. Robert Gold to
start the entertainment."

Sharon smiles at the other two and leads them
out in front of the divider. She begins: "The Fourth
of July was a few days ago and at this time of year our
thoughts turn to 1776 and the War of Independence,
led by General Washington with his valiant group of
men. We take you now to 1776 and the army as it was
then."

Wendy as an aide comes up to Sharon: "General
Washington, the new AOB class has arrived."

Sharon playing Washington asks: "What's an
AOB class?"

Wendy the aide replies: "AMATEUR Officers
Basic – very basic."

The three meet back behind the divider. Then
they all go out in front again, signaling a new scene.

Donna faces Sharon and Wendy: "Now, men,
here are forms 2031 and 1023. All married men
whose wives accompanied them fill out form 2031 in
quadruplicate and form 1023 in triplicate. All single
officers fill out forms 2031 in triplicate and form
1023 in quadruplicate. All married men whose wives
did not accompany them but who will join them
here fill out both forms 2031 and 203 in duplicate.
Married men whose wives won't be joining them fill
out only form 2031 in triplicate and disregard 1023.
Correction: Married men whose wives are here and
were married under the harvest moon …"

Sharon and Wendy hum the opening words to the song "Harvest Moon."

Donna frowns: "Order, please. As I was saying, fill out form 2031 in triplicate. Class dismissed."

Sharon and Wendy run back behind the divider. Wendy comes out wearing the doctor's white coat. She examines Donna. "Type blood – red. Heart – beating. Lungs – breathing. You're in good shape." Donna collapses onto the floor.

Sharon as Benjamin Franklin comes out from behind the divider. "Men, here are your manuals, hot from my printing press." She reads from her copy: "Oiling a Flintlock; Trading with the Indians; How to Spot a Redcoat; Assembly and Disassembly of the Fire – M1; Care and Feeding of the Horse; Crossing Rivers, Delaware, Potomac, Etc.; Hiding Behind Trees; Horse Recovery."

Sharon disappears behind the divider while Donna and Wendy stand at attention for inspection. Sharon reappears and says to Wendy: "You there, get a wig. We don't want any short-haired soldiers in this outfit."

Donna opens a manual and reads: "Maintenance of the Horse – The horse's left foot is on his left side. The left side of the horse is the side where the left foot is on. Which side is the left foot on?" She looks up from the manual. "The right?"

Sharon appears with Wendy wearing an apron over her fatigues.

"$140 a month for that tent! Forget it!" Sharon says.

"Let's try the Muldraugh Wagon Court," Wendy says.

Wendy reappears from behind the divider with a green bag on her face. Donna and Sharon walk past her.

"There goes an AOB class member," Donna says.

"How do you know?" Sharon says.

"He's a green lieutenant."

Back behind the divider again. Then Sharon appears out front wearing the MP helmet. She says "Halt!" to Donna riding on a stick horse.

"I was only trotting," Donna says.

"May I see your horse license?" Sharon says.

"What license?"

"That will be five nights at horse driving school for you."

Sharon dumps the MP helmet behind the divider, then reappears talking to Donna: "AOB? OMO. TDY? PCS! RA? USAR. MI? MP. EDCSA? 0-1-28."

Wendy walks over to listen. "I must be in the wrong company. They don't speak English here."

Now Sharon addresses Donna and Wendy. "Vol indef will give you 12 to 18 months in Boston. And, gentlemen, if you don't go vol indef, we'll send you straight to Valley Forge."

Donna holds up a sign saying "To Valley Forge" and Wendy holds up an "AOB Graduation Diploma." All three of them bow to signal the end.

From behind the divider they can hear barely any applause. "Maybe they didn't get it," Sharon says.

"Or maybe they were disappointed not to have a fashion show," Donna says.

"It was great," Wendy says. "I'm glad we did this."

They change back into their dresses and reemerge from behind the divider, taking their seats with the other women. The woman in the blue dress smiles at all of them. "Thank you for your presentation," she says.

"And now we have another special treat. We have diplomas for all of you for graduating this course on how to be an officer's wife."

She calls up the AOB class wives one-by-one by name. Sharon reads her diploma as she walks back to her seat.

The certificate reads "U.S. Army Armor School" at the top. Under the words "United Students Wives" are the words "check book, cook book, baby care." Then comes the formal "To all who shall see these presents greetings." The next words crack Sharon up:

> *Be it known that Sharon Gold having*
> *successfully completed and survived the required*

course in the feeding, care, and coddling of her
husband in
The U.S. Army Armor School
In testimony Whereof, and by authority vested
in us, we do declare her a
GRADUMATE
Given at Fort Knox, Kentucky, this 10th day of
July 1970

And it's signed by a brigadier general, a major general, and a lieutenant colonel!

Sharon would love to have shared a laugh with Kim over this silly diploma.

House rejects without debate
move to endorse the Senate-
passed Cooper-Church
amendment to curb U.S.
military action in
Cambodia ...
July 9, 1970

DONNA – VI – July 16

"After retreat and early evening, wear a cocktail type dress, shoulders covered, and gloves – but no hat."

Donna closes the suitcase. She's ready to leave for Ft. Holabird. In the bathroom Jerry inspects himself in his Class A uniform. In a few minutes they'll drive to the post for the graduation ceremony and their farewells.

How often will she see Sharon while they are both at Ft. Holabird? As she understands it, available rental housing is spread out all over Baltimore. She and Sharon may live far away from each other.

Donna's mother has promised to come to Baltimore on the way back from a visit to Puerto Rico, bringing green bananas for Donna's favorite treat. Donna and Jerry can have a party when her mother visits. Invite people over for fried green bananas. Sharon and Robert will come then.

Donna looks at the suitcase. If only those packed clothes were becoming tight on her! If only she would soon need the maternity clothes her mother started to make!

The doctor explained it was for the best. "The fetus may have been unviable. Or you may have had the German measles without knowing it. Sometimes adults don't even notice a slight fever," he said. "Even such a slight case can badly affect a fetus."

Jerry brought her home from the hospital the next morning. He threw her diaphragm in the trash. "We'll make lots of babies," he said.

"We can't have sex until the bleeding stops."

Jerry kissed her. "We can wait a week to start our family."

She asked him again, that night, when they were lying side by side in their bed. "Did you mean what you said about taking the exemption?"

"I understand how important it is to you," he said. "I'm giving my time to the army. I don't have to give my life when you need me so much."

She kissed him. She didn't want to excite him, but she couldn't restrain her happiness. Even Miguel's face, hovering above Jerry, couldn't squash it.

She isn't superstitious, doesn't believe that Miguel's ghost caused the miscarriage. There will be other pregnancies, successful ones. She knows it.

For the second time in 16 days, Senate votes to repeal 1964 Gulf of Tonkin Resolution cited by Johnson administration as authorization to expand the Vietnam War ...
July 10, 1970

WENDY – VII – July 16

"For receptions held later in the evening, a dinner dress is suitable."

Wendy studies the interior of the trailer. The bare Formica surfaces stare back at her, absent of any indication that she and Nelson have lived here.

Everything is now packed in the car. They will leave for Ft. Hood immediately after this morning's graduation ceremony. She's pleased about going to Texas. Although it isn't as good as going back home, it'll be somewhat familiar.

The phone rings.

"Mrs. Johnson, this is Mrs. Donovan."

Mrs. Donovan!

"I just called to thank you for your wonderful work at the hospital. The men have told me how much they enjoyed your visits. They'll miss you and the committee will miss you."

The other officer's wives! Wow!

She remembers her own manners. "Thank you, Mrs. Donovan, for calling. I really appreciate having the opportunity to help out."

"Good luck at your next post. You'll be able to help out there too in some capacity."

Incredible. A senior officer's wife calling just to say thank you. Maybe Nelson is right that army etiquette can make life easier for them.

Nelson comes back into the trailer from checking the car. "Are you ready?"

In the car Nelson flips on the radio and catches the end of "Smile a Little Smile for Me" sung by the Flying Machine. The song reminds her of the drive home with Kim – watching for a sign that Kim was okay.

Will Kim ever be okay? Donna remarried soon after her first husband's death. Yet Kim seems so much more fragile than Donna. Can Kim ever risk loving someone again after Jim?

Wendy shakes her head. She won't allow herself to think about Jim, about Donna's first husband. About Nelson going to Vietnam. She'll think only of settling into Ft. Hood, joining the officers' wives club there, making new friends. She'll call her parents as soon as they reach Ft. Hood, assure them that she and Nelson are fine. And they will try to stay just fine. Please God.

House Armed Services subcommittee report on the Songmy incident concludes mass killing did occur and was covered up by military and State Department officials in South Vietnam ...

July 15, 1970

SHARON – XVII – July 16

"Note that gloves are usually worn while proceeding through the receiving line."

The United States flag limps in the humid air. Sharon sits in the viewing stand with Donna and Wendy while their husbands in their Class A uniforms go through their paces. The AOB graduation ceremony flies by. The senior officers must be as affected as everyone else by the heat.

If only Kim could be sitting next to the women now and Jim out on the parade ground with Robert, Nelson and Jerry. If only, if only ...

"It's certainly hot out here," Donna whispers.

"Hot enough to melt," Wendy says.

Her friends. Sharon has come a long way from the person who arrived here – scared of an alien culture, convinced she would be all alone among people so different from herself.

For this ceremony Sharon wears the red felt hat that her sorority sister brought her from Florence. It's the only nice hat she has. And she can see there's a practical reason for wearing hats at outdoor official ceremonies – protection from the sun.

Out on the parade ground the men step up in turn to receive their graduation diplomas. Surely not as goofy as the wives' diplomas.

Now, the ceremony over, the men march off the parade ground. The women rush forward to kiss their husbands. It's time to say goodbye.

"Let's take a picture of all of us in front of the gold. So we can prove we were at Ft. Knox," Sharon says.

"Gold for the Golds," Jerry says.

She asks another AOB class member to use her camera. The six of them stand together for the last time: Donna and Jerry, Wendy and Nelson, Sharon and Robert.

"Say Mickey Mouse AOB," the cameraman says. They all smile.

The men wish each other luck and kiss the wives. The wives kiss each other. "Drive safely," they say.

Then Robert salutes Jerry and Nelson. They salute him back. "At ease," he says. They all laugh.

Sharon climbs into the passenger side of the Fiat. Her journal, new the first week in May, is now filled with her experiences here. And her friendships.

Robert drives the Fiat out of Ft. Knox and back onto Dixie Highway. They drive north, on their way to Ft. Holabird – one step closer to Vietnam.

EPILOGUE

SHARON – XVIII – April 1994

*"The receiving line should normally be formed from right
to left, although sometimes, due to the physical being of a
room, this may not be practical and necessitate the opposite."*

From a distance the grass appears unmarred,
stretching in a straight line from the front of the
Lincoln Memorial to the reflecting pond, then
rising slightly to the Washington Monument and
on to the Capitol building. Only as Sharon reaches
the actual location in Constitution Gardens can she
see the cutout in the ground for the memorial wall
designed by Maya Ying Lin for the Vietnam Veterans
Memorial.

The wall can be viewed by taking a downward
sloping path from either the east or west end. The
first black granite panel is a sliver on Sharon's left as
she starts down the path. The panels grow in height
from both ends, until at the bottom of the path the
two sides meet as tall wall panels.

The names of the dead cover the surfaces of the panels, name after name in continuous flowing lines.

A man parks his wheelchair in front of a panel. Sharon glances at his face. He's about the right age. Is he remembering his buddies?

And who has left the box of Cracker Jacks at the base of another panel? It's out of place surrounded by flower wreaths and miniature American flags, even a cap with the slogan "Reenlist."

A woman bends towards one panel, her left hand pressing a sheet of paper against a name, her right hand rubbing a pencil over the paper's surface. A rubbing. Like the rubbing of a tombstone.

An older woman leans on the arm of her middle-aged daughter, both their faces damp. Is the older woman here to honor her son or the middle-aged woman her husband? Or both?

"It was a difficult decision," Sharon hears a young man – probably in his twenties, too young to know firsthand – say to his companion. "Whether to go."

Two teenage boys turn to their mother. "Thanks for taking us, Mom," they say.

An African-American family is on the path in front of Sharon. The man pushes a stroller with a sleeping baby while his wife holds the hands of twin girls. Sharon flashes to Donna Lautenberg's description of the black woman standing in the clinic line at Ft. Knox feeding bread to her young son. The woman had been eight months pregnant with this son when her husband was killed in Vietnam. Is this man here to show his children his father's name on the wall, the father he never knew?

Ahead of Sharon appears the spot where the two sides of the wall meet. At the bottom of the last west panel is the date 1975 – the last year of casualties – with the inscription:

Our nation honors the courage, sacrifice and devotion to duty and country of its Vietnam veterans. This memorial was built with private contributions from the American people. November 11, 1982

At the top of the first east panel appears the date 1959 – the first year of casualties – with the inscription:

In honor of the men and women of the armed forces of the United States who served in the Vietnam War. The names of those who gave their lives and of those who remain missing are inscribed in the order they were taken from us.

"In the order they were taken from us."

How eerie to be walking this path now. Richard Nixon, the president who escalated and then ended the Vietnam War, has just died at the age of 81. Many of the Vietnam War dead lived less than one-fourth of that time.

Sharon stops at a panel and randomly counts the minuscule round indentations representing 10 lines of names. She is not looking for any specific name.

Above her at ground level Robert is checking the directory – the directory that will give the panel location of Kenneth's inscribed name. Sharon does not want to look in the directory for the names of Nelson Johnson or Mark Williamson. She prays their names aren't there, but she can't bring herself to find out.

Sharon reflects that clerks probably compiled the names of the dead for this memorial. And it is an unknown clerk who changed Robert's life. In October 1969 Robert was due to report to Ft. Benning, Georgia, for Infantry Officers Basic at the end of that month. He called the army personnel office in St. Louis and told the civilian clerk, "I haven't yet heard about my branch transfer request." She said, "Don't go. I'll put your orders on hold until you hear." A few months later the transfer to MI came through with orders to report to Ft. Knox in early May for Armor Officers Basic before MI training. The army clerk's delay by six months of Robert starting active duty coupled with Nixon withdrawing troops from Vietnam are probably what saved Robert's life.

Because, as it turned out, Robert had been right in the spring of 1970 at Ft. Knox during the AOB class members' discussions of whether to go voluntary indefinite. Robert had said then that, if Nixon wanted to be re-elected to a second term, he'd have to end the war in Vietnam. And indeed in the fall of 1971 the army began bringing home troops from Vietnam.

There had been one sentence in the special instructions section of Robert's orders to report to active duty that haunted Sharon – the reference to Vietnam: *Ultimate assignment to a short tour area.* Due to that fall 1971 troop drawdown, Robert never goes to Vietnam.

Sharon's fingers trace the chiseled lettering of the unknown name in front of her eyes.

What were all the American deaths in Vietnam for?

She flashes on the chaotic images of the American embassy at the fall of Saigon on April 30, 1975, captured on news footage: The last American helicopters lift off from the roof, desperate South Vietnamese civilians trying to cling to the helicopter skids. And in the embassy compound below, watching their last chance take off, are the masses of South Vietnamese who will become fodder for the brutality of the victorious Communists.

Rivulets of tears splash down Sharon's cheeks, blurring the names on the panel in front of her.

The perspiration drips down his face, oozing into his eyes and sliding over his mouth. He swipes at the beads dripping from his nose with the arm of his filthy fatigue shirt. "This heat is unbearable," the army officer says to the 19-year-old enlisted man quivering besides him inside the tank. "How do the Vietnamese survive?"

The officer pops the hatch, standing upright in the commander's seat to check the terrain. The enemy hides somewhere nearby.

He lowers himself back into the tank and buttons down the hatch. The 19-year-old drives the tank forward.

An officer's wife
Not an officer's widow.

35851452R00296

Made in the USA
Lexington, KY
26 September 2014